Enticing Taboos

Gray-Finn Productions

ISBN- 10: 061592672x
ISBN- 13: 978-0615926728

Cover design by Kari Ayasha of Cover to Cover Designs

Photos:
Cover photo © Depositphotos.com/Subbotina
Cover photo © Depositphotos.com/@ ssuaphoto

Author: Shantale Finnerty

Authorsfinnerty@gmail.com
www.facebook.com/authorsfinnerty

Acknowledgements

As I sit here compiling a list of names for the wonderful people that have impacted my life in such a positive way, I cannot help but think of how thankful and truly blessed I am. I wrote this book within a years' time while in the mist of raising two young children and a baby. I know all of the parents out there can relate when I say that it is hard to steal a little time for ourselves, but we make it happen.

To my Lord and Savior, I thank you for revealing my talent to me during one of many sleepless nights. I have been a wife and mother for so long that I didn't know who I was as an individual, but I can wash and fold a load of clothes like no other, break up fights quicker than a referee, and feed a baby while scheduling an appointment, and washing the dishes all at the same time. You have opened my eyes to the other side of me, and I thank you. To my husband Frederick Finnerty and my biggest supporter, I thank you for always being there, for placing our family on your back and carrying us, burdens and all. Thank you for the many years of love and affection and being that driving force I needed to achieve my goal, and lastly I thank you for allowing me to express myself in every way without judgment and without complaint. You mean the world to me. To my babies, Frederick III, Cianni, Yarri and Alexis, Mommy loves you and thanks you for your patience as I carried my laptop around everywhere with my face buried in the screen as I worked diligently on this book.

Thank you to my beautiful mother Carmalina Scott. The amount of unconditional love you have showered me with is immeasurable and I love you for reasons too lengthy to mention. I am who I am because of you. I have so much love and appreciation to my mother-in-law Germaine Finnerty, Robert Ross, and Tyrone Day. I appreciate everything you have done and continue to do for our family. I am forever grateful for your love and support.

This book is the result of hard work and dedication that would not have been possible without the real Lani, Ira, and Courtni, so to the best friends a woman could ever imagine, thank you Melody Hope-Hicks, Nicole Foots, and Patrice English for allowing me to use your incredibly unique and peerless personalities to build a realistically spicy storyline. I love you all and thank you for all of the years of love and support. Yalonda Rice, the woman who is more excited than I to see this happen. Thank you for the countless hours of work and guidance. You have become more of a mentor than an editor, and you are greatly appreciated.

Thank you to the abundance of supporters that continue to encourage me along this journey, as well as all of my siblings, family and friends. If I forget your name, please know that my memory isn't the best, but my heart is always in the right place. Kila Campbell, Lavinia Wishon, Mark Douglas, Nathalie Weekes-Douglas, David Rice, Thomas Scott, Torokah Gray, Michael Gray, Marcus Scott, Jazman Gray, Khadijah Gray, Eboni Gray, Marcus Lloyd and last but not least, thank you to each and every one of you that are reading this book. I can hardly wait to give you more.

I hope you enjoy. Now kick back, relax, and let the drama begin.

Foreword

Every woman is loved by their man in their own unique way. Since the beginning of time, it was never the plan for us to live our lives without companionship, and we often seek it at all cost. The overwhelming need to be in a relationship often leads women to look for love in all the wrong places. Women will knowingly bond with a man when the onset of the relationship is destructive and fruitless; but they forge ahead because the opposite is even scarier—being alone. Then you have women on the opposite end of this spectrum, their expectations are so high that they completely box themselves out of meaningful relationships because there is not a man who fits into their box. Welcome to *Enticing Taboos*.

I count it a privilege and an honor that Shantale asked me to write the foreword for this exceptional body of literary work. As her 6th grade teacher, I knew she was destined for greatness. As I was reading this novel, I often found myself wanting to bolster my own talents as an educator because it is written on the level of an expert and not a novice. Shantale was born with this talent that neither I nor any other could credit ourselves with imparting upon her. Her gifts were divinely ordered before she stepped into my classroom.

May God continue to bless her and keep her as she embarks on this new chapter of her life of being a published author.

--Kila K. Campbell

Prologue

"Is this what you want?" he asked as he stroked his long mocha colored shaft from its base to its mushroom shaped head. She sat mesmerized on the edge of the bed while nodding her head, ready for instructions. She wasn't sure what to do with it, but she was pretty sure she would figure it out along the way.

He came closer to her with his seductive smile leading the way, "You think you can handle all of this?" he asked never missing a stroke as he approached the edge of the bed where she sat, and seconds later the savory scent of his cologne flooded her nostrils.

"Yes," she spoke out loud. Her heart was pounding as her fingers toyed with a loose button on her plain white blouse. She had sat nervously for all of five minutes in the presence of this man, and managed to work the thin thread down to its beginning seam.

"Well turn around and bend that ass over," he said in a deep stern voice. She did as told and soon after felt his rough hands grip both cheeks. She closed her eyes enjoying the feel of this rugged man as he reached around her to unbutton her gray slacks. He pulled them over her hips as she lifted each knee one after the other until the slacks were on the carpeted floor.

"Tell me how you want it," he whispered in her ear as the heat from his minty breath cascaded down the side of her neck and plunged into her panties. "Do you like it rough," he asked as he palmed both of her breasts and pulled her closer to him, "or do you want me to take my time and give it to you nice and slow? Would you like for me to lick it, suck it, and then fuck?"

He spun her around awaiting an answer, but all she could do was hyperventilate. He smelled so good, and the feel of his hardness on her thigh made her even more nervous than seeing it, but damn did she want this man to do any and everything he wanted to do to her, so long as he put out the fire he ignited inside of her. "You know what," he paused and turned her around once more, "Get on your knees baby." Her knees were bent and she was assuming the position before it even registered to her that she was doing so.

"Are you going to eat that?"

She paused and turned around confused. What the hell was he talking about?

"Are you going to eat that?" he repeated himself, this time in what seemed to be a feminine voice. She turned around and stared him dead in the face, but didn't say a word. He was really blowing her mood.

"Hello," Lani's voice woke her from yet another fantasy.

Her eyes scanned the outdoor scenery confused for a minute, "Oh sorry, I'm so tired." Courtni said, trying to compose herself while sitting on a bench at Federal Hill Park. The park overlooked the Baltimore Inner Harbor, and their girl Ira's restaurant Hicks by the Docks.

"You can say that again," Lani said relieving Courtni of her last butterscotch cupcake, "but you can't sit here nodding off looking like a dope fiend Courtni."

"Shut up," Courtni laughed.

"That was no nod. That was a freaky fantasy," Jade laughed, and the girls joined in.

"Here comes Ira now. I wonder what she wants," Courtni ignored Jade, and all three ladies looked in the direction of the restaurant.

"Good I have to hit the gym before my date tonight," Lani said while scrolling through her phone. "I have to get back to the bakery. I told Arnie I would only be a minute," Jade said.

The girls stood as Ira approached them. They all hugged and sighed jokingly as they took a seat with all four of them squeezing onto one bench.

"Ladies, this fantasizing is getting completely out of hand, and it's crazy because I cannot control it since I never know when it's coming on," Courtni said.

"What are you fantasizing about?" Ira asked.

"Dick," Jade said.

"Well if you want to put it bluntly, yes that's what I think about."

"Then go get you some," Lani said.

"You know I cannot and will not do that," Courtni rolled her eyes. "I am not you. I want more than the meat, I want the man."

"I'm just saying, it wouldn't hurt for you to get your hands on a piece of meat for once. Just to feel it, touch it, stroke it, get to know it, name it..."

"Taste it," Jade interjected.

"Ok, Lani and Jade," Ira said. "Courtni don't pay them any mind."

"As usual I'm not," she said. "I think I need to find a hobby or something to occupy my mind. I've always thought that I would have it all by this time in my life, but I must admit, it's funny to see how life plays out."

"Just be careful what you wish for," Lani said.

"You may get more than you can handle little 'Miss Innocent,'" Jade teased.

"I can handle anything with God on my side. You ladies need to get to know him a little better," Courtni said.

"I can't argue with that," Lani replied.

"Ok Ira, why did you call us all here today?" Jade asked.

"Well, first I haven't seen my friends in forever, and I've missed you all, and secondly, I wanted to invite you guys to a party."

They all looked in Courtni's direction to view her expression. She was not big on partying.

"What," Courtni asked while rolling her eyes at the trio. "What party Ira?" she said in an unenthused tone.

"Robert May, one of Nick's friends from the Army is having a get together, and I wanted to stop by. He was so supportive when Nick passed, and I just want to show my face, but I don't want to go alone."

"Well I'm in, but I don't know about little 'Miss Innocent' over there," Lani said, nodding her head in Courtni's direction, "and the old maid over there," she added pointing her phone in Jade's direction.

"For your information, Trent has been working late at the office lately so I don't see a problem with me going," Jade said. They all fell silent, and looked in Courtni's direction.

"Fine, I'll be there. When is it?" Courtni asked.

"Good," Ira said elated, "It's this Saturday at six. Let's all meet at Jade's and I'll drive."

"Well since you don't plan on staying long, maybe we

can stop by my co-worker's house. She's having a house warming party that day, and I told her I would stop by," Lani said.

"Cool," Jade said. "Can we go now?"

"Yes, you're all dismissed," Ira said and they all began to walk toward the parking lot. They got in their vehicles, and went their separate ways as they had done many times over the years. Back in the day, they would all get together just to sit around and talk. Lately their gatherings have turned into quick meet and greets, due to their busy schedules, but they cherished the time they spent together. Everyone knows women can be ruthless, especially towards each other. Just the fact that they had friends that didn't judge them, and they loved each other unconditionally meant a lot to them. They had been through everything together growing up. Having each other's back was nothing new.

The four of them have been best friends since their days in elementary school. They have been a part of each other's lives for so long that they felt more like sisters than friends. Growing up in Cherry Hill, a place some folks like to call the hood, but they liked to call home was the best years of their lives. Walking around the neighborhood, going to the candy store with one dollar and coming out with a bag full of junk food, buying frozen cups and snowballs during the summer, or just sitting outside on the porch talking and being nosy, was the life back then. Although the girls grew up, they didn't grow apart.

They have always had big dreams as children, and dreamed of the day when they would all have nice homes, nice cars, and nice jobs. Years later they are all successful women. Defying the odds and making it out of the hood was hard work. They are not all college graduates with PhD's, Doctorates, or Certificates of Achievements lining the walls of their offices, but they are successful in their own rights.

The way things are now, growing up a teen in a rough neighborhood, with very little guidance, and not becoming someone's "baby momma" by the age of eighteen was success in itself. The one thing they didn't realize as young girls, wishing and hoping to become adults quicker than life allowed was there was no going back. No falling down and running to momma to kiss your boo boos. As adults you made your bed, and you lie in it. Life has been pretty good for the foursome so far despite their losses, trials, and tribulations. Life is not always rainbows and butterflies, and sometimes having a friend to lean on, means more than being successful.

*****

Courtni Tremaine Jeffries

I have always been the goody two shoes of the bunch. My whole life I've done right by everyone including myself. I am a twenty-seven-year-old virgin. That's right I said virgin, and will continue to be so until I meet Mr. Right. I could never figure out why life has always thrown me curveballs. I mean, is it asking too much to be given a good man. I know they're out there I just haven't crossed paths with any yet, but trust me, I'm waiting for the day.

I lost my mother at the hands of my father when I was six years old. If that's not a curveball, I don't know what is. My grandparents raised me and my brother Randy, and did a great job might I add. We're both College graduates, and successful people. I've often wondered about the person I may have become if my mother had raised me. That's why I've always lived my life in a way I thought my mother would approve, but yet and still, I haven't received the one thing my heart desires, a good man. I want a good man more than I want this Lexus truck I'm looking at online right now. I look forward to the day that I get married and start a family. I have big plans for my future and I plan on doing things in that order. The last thing I want to be is someone's baby momma. I don't want a man that bad. Some say my standards are way too high, but I say if you're not on, or near my level than it will not work. I refuse to take care of a man, who refuses to take care of himself.

I've spent most of my life in school, and it has paid off. I'm a child and youth counselor, and I absolutely love my job and the children I work with. I also counsel my friends in my home life. I care for everyone all the time. When is someone going to care for me? I know my God has something special in store for me. That's why I try so hard not to complain, but that's not the easiest thing to do when I see all of my friends around me either married with children or in a serious relationship.

Courtni sat her laptop down on her purple comforter then walked into the bathroom. She looked at herself in the mirror and recited Psalms 27:14 out loud to herself.

"Wait on the Lord, be of good courage and he shall strengthen thy heart; wait on the Lord I say wait on the Lord."

She turned the faucet on, and stuck both hands under the cold water then splashed a bit of it on her face. As she made her way out of the bathroom, she heard the sound of Chrisette Michele's "Fragile" begin to sound from her cell phone that lay on her night stand. She loved Chrisette Michele, and she knew that song indicated she had a text message. She picked up her phone, and saw the message was from Lani saying, "What do you think?" with a photo attached to it. Lani looked great in a strapless form fitting black knee length dress and a pair of black pumps with a single strap around her ankle. She sent a text back saying, "You go girl. I love it," then sat the phone back on her night stand.

"Look at me Colby," Courtni said to her little black shih tzu, "It's 8:15 on a Friday evening, and I'm in this house once again," she said walking into her living room, and flopping down on her chocolate colored sofa. Scanning the room, she felt a sense of pride enter her heart. She loved her home that she had only been in for about seven months. It was a brand new red brick condo with a view to die for. Her Boston Street home was a dream come true not to mention it overlooked the water at Fells Point. What she loved most about her house was that she had her own garage. No rushing home from work, parking her car, and walking everywhere she had to go to save her parking spot, like others in her neighborhood had to do.

After flipping through the channels on the television, she let out a light giggle as Bill Cosby did his best impression of a whinny kid. She loved kids. That's why she chose her profession, or as some liked to say, "Her profession chose her." She loved helping people especially children that has suffered any type of traumatic experiences in their young lives. Courtni discovered that most of the time all they needed was someone to talk to, and tell them what they have been through does not define who they are or where they are going. Although she loved children, she was afraid to have them after all of the stories her clients have told her. She didn't know if it was possible to protect a child the way they truly needed to be protected with all the psychos roaming around.

Thinking about psychos took her back to her childhood. Her father was a good man when he was sober, as far as she could remember. Thoughts of him coming home from work drunk, and starting fights with her mother crossed her mind. She had witnessed him strike her mother on more than one occasion until one day his abuse turned deadly. The day he stabbed her mother, and took her life was the day he died in her heart. She was now a motherless child, which left her feeling lost. She had lots of family that stepped in and tried their best to parent her and her brother, but even as a six-year-old, she knew there was no love like a mother's love.

She looked at her mother's picture that hung above her mantle, and smiled at the resemblance. She had inherited her mother's beautiful dark skin and gorgeous smile. Her face was flawless just like her mothers, and she loved every bit of it. The thought of her mother warmed her heart, and she knew she watched over her and her brother every day.

Courtni picked up her cordless phone and dialed her brother's number.

"Hey baby sis," he answered on the first ring.

"I take it you don't have any plans tonight either," Courtni said and her brother chuckled.

"Actually I am en route to a friend of mine's bachelor party," Randy said.

"Well, that confirms it. I am the only one without a social life."

"Your stubbornness hasn't changed much since we were kids," Randy said.

"I'm not stubborn Randy, I just don't have time for foolishness," Courtni replied.

"Well, just so you know I would love to have a few nieces and nephews, so if you could go ahead and snag a husband that would be great," he laughed.

"You first. You are older than me," Courtni said. Her brother was still living life care free at the age of thirty-two with no wife and no children.

"Hook me up with one of your friends," he said.

Courtni laughed, "You wish."

"No, but seriously sis, you have to get out and socialize. I didn't want to tell you this, but grandma thinks that you may be gay."

"What," Courtni shouted.

"Yeah, she told me that the other day, but she said she still loved you and accepted it."

"I'm not gay Randy," Courtni said annoyed.

"Ok," he said, but his voice sounded unconvinced.

"I have to make another phone call. I love you and have fun," Courtni said.

"I love you too sis, and hey," he paused waiting for Courtni to answer.

"Yes."

"Any man would be lucky to have you...or woman," he said.

"I'm not gay Randy, bye," she said and disconnected the call before dialing Jade's number.

"Hey girl," Jade spoke loudly into the receiver.

"Hey you," Courtni said back. "What are you and Trent getting into this evening?"

"Well, Trent is at the office. You know they are still trying to close the deal on that Hanover project, but the kids and I are getting our bowl on with this Wii sports. What are you doing tonight?" Jade asked.

"You know me, either paper work or nothing at all," Courtni let out a sigh.

"You know, you need to carry your butt down to Baltimore Street, and hit up a couple of those strip clubs to loosen yourself up a little bit. Shoot, hit up a couple of those corners, and get that cherry popped while you're at it," Jade laughed and Courtni couldn't help but laugh herself. She loved Jade's sense of humor, but sometimes it was a bit much.

"You know I was actually thinking about going down the street to the Black Jewel and see what their menu looks like,"

Courtni said.

"Sounds good, let me know how it goes," Jade said and Courtni could hear Trent Jr. in the background telling his mother it was her turn to bowl.

"I'll let you know. You go ahead and get back to playing the game with the kids. I'll talk to you later Jay."

"Okay be safe," Jade said.

They disconnected the call and Courtni went into her bedroom. She put on a pair of black leggings, then went into her closet and put on a purple shirt that hung off her shoulder. She didn't need to get to fancy just to get something to go, and sit at the bar and take in the scenery while waiting for her order. She slipped on a pair of black gladiator sandals, grabbed her keys and purse then headed towards the door, and made her way down to her red Volvo xc90. Her car reminded her of a ladybug, and her mother loved ladybugs. As she made her way to her destination, she perked up when someone was pulling out of a parking spot directly in front of the restaurant. She pulled into the spot and hopped out while a handsome young man held the door for her as she walked the pathway to the restaurant's entrance.

"Thank you," she said as she put a little pep in her step as not to keep the young man waiting.

"You're welcome Beautiful," the man said as he flashed a Colgate smile and walked off.

Why do they always do that? Give a compliment but never follow up, and why don't I ever make the first move myself? She thought to herself.

"Just one ma'am?" the hostess asked, interrupting her thoughts.

"Um, no, I mean yes, but I'm ordering to go."

"Okay, you can go over, and have a seat at the bar," the perky hostess said with a cheesy grin plastered on her face.

She made her way over to the bar, and before her bottom even hit the bar stool the guy behind the counter asked, "What can I get you ma'am?"

"Can I see your menu please?"

"Sure. Just let me know when you are ready to order," he said, and handed her a black menu with gold letters covering the front. She smiled and nodded her head.

"How you doing Gorgeous?" she heard a voice say from behind her. She felt herself get excited as she spun around on her stool, but the smile dropped from her face once she saw where the voice had come from. The scrawny little thing standing in front of her had to be kidding. She was not obese by a long shot, but she was a thick woman. At five foot eight, one hundred and ninety six pounds, ninety of it being boobs, she would hurt this boy, or man, or whatever he wanted to call himself.

"Hi," she said dryly.

"Can I sit here?" he asked pointing to the stool next to her.

"Of course," Courtni said trying to be nice while giving him the once over. He wasn't that bad. He stood about six foot one, with a caramel complexion. He was dressed in a pair of black slacks, and a blue button up shirt. He smelled good too and that was a plus.

"So what you drinking Ma?" he asked.

What are you drinking she wanted to correct him, but didn't. "I'm not drinking. I'm just placing an order to go."

"Oh, well, you care to buy me one?" he asked with a crooked smile on his face, and winking his eye as if that was the sexy thing to do.

"Are you serious?"

"Hell yeah I'm serious," he said confidently. "And it'll be well worth it too Shorty. Wait 'til you see what I'm working with. You gon' wish you bought me the bar."

She wanted to tell him to go play somewhere, but instead she just said, "Child bye," and turned back around. He sucked his teeth, and mouthed something as he made his way back over to his seat. She looked over the menu and decided she didn't want anything, and asked the bartender for a virgin daiquiri.

"Sure," he said with a chuckle.

He could chuckle all he wants. She drank occasionally, but never when she was out alone. She sipped her drink and took in the atmosphere. The place was pretty nice, not too packed or rowdy, and seemed to have a pretty mature crowd, aside from the mess that had just approached her. She checked her watch, it was quarter to ten, and she was not ready to go back in the house just yet. She didn't know what it was, but as of lately she has been itching to do things differently and wanted to have fun. Be spontaneous. Get a little wild. Her nipples hardened at the thought of her being free of all her inhibitions. She snapped out of her day dream, paid the bartender, and went home.

At home, she went straight to the bathroom, ran a hot bath, and stripped out of her clothes before grabbing her book out of the night stand. She eased her way into the tub and leaned her head back on her bath pillow that took her forever to blow up and closed her eyes. Her thoughts immediately turned dirty. Usually that didn't happen until after she had read a bit of her book. Thoughts of the guy at the bar and what he really may have been working with took over her thoughts. She didn't know anything about the kind of pleasure a man could bring, but if it was anything like her fingers she couldn't wait to experience it. She brought her hands up to her 40DD breasts and began to rub them slowly. She knew she shouldn't do things like this, and she felt so dirty afterwards, but man did it feel so good. Her friends introduced her to masturbation. At first, she was reluctant to try it since she wanted to save everything sexual in nature for someone special, but the more stories she heard the more eager she became.

She grabbed her body wash and began to wash with her sponge. After drying off, and moisturizing her body she slipped into a satin night gown, and climbed into her bed. Smelling good, nipples hard, and ready to put herself to sleep, she pulled the top of her gown from over her right breast and let it escape from underneath. She took her dark chocolate nipple into her mouth, and sucked it as hard as she could. The intensity made her left nipple harden so she pulled her gown down a little more and let the other one free as well. She took her tongue and flicked it over her nipple then took it into her mouth, and just then that little devil appeared on one shoulder, and an angel appeared on the other. Her conscience was working over time, but the thought of some mystery man planting wet juicy kisses all over her body took over. She said a quick Lord please forgive me, and let her fingers explore the place where no man has ever been.

Her kitty was warm and wet as she took her middle finger and eased it inside enough to get the tip in. She didn't know what that was supposed to do, but she did it anyway then took her hands out and started rubbing her clit first slowly then increased her speed. Her mystery man was now in between her legs licking away. She felt her clit growing and reached over to grab her tiny bullet vibrator. She turned the vibrator on to finish the job, and moved it around in circles, while doing the same thing with her hips in the opposite direction.

"Oh yes," she said out loud as her breathing began to pick up. She turned the vibrator up a notch. The buzzing became louder and so did her moans.

"Oh yes, yes, yes."

Colby came running into the room, jumping on the bed, and barking at the vibrator.

"Aw man, Colby get out," Courtni yelled.

Colby barked, still staring at the buzzing vibrator in Courtni's hand. She jumped out of the bed, grabbed Colby, and put him out of her room then slammed the door, and went over to turn the vibrator off. When she couldn't find it she lifted the covers, moved the pillows, and checked under the bed.

"Come on now. Where is it?" She got up and ran to the door.

"Colby, give it to me," she said playing tug of war with the dog. He had the thin cord in his mouth while the bullet dangled and continued to vibrate.

"Let go," she said sternly and he did as told. Masturbation was completely out of the question now. She tossed the vibrator over the towel rack in the bathroom, got in bed and closed her eyes. She asked God for his forgiveness, and to rid her of all ungodly thoughts, and to keep her near his cross. Boy did she need it.

*****

Jade Serene DeVoe

I don't know how many times I have to tell these kids to put their toys away, and I don't know which is going to give me gray hairs first, them or my bakery. Speaking of my bakery, that's where I should be headed. I open at 11 a.m., and it is now 7:45 a.m. I like to get there by 8 a.m., so I can get everything baked, and put out before the customers start rolling in. Sometimes I feel like there is not enough time in a day, but that's okay tomorrow I will find time to relax, maybe catch up on some reading. I try so hard not to complain. I know I am very blessed to have a hard working man, two healthy children, and my dream bakery. I just, well I don't know, I guess I'm just in need of a vacation.

"Hey baby," Trent says as he walks over to give Jade a kiss on the lips, then headed towards the kitchen where the kids were stationed.

"Daddy," they both screamed from the table.

Jade stood in between the dining room and the kitchen and watched her husband as he greeted the kids with kisses. She noticed he was dressed in his work attire and instantly became irritated. Even though she had to work herself, her husband usually didn't work weekends, but this was becoming a regular occurrence and she didn't like it not one bit. Saturdays and Sundays were the only days she could come home to her husband, and now that was a thing of the past. She understood he had a business to run, and he was very hands on, but he had two partners in this business, and she thought the work load should be equal.

Her husband was very meticulous when it came to work of any kind. Whether it was designing a new building or washing his car. Things had to be perfect, so she knew he wouldn't rest until things were up to par, but that didn't stop her from getting upset.

"So you're working again on a Saturday?" Jade asked, while Trent stood in front of the toaster waiting on what seemed to be his breakfast of choice lately.

"Yes, hence the reason why I asked you to get your mom to watch the kids. You know we need this deal," he kissed his wife on the lips.

"I know that, but what are Greg and Sheldon there for? To help you, right? Why does it seem like you are the only one working at that place?"

"Trust me babe they're working just as hard as I am, on this and other projects."

She decided to drop it for now since she needed to get

going, but she didn't like feeling uneasy so this subject would definitely be brought up again. She went into the closet to grab an umbrella since the weather called for rain, and soon after she heard the doorbell, and her husband greeting her mother.

Jade walked back into the kitchen, kissed her mother and kids and walked out of the door with Trent on her heels. He opened the truck door for her and she climbed in.

"I'm headed out behind you. I'll call you in a few."

"Ok," Jade said and began to back out of the garage.

She loved her Gibson Island home, but fighting that downtown traffic was a headache. Today will not be as bad as the weekdays, but nevertheless there will be traffic jams. She reached her bakery on the corner of Howard and Centre Street at 8:51 a.m., and went straight to work. She started her ovens, then started mixing the batters and cookie dough.

At 9:15 a.m., she got a text message from Arnie saying, "I'm pulling up. I'll be at the door in five." Arnie was her right hand man at the bakery. He was such a good worker and very reliable. Jade relied on him to keep things afloat when she had other things to do, and to help Stephanie, her newest employee out until she got the hang of things. Jade stood by the door until she saw Arnie's fuchsia-colored apron that matched the fuchsia and teal colored interior of the bakery, then unlocked the door.

"Good morning Beautiful," Arnie said leaning in to give Jade a kiss on both cheeks.

Jade giggled and locked the door, "Good morning Arnie, guess what?" Jade said with excitement, grabbing both of his wrists.

"Gurl what?" Arnie said, ready to hear something juicy.

"Our cookie of the day is your favorite, raspberry macadamia."

"Jade don't do that," he rolled his eyes. "Got me all riled up, and ready for some action. You know I'm lonely honey. I can use any type of action in my life," Arnie said while washing his hands. He put on a pair of gloves and joined Jade in the back.

"So you and Paul didn't make up yet, huh?"

"No, and you know what? I'm so over dealing with closet freaks. He don't know what he wants, and I'm not fittin' to tell him honey. I'm leaving on that 'midnight train to Georgia,' cuz I don't got time for that mess. You hear me boss lady?" Arnie placed his hands on his boney hips.

"Loud and clear, but I've also heard this song before," Jade said laughing at the expression on Arnie's face. "Don't look at me like that. You and I both know that man is your weakness."

"Jade, every man is my weakness honey."

They both laughed and finished prepping the pies.

Eleven o'clock came quickly and before they knew it they were greeting one of their favorite customers.

"Good morning Mrs. Carol, how are you today?" Jade said.

"I'm good suga', how about you?"

"Pretty good, are you having your usual decaffeinated coffee and carrot cake today?"

"Why yes I am, but I have a bone to pick with you first," Mrs. Carol said with her hands on her wide moo moo-covered hips.

"Oh no, what did I do?"

"You need to think about opening a little earlier for us early birds."

"Now Mrs. Carol, you know you do not need to eat sweets any earlier than you already do."

Mrs. Carol laughed, "I guess you're right. I'm going to go have a seat."

"Ok, Arnie will be right over," Jade said.

Arnie helped Mrs. Carol while Jade waited on the other customers, then they had the afternoon crowd. That's why Jade chose this location. No matter what time of day it was, folks were always roaming around downtown Baltimore. During the week she opened at seven, so she could feed all of the hungry men and women in business suits. Those are the days she makes croissants, bagels, and turnovers. They seem to be a crowd favorite. She had to admit, some of the people that walked into her store were rather rude, and some just downright nasty, but she liked to think she could handle her own. Besides she also had some of the best customers in the world. She has been given birthday gifts, Christmas presents and even had a customer name her child after her. If that's not love, she didn't know what was.

Around 1:30 p.m, a woman walked in wearing a black,

suede jumpsuit and an oversized purse. She stood at the door and scanned the room looking at the few customers sitting at tables chatting and enjoying their pastries. The woman wore dark shades, and didn't bother to remove them as she entered the building with her shoulder length bang wrap surrounding her face but her distinctive oval shaped birthmark was clearly visible from where Jade stood.

"Can I get you anything?" Arnie asked the woman from behind the counter as Jade made her way to the back.

She grabbed her flour, butter, salt, sugar and a half cup of water, and began preparing her butter pie crust. After looking through the small, rectangular shaped window on the swinging door that lead to the dining area, she saw Arnie walking toward the back where she was, wearing a mug that said, "Oh hell no," as he would say. Jade couldn't help but smile since she knew he was about to come in the back and say something cynical.

"Did you see the superstar that just walked in here?" Arnie asked with one hand on his hip, and the other hand on the steel prepping table.

"As a matter of fact, I did."

"Jade girl, now you know she knows better than to be wearing something like that. If I had a uterus I'd smack her ass, and I wouldn't even tell her why I did it 'cause she should already know."

Jade laughed, "Arnie boy you are a mess. Be nice. You don't know what that woman's day has been like. Now, what I would like to know is what is up with the spy look?"

"No Boo, the question is who the hell let her out of the house with all that damn velvet on," Arnie said. "And she seems to be a fan of yours." He added as he dramatically turned his back and looked over his shoulder waiting for Jade to inquire more about the woman.

"Why do you say that?" Jade asked.

"Girl, I asked her would she like anything, and she asked me if you were the owner." Arnie said. "I said yes, and she had the nerve to say, "She's not what I expected," with her mug broke down as if she smelled something funky," Arnie rolled his eyes. "So I asked her what did she expect, because I mean—," he popped his lips, "If she wants to go there we can go there."

"Oh gosh Arnie, don't feed into that mess," Jade said.

"Honey she knew better her reply was, "Oh nothing," he altered his voice.

"She's a strange one," Jade said.

"Tell me about it honey, she even asked me what time you usually leave," Arnie frowned.

"Why the hell does she need to know that?" Jade said.

"I don't know Boo, but she was on yo' ass like flies on shit."

Jade laughed at the twisted state Arnie's face was froze in. "I'm sure she has her reasons for her questions. Maybe she is opening a bakery in the area and wanted to check out the competition, but you have to take the good with the bad Arnie."

"Not if I get this job swinging around somebody's pole," Arnie rolled his eyes and folded his arms.

"You wouldn't leave me, would you?" Jade poked her lips out.

"Of course not honey," Arnie came close and wrapped his arms around Jade. "You gon' be swinging around the pole next to me."

Jade laughed, "Get away from me," she said.

She looked through the window, and saw the woman getting up from her seat.

"Well time to send her off on a good note. You know every customer that comes into Jade's Sweet Treats get treated the same," Jade said as she watched Arnie walk through the swinging door.

To Jade, it didn't matter that this woman had a bad attitude. She knew better than anyone with all the sisters she has that some people carried themselves that way, and who was she to judge her? This woman was a paying customer, so as far as she was concerned she would give her the utmost respect, whether she was receptive to it or not was on her.

By the time five o'clock rolled around, Jade was happy she had met her goal for the day. Saturday's are typically slower than the week days, because all the office buildings in the area were closed. Arnie bagged up all the baked goods they had left over from the day, and they headed for the door. She always fed Gerald, who was the homeless man that slept on the side of her bakery at night. Trent didn't like the fact that he was there every day. He said it's hard to trust a man who has nothing to lose, but he was there before she even bought the place. She asked him not to loiter during business hours, and he did as told. She felt bad for making him leave the place he had slept, and took shelter from the rain for so long, seven years he says, but there was no way he could stay there, and solicit money from her customers. Although she didn't want him sleeping near her bakery at all she didn't complain since he kept the area clean, and made sure not to do his business near her bakery.

"Now Gerald, don't you give all this stuff to your so-called friends sitting over there." Arnie said, gesturing toward the other homeless men that seem to migrate toward Gerald when five o'clock neared. "This is for you honey, ok?"

"O…o…o…ok," Gerald said stuttering.

"Be safe Gerald," Jade said while locking the doors. She pulled down the metal roll down gate, and she and Arnie walked around the corner to the parking lot. Their routine was to wait until they were both in their vehicles and then leave. They were parked a few spaces away from each other so Arnie went one way and Jade went the other. She fumbled for her keys, and heard Arnie's car start up. As she opened the door to her truck she noticed both tires on the driver's side were flat.

"Shit," Jade screamed. She was so pissed she could see red. All she wanted to do was go home, so right now, was not the time for this.

"Come on now Jay what's taking you so long to…what happened boo?" Arnie said when he finally noticed why Jade was still standing outside of her truck. "I know that trick did not do this. Uh uh…uh uh," Arnie said loudly while walking around to the other side of her truck. "Child and she done fucked up both sides. This bitch needs to be cut. Let me call my sister Mooky she gon' lay hands on that heifer. I'm telling you now," Arnie walked away dialing numbers on his phone, while Jade stood there staring at her flat tires.

"Girl, call Debbie and them—," she could here Arnie talking to someone in the distance.

Jade didn't know what was happening. To her knowledge she did not know that woman. She knew her memory wasn't the best, but she was positive that she had never had any altercations with that woman, or done anything remotely close to what had just happened to her. She pulled her phone out from her purse and dialed Trent's number.

"My tires are flat Trent," she spoke into her cell phone as soon as he answered. "Don't bother asking who, what, when and why please, because I don't know. Just tell me what I need to do."

He sighed loudly "Just stay there I'm on my way. I'll call a tow truck are you still at the bakery?"

"Yup."

"Alright I'm on my way."

"Mooky said just give her the word, and she's on it, honey," Arnie said returning to her side. She had to laugh at Arnie, because neither of them knew that woman, so of course they didn't know if she was the culprit, but yet he was willing to go out of his way to make sure she paid for what she may have done. She loved how Arnie was professional while on the clock with the customers, but like one of her good friends while they were alone.

"Tell Mooky I'm fine, and thanks. The only thing I need you to do is stay here with me until Trent gets here."

"Child, she's delirious right now. I'll call you later," Arnie disconnected his call, and turned to Jade, "Are you sure you're ok Jade. Is something going on that I don't know about? I mean I know you're my boss and all, but you know I'm here for you."

"Nothing is going on. I don't know what this is about Arnie. Maybe it's just a random act of stupidity."

"Maybe, but why only your truck, huh?"

"I don't know. I haven't done anything to anyone."

"Well you better think harder honey, 'cause somebody don't like you boo boo, and they may be watching you."

Those words struck a nerve. Why would anyone be watching her? She thought about how boring of person she was, or so her friends say. Her routine was basic. She worked, picked up her kids, cooked then usually did something around the house until she decided to go to bed. Her idea of excitement was purchasing a new book, or having date night with her husband.

She thought back to her younger years, her pre-Trent days when she was dating, and tried her best to think of anyone who would still hold a grudge after all these years, and that was a lost cause. She had so many girls back then that didn't like her, usually for the same two reasons, either a guy they had their eyes on wanted Jade, or they thought Jade was snooty; when in reality, she was just the exact opposite, but didn't bother telling them that. If you would judge someone without ever conversing with them, and getting to know them for yourself in her opinion they were not worth the energy of trying to prove who she really was to them. She hated when she heard girls whispering to each other about her. Things like "She thinks she's all that." Of course she did. What was she supposed to think about herself, and further more why did they even care what she thought about herself?

Growing up she never had the latest fashions, or the hippest hairstyles, but no one could tell her she wasn't a beautiful person. Even with her hand-me-downs, and no-name sneakers, she thought she was cute. Her mother always said they had to make do with what they had, and that's what she did.

The first five years of her life was great. They were what folks called hood rich. Her father was a small time drug dealer who was always in and out of jail for minor charges, and would be out a few days after his arrest. Her mother was always very timid. She cared for her children, and adored this man who had swept her off of her feet. He was her first love, even though he cheated on her multiple times. He even made children with two other women while still with her mother. When her father was around her and her brothers had the best of everything. Even though they lived in the projects, they had a nice car, nice shoes, nice clothes, and didn't want for anything. Jade was a daddy's girl. She loved her father and how safe she felt whenever he was around. That's why the memory of the day he left them will never fade. No matter how much she wishes it would. Her father left them for a woman he had been seeing, and never turned back. He left her mother pregnant with two other children to care for with no job, and no money. That's when she saw her mother's strength. She picked up the pieces of their shattered life, and made things work as best as she could. She has always thanked God for blessing her with a strong woman for a mother.

"Hello. Earth to Jade," Arnie said, snapping his fingers and interrupting her stroll down memory lane. "Your husband is here suga, snap out of it."

Jade looked through her windshield and saw Trent's truck at the light on Park Avenue, and was not in the mood for the interrogation she knew she was in for. She knew how Trent was if she said she didn't know he wanted her to make some shit up. She got out of the truck thinking, "please don't start."

"Hey Baby what happened?" Trent said walking around the vehicle and inspecting the damage.

"Someone slashed my tires."

"Why? Have you been having problems with somebody and haven't told me?"

"No Trent. I don't know who did this, or why they did it. I'm just as puzzled as you are. We had one rude customer today, but she was rude to Arnie not me."

"Did you know her?" Trent asked.

"Nope, I have never seen that woman a day in my life."

"What about you Arnie? Did you know her?"

"Hell no, I didn't know that wench," Arnie said rolling his eyes, and placing his hands on his hips.

They all looked in the direction of the entrance into the parking lot when they heard the reverse beeping sound of a truck. The tow truck driver backed up as far as he could without running them over being as though they all just stood there.

"Whoa someone was mad," the truck driver said looking at her vehicle and shaking his head. "Do you have a repair shop you want me to take the truck to?" the driver asked Trent.

"Yeah a friend of mine has a shop on Patapsco Avenue. I'll get the address for you," Trent said as he walked over to his truck.

"Well Jade I'm gon' head home. Are you good?" Arnie asked.

"Yes I'm fine. I'll call you later and thanks for staying."

"Okay smooches honey. I'll talk to you later," Arnie hugged Jade and walked off.

"Here you go," Trent handed the tow truck driver a piece of paper with his friend's shop address on it. "Somebody should be there. I'll call them to let them know you are on the way."

"Ten-four," the driver said, and then hopped into his truck and began to slide the bed of the truck down.

Jade made sure to retrieve her purse from the vehicle before the driver hooked it up to his truck. Looking at her truck on top of the bed angered her all over again. She felt completely violated and for what? She looked over at Trent, and was surprised to see him a lot calmer than she thought he would be talking on his cell phone. Trent was usually very protective of her sometimes a little over protective, but surprisingly today he was handling things a lot better than he has in the past. She didn't know what to make of it, and quite frankly all she really wanted to do was be done with this day, so she made her way over to Trent's truck, got in, and leaned her seat back. She thanked God tomorrow was Sunday, and her bakery was closed.

As soon as they walked through the doors of their home, the kids came running toward them. That is what makes every parent want to keep going. Jade picked up her daughter Dani, and hugged her son Trent Jr. then flopped down on the tan-colored sofa, and began to tell her mother about the day she had. Watching her kids play brightened her day. Children were so care free. It almost made her wish she was a kid again.

She looked at her husband when he entered the room.

"You're staying home?" Jade asked.

"Yeah, I'll just start fresh on Monday."

Jade smiled. She was happy to have her husband home with his family at a decent time. She thought about the person that was responsible for vandalizing her truck, and what their problem may be with her. A part of her wanted to just forget about what took place today, but a part of her also wanted to be alert and stay on her toes. You never know what people are thinking nowadays, and she would rather be safe than sorry.

After dropping her mom off, she opened the sunroof, and put down the windows. The cool April breeze brushed across her face and soothed her anxiety. She thought about returning home to her husband, and relaxing the rest of the weekend. Looking in the rear view mirror, she checked on the kids. They were struggling to hold their eyes open, and to any spent parent that was a wonderful sign. After their baths they will be asleep before you know it, so as soon as they were in the house she went straight up the stairs, ran a bath for her daughter, and started the shower in the master bedroom for her son. Forty minutes later, they were in their rooms out like a light. Jade showered while Trent sat in the den watching "Sports Center." The warm water was so invigorating. She stood under the steady stream of water and let it fall to her face. The steam filled room opened her nostrils, and soon after they were filled with the scent of her Japanese Cherry Blossom body wash. There was nothing like a nice hot shower after a long day, but as wonderful as the shower felt all she wanted to do was lay down, and watch *Sports Center* with her husband. She turned the water off, dried herself with a towel and covered her body in her scented body cream.

Once she opened the bathroom door she could have sworn she heard her bed calling her name, so she answered it as she walked over to the bed and fell onto her stomach. Her face was buried into the burnt orange colored comforter and she didn't move a muscle.

"Can I taste my pussy?" she felt Trent's hands moving up the back of her thighs before she heard his voice.

"That depends," she said as she turned her head, "how much money do you have?"

"I'll write you a check," he said flipping her over on her back. He wasted no time getting on his knees, and planting his tongue inside of her walls. She laid there in ecstasy for a while, just letting her husband please her. His tongue was lethal, and he knew it. She lifted her head to get a better look at Trent putting in work, and to her surprise he was already eyeing her. Jade gripped the back of his head with her hands, and pulled him closer to her. His tongue went deeper, and she enjoyed every plunge. A feeling of electricity raced through her body. It started at her toes, crept up her thighs, made her clit pulsate, hardened her nipples, and finally escaping through her mouth, and coming out as a moan. She started to feel that undeniable feeling and Trent noticed. He pulled back a little, and began to lap up her juices. Making slurping sounds knowing that turned her on. He took his tongue and began to brush it back and forth against her clit repeatedly. She felt her orgasm building, and he pulled away again. She knew he enjoyed pleasing her, but she needed to release the frenzy that was brewing inside of her. Her legs started to twitch, and she begged her husband to relieve her of her orgasm.

"Trent please don't tease me," she moaned, "Make me cum."

Just like that he got her where she needed to be, convulsing and screaming his name out in erotic bliss. She lay there out of breath, and staring at the ceiling while Trent stood over her smiling. She couldn't even say anything, so she reached for a pillow and tossed it at him.

"Who's the man?" he said, slapping her thigh. "I'm the man. Remember that," he added bending down, and planting a kiss on her stomach. "I'm going to take a shower."

"Cool." Jade said in a voice barely above a whisper. That was the last thing she said before her eyelids met. Damn she loved that man.

*****

Lani Alona Wilkes

I smiled as the guy in the black mustang next to me is trying his best to get my attention before the light changes. If he hasn't noticed by now, I'm not interested. Now a few months ago, depending on my mood I may have given this fool a little bit of my time, until I got bored with him, and tossed him aside. To be honest with you, I just spared this man the agony of my premature departure from his life. As my friends say I have the tendency to chew men up and spit them right back out. That's why Jade calls me a man eater, but that is not the case.

Let's get one thing straight. I do for myself. Never have I needed any man to carry me, and if they did it was because they wanted to not because I needed them to. Granted, I have always been a little all over the place when it comes to jobs, but I have always had one. I have been a dental hygienist for a few months now, and for once, I'm actually content with my line of work. That was my biggest fear going into this process. I was afraid I would get through all of my classes and internships at the dental school and in the end dislike my job, but that didn't happen. I love my job, and the people I work with and that's a far cry from the songs I've sung in the past. I have done everything from retail to medical records. I have even done a brief stint at a day spa, but that's all behind me now.

Growing up the youngest of three children, I could honestly say that I have been spoiled, and never wanted for attention. The men I have come across in my adult life only added to that. Some of the men I've known, we've never had a sexual relationship. They always stuck around with the hopes of getting the goods sooner or later, and I kept them around because, well, I guess there's a part of me that likes the chase.

At five feet five, one hundred and forty pounds, nice shape, light golden brown complexion, and long, dark black hair most people I meet think I'm Latina, but I'm not. I'm used to guys drooling over me like dogs in heat, but that has never affected my attitude. I am one of the nicest people you will ever meet. I just do men that I know are no good like my man Snoop says, I treat them how they want to be treated, but not this man. The gentleman I have been seeing for the past two years is the exception to the rule, and this time around I am going to treat this gentleman like a king.

Lani pulled into the complex in Ellicott City, Maryland. It was a nice neighborhood and all, but she wished Jackson would take the time from his busy schedule to search for a nice single-family home. She set the alarm on her smoke gray Toyota Sequoia, and proceeded up to his second floor unit. The all-white exterior of the gated complex was beautiful. She inserted her key into the lock of apartment 209, and her man came rushing out of the kitchen smothering her in kisses.

"Well hello to you too," she giggled, wrapping her arms around his well-built shoulders.

"I've missed you," Jackson said.

"You've missed me? You just saw me Friday and it's only Sunday."

Jackson pulled away from her, and looked her in the eyes "You know you're my baby, right?" he said.

"Yes I do," Lani said with a grin on her face. She knew what was about to happen whenever he said that.

"Well, then you should know that I'm about to put you to bed."

"Oh, really? At four o'clock in the afternoon?"

"That's right," he said pulling her over to one of his over-sized recliners. Before he instructed her to sit down, he unbuttoned her high waist denim shorts, and pulled them down along with her pink Victoria Secret lace thong. Once she was seated he said, "Now spread them," and like a good girl she did as told. Her motto in life was to never look down on anyone, unless they're giving you head so she watched Jackson devour her for a few minutes before she closed her legs and stood up.

"Now it's my turn," Lani said pulling her pink blouse over her head, and reaching back to unhook her bra.

Like a sixteen year old boy, about to get his first blow job. He was out of his slacks in record time, and stretched out on the white carpet. She didn't have to do much since he was already standing at attention, so she teased him by licking from the base of his thick penis up to his large head. He let out a deep sigh.

"You like that don't you, Doctor?" Lani asked. Doctor was what she liked to call him while they were having sex. She loved the sound of it.

"You know I do."

"Well, lay back and relax. I got this," Lani said as she pleased Jackson like he says only she could do. She stuck her tongue out, and eased his thick, saliva soaked eight and half inch dick down her throat. She felt sorry for all the women that knew what gag reflexes were because she sure as hell didn't. The further his dick went down her throat, the more her juices started to flow. She reached between her legs and stuck two fingers into her drenched pussy, and fed it to Jackson. He took her fingers into his mouth, and sucked every bit of it off.

"Damn you taste good," he said licking his lips.

Lani climbed on top of him and wasted no time bucking. She knew that drove him crazy, so she rode him until he finally exploded inside of her, and they both lay side by side on the floor allowing their orgasms to dissipate.

She wondered when he was going to ask her to stay with him. She had her own home, but she wanted to hear him say those words. She would rather hear him say will you marry me, but she was not going to press the issue. Although she knew they were exclusive, she wanted more. How often does a woman come across a handsome thirty-five-year-old single doctor? This was one fish she wanted to keep on her hook.

Lani met Jackson two years ago while on her lunch break at the University of Maryland. She decided to go over to the main buildings café, instead of her usual lunch spot at Lexington Market. She recalled passing an unexpected exam at the dental school and wanted to treat herself. Once inside of the hospital she opted for Subway instead, since the café's line was way too long. When she went over to the seating area in search of a table she couldn't find one unoccupied so she went over to a young woman sitting alone. Lani asked if she could join her.

"Sure," the girl said, "I'm finished eating. I was just passing time by." She began to stand, "The table's all yours," she smiled at Lani while gathering her things. She thanked the woman, as she walked away. A few minutes after Lani had taken a bite out of her chicken bacon ranch sandwich, she was interrupted herself.

"Excuse me, but do you mind if I sit with you?"

She looked in the direction of the deep voice.

"There aren't any available tables," the fine ass man towering over her table added.

He was unquestionably drop dead gorgeous with his milk chocolate complexion, deep dimples, and thick eyebrows that sat above the most exquisite set of almond-shaped eyes she had ever seen. His five o'clock shadow was just starting to reveal itself, but he was dressed in a pair of black slacks and a white button down shirt which gave him the look of a professional.

"Sure, have a seat," is what came out of her mouth, but, "Hell, yeah, sit your fine ass down," is what came to mind.

"Thank you. You will not know that I'm here," he said as he took a seat, and began to remove the paper from his sandwich.

"So are you a student at the dental school?" he asked.

"I thought you said I wouldn't know you were here," Lani replied.

Just then the sexiest smile crossed his face, and it made her pussy twitch. She scanned his finger for a ring, and was satisfied when there was none.

"Yes. I am a dental student, but the question is how did you know that?" Lani said, now picking at her food.

"Just a guess," he said taking a bite out of his sandwich, and swallowing it, "and your badge hanging from your shirt," he said wiping mustard from the corner of his mouth.

Lani looked down at her identification badge and said, "Ha ha ha." She completely forgot her badge was still clipped on to her shirt. Not sure what else to say to the fine specimen of a man sitting across from her she introduced herself.

"I'm Lani, by the way."

"Oh," he said reaching for a napkin and wiping his hands, then extending one to Lani, "Jackson," he replied with that gorgeous smile that made her instantly wet.

"Well it's nice to meet you," Lani said shaking his hand.

Her hand became completely engulfed in his. She looked at his huge hands, and dirty thoughts flooded her mind. They made small talk for about twenty minutes until he broke the news that he had a seminar to attend and didn't want to be late. That is when he informed her that he was a doctor, and she informed herself that she had to get his number. As he stood and cleaned the area where he was eating, he placed two business cards on the table.

"Would you mind if I called you sometime?" he asked.

Would a dog in heat mind some doggy dick? Hell no, they wouldn't mind, she thought to herself, but managed to say, "I think I'd like that."

"One is for you to keep, and use sometime, and the other is for you to write down your number for me," he smiled that million dollar smile again and the rest is history. He has been just as charming as the day they met. She loved this man, and not just because the sex was ridiculously good, but because he treated her like a queen. He sends her flowers, takes her on romantic dates, and constantly tells her how much he needs her in his life. She has always loved the way he made her feel. That is why she thought he was made just for her, and she was going to please him any and every way possible. You know what they say, what you will not do another woman will, and she didn't want to have to put her foot in anyone's ass for trying to take what was hers, but sometimes you got to do what you got to do.

She turned her head to the right where Jackson was laying and rested her head on his chest. She could hear a light snore coming from his mouth, and she smiled because her man was fine, snoring and all. She got up off the floor, walked into the bathroom, grabbed a washcloth and cleaned herself up, then used his mouth wash to wash away the last hint of sex that lingered around. She heard Jackson's cell phone ringing, and him quickly answering. All she heard was "Hello, yes, I'll be right there," then the call ended.

"Who was that?" Lani asked walking into the living room, and startling Jackson.

"Work," he said as he walked past Lani and into the bathroom.

Jackson was a primary care physician with his own practice, so he did not have to "work" on the weekends, but he chose to do so. She knew he went out of the way to meet the needs of his patients, and she could respect that. He was a stand-up guy who would give his last to anyone in need. He was raised in a family full of doctors. His father is a retired neurosurgeon and his mother is an obstetrician. Lani has never met his parents. They lived in Atlanta, and the one time they were here in Maryland, she had to be by her friend Ira's side when her husband passed away.

She couldn't wait to become a part of the family, and pop out a few doctors of her own. Jackson wanted children, which was a plus because someday Lani wanted children of her own with him.

"Hey babe," Jackson called from the shower. Lani walked into the bathroom, and leaned against the sink taking in the view through the glass shower doors.

"Are you going to be home around nine or nine-thirty tonight?" he asked.

"Yup, why?" she replied.

"I'll call you then," he said not answering her question. He stepped out of the shower, and grabbed a towel while she eyed his toned chest and ravishing brown-skinned penis. This man was nothing but pure eye candy.

Yup, she would definitely smack a bitch if need be. Not that she was the fighting type. In fact one of her rules was to never fight over any man, but hey rules were meant to be broken.

"What are you looking at? You want some more?" Jackson said with a sly look on his face.

"Don't tempt me mister," Lani said, as Jackson laughed and walked into the bedroom.

Lani stood looking at herself in the bathroom mirror. She wanted to ask him about moving in together, or spending a weekend together with no calls, and no interruptions, but she knew the only thing he would say is "I'm a doctor all day, every day. Just because my office is closed does not mean I no longer care. Yadda yadda yadda." She got it; he cared, but how about not caring for just one weekend. That thought may be selfish, but all she wanted was what was rightfully hers all to herself. At least if they lived together she would get to see him every day when he came home. Lord knows that if that were the case they would be humping like rabbits. Everyone that knows her knew she absolutely loved sex. If her man was not available she would simply take care of herself. After all, who knows your body better than you do?

"Don't forget to lock the door on your way out," Jackson said hurrying past the bathroom and adjusting his tie. Lani walked out of the bathroom, and saw Jackson grabbing his keys from the marble bar countertop, then grabbing his briefcase from the dining room table. He walked over to Lani and slipped his tongue in her mouth.

"I love you woman," he said before disappearing behind the door.

That man was something else. She couldn't put into words how he made her feel. She grabbed her purse from one of the chairs and a bottle of water from the fridge. There was no need in her being there if he wasn't. She could lounge around her own home for that matter, so she left the apartment, and double checked the lock. Once she reached her truck, her cell phone started to ring from inside of her purse. She felt around for her phone then hit the talk button, as she climbed in and closed the door.

"Miss me already?" she teased after seeing Jacksons name displayed on her screen. She put the call on speaker, and set the phone in its holder as she looked over her shoulder, and began to back out of the parking spot.

Jackson laughed, "I just wanted to tell you that I have a surprise for you."

"What kind of a surprise?" Lani asked inquisitively.

"The kind you're going to love."

"Well can I have it today?"

"I don't even have it to give to you today. I'll have it tomorrow evening."

"Alright, well I'll be waiting for it. Love you," Lani said.

They disconnected their call, and she thought about all the things Jackson has done, and continued to do. This man was too good to be true. She beamed all the way down Route 1 to her Elkridge, Maryland home on Middleton Road before pulling into the driveway of her white two- story home, with black shutters along the windows. This was yet another one of Jackson's many surprises. He knew she had her eyes on this particular house, and he gave her the down payment for it about four months ago. Lani knew with Jackson she did not want for anything, but she paid her own mortgage. She made sure he knew ahead of time that this was going to be her home. That's why she informed him that his name would not be on any of the paper work, and especially not the deed. She loved him and all, and wanted nothing more than to be with him, but just in case things went south she needed to know that her home would not be in jeopardy.

She spoke to her nosy neighbor Mrs. Steinberg and tried her best to hurry up the curved walk way. Mrs. Steinberg was an older woman who lived across the street, and had a lot of time on her hands. She was widowed and her two children barely come to visit her, so that leaves her with a lot of time to sit and signify all day long. Every now and then, Lani would stop and give her a little bit of her time, but that woman could talk, and she knew everybody's business from the east coast to the west coast. If she was not on her porch, or in her yard acting as if she was gardening, she was in her house looking out of the window. If you have a secret and wanted to keep it that way, your best bet was to stay as far away from Mrs. Steinberg as possible, because she could smell a secret from a mile away. Not to mention she couldn't pronounce Lani's name for shit.

"Loni," she yelled from across the street as she made two attempts to get up from her rocking chair.

She was a heavy set woman that wore floral print most of the time, and always smelled like fresh flowers. Lani walked to the end of her drive way. She knew there was no getting out of this encounter. She would just knock on her door until she answered it.

"Lena, you missed all the action today. You know that woman down the street with all the children? Well one of the kids father came and took the child from her," she said nodding her head up and down adding emphasis to her own statement.

"Oh, ok, I'm sorry to hear that," Lani managed to muster up. She was not worried about anybody else and their problems.

"Well don't be. I've seen those kids outside by themselves numerous times, sometimes without any garments on. That woman is an unfit mother, and I don't blame the father for taking his kid. I think we should find the rest of the fathers, and tell them to come and get their children also."

She must be out of her damn mind. "Umm, I think we should just stay out of this. I know I am, and I think you should follow my lead on this one."

"Well maybe you can just stand by and watch but I can't," Mrs. Steinberg said as she started to back away from Lani. That was one way to get rid of her, just disagree with whatever concoction she'd thought up that day, and keep it moving.

"Ok well I'll talk to you later," Lani said high stepping toward her door. She was relieved when she was safe inside of her home. She checked her messages and had one message from Ira saying she couldn't reach her on her cell phone, and one from Jade saying to call her because she had issues. She laughed at Jade. She could be so dramatic at times. She would call them both later, but right now she needed to shower and to get comfortable. Tomorrow was Monday, and she was not looking forward to hearing her alarm clock sound at six o'clock but she would be ready.

*****

Ira Annalee Meadows

"Yes, Frank someone will be waiting for you this evening, and I do apologize for the wait last week, but we were flooded with customers at the last minute," Ira spoke into the receiver of her home office phone.

"I understand that Ira, but my men have a schedule to keep, and they cannot be kept waiting outside for your staff to let them in."

"I know, and it will not happen again. See you tomorrow," she hung up the phone.

This man is a thorn in my behind. Frank and his sons are the owners of Fresh from the Bay, the business where I order all of my seafood products. If it weren't for his reasonable prices I would take my business elsewhere. Oh who am I kidding, I wouldn't be able to bring myself to fire anyone. I'm just not that type of person. Most people I know don't understand how I can run a successful business with such a modest personality, but I seem to do alright. I do have the tendency to let apathetic employees remain on my payroll a little longer than they deserve, but I believe in second chances, and thirds, and fourths. I'll be the first to admit it is very hard for me to tell a single mother or struggling student that I no longer require their services. Even as a woman I am still working on myself as a person, a mother, a boss, and a friend. Everyone is constantly telling me how strong I am, and it's greatly appreciated, but truth be told I believe my Lord and Savior upholds me on the daily basis.

With all of the family and friends I have showering me with love I am still a lonely woman without my husband. When I lost him two years ago I didn't think I would ever recover from the tragedy. Thank God for my two babies, Nicholas Jr. and Tij. They have kept me sane over the years. At seven and three years old, they don't know how much of a role they play in my rise as a courageous woman. Things are getting better for me I must say. I know I will see my husband again very soon, and I take comfort in knowing I have my very own angel watching over me.

Ira checked her emails before she called it a night. She noticed she had one from Frank, and decided not to open it. He was a very punctual man whom she understood, but he could be a nuisance at times. She loved the fact that she had a close business relationship with the companies she conducted business with, but it was a Sunday night and she wanted to relax before manic Monday hit.

She walked upstairs to her bedroom and sat on the edge of the bed before lying back on her all white down comforter. Sometimes she felt so overwhelmed with responsibility. Her restaurant was like her baby, and she loved being a business owner but there was a lot involved in keeping it afloat. Her husband used to be that sanctuary for her, and he would always tell her not to worry about anything. She was glad that she was to the point where she could think about her beloved husband without crying.

She looked over at her husband's picture on the night stand. Sergeant Nicholas Meadows, God did she miss him. Even though he was in another country three months before he passed, she always felt so close to him. Ira remembered that dreadful day like it was yesterday. As soon she saw the two uniformed men approaching her home, as she and her boys made their way to her car, she knew they weren't bearing good news. Before they even spoke one word she dropped to her knees. She remembered the two soldiers standing over her giving her their regards and her boys crying asking her what was wrong, but she couldn't speak, she couldn't move, she couldn't catch her breath, and surely she could not tell her babies that Daddy was not coming home.

It took her months to actually come to the realization that he really was gone. She loved her husband with all of her heart and soul, but she didn't like the fact that he chose to re-enlist in the Army. He had a family to live for, and they should've come first, but he felt as if it was his duty to fight for his country.

It has been two years and five months since Nick has passed, and she was still trying to move on with her life.

Usually on nights like this, when she was restless she would pick up a pen and paper and write to Nick. She laughed as she recalled her failed attempts at writing freaky things to him. She was not good at those things. Her private nature prevented her from fully letting go. Nick was the only man she had ever opened up to even then she shied away from certain things, but what she wouldn't give to do whatever he asked of her now. He had the best loving, the best wet juicy kisses, and the softest touch. His dark chocolate skin and masculine stature was just right, even down to his pudgy stomach. She wish she could rub her hands over his thick head of hair while gazing into his dark brown eyes, and him ruining the moment by saying, "What are you going to give me some tonight?" she laughed to herself, but felt sadness coming on, so she opened her dresser drawer and pulled out her bible then flipped to her bookmarked page and recited one of her favorite scriptures.

"Don't let your heart be troubled. Trust in God and trust also in me. There is more than enough room in my Father's home. If it were not so would I have told you that I am going to prepare a place for you? When everything is ready I will come and get you, so you will also be with me where I am, and you will know the way to where I am going."

Those words made her feel a little better. She was ashamed to say that lately she missed her husband's companionship more than anything. She missed his physical presence don't misunderstand, but she wanted to feel him and only him inside of her again. She knew she would never be able to love another man the way she loved Nick. That flame that her husband sparked had been completely doused, and she didn't think any other man had what it took to reignite it. That's why she vowed not to love another, it just didn't seem right. Putting herself back on the market was out of the question. She would just live off of her memories, and love on her children that much more.

She went over to her black floor length mirror that stood in the corner of her bedroom and eyed herself from head to toe. Her pink and black Joe Boxer pajama's with polka dots on the shorts was her favorite thing to wear. All of that lacey stuff was not for her. She marveled over the fact that she could still pass for a twenty-year-old. Her thin frame she had inherited from her father and her caramel complexion she had gotten from her mother. She spun around and looked over her shoulder at what her husband liked to call "her apple." It stood out from the rest of her body. Not quite as much as Jades who they affectionately called, "Big booty Judy," but it was definitely nice. She puckered up her plumped full lips and made a smooching sound with them then laughed at herself again. After surveying her body she thought to herself, whatever she lacked in the front with her A cup, she made up with in the back. Too bad no one else was going to enjoy it.

"Mommy, I got to go pee," her three year old Tij stood sleepily in her doorway.

"Ok come on," she said ushering him into her bathroom.

"Can I really go the rest of my life without companionship?" she asked her reflection out loud in the bathroom mirror, while her son stood over the toilet hitting everything, but the water inside of the toilet bowl. That's the only thing about little boys. Their aim at that age is really off.

"Yes, I can," she continued. "He would have done the same thing for me."

"Who mommy?" her son asked.

"Mommy was just talking out loud. Come on lets go back to bed," she picked her son up and held him on her hip. Even after asking a question he was asleep by the time she placed him back in his bed.

She went back into the bathroom and cleaned up her sons mess, but her thoughts were still in the same place. Thinking about her husband did something to her. She felt awakened all of a sudden. She washed her hands and made her way over to her bed fighting the temptation to pleasure herself.

"I've read my bible for the night, and that is all the stimulation I need," she said giving herself a pep talk. Her kitty was purring and being very disobedient. She covered her face with a pillow. She needed a release, but wanted to believe that she was mentally above sexual stimulation. If she wanted to remain true to her husband she would have to adhere to that. Her marriage vows said until death do us part, but she couldn't help thinking that Nick would be watching her stroke her kitty, and that made her feel uncomfortable. She had only pleasured herself once since Nick has passed, and even then she felt ashamed afterwards.

Laying back on her bed her thoughts shifted from her husband to her restaurant to the throbbing in between her legs.

She had to get some rest soon, since the crack of dawn was not far off.

Remembering she was given a phone number earlier at work, she got out of bed and walked down the stairs. She pulled the number from her purse that hung off the edge of the black kitchen bar stool. According to her staff it was an older woman that left the number, and said it was in reference to her husband. She looked at the paper and read the note written at the bottom, then checked the time on the microwave above the stove.

"Well it says call anytime," Ira mumbled.

She wouldn't be surprised if the woman was a debt collector. In the past two years anyone that has ever done any business with Nick has made their presence known. In her opinion his debt should have been buried right along with him, but she would hear what the woman had to say, make a note of it, and pass it on to her lawyer.

When no one answered after the fourth ring she waited to hear a voicemail greeting to see if she recognized the voice. When she heard the automated system she decided not to leave a message. If it was important enough for the woman to come to her restaurant then she would find some other way to get in contact with her.

She sat the phone on its base, and it began to ring. The number displayed on the caller ID was the same number she had just dialed, so she answered it.

"Hello?" she said and was met with silence.

"Hello?" she said again and got the same response. She hung the phone up and passed it off as a bad connection. Surely an older woman would not play on her phone, so she turned the kitchen light out and rechecked all of her locks. The motion censored lights lit up the patio, as she scanned her back yard. After checking on her boys who were asleep in the same bed, even though they each had their own rooms she tucked herself into her own bed. Tomorrow would come sooner than she'd like, so she tried her best to push all of the thoughts that have been weighing heavy on her mind to the back of her head. Her goods would have to throb away since her plan was to say a prayer and closed her eyes.

Chapter One

"Forty, what did she mean forty?"

"How old are you Ms. Jeffries?" Six years old, Nicah asked as she sat across the table from Courtni. She was coloring a picture that was supposed to represent her family.

"How old do you think I am?" Courtni asked the child while scribbling notes on her note pad.

"Like forty," the child replied, never looking up from her drawing.

Forty? What did she mean forty? Courtni thought to herself.

"Why forty?" Courtni asked trying to mask her disappointment.

"Well," Nicah said, dragging the word out way longer than its four letters intended. "You talk like an old person and you dress like an old person."

"Well, forty isn't old, you know?"

"Yes it is," Nicah giggled in between switching crayons.

Courtni laughed at her squeaky voice. She was such a bright child and Courtni loved working with her. She wished she had more time to spend with Nicah, but both of their schedules were pretty tight. Her family had her in all types of after school and recreational activities to buy them time to finish whatever business they had to tend to.

Nicah was like most of the children she worked with. She lost her father over a year ago and her mother just a few months ago. From her sessions with the child, it seems as if she spent a substantial amount of time with her grandmother. Courtni was not sure what her mother's occupation was, but it must have taken up a lot of her time. Nicah's grandmother was now hospitalized, and her twenty-year-old aunt has been caring for her. Courtni was praying for her grandmother's speedy recovery. Nicah needed her more now than ever. In her short period of time on this earth she has had a great amount of heartache come her way, but you wouldn't think so after having a conversation with her.

In the two months that Courtni has known Nicah she was always very upbeat and positive, but Courtni knew from experience that was all a cover up. Her goal was to break through that shell, and let her know it was okay to cry for her parents, and enlighten her on ways to cope with her loss. She was a beautiful child with a tan complexion and big round eyes. Her long and dark eyelashes gave the impression that she wore mascara. Her lengthy hair was kept in a bush ball on top of her head. She also had a very extensive vocabulary for a six year old, and was very attentive so Courtni wouldn't be surprised if she knew a lot more about what went on in her parent's lives than she let on.

"I need for you to finish your picture while I finish my paper work before your Auntie comes to pick you up okay?" Courtni spoke to Nicah while inching her way out of the tiny chair that sat in front of the preschool like table.

"Ms. Jeffries?" Nicah called out.

"Yes?" Courtni stopped in her tracks.

"I really miss my mommy," she said and Courtni sat back down, "and my daddy. My daddy was going to take me to Disney World," she said excitedly.

"He was," Courtni said returning the excitement.

"Uh huh, he said when the time was right we would go, but then he went to heaven. Do you know where heaven is? It's in the sky," she said answering her own question.

"How do you feel about your daddy being in heaven?"

"Good. I like heaven. There are angels in heaven, and mommy said daddy still comes to visit me just like he used to. I just can't see him now."

"Did daddy live with you and mommy?"

"No," she said and dropped her head. Courtni could tell she was about to shut down, so she changed the subject.

"So what do you have planned for tomorrow?" Courtni asked.

"I have a soccer game. I like soccer."

"That's good Nicah. I hope you have fun, and score lots of goals," Courtni said and Nicah giggled. There was a knock at the door, and Amy Courtni's secretary stuck her head in.

"Ms. Camille is here to pick up Nicah."

"Okay, send her in."

"Ok," Amy shut the door and a few seconds later Camille walked in.

"Hi Camille."

"Hi, I'm so sorry I'm late. I had another job interview today. Things have been kind of hectic lately," she said as she walked over to the coat rack in the corner, and grabbed Nicah's jacket.

"I understand, and it's not a problem."

"Thank you. Come on Nicah we have to go before we miss our bus," she said while Nicah put her arms into her jacket. They headed towards the door and Courtni followed.

"How is your mom doing Camille?"

"Okay, I guess. They are starting her on some new medication and, so far so good. Please continue to pray for us."

"Will do," Courtni stooped down to Nicah's level, "Thank you for cleaning up your crayons Nicah. I'll see you next week okay?"

"Okay," Nicah said letting go of her aunts hand and wrapping her small arms around Courtni.

She waved as they made their way toward the elevators. Courtni shut and locked her door. Her job was done for the day, and she was ready to get out of her work clothes and into something a little more comfortable. She checked the time on the clock that hung above the coat rack, and noticed it was 5:10 p.m., so she picked up her office phone and dialed Lani's number.

"Hello," Lani said.

"Hey, are we still going to Hicks tonight?"

"Yup, as far as I know. Have you talked to Jade at all today?"

"Not yet. Hold on a second," Courtni said. She clicked over and dialed Jades number.

"Chello," Jade answered playfully.

"Hey what are you doing?"

"Closing up the bakery."

"Hold on Jade. I have Lani on the other line," Courtni said clicking over and joining the girls on a three way call.

"Hello, Lani…Jade?" Courtni said waiting for a response from both girls.

"I'm still here," Lani said.

"Me too," Jade said.

"Okay, so eight-thirty we're at the spot, right ladies?" Courtni asked.

"The spot?" Lani said confused.

"I'm sorry, but what the hell is the spot? I'm lost," Jade said.

Courtni sucked her teeth. "It's Ira's restaurant. Gosh, you two are slow. Are we still meeting there tonight?"

"Yeah, but the spot Court? I'm still lost," Jade said laughing.

"Are we trying to sound hip today?" Lani said.

"Look, forget I said that. It just slipped out and—"

"Yeah, but why?" Jade said.

"I don't know why Jade, it just did so let it go, and Lani stop laughing. She's really not that funny. Are you coming or not?

"Yes, I'll be there," Lani said still laughing at Jade. She had a way of annoying everybody especially Courtni. Courtni is very easily bothered and Jade got a kick out of doing so.

"All I'm saying is if you are going to start speaking in codes you have to let at least one person in on the codes," Jade said laughing along with Lani and Courtni joined in on the laugh.

So, "the spot" wouldn't be her normal choice of words, but she was trying to relax a little, and not be so uptight. She couldn't believe a six-year-olds comment had stirred those subconscious thoughts that she have lived with for so long. Courtni has always known that she was way ahead of her years, but her goals were all she saw in the distant when it came to having fun, and letting down her hair so to speak. In her mind, partying could wait, but now that her goals were accomplished, she could mitigate her apprehensive personality when she did not have to be professional.

"I'll see you two later, and someone remind Ira," Courtni said.

"Okay. I'll call her," Lani said and they disconnected their call.

Courtni loved her friends despite their sometimes vexing ways. She knew they loved her, and if she really had a problem with anything they did she had no problem putting them in their place.

After storing her handwritten notes from Nicah's session, she thought about her forty-year-old comment. Courtni looked down at her two-inch brown wedges, and brown slacks with the matching brown blazer that did nothing for her figure. She didn't dress like this all the time. This was her professional look, but one thing she knew was children were some of the most honest people in the world, and if Nicah said it she more than likely meant it. Yes, she was a child, but children are a lot smarter than we give them credit for.

Courtni stood up and walked over to her closet, and pulled open the dark wooden door. Her image appeared in the mirror that hung on the other side, and she liked what she saw, but had to admit now that it had been brought to her attention she did look a little older, not forty, but older. She put her hands on her hips and turned from side to side.

She said out loud to her reflection, "You're going to start acting your age. You will not be in your twenties forever," she smiled, and was excited to make some mild changes in her life. She would start with clothing and would go shopping soon, but today was Friday and she was hanging with the ladies.

By the time Courtni reached her home and showered it was almost eight o'clock. She called the girls to see where they were. She would leave out once she knew they were in route since she only lived about ten minutes from the restaurant. Jade said she was on Key Highway, and Lani was on Washington Boulevard, so Courtni reached in her closet and grabbed her brown cowboy boots to go with her denim shorts and burnt orange colored blouse. She grabbed her purse and locked up her home.

When she got to the restaurant, she saw Jade standing outside leaning against the building. She was talking on her cell phone, and Courtni was sure it was Trent on the other end. From the side all you could see was ass. Jade wore a pair of black leggings, black peep toe booties, and a blue silk belted blouse.

When she noticed Courtni she waved and placed her phone in her purse.

"Where is Lani?" Jade asked as soon as Courtni was within earshot.

"She's on her way. You know she's always late," Courtni said and they entered the restaurant.

Once inside they stood behind the other customers waiting to be seated, until Julia, the hostess, sat them at their usual table. The table was located in the back of the restaurant with four sets of silverware wrapped in red cloth napkins, and a red candle holder in the middle of the table. Julia placed their menus on the table and lit the candle before informing them of the special of the day.

"You are missing one, aren't you?" Jonathan asked in a thick Nigerian accent.

"Yes, she's on her way," Courtni replied.

Jonathan was the manager of Ira's restaurant. He was also the subject of many of Courtni's naughty dreams, but she wouldn't dare let that cat out of the bag. That will be her little secret. His beautiful dark eyes and square jaw line was very appealing to her. If any of her friends caught wind of her little school girl crush they wouldn't waste any time running down her resume to the man, and informing him of how lucky he would be to have her on his life. In other words they would embarrass the hell out of her, so yes she would keep that to herself.

"Courtni," Jade said snapping her fingers, "The man asked you a question."

"I'm sorry, what was the question?" Courtni asked feeling embarrassed.

"That is okay. I asked if you would like anything to drink," Jonathan said smiling at Courtni.

"Oh, yes I'll have a sweet tea. Thank you," Jonathan nodded his head and motioned for the waitress to come over.

"Hey honey buns," Lani said as she approached them. She sat her compact purse on the table, and pressed the back of her black baby doll dress against the back of her legs before taking a seat.

"I ordered you lemonade like me. You know since you weren't here to order for yourself," Jade said with a forced smile on her face.

"Well I'm sending it back, because that's not what I want," Lani said sticking her tongue out. "Ira's not ready to eat yet? I'm hungry."

"No she's still in the front somewhere," Courtni said, and they all looked in the direction of her glare.

They spotted Ira greeting customers with a huge smile on her face. She wore a pair of dark wide legged jeans and a pale pink fitted tank top. Her pants were too long to even see the shoes she had on, but her bobbed hair cut was on point.

"Here you go ladies," the waitress said placing their drinks in front of them. They placed their orders and ordered Ira a plate of fried shrimp which they were sure she was going to order anyway, since that's all she ever ordered even at other restaurants.

Ira was now talking to Jonathan, giving him the run down on what to do, and what not to do while she was not around as if he didn't already know. He has only worked for her for the four years that she has been in business.

"Hey ladies," Ira said taking a seat beside Lani.

"Girl, it's really busy in here tonight. Business must be pretty good," Lani said, and Ira smiled.

"I know. I thank God for that. We were pretty slow last Friday, but not today."

"That's good. We ordered you fried shrimp by the way," Jade said.

"Ummm, that sounds good. I'm starved."

"Do you want a drink Lani?" Jade said staring across the table. "You're staring at that cocktail menu like Courtni was just staring at Jonathan."

"Courtni you was staring at Jonathan?" Lani asked.

"You like Jonathan, Courtni? Do want me to hook you up with him?" Ira asked.

"What? No, I was not staring at that man. Do not start Jade."

"Who had the stuffed flounder?" The waitress asked as a male server carried their food for her on a large tray.

Courtni was happy she had come at the time she did. The last thing she wanted was to get the third degree from the wolf pack at the table. Whenever they had the tiniest inkling that she was interested in any man they were all over it. She knew they meant well, and only wanted her to experience life with the opposite sex, but that would happen when it was supposed to happen. She knew God was at work three hundred and sixty five days a year and her time would come.

The waitress left them to enjoy their meals. Ira's restaurant had the best seafood, and although expensive, it was well worth the money. You received nice portions, and no one left without a full belly or the "itis" as they like to say. Ira and Nick worked so hard to make her dream a reality, and Ira has worked twice as hard to keep things together after Nick left for Afghanistan where he was stationed when he passed. That time she spent away from him gave her a little bit of independence, and forced her to make executive decisions on her own. All in all it made her a much better business woman.

"So what's been going on with everyone? Ira asked while pulling apart her jumbo fried shrimp.

"I have a brand new BMW 335i coupe," Lani said still eating her chicken alfredo.

"Well damn," Jade said.

"Wow, when did you get that? Ira asked.

"Sunday."

"What and you didn't tell us about it? I can't wait to see it. What color is it? Did Jackson buy it for you?" Courtni asked firing off an abundance of questions.

"I didn't tell you guys because I wanted it to be a surprise when I pulled up on time today, but since I was late things didn't work out that way," she laughed, "It's silver and yes, Jackson bought it for me."

"You don't sound like a woman who is now driving a top of the line vehicle," Ira said, "Why aren't you jumping for joy?"

"Because I did that Sunday and I am happy, very happy," she said nonchalantly.

"No she is not," Jade said, stuffing a forkful of crab meat into her mouth.

"I don't know. I think my womanly intuition is trying to tell me something."

"You mean something like you wanted a different color, because I don't see what the problem is," Jade said.

"No Jade," Lani said rolling her eyes. "I mean like some things aren't sitting right with me."

"Like what?" Courtni asked.

"Like, I have only seen him twice since he gave me the car. We talk all the time, but this is new to me and to our relationship. I have been trying to get him to stay with me or me stay with him a little more, and it seems like I'm just pushing him further away," Lani said pushing her plate towards the middle of the table. "I cannot begin to put into words how much this man means to me," Lani continued and tears began to form in the corners of her eyes. "I love him," Lani said. Her tears were now flowing freely down her cheeks.

"It's okay Lani," Ira said rubbing her back, "Maybe you are feeding a little bit too far into this. He is a doctor and a very busy man. You have said yourself that he is constantly on the go. You watch and see, soon he will be calling and telling you to pack your bags and come along with him on one of his business trips as usual."

Lani wiped her tears with her napkin. "He called me yesterday and we talked for a while. He told me he would stay at my place tomorrow night, and everything was fine. Then we disconnected the call and he called right back. When I answered he said, "Hello," as if he didn't recognize the voice. He claimed he was trying to reach his parents and accidently dialed my number, but I don't know."

"Did you ever stop to think that maybe he really was trying to reach his parents?" Jade asked sarcastically.

"Yes I did as matter of fact, but shouldn't he know my voice by now?"

"Not if he planned on dialing his parent's house and you answer the phone Lani. That man loves you. For the first time in your life you are in love with a great man, and your insecurities are starting to rear its ugly head and that's normal. We all have insecurities, but you have to have trust in your relationship. That's the only way things are going to work," Jade said.

"Do you trust Trent, Jade?" Lani asked.

"With everything in me," Jade stated and Lani smiled.

"Well I need to get there. I know he is not doing anything. I just want him to want me the way that I want him. He can keep the car and just give me all of him."

"In time that will happen, but you cannot force it," Ira said.

"Look, there is nothing wrong with your relationship. That man loves you dearly," Courtni said, rubbing Lani's hand from across the table. "Come on let's join hands and pray," Courtni said taking Jades hand.

"Courtni you don't have to do that," Lani said. Prayer was always her and Ira's go to response to everything.

"Yes I do. I will leave you with a prayer tonight. Even if I have to call and pray with you over the phone, it will get done."

"Okay then, lets pray," Lani said. They all held hands, and bowed their heads while Courtni led them in prayer.

"Lord we come to you today to seek your guidance. Please watch over Lani, comfort her and place your healing hands over her heart. Let her always come to you in her time of need, and let us all remember that you Lord show your servants your greatness and your strong hand. We shall love you Lord with all of our hearts and with all of our souls, and with all of our strength. From heaven Lord you look down and see all mankind. Surely you are our help Lord; you are the one who sustains us. Let us always remember that you are our salvation and our honor depends on you Lord. You are our rock and our refuge. For you will never forsake us Lord in Jesus name we pray. Amen."

"Amen," they all said in unison.

"Well, I don't know about you all, but I feel better," Lani said.

"Yes-sa," Jade said, closing her eyes and waving hands in the air.

The waitress came over to the table right after, and they knew she was waiting for the right time to come over instead of interrupting their extensive conversation. That was a smart move since no one likes an awkward moment. Courtni probably would have made her sit down and join hands with the rest of them. The waitress took their food to box it and cleared the table.

Ira introduced her to everyone. She was new to Ira's team, but Ira seemed to adore the young the lady, then again Ira adored everyone. She was just an all-around sweet person, and they loved her for that.

"Okay, enough about me. What's going on with everyone else?" Lani asked.

"Well, I have decided to start living a little," Courtni said.

"Good for you," Jade said, "Now what exactly does that entail?"

"Well, I'm going to try my best to loosen up, and get out a little more. You know, things like that."

"I can dig it," Lani said.

"Well, I'm not doing much. I just hired a nanny for the boys. She's going to be staying with us throughout the week, and she will have the weekends off," Ira said taking a sip of her drink.

"Umm, do you know this woman?" Courtni asked.

Ira laughed, "Yes I have met her a few times. She was my neighbor's nanny for a while, but my neighbor is now a stay-at-home mom, so they let her go. Her name is Naomi and she is twenty-five -years old. She comes highly recommended by not only my neighbor's, but the company she works for. Not to mention I've seen her in action myself, so I'm pretty confident that things will work out for the best."

"Can I drop my kids off or will that be extra?" Jade said with a serious face then burst into laughter. "Well I don't have anything going on right now. My tires are still intact, and we are all doing well at home."

"Did you ever find out who did that?" Ira asked.

"No, and I have been wrecking my brain trying to figure that out, but I'm over it now."

"Well make sure you all are ready to go tomorrow. I'll stop and grab a cake or something to take to Robert and Maria's house, and I will be at Jade's by six. The party starts at five so we'll mingle a little bit, and then get out there before someone brings up how sorry they are for me and make me cry," Ira laughed.

"Oh, and afterwards I would like to stop by my coworker house warming party. If I don't go I will never here the end of it," Lani said.

No problem," Courtni said, and they all looked at her shocked. "Hey, I said I would start to live a little, and a little house warming party is just what I need to get my feet wet."

"Alright, see you all tomorrow," Jade said reaching in her purse along with the other girls for money to tip the waitress.

Ira walked the girls outside, and they all went to Lani's parking spot to check out her new car. The silver BMW had Lani written all over it. It was sporty and most of all it was fast. Everyone knew Lani had a heavy foot and loved to drive fast. After viewing Lani's car they all went to their respective vehicles and Ira went back into her restaurant. Courtni let her windows down to enjoy the cool May breeze while taking in the sites that surrounded the Inner Harbor. Tomorrow morning she would treat herself to some retail therapy and pick up something to wear to the two parties she would be attending with her friends.

She arose Saturday morning feeling refreshed and ready to shop. She would ask one of the girls to go with her, but she knew they were all preoccupied. Lani would be "boo lovin" with Jackson since he stayed over with her last night. Jade would be at the bakery, and Ira would be at her restaurant. That was okay, because she didn't mind shopping alone. No one was there to distract her, and no one to wait for when she was done shopping for herself.

She went into the kitchen and poured Colby's dog food into his bowl. Then grabbed a frying pan and made herself a few strips of turkey bacon, and two eggs. After eating, she showered and threw on a pair of jeans and a shirt, walked Colby then headed to mall.

It seems like everyone had the same idea this morning. It was a little after ten and Towson Mall was packed with vehicles. She headed straight for Nordstrom, and after searching the racks she found a pair of black and white leopard print leggings and fell in love. She loved animal print, but preferred not to wear it often. She had a pair of pumps she bought a few weeks ago from the Jessica Simpson Collection that would go really good with those leggings. She found a shirt to match the leggings, and somehow managed to buy $197 worth of clothing. This is why she didn't shop very often.

On her way out of the mall she purchased a cinnamon roll and a Creamy Retreat ice cream dessert. She knew she shouldn't be eating junk food as much as she has been lately, but it happened every time she came to the mall. Her plan was to lose twenty pounds before the summer, but she has yet to put that plan into action. This summer she had plans to travel a little and wanted to wear a bathing suit comfortably. She was a nice size and thick in all the right places except her backside. The good Lord gave her more than enough boobs but not nearly enough booty. She wouldn't complain though things could always be worst. All she really wanted to do was work on her stomach. Right now it was just a little bulge, but if she didn't work on it soon she knew it would become a pouch. Once in the garage, she sat in her truck for few seconds trying to enjoy her Creamy Retreat before it melted, and she noticed a car with its blinkers on in her review mirror.

"Oh come on, I can't even enjoy my snack without somebody rushing me along," she said out loud to herself with a mouth full of dough. She placed her foot on the brake, put the truck in reverse and began to back out of the spot. She would go home and relax until it was time for her to get dressed and head to Jade's.

Chapter Two

"You have got to be kidding me."

"Today has been pretty busy," Jade said while packing two blueberry muffins into a small, teal-colored box for the young man on the other side of the counter.

"Yes it has. We have been through eleven pies today and it's only two thirty. Here you go sir and thank you for stopping in," Arnie said giving the man his order. "What time are you leaving today?"

"Around three, are you sure you and Stephanie will be okay in here? If you need me to stay, I will," Jade said.

"Girl we will be just fine. Stephanie is on point. I really like her Jade. She's a sweetheart, and she is really good with the customers. Just look at her over there with that woman. She's having a good old time," Arnie said, and Jade looked across the bakery at Stephanie.

She was standing next to a customer who was sitting, and they were laughing at something obviously very funny. Stephanie seemed to be a very passive person. She had a very calm demeanor, but the customers absolutely loved her. Her plumped cheeks were rosy and gave her a childlike innocence along with the floral print headbands she wore, but she had a small piercing above her lip that showed a hint of rebellion. When Jade first met her she couldn't pass up the opportunity to be someone's first employer.

"Yes, she is Arnie, and thank you again for closing for me. I'll take the deposit bag to the bank Monday morning."

"That's fine by me honey. The bank will be closed by the time we get out of here anyway, and I'm gonna high tail my behind to Jumpies Bar," Arnie said bouncing his shoulders and pressing his lips together.

"You like that place huh?" Jade asked, and started cleaning the table behind the register.

"Woo girl, it's the best thing since frank and beans."

"Wow, that's good Arnie," Jade said. She knew his metaphor was not that of hot dogs and pork and beans.

"Girl, I walked in there last weekend and damn near fainted when I saw all those glistening honeys just sweating and pumping and gyrating. Girl my bitch had to catch me. I ain't lying."

Jade laughed at Arnie. He was hilarious and had the funniest facial expressions. He called all the other gay men he hung with his "bitches." Together all of them were a force to be reckoned with. Sometimes when they went out they all dressed in drag, but looked ten times better than some of these women that pack on tons of makeup and call themselves Barbies.

"Well you try to behave yourself tonight," Jade said.

"No thank you Mrs. DeVoe. I already have plans to don't stop get it, get it," Arnie said pumping his fist in front of chest a few times, and then looking over his shoulder to make sure none of the customers saw him. "Where are you going today anyway Miss Lady? Why are you leaving early?"

"I'm going to a little get together with Ira and the girls, and then we're stopping by Lani's friend's house warming party, which we are going to be late for, but Lani says it okay."

"Tell all the girls I said hey, and I'll see you on Monday, or maybe I'll call you if my night isn't as exciting as I want it to be."

"Okay, I'm going to grab my purse and then head out. You two take care of my baby," Jade said, as Stephanie made her way to the front with Jade and Arnie.

"I will, and I'll see you Monday Mrs. Jade," Stephanie said.

"Stephanie, you don't have to call me that. I actually prefer for you to call me Jade. You're a part of our little family now," Jade said pinching her chubby checks.

"You wait until she comes in here with one of her nasty attitudes. You gonna be calling her plenty of other names under your breath," Arnie said to Stephanie, and she laughed.

Jade shoved Arnie playfully and grabbed her purse from the back on her way out she stopped and thanked all the customers that were still in the store for their business.

"Thank you for hiring me I like it here. You two are funny," Stephanie said.

"Well, thank you," Jade said. "I'm headed to Five Guys. Would you two like anything?" Jade asked and they both shook their heads no. "My treat," Jade added.

"Oh well in that case, I'll have a small burger with everything and some fries. You know I don't turn down free food," Arnie said.

"I'll have the same," Stephanie said.

"You two are something else. I'll be back," Jade said, and exited the building.

Once inside Five Guys, she decided to buy Trent and the kids something as well. She sent him a text to ask what he would like, and his response was, "You choose." The line was long as usual, so she had more than enough time to make a decision.

Her total came to over fifty dollars, and she instantly regretted her kind gesture. She could have cooked them all a home cooked meal for less than that. She placed the rest of the food in her truck before going back to the bakery. As she turned the corner and started towards the bakery she noticed a familiar face crossing Centre Street and coming towards her.

She watched as the same young woman from her bakery crossed the street and neared her wearing the same dark shades, but this time a gold and white head scarf covered her head and ended in a knot under her chin. Jade slowed her pace as the woman walked past without saying a word. Her eyes were pointed in the direction of the concrete as Jade watched her walk past the parking lot making sure that she didn't touch her truck. She was positive the woman was not wrapped too tight, and although she didn't seem like much of a threat, it still bothered Jade that she questioned Arnie about her the other day, then her tires were mysteriously slashed. She hurried to drop off Arnie and Stephanie's food so she could make it back to her vehicle, just in case.

Once she was on the road, she pressed the button to open the sunroof and let a little fresh air in. Her husband used to own a Navigator a few years ago. Over the eight years they have been together he has had about ten different vehicles, but she fell in love with the Navigator. When he traded it in she decided she would invest in one for herself, and once the money from her bakery started to roll in she did just that. They were blessed beyond measure and she was very thankful for everything the Lord has given them.

She had a rough time when Trent's business began to pick up and he was away from home a lot more. When she asked him to invest in her and help her open a bakery, he didn't hesitate. He has been very supportive from day one. Both of their businesses were booming, and things have been going very well for their family. Her husband has been home before night fall these past few weeks. For a while he would come home all hours of the night. She would call his office before she went to bed just to say good night and to see if he was really still at work. Let's be honest, any woman would think there was something fishy going on if their man claimed to be at work all day and all night, but he passed all of her test that he never knew he was taking.

Men should always remember that women are always two steps ahead of them. After countless days of Jades complaining, Trent finally started to comply. It felt good being wrapped in her husband's arms at night. She absolutely adored her husband. They grew so close over the years that she felt like she needed those hugs and kisses on the daily basis.

She pulled into the drive way of their three-story Victorian style home and saw Trent's black Range Rover parked in the drive way. Her face lit up and she gathered her things before opening the door. She saw Trent coming out of the house through the open garage door.

"Hey baby," Trent said walking towards her.

He was dressed in a pair of old jeans, a white shirt, and a pair of old Timberland boots he kept in the garage. She had one fine ass white man on her hands and she knew it. The closer he got to her, the more pronounced his scruffy five o'clock shadow became and she loved that. There was nothing like a manly man in her opinion, and this one was all hers.

"Hey, what are you doing?" Jade asked as Trent approached her and took the food out of her hands.

"I had to bring your son's footboard down to fix it for the one hundredth time. I'll put a couple of screws in it when I take it back up," he said digging into the bag and pulling out a fry.

"Why does he have to be my son when he does something bad?" Jade said following Trent through the garage door and into the kitchen.

"Because he does not get that from my side of the family," Trent said laughing. "What did you get me?"

"The same thing I got myself since you were undecided. Where are the kids?" Jade asked taking her jacket off and placing it on the back of the kitchen chair.

"They are with your mother. She asked me to bring them over there about two hours ago. She wanted to take them to some kid's party."

Jade loved that her mother always wanted the kids, and was very reliable, but she disliked the fact that she didn't drive. That meant as soon as they got comfortable, she would call for them to come pick the kids up, but instead of complaining she counted her blessings. There were many people in the world who would give anything to have a wonderful mother like she had.

She stood at the sink washing her hands and Trent came up behind her and kissed her on the neck. She hunched her shoulders trapping his head in between her shoulder and cheek. He knew that was her spot and where things were going to lead to if she let him continue.

"I love you," he said smacking her on her ass. "I'm going to take a shower."

"Suit yourself," Jade said sitting at the table and wasting no time tearing open one of the burger wrappers.

Trent disappeared up the stairs while Jade dug into her food. A few minutes later she heard an alert coming from Trent's laptop in the living room indicating he had mail, which was nothing new so she didn't pay it much attention. Then she heard it again, and again, and again and her curiosity was piqued. She wiped the grease off of her hands with a napkin from the Five Guys bag then went into the living room. Four new messages from DarkSkn21 displayed on the screen, and her mind went from zero to sixty in one point five seconds. A million different thoughts flooded her head, but the main one was, "Who the fuck is Darkskn21?" Jade said out loud.

She has never checked her husband's computer or phone, because she never had a reason to. She trusted him and always has, but there is a first time for everything. She walked over to the stairs and stood where she could hear the water running. Satisfied with what she heard she went back into the living room and knelt down in front of the coffee table. She clicked on the instant messaging box at the bottom of the screen, and the box expanded, revealing five new messages from the sender. Trent must have been chatting with this person prior to her pulling into the driveway and deleted the conversation. She scrolled up to view the first message then began to read:

Darkskn21: You're right. Sorry it will not happen again.
Darkskn21: Hello?
Darkskn21: Are you still there?
Darkskn21: Ok, well, Mr. Davenport will look over the proposal on Monday morning, and we will be in contact with you shortly after.
Darkskn21: TTYL

Jade minimized the small box, and walked back into the kitchen. She didn't know what to think about what she had just read. Obviously the messages were business related, but who would conduct business under the name Darkskn21? She knew her husband and dark skin was right up his alley. Her husband has never been with a white woman. Black women were just his preference, one of the many things that attracted her to him. There was something about a man that thought black women were beautiful and not just any black woman, but dark skin black woman. So frequently you see and hear about many men looking past the dark skin beauty to the lighter pigmented sister, and in some cases, looking past sisters all together to the more exotic looking woman.

She never regretted stepping outside of the box herself, since she landed a great man whom gave her two wonderful children. The fact that her husband loved every inch of her dark skinned, five-foot-six inch frame was a beautiful thing. Even after giving birth to two huge babies, she carried her one hundred and fifty five pounds well. Most of her weight she carried in her backside. Her huge booty was past down from generation to generation. She had inherited that from her mother who had inherited hers from Jade's grandmother. Her milk chocolate complexion she had gotten from her father. The only thing she felt was missing were a nice set of perky D cups to accentuate her small waistline and round booty. Her husband claimed to love her small B cup breasts, but she knew any man would love a nice set of knockers knocking them in the face while the woman rode him like a jockey.

Trent broke her train of thought when he walked into the kitchen. "I'm starving. Which one is mine?" he said searching through the bag of food. He wore only a pair of black boxers and the scent of his Jean Paul Gaultier cologne. Jade pointed to the grease stained bag in the middle of the table without saying a word. She didn't exactly know how to handle the situation without shouting and screaming. She has never been placed in this position, and even though he technically didn't do anything she still wanted to scream. The messages said one thing, but her interpretation of the messages said another.

"What's wrong with you?" he asked with a mouth full of food.

She looked up at him from her now cold burger. "Nothing," she said.

"Well, it sure does look like something is wrong with you." Trent said before taking another bite out of his food.

She wanted so badly to yell at him about this Darkskn21 person, but she didn't want to look foolish jumping to conclusions. In her mind that is what an insecure woman would do. A woman like herself who has never had any problems within her marriage and no reason to distrust her husband would not feel threatened so for a happily married woman with no concerns this was nothing. She knew her husband was faithful to her, and would never step outside of their marriage so she had nothing to worry about.

"Who is Darkskn21?" she blurted out. The little pep talk she gave herself did absolutely nothing.

"Who?" Trent replied with his mouth open ready to bite into his burger again.

"You got a message when you were in the shower, five to be exact," Jade said crossing her arms across her chest.

"Oh, that's Mr. Davenport's secretary. I think we are really close to settling this deal. This could be huge for us," he said popping french fries into his mouth one after the other. He was completely unfazed by the mention of Darkskn21 and Jade's flustered appearance.

"Why does a business woman conduct any type business under the name Darkskn21?"

"It's her personal username and email address. We all have each other's work and personal addresses. It's really not a big deal. It's just business baby, and since when do you have trust issues with me?"

"Since a chick named Darkskn21 popped up on your damn computer screen."

He laughed but Jade didn't see a damn thing funny. She got up from the table and started putting her food wrappers in the trash can under the granite counter. She may have been over reacting, but he should place himself in her shoes, and think about how he would feel if the shoe were on the other foot.

"If it'll make you feel any better I will tell her we can only conduct business under our company addresses, okay? As a matter of fact I'll do it right now," he said, as he walked into the living room, grabbed his laptop, and walked back into the kitchen with Jade. He placed the laptop within clear view of Jade and sent an email informing Darkskn21 that it was unprofessional to conduct business under personal addresses, and moving forward all work related issues was to go through the corresponding companies. She quickly complied.

Jade wanted to question him about the fact that the conversation was evidently cleared before she came in the house. She wanted to know why the woman was apologetic, but didn't ask. She decided to let it go and sat back down at the table. He was a good man, and she had to trust that even if the woman did over step her boundaries he must have put her in her place. Maybe that was the reason for the apology.

She watched her husband as she sat across the table. The way he licked his lips, and looked at her like she was crazy for looking at him lightened her mood. She thought about her husband's loving and how good it was. Then those thoughts were replaced with him possibly giving that loving to another woman as if his wife didn't even exist, but those thoughts were quickly abolished. There was no way her man would ever be foolish enough to step outside of his marriage and ruin everything they have worked so hard to build together.

Jade looked into her husband's green eyes, and he smiled at her with that one dimple on his left cheek displaying itself through his scruffy beard. He was still as fine as he was eight years ago when they met, while she was waiting tables at a restaurant that was now closed. A few of her coworkers noticed that he couldn't keep his eyes off of her and made a bet with Jade to get his number before he left. She was never the type to chase, since she never had to. Guys were more than willing to try their luck with her, and wasted no time trying to shove a phone number down her throat. Long story short she started up a conversation with him, and they exchanged numbers. She won the bet and the man.

"You know the girls will be here at six, right?" Jade asked from across the table.

"Yes I know, and I'll be up the stairs away from all of the giggling and girl talk," he said. Trent thought they were so annoying when they were all together.

"We have an hour before they get here," Jade said, giving him her come get some stare.

"Yeah, I know," he said while balling his food wrapper up into tiny ball, and shooting it into the open bag in the middle of the table.

"So we have time to do some things."

"You're right, and I have a million different things I could be doing right now."

Jade rolled her eyes. She hated it when he didn't catch her drift. As out spoken as she is, Jade couldn't bring herself to talk dirty to her man. She didn't know why, she just felt awkward. The things she wanted to say didn't come out right when she did try, so she left the dirty talk up to him.

"Oh," Trent said. The light bulb finally went off in his head. "You know I'm ready when you are, and you know we haven't officially broken this house in," Trent said. He got up from his chair and his face wore a mischievous grin as he walked over to Jade and pulled her up out of the chair. He placed his soft lips on hers while unbuttoning her black slacks, and let them fall to the floor along with her white panties then lifted her onto the table. When her bottom touched the cold surface goose bumps appeared on her body while Trent positioned the chair she was sitting in between her legs and took a seat.

"You already know what I want," Trent said, biting his bottom lip. "Feed it to me."

Jade did as she was told. She scooted her bottom toward the edge of the table until his tongue met her goods and then she leaned back onto her elbows.

"Damn" she said out loud as Trent spread her outer lips and went straight for her pearl. She rotated her hips in circles and took pleasure in the feel of her clit growing in Trent's mouth. He sucked harder and held on to it for dear life then twirled his tongue around causing friction against her erect clit. When he did that she didn't know whether to give into the sensation or savor the prurient moment. She allowed him to continue for a while before placing her hands on his forehead and pushing him back.

"Take your boxers off," Jade demanded, and got a little more excited from the sense of control she felt.

Trent leaned forward and took one last lick. "Um um um," he said lifting his hips and sliding his boxers off and onto the floor. Jade slid down off the table, and onto her husband's lap. She stroked his thick erection and stuck her tongue into his mouth while grinding on his lap. Never ending the kiss, she placed the beefy head of his dick at her opening, and slowly allowed him to part her walls. Her vaginal muscles gripped his dick as she began to slide up and down while wrapping her arms around his neck. She increased her speed while arching her back giving her big booty permission to bounce off of his thighs.

His hand landed against her left ass cheek. The sounds of their skins slapping sounded throughout the house. Jade was so aroused. They have never got it on in the kitchen, and she would have to see to it that they did it again real soon. She stood up and turned around giving him full view of her ass, then she bent over the table.

"That's how you want it baby?" Trent said coming to his feet and fondling his wet dick.

"Yes," Jade said right before Trent entered her from the back. She placed her face on the table, and pressed her hand against his stomach. She couldn't take it too deep from the back right off the top. Her husband was well hung, so don't believe the hype about white men lacking the goods.

Trent slowed his pace and Jade relaxed and placed her hands on the table. She pushed past the pain, and backed her ass up until she felt that undeniable feeling of him hitting her spot. Her eyes closed and soon after her legs began to shake. He pulled out of her and dropped to his knees right before burying his face between her cheeks, and sucking her swollen clit into his mouth. He took his tongue and made it pulsate against the head of her clit, and her body began to tremble. She didn't know how much longer she would be able to hold her balance, so she braced herself by gripping the edge of the table.

Just when she thought she was about to have an explosive orgasm Trent removed his head and replaced it with the other. He wasted no time spreading her ass and plunging deep inside of her while using his right hand to play with her clit. The sensation was so strong her fingers and her toes were curled. The next thing she knew she was screaming "I'm cummin" so loud her ears rung.

She saw the sun, the moon, the stars, the trees, the birds and the bees, as R. Kelly would say, "She touched a dream." Trent collapsed onto the chair behind him, and Jade lay with half her body on the table and her spaghetti legs barely touching the floor. Jade couldn't catch her breath, and apparently Trent couldn't either. She thought about the last time she had an orgasm of that magnitude and couldn't remember, but damn if she didn't want to have another one as soon as possible.

The sound of the phone ringing caused her eyes to open, but she lay there for a second to see if Trent was going to get it.

"Are you going to get that?" Trent said still out of breath.

"No."

"That's fine with me, but you better get up and get ready. It's past six," Trent said, and Jade popped her head up and checked her watch.

"Shit," she said getting up and standing on her wobbly legs.

It's a good thing her friends are always late. She made her way up to their bathroom and hopped in the shower. Knowing her friends she had a good thirty minutes to get herself showered and dressed. Her plan was to make it quick, but the warm water along with her raspberry scented body wash was so soothing. She stood there with her eyes closed allowing the water to wash away all of the days contentions.

After cutting the water off, she slid the glass shower door aside. When the bathroom door opened, the cool air ambushed the room clearing the mirror of steam and completely violating Jade's body.

"Ira and Courtni are here," Trent said.

"Ok, did you tell them I was coming?"

"Yup, what time do you think you will be home? I'm trying to decide if I should wait up for you," Trent said smiling and stepping aside while Jade made her way into the bedroom. She sat on the bed and began to coat her body with Shea butter lotion.

"I'm not sure, but I'll call you, and you didn't forget you have to pick up the kids, did you?"

"No I didn't. You didn't forget about Mr. Davenport's fundraiser tomorrow did you?" Trent replied with a question of his own.

"No, I didn't forget, but you never told me whose fundraiser it was. Will Ms. Darkskn21 be there?" Jade said, coming to her feet and stepping into a pair of denim skinny jeans. She pulled a peach colored blouse from the closet then turned around to face Trent who was now sitting on the bed flipping through the channels on the television.

"Yeah, I guess. She is his secretary."

"So, how does she look?" Jade asked.

"I don't know what you want me to say. She's average looking," Trent said shrugging his shoulders.

"Describe average looking to me. I imagine she is a dark skinned woman because of the name she chose, but is she tall or short? Big or small, Cute or not so cute, and how old is she?"

"I don't know Jade. I'm not that familiar with her," Trent

said, and Jade could tell he was becoming irritated, but she didn't let up.

"So, are you going to answer any of my questions?"

"No, and I don't want to talk about Tamra anymore."

"Tamra?" Jade said, surprised, "Wow, Trent, you're on a first name basis with her?" She placed her foot into a pair of brown plat formed pumps, and walked over to the mirror.

"You know that's how we like to handle business Jade. Clients start to see you as a person as opposed to a pest trying to take their money."

"You don't address Mr. Davenport by his first name."

"Jade," Trent shouted, "That's enough. You're starting to sound really childish. I only have eyes for you and only you," he stated, and Jade rolled her eyes.

The attitude was unnecessary, and if it weren't for her friends waiting downstairs she would have expressed that to him, but instead she just sprayed on a little Glow by J. Lo and walked out of the room.

When Jade got downstairs all three ladies were sitting in the living room looking through an old photo album book. She had to check her attitude before she walked into the room, so they didn't inquire about her mood.

"Hey girls, ready to go?" Jade said, trying to sound upbeat. "That's a cute dress Courtni. I'm very surprised to see you in it, but it's very cute," Jade said, checking out Courtni's knee-length leopard print dress. Her thin spaghetti straps were barely able to support her bodacious mounds, but she wore a black cardigan over her shoulders which made the outfit look classy.

"Thank you, I picked it up today at Nordstrom. I thought it went well with my new attitude," Courtni said standing up and striking a pose.

"I know my mouth hit the floor when I saw her," Lani said. "Now, she needs to get rid of that cardigan, and let the girls come out and play."

"No, she doesn't she looks fine just the way she is." Ira said.

"Stop cock blocking Ira," Jade said.

"I'm not cock blocking. She is not on the prowl for a man today, and you two are not on the prowl for her. We are simply going to a gathering and a house warming party. There is nothing provocative about either of the two," Ira said.

"Whatever, can we go now mommy dearest?" Jade said, grabbing her purse from the chair. They all followed Jade out the door and into Ira's white Infinity JX.

"Ira is right," Courtni said once they were all seated in the SUV. "I'm not in search of anyone or anything besides a few laughs with my girls, and a lot of fun. I'm letting my natural, kinky hair down tonight."

"At a house warming party Court?" Lani said and Jade laughed.

"Yes, I'm taking baby steps, and my next step is going to a jazz club. I've always wanted to go so Paula from work said she would accompany me," Courtni said.

"Does Robert know you are bringing a group of people with you to his gathering Ira?" Jade asked.

"Yes he does. He remembers all of you from my house when Nick passed."

"That sucks because I don't remember him, so now I have to fake the funk," Jade said.

"Me too," Lani said.

"He is the tall guy with the really pretty Chinese wife, Marie," Ira said.

"Oh, now I remember," Jade said.

"I don't," Lani said from the back seat.

"Just act like you do Lani," Courtni said.

They drove the rest of the short distance jamming to an old school CD that Jade made for Ira. They all sang Bobby Brown's "Every Little Step" in unison while mimicking the dance he does in the video. Whenever they got together they had a good time. They permitted the teenager inside of them to come out just a little, since at the end of the day they were still adults with responsibilities, so the teenagers couldn't fully expose themselves.

Jade sat in the passenger's seat, and focused her attention on the wooded area along the highway. She thought about her situation at home with Trent, and wondered if she was handling things all wrong. The last thing she wanted to do was cause trouble within her marriage over something senseless. She had become accustomed to other women hitting on her husband, sometimes while she was with him. Some women can be very bold, but Jade found them to be comical.

Jade has always trusted her husband, and she felt in her heart that he loved her with every fiber of his being. The fact that she could appreciate a beautiful woman was just an added bonus for Trent. Like other marriages they have had their fair share of ups and downs, and managed to make it through the storm hand and hand. The first two years of their marriage Trent had a very serious drinking problem. He was what they called a functional alcoholic. Although there was not a day that went by that he did not have a drink, he never missed a day of work and was always very productive. He has always been a working man, and made sure his family didn't go without any of their needs and many of their wants. There were times during his drinking days that Jade didn't think they were going to make it. All of the sleepless nights she spent praying her husband made it home safely was starting to take a toll on her, but six months of AA meetings, two DUI's, a short stint in jail, and thousands of dollars in court and lawyer fees later they are still going strong. The power of prayer is amazing. She thanked God every day for rescuing her husband, and recovering their marriage.

Ira made a right turn into a suburban neighborhood with similar looking houses on both sides of the street. They slowed down to allow a few teens to cross with their skateboards and bikes then came to a two story home with tan aluminum siding, and wind chimes dangling everywhere. Jade thought about how annoying that must be to the neighbors as they drove meticulously passed the house in search of a parking spot. There were cars parked bumper to bumper along the side walk. Ira found a small but big enough space to squeeze into behind a fire hydrant, and Jade was the first one out of the car. She looked down the street to the house with the wind chimes, and noticed there was an American flag blowing freely in the yard from what looked to be a flag pole.

"I guess that's where we are headed," Jade said pointing to the house.

"Did the flag give it away?" Ira asked while grabbing her purse and seafood platter from the back of the truck.

"Just a little bit," Jade said, and they walked toward the house.

There were two kids playing in the yard, and an Asian woman sitting in a lawn chair supervising them. She looked so relaxed rocking in the padded chair, and sipping on something red from a glass.

"Ira, how are you?" the woman said, getting up from her chair and embracing Ira.

"I am good, I can't complain," Ira said. "These are my friends in case you don't remember, Lani, Jade, and Courtni. Girls this is Marie." Ira introduced them, and they all gave Marie a friendly hug.

"You all make yourselves at home. I'll be in shortly. The boys wanted to come out and play for a while, so I'll let them burn off some steam," Marie said. "Robert is going to be so happy to see you." She embraced Ira again, and then pulled back and gave her a compassionate gaze that lingered a little too long for Ira.

Jade watched as Ira pulled away from Marie, and showed her the seafood platter she brought with her. Ira didn't like all the sympathetic looks, and comforting words she still received from lots of people. She appreciated everyone's kindness, and knew that they all meant well, but those words that were meant to comfort her only reminded her that she was widowed. Her one and only true love was gone.

"I really hope they get all of their sad looks, and uncomfortable stares out of the way as soon as I walk in." Ira said as they stood in front of the door. She wore the face of a despondent woman. She knew what she was in for, but hoped for the best.

"Are you ready?" Courtni asked Ira. She had her hand on the door knob ready to open it.

"Yes, I can't hide from them forever," Ira said, and entered the house.

They could see people in the distance sitting in the living room conversing on a large green sectional sofa. Ira walked to the right into the kitchen, and placed her platter on the counter.

"Hi. Jade right?" a voice said from behind the girls.

"Yes. How are you?" Jade said shaking the man's hand. He was the same man she had met at Ira's house, and saw at Nick's funeral.

"I'm good, and let me guess, Lani and Courtni?" Robert said, as he pointed at each girl.

"Correct," Courtni said, and she and Lani shook his hand.

"And I know who this beauty is," he said making his way over to Ira.

"How are you Mrs. Meadows?"

"I'm good Robert. How are you?"

"I'm here," he said smiling with his arms open. "Come on and let me introduce you all to the others." They walked into the living room and there was a few men and woman sitting around. They all stopped and turned their attention to the five standing in the opening. Jade scanned the room and took in all the sad faces with their gaze focused on Ira.

"Everyone this is Nick's wife, Ira Meadows and her friends Lani, Jade, and Courtni," Robert said and everyone stood up and walked over to the girls. Ira seemed to be familiar with most of the people there. Lani was in between Jade and Ira, but Jade could hear everyone confessing their love for Nick, and giving her their condolences even though most of them expressed that two years ago.

"Are you ladies hungry? I have my good friend Billy on the grill out back. He makes a mean steak," Robert said.

"I'm not really hungry, but I did bring a seafood platter for everyone to enjoy," Ira said as a few of the guys made their way into the kitchen.

"I didn't bring anything, because I think I temporarily lost my manners. Sorry," Jade said.

"Don't be silly. No one brought anything, but Ira," he laughed. "We have plenty of food to go around. Please help yourselves."

"Thank you," Jade said, and they all walked through the glass double doors that led to the deck. Once outside they saw a group of men sitting around drinking beer and dressed in U.S.

military gear. They all addressed the women and offered them a seat.

"Hi, I'm sorry for your loss. Nick was a good man. We were in the same platoon in Afghanistan," said a young man wearing military attire haircut.

"Thank you," Ira said, and Billy sat his spatula down next to the grill and come over to hug Ira.

"Anything you need I am here so please do not hesitate to ask us for anything and I mean that."

"Well, I'll take a hot dog," Jade said, trying to lighten the mood and it worked. Everyone laughed and Billy went back to grilling.

"One hot dog coming up; and what would the rest of you ladies like?"

"We'll have the same," Lani said.

"Coke, orange soda, or iced tea?" A guy standing over by the blue and white cooler asked.

"You can give us all an orange soda," Lani said, and Jade looked at her like she was crazy.

"I don't want orange soda," Jade said low enough that the guy wouldn't hear her, but loud enough so that Lani would.

"Drink it anyway, like I drank that lemonade you ordered me yesterday," Lani said.

They took their sodas and walked over to the four empty chairs the men had given up for them. The chairs faced the huge fenced in back yard. There were three small children chasing a golden retriever who had a toy in his mouth. Being as though there were no women in sight Jade guessed the men were supposed to be watching the children, but of course they were in their own little world. Billy brought them their food, and they went inside to get some of the platter Ira had brought over. To their surprise the platter was gone. The plastic plate that once housed the food was now sticking halfway out of the trash can.

"I take it they liked the platter," Ira said, and began to lift the lids on the rest of the pans that sat on the table. They weren't disappointed for long when they saw the shrimp and pasta salad, seafood salad, deviled eggs, crab pretzels and spinach dip.

"Now this is my kind of party," Lani said.

"I agree," Courtni replied.

"Are you okay, Ira?" Courtni asked.

"Yes, I'm okay. Are you all ready to go?"

"Yes," Jade said before Ira finished her sentenced. She threw her soda can in the trash. "Could y'all move any slower?"

"I'm coming Jade," Lani said. She gathered her empty plate, and purse as they followed Ira through the kitchen and into the living room area.

"Hey ladies, are you going to join us in a game of charades?" Robert asked from the sectional sofa.

"Oh no Robert, we're going to head out. We have another function to attend," Ira said, and the rest of the girls stood behind her looking like deer's caught in a set of headlights. They were the center of everyone's attention. Ira made her way over to give Robert a good-bye hug, and he made one last plea.

"Come on, we're going to bring the wine out and other drinks. It'll be a lot of fun."

"We'll have to pass, but thank you so much for inviting us into your home, and it was nice to meet you all," Ira said turning around to acknowledge the guests behind her.

"Well, please don't be a stranger. Bring the boys over sometime, and we can catch up while the kids play," Marie said. She embraced Ira, and walked over to the rest of the ladies. "Thank you all for coming."

The sun had set and left the sky blue with reddish orange waves scattered about, while the warm breeze was now mildly brisk. Jade was glad she had packed a sweater in her oversized purse.

"It's getting a little nippy out. Maybe this dress wasn't such a good idea," Courtni said.

"Beauty is pain Court so suck it up," Lani said, and laughed at her own joke.

"Where is your friend's new house?" Ira asked Lani.

"When we get to the truck I'll call her."

"Turn that up," Courtni said, referring to the heat as they entered the car.

"It's not that cold," Jade said, turning the heat up a notch.

They sat in the same parking spot waiting as Lani contacted her friend. Whatever was happening on the other end of the phone appeared to be live. They could hear laughter in the background, and music playing so loud that whomever Lani was speaking with had to scream into the phone so Lani could hear them. After making note of the directions and address, Lani relayed the message to Ira. They had a forty-minute drive ahead of them, maybe an hour since Ira was driving, and they were headed to Silver Spring, Maryland.

"Does your friend live in an apartment?" Ira said to Lani's reflection in the rearview mirror.

"No, she said her fiancé bought the house for them," Lani said.

"That was nice," Ira said.

"The only thing I'm still in the dark about is what her fiancé does for a living."

"Even though that's none of your business, did you ask her?" Jade said.

"Yes, and when I did, the response I got was, "He does a little bit of everything," Lani said altering her voice to sound like her friend.

"That doesn't sound good," Courtni said. "If your man is successful in his line of work, wouldn't you want the world to know that you chose a winner?"

"Not unless he was into some illegal activity," Lani said.

"What are you getting us into?" Ira asked.

"Hey, I'm just as puzzled as you are. All I know is that she has been bragging about this huge new home she has, and how glamorous it is for a month now. You can tell when folks aren't used to having the finer things in life," Lani said.

"Well, maybe it is a huge and glamorous house," Jade said.

"I doubt it. I bet you we will pull up to a single family home in a nice neighborhood with a garage, and a well-manicured lawn just like the neighborhoods we all live in," Lani said. She pulled her lip gloss from her purse, and smoothed it over her lips. "I don't want to make her out to be a storyteller or anything because I really do like her, but I just think her description of the house is a little far-fetched."

"There is nothing wrong with being proud of what you have. We all have over exaggerated about something at some point and time," Ira said.

"Yeah, but a mini mansion Ira, come on now," Lani said.

"Did she say that?" Jade asked.

"Yes she did."

"Well I don't think she would lie about her home, and then invite everyone from her job to visit," Jade said.

"Okay," Lani said dropping the subject.

"I just hope she keeps her job so she will have some sort of economic and financial security to fall back on if he ends up where most men trying to make a quick buck ends up," Courtni said.

"Amen to that," Jade said.

"That's why I am still single."

"Is that why you are still single Courtni, or is it because your list of requirements is a mile long?" Lani said.

"See that is where you are wrong Lani. My list is there to save me; I don't want to waste anyone's time. Unlike you all I will not put myself through all the ups and downs of a fictitious relationship, and spend months, maybe years, with a man who has no intentions on settling down with me, and making me his lawfully-wedded wife. Now I know you all have found Mr. Right, but there were a few imbeciles in your past, and I plan on sparing myself the heartache by avoiding all inadequate candidates."

"Those were teenage love affairs you speak of, and women who create a list of qualifications they want in a man are always let down," Jade said. "See what happens over time is most women realize how difficult it is to find someone who meets the criteria, and somewhere along the lines they come to their senses and focus on what is truly important."

"I know what is important. I want a man to love me for me. All of me, all of my curves, all of my faults, all of my flaws, and I'm going to love him the same way in return. I know you all think I'm all brains and no common sense, but that's not the case. I know the possibility of revealing my list to a man, and having him check each one off before we go galloping into the sunset is next to impossible. All I want you all to know is that at this stage in my life I know what I want, and I will not cheat myself, because I am going to make some lucky man very happy someday," Courtni said, clamping her fingers together and placing them in her lap. "Now, tonight, I just want to have fun, so hopefully I find it at this mini mansion," Courtni laughed, and they all joined in.

After exiting the freeway they came to a residential area with huge, alluring homes that was secured behind a black iron fence, and a heavy-set security guard that sat inside of a tiny booth. They hadn't spoken a word, but Jade was sure they were all thinking the same thing.

"Wow, she really does live in a mini mansion," Lani said. Her eyes were opened wide as she took in the neighborhood.

Ira pulled up to the security gate next to the sign that read "Barberton Estates," and waited for him to put his magazine down and do his job.

"Hi, we're here to see Deidra Finley," Lani said from the back seat.

"I need to see ID's from everyone," the top-flight security guard said. He leaned forward, and stared into the SUV while they all dug for their driver's licenses. His broad shoulders barely cleared the tiny window.

"Y'all late aren't you?" He said as Ira handed him all four ID's. He grabbed a clip board with a stack of papers attached to it, and began to write down their information.

"We are coming from another party actually," Ira said.

He looked down at her, but didn't respond. Jade pegged him as one of those security guards that thought he was actually a cop, and that he was more significant than what he really was, when in reality, if some shit went down he would have to call the police just like the four of them. Why he was acting so cold was beyond her. He knew damn well he was sitting there bored out of his mind before they pulled up. He ought to be glad he had some company.

"You have four young ladies here to see you. Their names are Jade DeVoe, Ira Meadows, Courtni Jeffries, and Lani Wilkes. Do you want me to send them around?" He bellowed into the phone receiver then handed their belongings back to them. "Y'all can go ahead through."

"Can you tell us where the house is? This is our first time visiting," Ira said.

He let out a sigh, and pressed his lips together.

"Keep straight and you're going to hit a curve. Once you clear the curve, you'll run right into the property," he said and closed his Plexiglas window without confirming whether they understood the directions or not.

"Asshole," Jade said as they pulled away.

They marveled over the beautiful homes within the gates. It reminded Jade of an MTV "Cribs" episode. Every home had more than one expensive car in the drive way. She spotted a Porsche, a Lamborghini, and a Maserati. She was officially astonished, but not as astonished as Lani.

"What the hell is going on? I cannot believe this shit," Lani said. "She is really living large over here. Now I know I need to find out what her man does for a living," Lani continued as they passed a prodigious white brick home with a crystal chandelier illuminating the stairwell in their home. The sight was so enchanting, and Jade could tell Lani was having a hard time wrapping her head around it.

"Well, she's definitely not a liar," Courtni said.

"I thought I hit the jackpot, but damn," Lani said. "I think I'm going to bring Jackson by this place and show him how we could be living."

"Make sure you pick Trent up," Jade said.

Once they cleared the end of the road they came to a curve which had cars parked along the left side, and the same black iron fence along the right, which surrounded a lake. Ira parked behind the last car, and they made their way around the curve and up to the house. It was a beautiful home which sat on a lawn the size of a football field. The home was also white brick like the other homes they've passed, but this one had four huge circle top windows embedded in the front of the home. The biggest window was above the dark wooden double doors that sat on top of twelve steps and a concrete porch. There were two circle top windows above the two-car garage to the right of the door step, and another window on the left.

All of the lights in the house were on, and there were people standing around on the lawn, and leaning against the cars that were parked in the driveway.

"This house is amazing," Ira said, and they all agreed as they migrated through the crowds of people.

"I know one thing. This is nothing like any other house warming party I've ever attended," Jade said.

"That makes two of us, but I'm not surprised by the outcome. She invited anyone and everyone she crossed paths with, and now I see why. I would want to show off my home too if it looked like this," Lani said.

"How y'all doing?" One of the guys leaning against a car in the driveway asked. He was a short, light-skinned guy with a small afro, and a mouth full of gold teeth, and was accompanied by two other gentlemen who had drinks in their hands and droopy eyes.

"We're good," Lani said.

"That's good, that's good," he said as they made their way up the driveway and onto the stone pathway that led to the entrance of the home.

It was dark out, but the area around the house was well lit, and they could see all the people moving about on the property. As they approached the steps in front of the house they could hear music playing from inside, and the ladies sitting on the steps seemed to be bouncing to the beat and having their own little party outside. They stood up to make way for them to walk up the stairs, but never stopped swaying and snapping their fingers.

"Thank you," Lani said as they walked past the girls, and onto the large porch which also had people lounging around on a few chairs and leaning against the railings.

"Oh gosh, this is not what I expected. I don't know about this," Courtni said.

"Will you relax? These people are not worried about us, and I'm sure they are all Deidra's friends," Lani said as she looked past Courtni at the guy leaning against the rail on his cell phone with his pants damn near down to his knees, "and possibly her fiancée's friends, but that doesn't have anything to do with us. Besides weren't you the one who wanted to let loose a bit? Well here's your chance."

"Yes, but I thought we were going to a house warming party not a house warming turned club."

"Courtni, you're fine. Let's go," Jade said as they entered the house.

The foyer was grand with its high ceilings, and a beautiful Ironwood light-rusted chandelier and tropical plants along the walls. From the foyer you could see straight into the large living room area that was filled to capacity, and there was a semi-spiral staircase to the right covered in a dark beige-colored carpet.

"Excuse me," a young lady said breaking their trance as she exited the house.

They all stepped aside, and continued inside of the home as the young and old roamed about and intermingled with each other. They passed a couple who didn't seem to mind that they had an audience, while they were doing some serious groping and lip locking on a chair that sat in the foyer.

"Hey, take that outside," a short brown-skinned woman said to the couple. She wore an apron with the words, "Do not kiss the chef" on the front. "Hi, can I help you ladies. You look kind of lost," the woman spoke to them.

"Yes, we're looking for Deidra," Lani said.

"I should've known that. You look more like one of Dee Dee's friends, and not one of Laurence's knuckle head buddies. I'm Yvette, Deidra's mom," she said.

"Hi, I'm Lani Deidra's coworker, and these are my friends Ira, Courtni, and Jade."

"It's nice to meet you ladies. Dee Dee is right over there," she said pointing into the living room.

Jade couldn't tell where she was pointing. There were so many individuals in the same area, but she was sure Lani would find her.

"Y'all better get a plate before everything is gone. I'm done in the kitchen," Yvette said. She threw her hands up in the air to add emphasis to her statement then walked away.

"Well, I don't know what she is going to do with this Pier One gift card I got her. It looks like she has everything," Lani said, pulling the card out of her purse.

They followed Lani through the crowd and over to a woman who looked like a younger version of Yvette. She was sitting on the lap of a thin man who was rubbing her thigh and whispering in her ear. There were scantily-clad women dancing around them, but he didn't seem to pay them any attention.

"Hey Mami," Deidra said to Lani after jumping up off of her man's lap. "This is my soon-to-be husband Laurence." Laurence came to a stance, and nodded his head at the ladies.

"These are my friends—" Lani said, but was cut off by Deidra.

"I already know. She talks about y'all all the time. You must be the virgin," she said to Courtni. "I think that is a wonderful thing, and I just want to commend you for that." She said bowing down in Courtni's directions.

Courtni gave Lani a look of anger then rolled her eyes. Jade looked at Lani who cleared her throat, and shrugged her shoulders. Courtni would definitely bring this topic up as soon as Deidra was not around.

"Thank you," Courtni said.

"Alright y'all I just got word that Mrs. Yvette is out of the building, so let's get this party started," the DJ said over the microphone before turning the music up and bopping his head to R. Kelly's "Fiesta."

Laurence opened the doors to the deck to allow the music to travel outside of the home. Everyone in the house started dancing, and shouting, and singing along with the music. It was as if they were in the movie *House Party* without the choreographed routines.

"Come on, you're coming with me," Deidra said as she pulled Courtni by her wrist, and Courtni in turn pulled Jade by arm to come with her.

"Don't worry we'll be right here when y'all get back," Lani screamed. She grabbed Ira's hands, and they started to dance to the music.

Deidra took them into the kitchen where there was an older man with salt and pepper hair standing on one side of the island. There were all kinds of alcohol atop the counter, and plenty of people standing around guzzling it down. The older man stood concocting a drink for a tall white guy who looked like a frat brother. He took his drink and bopped out of the kitchen.

"Hey there, sweetheart," the older man said to Deidra.

"Hey Uncle Marty, I need you to make them a couple of drinks. Make her something strong," she said lifting Courtni's hand in the air.

"Oh, I'm okay. I don't drink much," Jade said.

"I don't either, so I'll just take an apple martini," Courtni said.

"Uncle Marty is the man for that. He makes the best martinis, and he knows alcohol inside and out," Deidra said, snapping her fingers and rocking from side to side.

"Well, you look mighty nervous Gorgeous. Why don't you start with a shot?" He said pouring Rumplemintz and Jagermeister into the empty shot glass. "See if that calms your nerves," he said as he handed Courtni a shot glass. She looked at Jade then chugged the drink. Her face contorted as she stuck her tongue out of her mouth.

"Whoa, you took that like a champ Court," Jade said.

"Yeah, make her another one Uncle Marty," Deidra said.

"You think you can handle another one Court?" Jade asked.

She looked at Courtni's face which was just returning to its normal state and laughed. This was surely something new for Courtni, and it was amusing to see her in that light.

"I don't know, that was kind of strong, and I'm a light weight. I don't need anymore."

"How about if I have one with you?" Jade said.

"Hey, well make that three shots Uncle Marty. I'll have one also," Deidra said joining in. Her uncle poured their shots and the three of them downed their drinks at the same time.

"You were right, that is strong," Jade said. Her eyes were closed tight, and her hand was on her throat. She felt a burning sensation in her chest, but sucked it up, and sat her glass back down.

"Can I have my lady back please?" Laurence said coming up behind Deidra, and wrapping his arms around her.

"Yes, you may," Jade said, and watched as they walked out of the kitchen intertwined. When she turned back around Courtni was downing another shot. She threw her arms up in the air like a champ and made a thirst quenching sound.

"Maybe you should let up on these shots Court," Jade said in Courtni's ear instead of shouting over the music.

"It's okay, I'm with you all, and I know my limit."

"I don't know Court, you have never had this stuff," Jade said, picking the bottle of Rumplemintz up, and sitting it back down on the marble counter top. Uncle Marty snatched the bottle out her hands before it hit the counter.

"Oh, y'all ready for some more shots?" he shouted.

"Yes," Courtni said.

"No," Jade said. She pushed the two shot glasses they were drinking out of toward Uncle Marty.

"She doesn't want me to take any more shots," Courtni said, leaning closer to Uncle Marty and turning her nose up at Jade.

"Okay, well how about a drink?" He said.

"Wouldn't that cause more damage than a shot?" Jade asked.

"Jade, have we switched roles here? You know I would not do this customarily, and more than likely I will never do this again. So stop worrying about me. I conduct myself as a lady at all times, and today will not be any different," Courtni said.

"Fine, I'll be back. I have to find the bathroom," Jade said, and turned to walk out of the kitchen. She had a feeling that tonight was going to be a long night so she pushed her way through the dancing crowd in the foyer that had appeared out of nowhere. She knew a home this big had a bathroom on the first level, but she wasn't up for the challenge of trying to find it so she headed for the stairs, and even though it was within eye shot it took her forever to reach it.

"Damn baby, where you going girl?" She heard come from behind her, and then felt a set of hands on her waist. "Shake, shake, shake that ass girl," the boy said, singing along to 50 Cents "Disco Inferno."

Jade turned around, and gave him her "You better back off" look and his hands dropped from her waist.

"Keep your hands to yourself little boy," Jade said.

He sucked his teeth and quickly found another female to grind up on. She reached the stairs, and before she could place her foot on the first step someone else was trying their luck.

"Can I go up there with you?" a voice from behind her said. She turned around and it was the short guy from the driveway displaying his raggedy mouth. She held her ring finger up, and he stood there with a dumbfounded look on his face as if he didn't understand what the ring signified.

"I am married, and no I cannot have any friends. No you cannot have my number, and do not follow me up these stairs. I'm not interested," Jade said and continued up the stairs.

She looked over her shoulder to see whether the guy took heed to her words. He was not following her so she continued on her quest. After opening three doors she finally found the bathroom. It had marble tile everywhere, and a glass see through shower with a large shower head that hung from the ceiling. She called Trent and told him she would be home soon before leaving the bathroom. Once she reached the lower level she went back into the kitchen to check on Courtni.

"What is that?" Jade asked referring to the red plastic cup Courtni had up to her lips.

"Well," Uncle Marty said.

He tossed a bottle from one hand to the other then did a Temptations-like spin. The maneuver had to take all of two seconds, but Uncle Marty was so slow with his moves that it felt more like ten long seconds. She could tell this was the most excitement he'd had in a long time, and he was enjoying every moment of it.

"We got to talking about her job, and her man issues, and I decided she needed something a hell of a lot stronger than a damn apple martini. That right there is the best I have to offer," he said pointing to Courtni's drink, and she gave him a high five with a sour look on her face. Jade could tell she was trying her best to hold the alcohol down.

"Okay, so what is it?" Jade said.

"It's a Slow Death," he chuckled. He was so proud of himself, and it showed all over his face. "It's Everclear, Jagermeister, Rum, Southern Comfort, and this here Snappes, but don't worry I gave her more Jagermeister than Everclear."

"Everclear, what the hell is that?" Jade said as she searched the alcohol filled table for the bottle. She found it without a problem, since the tall clear bottle stood out from the rest. She picked the bottle up, and read the contents under the label. After reading that Everclear contained ninety five percent alcohol, and was one hundred and ninety proof she concluded that Courtni was about to be drunk as hell. Uncle Marty's attempt to ease Jade's tension didn't work at all. She was no expert on alcohol, but she knew ninety five percent of anything was a generous amount.

"You are out of control," Jade said to Courtni.

"I'm fine Jade," Courtni said calmly, and she actually did sound as if she had everything under control.

Jade studied her face, and her tension softened. Maybe Courtni did have things under control, and she was worried about nothing.

"I'm going to go see what Lani and Ira are up to. Are you staying in here?" Jade asked.

"Yes, Uncle Marty is pretty funny. I'm going to sip a little of this drink, and then go to the bathroom. Where was it?" She asked.

"It was up the stairs, the fourth door on the left. I'll be back," Jade said.

She made her way through the crowd again. This time she bulldozed her way into the living room area, which was much more effective. She went over to the corner where she had left Lani and Ira, and they were nowhere to be found. After spotting an empty suede stool she stepped up on it to give her leverage over the crowd, and spotted Ira up against the wall with her head down. Jade knew she was texting Jonathan about the restaurant, even though it was well after eleven o'clock at night. She stepped down and made her way over to Ira.

"Where is Lani?" Jade asked.

"I don't know she walked off with a couple of her coworkers that came over. Where is Courtni?"

"She's in the kitchen getting fucked up," Jade yelled in Ira's direction since the music was so loud in that area.

Ira placed her phone back in her purse, and started to bop her head to DJ Kool's "Let Me Clear My Throat."

"I don't believe that," Ira said.

"Well believe it," Jade said. She stood next to Ira, and observed the crowd. Everyone was dancing, and sweating, and having a good time. At that moment no one had a care in the world. It was actually a pretty cool sight to see.

"Alright, alright, I'm about to take it back for a minute," the DJ said. "I want every guy in the room to grab a girl, and every girl in the room to grab a guy. Shit, every girl in the room grab a girl. I just want everybody to get on the motherfuckin' dance floor and act like it's 1988 up in this place."

Jade watched as everyone grabbed a partner, and she told a few guys that she and Ira were together. They laughed, and continued being wall flowers while everyone else waited for further instructions. "Are y'all ready?"

"Yeah," the crowd screamed.

"Well I'm gonna hit y'all with a little something like this," the DJ said, and then the go-go beat of E.U.'s "Da Butt" sounded through the speakers. The crowd went wild, and so did Jade and Ira.

"That's my song," Jade said. "Come on let's dance." She grabbed Ira by the hand and pulled her from the wall. They did their best rendition of the dance. With one hand on their head, and the other hand on their hip, they bent their legs and took it down to the floor. Jade couldn't remember the last time she had danced to some old school music with her girl. Ira stood up and turned around and shook her butt in Jade's direction. They laughed and took turns dropping down to the floor and waving their hands in the air.

"Now on the count of three y'all know what to do," said the DJ.

They looked at each other, and hunched their shoulders, not knowing what the hell he was talking about.

"I said a one...two...three...now switch," he screamed, and before she knew it she saw Ira being spun around by some guy with a white shirt on, and soon after that she was spun around by a pair of tiny hands. She focused on the person in front of her and realized it was a girl.

"Okay, I can do this," she said out loud. Trent wouldn't mind if she danced with another woman. It was men she needed to avoid. He was not here to see anything, but he would surely inquire about tonight's events, and she didn't want a guilty conscience. Her new dance partner had both her hands on the top of her head, and rocked her hips from side to side. Jade played along and placed both her hands atop her head, and imitated the dance.

"Hold up now," the DJ said. He cut the music, and everyone started fussing and complaining. "You know what I want y'all to do? I want y'all to bust it," he said, and everyone stood in place discombobulated. All they wanted him to do was turn the music back up and quit talking.

"That's right I want y'all to bust a move," he said, and then the funkadelic sounds of Young M.C.'s "Bust a Move" filled everyone's ears, and they picked up where they left off. Jade turned back around to dance with Ira to no avail. Ira was no longer behind her, and it seemed her dance partner wanted to do the bump by the way she kept bumping her hips into Jade's butt. After searching a little harder she saw Ira a few feet away doing the Wop with a different guy. She must have danced herself halfway across the room, so Jade joined her partner and started to bump back. They laughed and Jade switched it up by doing the running man. The fact that she had on six-inch heels entered her mind, and she slowed it down and decided to follow Ira's lead and do the Wop.

"This next one is by request," the DJ said. "My man Laurence wanted to dedicate this to his soon to be bride Deidra. Congratulations on y'all upcoming nuptials," as Jodeci's "Forever My Lady" played through the speakers.

Jade gave her dance partner a friendly pat on the shoulder, and made her way through the crowd towards Ira. When she reached her Ira was in a lovers groove, dancing with a guy. He was a medium-built guy with a close shaved haircut. Ira's head was resting comfortably on his chest, and they swayed from side to side in unison. Jade decided to let Ira do her thing. The fact that she was even dancing with a man was a big step for her. She slid past all the bumping and grinding couples trying to reach the kitchen where she had left Courtni. This trip was fairly easy since everyone was wrapped in someone else's arms.

"Hey there Sweetness," Uncle Marty said as Jade entered the kitchen.

She did a quick scan of the room when she saw that Courtni was not standing in the same spot.

"Hey, where is my friend?" Jade asked.

"Oh, you're talking about dark and lovely?" He chuckled. "Man she is beautiful, you know that? Back in my day I would have—."

"Excuse me, but can you just tell me where she is?"

"My fault I get to talking sometimes, and I just start to ramble on and on. She's in the bathroom. Been in there for a while now. My guess is she on that toilet. That liquor runs straight through some people," he said while shaking his head.

Jade walked out of the kitchen and through the crowd of sweaty people in route to the stairs. She wanted to check on Courtni who more than likely had her face buried in Deidra's commode. That's the price she will pay for turning things up a notch. She should have just had the damn apple martini instead.

"Where are you going?" Lani said from behind Jade. She turned around, and grabbed her by her wrist.

"I'm going to check on your sure-to-be-drunken-ass friend Courtni, and you're coming with me." Jade said. She tugged at Lani's arm as she trudged up the stairs. "Where have you been any way?"

"Girl I was dancing and having a good time with some of my coworkers. You see my hair?" Lani asked, as they reached the top of the curved stairwell.

Jade looked at her hair which was wet and frizzy. She tapped on the bathroom door, and no one answered.

"Wow, what did she have to drink?" Lani said.

Jade knocked again, this time a little harder. "She had a Slow Death, and you don't want to know what was in it"

"Yes I do."

"Well I don't feel like telling you right now," Jade said, as she turned the doorknob and stuck her head inside. She opened the door as far as it could go, and Courtni was not there.

"I thought you said she was in the bathroom," Lani said.

"That's what Uncle Marty said. Maybe she went back down stairs somewhere looking for one of us."

"Or maybe she took a nap in someone else's bed." Lani said. She was pointing to a room at the end of the hall with the door ajar. From where they stood they could see Courtni's black cardigan at the foot of the bed lying across her purse.

"I know damn well she did not take her ass to sleep," Jade said.

They headed for the master bedroom so they could grab Courtni, and get her out of Deidra and Laurence's bed before they came up the stairs.

Jade pushed the door open, and they got the shock of their lives. Courtni was lying on top of what appeared to be a man. All they could see was his hairy legs as they stuck out from under the blanket. Jade stood there in disbelief. She looked at Lani whose mouth was wide open and eyes ready to jump out of her head.

"What the fuck is going on?" Lani said.

"I don't know, but we have to get her out of here before someone sees her," Jade said.

"What are you two doing up here?" Ira said as she entered the room, and stood beside Lani. She froze and placed her hands over her mouth. "Is that Courtni?" she asked.

"Yup," Lani said.

"Come on, we have to get her up," Jade said.

They walked closer to the bed. Jade and Lani walked to one side, and Ira went to the other. Jade looked at the guy's face, and he was clearly out of it. They both reeked of alcohol, and were snoring lightly.

"Courtni," Jade whispered close to her ear, and she didn't move a muscle. "Courtni," she whispered again, and nudged her a little. She let out a deep sigh, but did not respond.

"Jade she is knocked out. We are going to have to help her up," Lani said. She pulled the covers back, and they all covered their mouths in shock.

Courtni's dress was pulled up above her waist, and they were both nude from the waist down.

"Oh shit, oh shit, oh shit," Jade said as she began to back away from the bed. "She fucked him. She had sex," Jade said.

"You don't know that Jade. Maybe she was about to and they passed out," Ira said.

"Bullshit, I know what cum smells like."

"Oh God, I cannot believe this is happening. Are we sure that she is okay? Is he okay?" Ira said.

"Yes they are okay. They're just highly intoxicated. I should know since I've been there a few times," Lani said.

"She's going to be so pissed when she sobers up," Jade said.

"Come on let's just get her up," Lani said.

Ira pulled from the opposite side of the bed, while Jade and Lani pushed Courtni towards her. Courtni's breasts were outside of her dress, and her underwear was at the foot of the bed. She now lay next to her companion who was unfazed by all of the movement. His stomach lifted and fell rhythmically from under his wife beater, and his muscular shoulders and arms lay flat against the bed. He appeared to be very handsome with chocolate brown skin, and a head full of long dreads. He could easily pass for the model Ryan Gentles, and was the complete opposite of what Courtni would go for, but dammit if he was not well hung. Jade was now convinced that Courtni did not engage in sex with this man. Although she was drunk, there was no way a virgin could handle what this man was working with, and she most definitely would not be the one running the show.

"At least she has good taste," Lani said, and Jade giggled.

"Will you two get it together. This is not a laughing matter," Ira said.

"Ira, tell me this man isn't fine as hell," Lani said as she lifted the man's shirt to expose his impeccable chest, six-pack, and luring V shape that led to the monster between his legs.

"Yes, Lord he is fine," Ira said, "but we have to go."

Ira grabbed her black panties, and placed them on Courtni, while Lani reached across the guy to lift Courtni's hips. They pulled her dress down, then Jade and Lani went to the other side of the bed with Ira.

"Ira, you should get her things, and pull the truck around to the end of the driveway," Jade said.

"Good idea," Ira said. She gathered Courtni's cardigan, purse, and shoes and headed for the door while Jade and Lani sat Courtni upright and placed her feet on the floor.

"Courtni, come on you have to wake up," Jade said. She tapped her face softly with her hand. "Courtni, wake up, wake up."

"Maybe water will help," Lani said. She ran to the master bathroom and returned with a soaked towel. As she stood over Courtni she twisted the towel to release a stream of water. Courtni moved her head sluggishly, and they took advantage of the slight consciousness. They both grabbed an arm, and placed it on their shoulders. Courtni's eyes were still closed, but her feet were moving along with them. She was slurring her words trying to say something, but all they wanted to do was get her outside.

"We're taking you home Court just bear with us," Jade said.

Courtni's head hung low and wobbled from side to side as they maneuvered down the hallway. Courtni's mouth erupted like a volcano. Her stomach muscles contracted, esophagus opened, and all of the unwanted food and alcohol was propelled from her body. Spewing an alcohol filled mixture on Deidra's nice clean carpet.

"Oh, come on Courtni," Lani said, as chunks of ejected food landed on their legs and feet.

"You have got to be kidding me," Jade said. She looked down at her platform pumps, and a grimace look covered her face.

"This is so disgusting, and Deidra is going to kill us," Lani said.

"No she is not," Jade said. She took a few steps to the side, so she would not step in the puke, and elongated her body to keep her grip on Courtni. "She will never know who did this, because we are leaving, so let's go."

Once they reached the stairs they braced themselves, and gradually walked down until they reached the bottom. They excused themselves a million times as they approached the door, and stepped outside. Jade was glad they had made it out of the house without causing suspicion. Even though they did not know these people, she didn't want anyone thinking her best friend was some sort of slut that had sex with random guys.

"Is she okay?" Deidra asked. Jade didn't even notice her sitting out on the porch with Laurence.

"Yes, she is fine. She just had a little too much to drink," Lani said, and forced a smile on her face.

"I'm sorry, I didn't mean for her to get drunk. I just wanted her to have a drink or two, and have a little fun," Deidra said.

"Well she definitely did that," Jade said, and Lani sucked her teeth.

"Girl she will be fine, and I will see you at work on Monday. Thanks for the invite," Lani said as they took their time walking down the porch steps.

"I hope you guys had fun," Deidra yelled from the porch.

"We did. Thanks again," Lani said.

They picked up the pace once they reached the bottom of the stairs. Walking the pathway was out of the question. Courtni was getting heavy, and dragging her feet, so they walked across the grass to Ira's truck. They placed Courtni in the passenger's seat, and reclined the chair to keep her head from bouncing around while Lani and Jade took a seat in the back. They all sat in silence trying to let the nights events sink in. This had to be the craziest night Jade has ever experienced. She couldn't shake the fact that Courtni possibly was not a virgin anymore, and to make matters worse she didn't even know the fellow she was with or did she? Her head was spinning and she wanted to rewind the past hour or two, and start all over again. She would not have let Courtni have that Slow Death, and they all would have stayed together.

When they were younger they had a saying that they lived by. "When one go, we all go" that saying came about when Ira would run off with Nick as a teen, but they were all tortured for it by punishment.

"Ira, you can drop Courtni off with me." Lani said.

"Okay," Ira said. She let out a sigh as she wiped the sweat from Courtni's forehead, while they were at the light.

"She didn't do anything," Ira said. "There is no way Courtni would be so foolish. I don't care if she is inebriated. She would never go that far."

"Yeah, I don't think so either," Lani replied.

"Well, let us all get a good night's sleep, and talk to her in the morning. We will not get anywhere by speculating," Jade said.

She laid her head back on Ira's leather head rest, and said a silent prayer for her friend. She knew how much Courtni's purity meant to her, and although she joked with her about it a lot she didn't want things to happen this way. She left all her troubles in God's hands and let it go.

Chapter Three

"I'm sorry, but do I know you?"

The phone ringing woke Lani out of her sleep. She grabbed her cell phone and squinted her eyes as she read the caller ID. Jackson's name was displayed on the screen.

"Hello?" She whispered into the phone.

"Good morning Beautiful," Jackson sang into her ear.

"Good morning," Lani said tiredly.

"Are you still sleeping? What time did you guys get in last night?"

"A little after one. What time is it?" Lani said. She looked at her alarm clock the same time that Jackson answered her question.

"It's ten minutes after eleven. Did you have fun?"

"Yes."

"Well from the short answer I take it you don't care to talk about it," Jackson said.

"It's not that, I'm just tired. Am I going to see you later?" Lani asked.

"Yes, I'll be over this evening. What's on the agenda for tonight?"

"I'm not sure, what would you like to be on the agenda?"

"Preferably you in your birthday suit standing over a hot stove cooking me dinner, and then me in my birthday suit serving you dessert," Jackson said, and Lani felt herself becoming aroused.

"I think I can make the first part of that sentence happen, but the second part you'll have to work on."

"That's not a problem," he said.

"Good, now let me go and check on Courtni."

"Check on Courtni? Did she stay over last night?"

"Yes, she had a little too much to drink," Lani said.

"Courtni?" Jackson asked and Lani laughed.

"Yes Courtni. I love you, and I'll see you later."

"Love you."

Lani slid her feet into her fuzzy slippers then went into the bathroom. Her morning ritual of showering and flat ironing her hair would have to wait. She brushed her teeth and washed her faced with a warm washcloth then made her way down the stairs. Her house had three bedrooms, but neither she, Ira nor Jade were up for the task of dragging Courtni up a flight of stairs, so they opted for the couch instead. Courtni's face was buried under the thick blanket Lani placed on her last night. She lifted the blanket to uncover Courtni's face, and allow the cool central air to connect with her skin. Her normally shiny natural curls were now dull and flat, but her brown skin was still silky and flawless.

Lani walked over to her windows, and drew the blinds. She cut off the air and cracked the windows. The sound of birds chirping entered her home, and she went into the kitchen to prepare the two of them breakfast. Courtni was sure to have a hangover when she woke up, so she knew a little breakfast would help if she was willing to eat.

"Rise and shine ladies," Lani heard coming from the living room where Courtni was, but she was sure it was Jade's voice she heard. She rushed out of the kitchen to silence Jade's big mouth.

"Will you be quiet? Courtni is still asleep," Lani said. Ira was just entering the house, and closing the door behind her. Lani motioned for them to follow her into the kitchen. "What are you two doing here, and why do you have a key to my house?"

"I don't know," Jade said and hunched her shoulders.

"What do you mean you don't know? I guess I can stop wondering where my spare key disappeared to now," Lani said. She turned back around and placed six strips of bacon in a frying pan, and mixed four eggs with milk in a medium sized bowl.

"I just wanted to stop by on my way to work," Ira said. She poked her head around the kitchen wall to look at Courtni who was still asleep. "Has she been asleep since last night?" Ira whispered.

"Yes, and she is not going to be a happy camper when she wakes up. I'm sure she is going to feel like shit," Lani said.

"Well I don't think we should bring up what happened, or did not happen last night unless she does," Jade said.

"No, I think we should talk to her about it, and let her know that drinking is not for her," Ira said. "Anything could have happened, and we still don't know if this guy persuaded her up to that room and took advantage of her."

"You're right we don't know, but we cannot accuse a man of rape when she was clearly on top of him," Jade said.

"I didn't say the word "rape." I said he took advantage of her."

"Well either way I think we should keep it hush-hush. Shit, she may not remember a thing from last night."

"If that happened to you Jade, would you want to know what happened?"

"Hell yeah."

"Okay then we need to tell her what occurred," Ira said.

"But that's just it Ira. We don't know what occurred," Jade said.

Lani stood over the stove, and listened carefully to the whole conversation. She didn't know what to say to her friends, because she could relate to what the both of them were saying. She thought Courtni should know that things got a little out of control last night, but what all could they tell her besides they found her passed out on top of some fine ass man?

"I don't know, I think we should just play this by ear," Lani said. She turned her burners off and placed two pieces of bread in the toaster. "If she asks any questions I think we should give her answers if we can," Lani said.

"Let's be honest," Jade said. "There is no way we can keep anything from each other, and Ira is right not mentioning it would be wrong," Jade said.

"Yeah, I guess," Lani said. "Well let's at least see if she brings it up first. I don't want to ambush her with all of this as soon as she wakes up."

They all turned their heads in the direction of the living room area. The sound of the bathroom door shutting startled them. They all looked at each other confounded.

"Do you think she heard us?" Lani whispered as she stepped closer to Jade and Ira. They both hunched their shoulders, and stared blankly at Lani. The toaster sprung the bread forward, and startled them again. Lani took the toast from the toaster and placed them on a plate. She loaded Courtni's plate with four pieces of turkey bacon and majority of the eggs.

"Damn Lani, she's hung over not dying of starvation," Jade leaned forward, and whispered in Lani's direction.

"Well I don't see you doing anything Jade," Lani whispered back.

"That's because this is not my house, Lani."

"Well you could have fooled the hell out of me earlier, walking in here with your own damn key like you own the place."

"Hey, you gave me that key," Jade whispered.

Lani scrunched her face up, "No I didn't."

"Yes you did."

"Both of you shut up," Ira said.

"What the hell happened last night?" Courtni said from the kitchen's entryway. Her eyes were low almond shaped to begin with, but they were barely open now. Her hair was disheveled, and she looked like something out of a zombie movie.

"Umm, Lani tell her what happened," Jade said.

"What, I don't know, I…"

"Why don't you just have a seat Court, and put something in your stomach," Ira said.

"Don't give me that shit, Ira," Courtni said, and Ira sat back in her seat with her lips sealed. "I can't believe you all have me cursing on a Sunday morning. Now I want to know why the hell my vagina feels like it's been ripped apart then sown back together. No, I do not know what that feels like, but what the hell happened?" She screamed. "I don't want to hear it Jade," Courtni said as she held her hand up in Jade's direction to stop her from saying whatever it was she was about to say. "It gets worse, I urinated and wiped myself as I always do, and what do I see?" She said, and they all looked on in silence. "Blood. Blood was on the tissue."

"Was it a lot?" Ira said.

"No, but that's not the point."

"Is it that time of the month?" Jade asked.

"Jade, do not play games with me right now," Courtni shouted again. "One of you better tell me what the hell happened at that party, because I don't remember a thing after having a drink in the kitchen, and if my recollection serves me correctly I was on my cycle a week in a half ago, so why am I shedding blood from in between my legs again?"

They all were hesitant to reply. Afraid she may silence them again. A few seconds tick away before someone spoke up.

"We found you in Deidra's bed with a man," Lani said.

"What?" Courtni shouted. She took a seat in the empty chair next to Jade, and placed her head in her hands. She was visibly shaking, and Lani felt so sorry for her friend. "Why did you all let me do that? I would never do that to any of you," she said. She lifted her head and her eyes were filled with tears. They fell onto the tabletop before she had a chance to wipe them away. "Who was the man? Was it Uncle Marty?" she said.

"Eww, hell no," Jade said.

"We don't know who the guy was Court," Ira said and Courtni's tears began to pour out. They all embraced their friend, and tried their best to comfort her.

"Did he rape me?" Courtni said.

"Umm, we don't think so, but we don't know," Lani said.

"Well, why don't you think I was raped?"

"When we found you, you were asleep on top of him."

"Oh God, please tell me this is dream. This cannot be happening to me," she sobbed.

"Do you remember running into someone you may have known there?" Jade asked, and Courtni shook her head no.

"Come on Court, you have to think. Give us something to work with, because right now we are just as confused as you are."

"I don't know," she sobbed. "The last thing I remember is sitting on a stool in the kitchen watching Uncle Marty mix drinks for random people."

"Do you remember going to the restroom?" Ira asked.

"No."

"Well Uncle Marty said you went to the bathroom, so I

think maybe that is where you came into contact with that guy."

"Why is this happening to me?" Courtni said. She held her head low while her tears continued to fall onto the table.

"Don't worry about that right now Court," Lani said as she placed a plate of food in front of Courtni, and a bottle of Deer Park water. "Try to eat and drink some water."

Courtni pushed the plate toward the abstract marble centerpiece in the middle of the table. "Just the smell of that is making me nauseous, and my head feels like it's about to explode."

"I'll get you some Alka Seltzer," Lani said. She walked over to the wooden cup board in the corner of the kitchen, and pulled out a tiny blue box. "This will help settle your stomach," she continued as she poured Courtni's unopened bottle of water into a cup, and watched the two dissolvable Alka Seltzers disappear while tiny bubbles arose, and caused the mixture to make a fizzing sound.

"I really don't want anything Lani. I'm so embarrassed, and hurt on top of being disgusted with myself," Courtni pulled the paper towel from underneath the plate of food, and wiped her face with it. "My grandmother is going to be so upset, and my mother…" she paused, "she's probably turning in her grave."

"That's not true Court. We all make mistakes sometimes, even you." Ira said. "You are not perfect, and your life is not always going to go as planned."

"Who knows what this guy has. I could have some type of foreign virus or bacteria or disease in my system right now," she paused again, and gave them all a serious look. "Please tell me he wore protection?"

They all looked at each other, but did not speak a word. Lani didn't want to break the bad news to her, and suddenly she realized that they were all so wrapped up in the fact that Courtni slept with someone that no one noticed the act was unprotected. She could not believe that thought did not enter her mind at all. Lani wanted nothing more than to look her friend in her eyes and tell her that the mysterious man had worn protection, and that everything was going to be okay, but she knew lying would not help the situation any.

Sexually transmitted diseases does not discriminate, and

nor does the HIV virus. After looking at her friends she knew they would be in prayer mode today and all the days to come. Praying for their friend's health would become a priority until she was tested and cleared of all infectious diseases and viruses.

Courtni broke down again from the silence and Jade clutched Courtni tightly. The anguish in the room was suffocating. Lani and Ira joined in the embrace and cried along with Courtni. She couldn't imagine her life without any of her friends, and the thought of Courtni's health being threatened hurt her to the core. Lani felt Jades hand soothing her by rubbing her back. She reached over Lani to Ira, and comforted her as well.

"Listen, everything is going to be fine. Tomorrow you will call your doctor's office and make an appointment. They will run as many test as you'd like, and they will call you within seven days with the results," Jade said, and they all latched onto each other's hand.

"I'll lead us into prayer," Ira said, as she bowed her head. "Dear Lord, we come to you in need of your healing touch, a touch that only you possess Lord. Heal Courtni's body of any possible threat. Heal us all Lord, for we are in need of your merciful redemption, your forgiveness, and your guidance. In Jesus name we pray. Amen."

"Amen," they all sang.

"Do you want me to stay with you today? I can call Jonathan, and tell him I'm not going to make it in," Ira said.

"No, I'm going to go home and recuperate so I can make it to the evening service later," Courtni said. She stood up from her chair, and began to exit the kitchen, but stopped short of the entryway. "I can't believe my first time has come and gone without me having any recollection of the occasion," she let out a sigh. "I'm going to take a shower." Courtni walked out of the kitchen and disappeared up the stairs.

"Well I guess I will make my way into the city," Ira said as she came to a stance. "Tell Courtni to call me if she's feeling up to it."

"Ok," Lani said, and watched as Ira walked out of the kitchen and through the front door.

"You think she'll be okay?" Jade asked.

"Yeah, I think so. Where are Trent and the kids?"

"They're all home. We have a fundraiser to attend tonight. I'm really not looking forward to it."

"Why?"

"You know what I like to do on Sundays, and it doesn't involve me leaving my house."

"Whose fundraiser is it?" Lani asked.

"Trent's business partner."

"Well, that is sure to be boring."

"Tell me about it. There is nothing but a bunch of rich folks walking around with their heads held high enough for you to see clear up their nostrils, with their mink coats, fox hats, and gator shoes. Girl, it always looks just like a damn zoo in those places."

"Do you have a clowning buddy?" Lani asked.

"A what?"

"A clowning buddy, someone you can hang with when you are at these events, like one of the other wives in attendance."

"Yeah Sheldon's wife Elaine, but she's very demure, and not much fun."

"Oh well, suck it up. While you are at your little fundraiser I will be raising hell in my B.E.D. with my M.A.N," Lani said. She did a little dance that looked like she was spanking someone while rocking her hips from side to side.

"Didn't we just say a prayer? That dance and this conversation is very inappropriate at the moment Ms. 'I am not married just yet.'" Jade said, and let out a light chuckle.

"That's alright, because he will be putting a ring on it after I have my way with him tonight."

"You go ahead and bag you a doctor, so at your wedding I can stand up in front of everyone and give a nice speech, and say, "This is for all the hoody hoodrats in the building. If she can do it you all can," Jade laughed, and Lani shoved her playfully.

"I have never, and never will be considered a hood rat."

"True, I'll call you and Court later—See ya."

Lani walked Jade to the door and watched her get into her truck. She would shower after Courtni was done in the bathroom, and later prepare for Mr. Jackson. She walked up the stairs to retrieve her phone from the night stand. Jackson had sent her a text message ten minutes before she got to the phone. She smiled when she read "Can you meet me at my apartment at three? I can't wait to see you." Although she wished he would have stuck to the original plan of coming to her place that evening, she complied and lay back on her comforter.

Courtni tapped on her bedroom door, and walked in without waiting for an answer. "Do you mind running me to Jade's house so I can get my car?"

"No, I don't mind, but I need to take a quick shower."

"Okay, I'll wait. I thought they would still be here by the time I was done. That way I could have rode with Jade. I'll be down stairs."

"Are you okay? I mean do you feel okay?" Lani asked.

"I don't know how I feel Lani. I just want to go home and lie down for the rest of the day."

"Well make yourself comfortable. I'll be out in a few," Lani said as she left Courtni in her bedroom.

She grabbed a towel from the linen closet, and went into the bathroom. Her mission was to wash as thoroughly and as quickly as possible. It was vastly approaching one o'clock, and she had to drive from one county to get to Jackson's house then to another to get to Jade's. Her plan was to show up at Jackson's place wearing her trench coat that she had purchased specifically for a freaky encounter. Since Jackson has always raved about her spontaneity, she knew he would love the fact that she would be partially nude underneath. She smeared her honeysuckle scented body wash over her body, and paid extra attention to her goods. Satisfied with her wash job she turned the water off, and stepped out of the shower. After applying her Caramel Apple scented lotion she was indubitably turned on. Jackson loved that scent on her, and she couldn't wait for him to place his hands all over her body.

Lani stepped out of the steam- filled room, and did a half skip half run through the chilled hallway and into her bedroom. Courtni must have made her way down the stairs, and Lani couldn't have been happier. She knew that with the night Courtni had she would not want to see or hear her talk about getting her freak on, which was sure to happen. Her black Balconette bra was at the bottom of her dresser draw waiting to be retrieved, and starring as the opening act in her freaky, erotic show. Shimmying her hips into her matching black thong, she slipped her feet into a pair of black pumps, and gave herself a quick inspection in the mirror. A frown displayed on her face when she checked her closet for her black trench coat. It was more than likely in the living room closet with the rest of her coats. That meant she would have to walk down the stairs in front of Courtni as is, or fake the funk and put on some clothes. She yanked a blue dress from its hanger in her closet and pulled it over her head. She would just have to take it off when she got to Jacksons place.

When she retrieved her trench coat from the closet Courtni looked as if she wanted to comment, but kept her thoughts to herself. They drove the distance to Jade's house in silence since she didn't want to talk. Lani didn't know what to do to appease her friend. She knew if she were Courtni she would be devastated also. Courtni does everything by the book. Her bills are always paid on time. She almost never misses Sunday church service, and her credit score is out of this world. The only thing she has always wished for is a good man that she could give herself to, so Lani could only imagine how upset she must be.

"Thank you Lani. I'll call you soon," Courtni said as she exited the car.

"You're welcome, and I'll call you tomorrow. Make sure you get some rest."

"I will."

Lani watched as she climbed into her SUV, and drove off. She noticed Jade and Trent's vehicles in the drive way of their home and hurried to pull away before Jade spotted her, and started asking questions about Courtni. It was five minutes after two so she headed in the direction of Jackson's apartment. Tapping her fingers on her steering wheel, and humming her own little tune, she was as chipper as a kid in a candy store. It amazed her that this man kept her interested after all of this time. He was the first guy to date to succeed at such a task, and she loved him for that. Her appetite for spontaneity was rather large, but nothing Jackson couldn't handle. He satisfied her desires for never ending pleasure, and gave her an assortment of memories to shuffle through whenever he was physically unable to brighten her day. She knew that no amount of sensual pleasure would satisfy her for a lifetime. That is why Jackson was so special to her. He was so much more than the average man, and in her book, he was one of a kind.

She pulled into her usual parking spot a little after two thirty and placed her car in park. She couldn't wait to get out of that wrinkled blue dress she had on, so she lifted her hips and pulled it over her head then tossed it in the back seat. When she looked up she saw that she had an audience. A middle-aged man who was walking his dog had stopped in his tracks, and stared at her semi-nude upper torso through the windshield. She stared him down until he met her gaze then continued walking his dog.

After applying a coat of her pink lip gloss, and adding a little more lotion to her already silky smooth body she was ready for action. Jackson's car was nowhere in sight so she figured she could post up in one of his leather recliners until he came home. She tied the belt to her trench coat firmly around her waist and proceeded up to the second floor. Thoughts of Jackson's favorite chair entered her mind, and she knew that was going to be the spot she would lie and wait for her Prince Charming. His favorite chair was an osculating recliner so she would be able to face the door without forcefully sliding and turning the chair in his direction.

The sound of her pumps hitting the concrete stairs echoed inside of the closed-in stairwell. She placed her key into the lock's cylinder, and turned it until the bolt was removed from the strike plate. Eagerly she turned the doorknob and hurried inside. She took two steps back to confirm that she was indeed at the right apartment. The three numbers embedded in the center of the white door said one thing, but the short-haired woman sitting inside said another.

"I'm sorry, but do I know you?" Lani said to the woman. She stepped inside of the house but held the door partially open.

"No, you do not," the woman said in an unfriendly tone. She sat in Jackson's favorite chair with her arms folded across her chest.

"Well, how the hell did you get in here, and who are you here to see?"

"I got in here with these," she said, unfolding her arms and displayed a set of keys, "and I'm here to see you."

If looks could kill Lani would be a dead woman. She stood in front of the door confused for a second. She didn't know what was going on, but this woman needed to hand over those keys and get out of her man's house. Lani thought about all the groupies Jackson had and immediately placed the woman in that category.

"Look, Jackson must have misplaced his keys, and you picked them up. Thank you for returning them, but you do not have the right to be in here," Lani said. She allowed the door to shut behind her as she walked closer to the woman. "I'll take those," she said. She held her hand out for the woman to place the keys in her possession.

"How dare you prance in here as if you're me?" She said. She stood from her seat, and was now face to face with Lani.

"Get the hell out," Lani said.

"I have more right to be in here than you do, home wrecker."

"Home wrecker?" Lani said.

"Don't play dumb with me," the woman spewed through clenched teeth.

"What the fuck are you talking about?" Lani said lower than she would have liked to, but she felt as if the air was being sucked from her lungs. Her heart was racing, and instead of tears welling in her eyes she felt anger brewing within.

"Do you think I'm just going to sit around and let you take my husband away me?"

Lani watched as angry tears fell from in the woman's eyes while she held hers in.

"He is my husband and he belongs to me," she yelled in Lani's face before backing away and walking over to the counter to retrieve her purse. "I just wanted you to know that you are destroying a family. I don't know what your relationship is with my husband or how long this has been going on, but I do know one thing. I refuse to raise my children in a broken home," she said as the tears continued to flow.

Lani couldn't believe what she was hearing. She wanted to scream obscenities at the woman, but she couldn't help but feel like she was the one in the wrong. Her future with the man that she loved had just been ripped from her grasp. She wanted to yell, scream, kick, swing, and declare her undying love for the man that she has loved for two years now, but she was paralyzed with grief. Finally the tears escaped and began to roll down her cheeks.

"Where is Jackson?" Lani asked.

"He is at home with our son and our daughter," the woman said. She made sure to stress the words son and daughter which was like adding salt to Lani's fresh wounds. "If you had any sense at all you would not see my husband again. You're a piece of ass that I'm sure he taps whenever I am too tired to give it to him. You mean absolutely nothing to him. Just look at the place he keeps you hidden in," she said, looking around the condo. "Did you really think that I wouldn't find out about this?"

"I didn't even know that you existed," Lani said. This time she was the one with clenched teeth.

"Bullshit," the woman screamed.

"You can believe what you want," Lani said. She marched over to the door and prepared to leave, but the woman stopped her.

"I love him and I need him. Our children need him. A real woman would understand that," she said.

Lani's partially nude body filled with goose bumps, and she felt as if her heart was beating out of control. "Yeah well, I love him too but you can have him," Lani managed to say then walked out of the door.

She practically ran to her car, where she broke down. She was in so much pain, and wished like hell that she could take a trip to the local hospital and have a doctor write her a prescription that would take her pain away, and knock her out at the same time but she knew there was no cure for a broken heart. Her steering wheel served as her pillow, as she rested her head and sobbed uncontrollably.

Why would he invest so much into their relationship if she was just a mistress? This was a position that she has never been in, and never wanted to revisit. All of the plans she made for her future involved Jackson. This could not be true. Jackson would not do this to her.

She lifted her head from the steering wheel as if she just had a revelation. She took the back of her hands and wiped the

tears from her face, then exited the vehicle.   "I
don't know who the hell she thinks she is," Lani said out loud as
she headed back to Jackson's apartment. As she approached the
stairs she nearly ran into Jackson's self-proclaimed wife. Her
hands covered her eyes, and she tried her best to dry her
drenched face.

"Prove to me that you are Jackson's wife," Lani said.

"What? I don't owe you anything," she replied.

They stood face to face for what seemed like forever.
Lani wanted so badly for the woman to break. For her to say I'm
sorry I was lying and you can continue on with your life, but
those words never escaped her mouth.

"Just leave my husband alone please. I am asking you this
nicely, because I do not want to put on a show. I am a
respectable woman and I will not be out here fighting in the
streets. Now Jackson has been my husband for seven years, and
will remain my husband for many more years to come, whether
you decide to chase after him or not. He will never leave his
family, and I can guarantee you that."

"I don't believe you," Lani said with her arms folded.

"Well don't believe me, but this apartment will no longer
be in my husband's name," the woman said as she walked
around Lani. "How do you think I got his keys? Something told
me to check our financial statements, and lo and behold I
discover that my husband has an apartment," the woman said as
she placed one hand on her hip. Her tears began to flow once
more, and this time so did Lani's. "After that I checked his cell
phone, his emails, and whatever else I could get my hands on,
that's when I found your number, Lani." She said Lani's name,
and made a distorted face as if her name tasted bitter on her
tongue. "You can play dumb for as long as you'd like, but you
will be playing along by yourself," the woman said, and climbed
into a white Mercedes Benz that she was standing in front of. She
placed the car in reverse, and mashed the gas, never looking back
at Lani as she exited the complex.

As Lani made her way to her car she noticed all the nosy
neighbors either standing on their balcony or slowly making their
way around the complex. Shouting at them was not going to
happen. She had a feeling that she looked foolish enough. After

securing her seat belt she gave Jackson's apartment one last glance then backed out of the parking spot. Her drive home was all a blur. She didn't know how she made it, and was now sitting in her drive way. The taste of blood in her mouth brought her back to reality. She must have punctured her bottom lip while biting it to keep from crying. She reached into her glove compartment filled with an assortment of fast food napkins, and tugged at the stack. The entire pile fell to the floor, and Lani burst into tears. The pain she felt at that moment was unbearable. She would never be able to come to terms with the fact that Jackson was no longer a part of her life. He was someone's husband, and that someone was not her.

Lani shifted her head towards her passenger's side window. Mrs. Steinberg was tapping on the window trying to get her attention. She reluctantly pressed the power window control, and let the window halfway down. Mrs. Steinberg was the last person she wanted to see at a time like this. She was as nosy as they come, and would easily put two and two together without Lani saying one word.

"Hey Londa, are you okay? You've been sitting in your car for quite some time now. I was growing a bit concerned so I made my way over," she said.

Mrs. Steinberg gave her a look of concern, and placed both of her hands on the top of Lani's window. She wanted to peel each one of her aged fingers from her car, and kindly roll the window back up, but she didn't even have the energy to do that. The fact that it would have been blatantly rude eventually registered with her as well.

"Yes I am fine," Lani replied.

"Are you sure? It looks like you have been crying," Mrs. Steinberg said as she stuck as much of her face inside of the window as she could. Lani wanted her to just go away.

"No really I'm fine. I was just gathering my things."

"Well, what things? I don't see anything. Do you have groceries in the trunk?" She asked. "Come on I'll help you take them in the house, but only the light bags. My arthritis has been kicking my behind today."

"No groceries. I'm just tired Mrs. Steinberg. I'm going to head in now. I'm sure I'll see you in the morning," Lani said. She rolled the window back up, locked up her BMW, and headed towards her front door with Mrs. Steinberg following close behind.

"Did that doctor fellow make you cry? You know there was always something about him. I just couldn't put my finger on it."

"No, no one made me cry. I am just tired. That is all," Lani said as she unlocked her door. She stepped inside of her home and turned around to look at Mrs. Steinberg who was still insisting on getting answers.

"Well for what it's worth. I think he is a very charming young man. I just don't understand why he doesn't live with you. It's like he is trying not to commit. You know my Herby proposed to me just two months after we met. God rest his soul. Before we even thought about doing the wild thing we were married, and that is how a man is supposed to treat a lady. When you have something good you want to keep it, and all your doctor wants to do is play house with you as if you aren't marriage material."

"I have to go." Lani said. She felt her tears trying to make a comeback and tried closing her door, but Mrs. Steinberg held it open.

"All I'm saying is you are worth it and you are marriage material Loni."

"Thank you," Lani said before placing her back against the door and shutting it.

She slid down onto the floor, and welcomed the tears. Two years of her life she had given to Jackson, and all she was to him was a little something extra on the side. Something to indulge in from time to time or whenever he felt like being bothered with her. She couldn't believe how he had played with her emotions. He had her completely fooled, and now she was alone while he was at home with his wife and kids. How was she supposed to just move on like nothing ever happened?

"If you need me I'll be across the street," Mrs. Steinberg yelled from the other side of the door.

Lani pulled her knees up to her chest and wondered if

Jackson was thinking about her. Could he really just forget about her and all of the good times they had?

"Oh, and I'm having a Tupperware party next weekend, and you are invited. You don't have to bring anything," Mrs. Steinberg added.

Lani stood up and peeked through the peep hole. Mrs. Steinberg was still standing in front of her door as if she was going to open it and invite her in. Couldn't she see that she was upset? She watched as Mrs. Steinberg looked back at her door then started towards her own home.

It was only four o'clock in the afternoon, and her day was officially over. She untied the belt to her coat, and tossed it onto the couch then climbed the stairs to her bedroom where she buried her face into her pillow, and pulled the covers over her head. She prayed for relief of the pain that she felt and guidance. At that moment all she wanted was to be in Jackson's arms despite of the news she just received.

Chapter Four

"This cannot happen again."

Ira sat in her office at the restaurant working on her new revised seafood menu. She was excited to introduce her customers to her new dishes. Among the highly anticipated list was the seafood chowder which contained diced red peppers, minced thyme leaves, fresh bacon bits, shrimps, scallops, roasted potatoes, her special sauce, and much more. Her next step was advertising her business. Although her business was thriving she didn't think there was anything wrong with staying a step ahead of her competition. Going into business at the Baltimore Inner Harbor meant establishing herself around some of the best. In addition to being surrounded by the best she knew that area received a large number of tourists every year, and ultimately she wanted her restaurant to be one of their fondest memories.

"Jonathan what do you think about the menu?" Ira asked Jonathan as he sat across from her reading over the final list.

"I think you've did it again Ira. That chowder is going to be a hit," Jonathan replied. He stared at Ira with a wide smile upon his face.

"We did it again. You know you and I make a great team. We're a force to be reckoned with when it comes to the restaurant business," Ira laughed.

"I concur, my Queen," Jonathan said with that distinguishing accent.

Ira chuckled, but lately she had been getting different vibes from Jonathan, and was hoping that her intuition was wrong. He has always been a gentleman, and addressed most of the women he came across as Queen. It was the lingering stares and constant smiling that made her a little uncomfortable. There was no way she would mix business with pleasure, and she didn't even want to think about another man taking the place of Nick. Whenever she did she felt as if she was betraying her beloved husband. Everything between Jonathan and Ira was strictly business. She knew very little about his personal life, and wanted to keep it that way.

"So, have you spoken with Rex about the signage?" Ira asked.

Rex ran an advertising company, and was the closest thing to an A-list promoter in the Baltimore area.

"Yes, and he says the flyers should be ready on Wednesday."

"Great, thank you Jonathan. We have to get you on vacation soon. I don't recall you taking one since last year."

"Nonsense, unlike the majority of the people I know I actually enjoy my job. I love the people I work with, and I have a boss that folks would kill for."

"You are either too sweet or very smart," Ira said.

"I'll agree with you on the first part and I plead the fifth on the second," Jonathan laughed.

"Smart man indeed," Ira laughed along with him.

"Hey, I have learned a few things in my thirty five years on this earth."

"Well that is good to hear. Come on let's see how things are going outside," Ira said as she walked around her desk.

"After you my Queen," Jonathan uttered with his deep voice.

Ira exited her office, and thought about Courtni. She knew that Courtni had a thing for Jonathan, but didn't feel comfortable playing cupid without her consent. She knew at this moment Courtni could care less about any man, but she hoped that one bad experience didn't ruin her outlook on men and relationships. Sure it seemed as if there were more dogs roaming around than real men, but she believed that there was someone for everyone. That was partially the reason why she didn't want to indulge in the whole dating scene. In her opinion it would be a waste of time for both parties involved. Nicholas Meadows Sr. was her soul mate, and no one could convince her otherwise. She was very familiar with all the stories about finding love after losing it, but there was no way any man could bring her and the boys the joy that Nick brought to them. After all there was no reason to move forward with a man if they did not bond with her children, and she didn't think her children would be interested in bonding with any man that was not daddy.

"How is everything?" Ira asked two customers after introducing herself.

"Great as usual," the man replied.

"That's good. Please be sure to come back soon. Next month we'll be introducing a few new items, and I'm sure there will be something on the menu that you two will like."

"I'm sure there will be, and we will be back soon. We just moved into the neighborhood, and everyone here has been great. You have a wonderful staff."

"Did they put you up to this?" Ira joked, and the couple laughed.

"No, not at all," the woman replied.

"Well thank you for the compliment, and I will be sure to pass it on to everyone else, and just for being the wonderful people that you are here is a coupon to receive twenty five percent off of your next bill," Ira placed the coupon on the couples table.

"Wow, thanks. This place just keeps getting better."

"Yes, that's what I like to here. Enjoy the rest of your meal, and welcome to the neighborhood." Ira gave the customers a giant smile and continued to make her rounds.

"Are you closing up with us tonight, Ira?" Jonathan asked as Ira took a seat at the bar.

"Not tonight, remember we are trying our best to help the new nanny adjust to our home."

"That's right. How is that situation coming along?" Jonathan asked.

"Pretty good, she's actually with the boys now. I told her weekends off, but she said she promised them a trip to the carnival so today was a fun day for them."

"Sounds like fun. Where is the carnival?"

"It's in Glen Burnie. You like carnivals Jonathan?" Ira gave him a disbelieving look.

"Yes I do. Why the look?"

"Oh, nothing. You just don't strike me as the type."

"We should go sometime while they are in town."

Did he just make a pass at me? Ira thought, but didn't confront Jonathan. She would hope that Jonathan wouldn't even think about making a pass at his boss. That would be employment suicide.

"I mean just to prove to you that I do. Not like a date," Jonathan corrected himself.

"Thanks for the offer, but I will have to pass," Ira gave him a pat on the shoulder as she stood from the stool. "I'm going to head home since we aren't very busy. It should be a pretty calm night since it's a Sunday and folks are getting ready for manic Monday. I'll call you later to check in."

"Drive safely," Jonathan waved.

Ira gathered her purse and keys then said her goodbyes before making her exit. On her way home she thought about her boys and prayed they didn't give Naomi a hard time at the carnival. Today was actually her first day alone with the boys. They had a meet and greet last week just to see how well she connected with them, and they loved her. Ira had a feeling that Naomi's beauty played a part in her oldest son Nick's approval, and her youngest son Tij always went along with his brother. Naomi was a beautiful woman with shoulder length hair, and a light brown complexion. Her piercing dark brown eyes and pearly white teeth only added to the beautiful person she was on the inside. She was no stranger to either of them, and in fact they have spent quite a bit of time around her when she worked for their neighbor. That was the main reason Ira was so comfortable with her taking the boys out alone, but that didn't stop her from calling more than ten times today.

"Mommy," the boys screamed as she entered the house. The three of them were sitting on the living room floor playing Uno. Ira intentionally did not call to inform Naomi of her arrival just so that she could see what they were doing.

"Look what I brought home," Ira said as she held the pepperoni pizza in the air.

"We already ate dinner. Naomi made us baked chicken, macaroni and cheese, and green beans," Nick said.

"I ate all of my green beans," Tij said.

"You did? Well good job Tij," Ira said. "Thank you for making them dinner Naomi, but you didn't have to do that."

"It's okay, I love to cook," Naomi said.

"Hey boys, how was the carnival?" Ira said.

"It was fun. We got on the motorcycle ride, and the

swings, but Tij couldn't get on that one because he was too little."

"Yeah, I ate all the cotta canny," Tij said.

"You mean the cotton candy," Ira laughed.

"I hope you don't mind. I made sure that they brushed their teeth as soon as we got in."

"You know I don't," Ira gave Naomi an approving smile. "How were they today?"

"They were very well behaved. They listened well, and they danced to every song that played at the carnival," Naomi laughed.

Her sons loved to dance, so Ira could only imagine the show they put on. "Did you get settled in Naomi?"

"Not yet, the boys wanted to play Uno when we came in, so we have been doing that for about an hour. Thank you again."

"No, thank you and don't think that because you work for me now you have to be scared and uptight. I am still the same person that used to come over and visit when you worked for the Pearson's," Ira said.

"I know you have always been very down to earth, and a very beautiful person."

"Thank you, and back at you. Now, since it's after seven and I like for the boys to be in bed between eight thirty or nine o'clock, I'll get them bathed and ready for bed while you get settled in."

"Okay," Naomi said. She walked over to the corner to retrieve her suitcases, and headed up the stairs.

Ira couldn't believe that for once she was not rushing to get the boys fed, bathed, and in bed before nine o'clock. She started to think about what she would do with the extra time she will have at the end of the night. Maybe she could finally finish that book Jade loaned her months ago, or maybe she could catch up on some of her favorite shows.

After the boys were in bed she showered, poured herself a glass of wine, and grabbed Jade's book from the bookshelf. She sunk into her lonely king sized bed, and sipped her wine. She quickly became indulged in the love story and steamy sex scenes that were in the book. Her mind was going places once again and she was sure the wine was not helping. Suddenly her silk gown became one layer to many.

The boys had been asleep for a while, and she thought about how quiet it has been, and figured Naomi must have fallen asleep as well. Ira sat up and pulled her night gown over her head. She hadn't slept in the nude since her husband was alive and it felt so good. She slid her legs from side to side along the white cotton sheet than did the same thing with her arms. The feeling she felt at that moment was magnificent. Since she was not a drinker just a little wine made her head spin. The wine had been given to her and Nick for their anniversary, so she grabbed her glass and held it up toward the ceiling,

"I miss you Nick," she said out loud, then she downed the rest of the wine in the glass. Contentment covered her body. She was not sad nor was she unhappy at that time. Maybe a little "me time" was all she needed.

"Ira, are you still awake?" Naomi tapped lightly on her bedroom door. Ira panicked briefly than pulled the blanket up above her breast, and hoped Naomi didn't think she was doing anything strange. "Yes, I'm awake."

Naomi walked in and stood at the foot of the bed. "Do you mind if I make some hot chocolate or a glass of warm milk? It helps me fall asleep at night."

"Not at all, that actually sounds pretty good," Ira said trying not to sound as uncomfortable as she was.

"Can I ask you a question? I don't want to impose, but I have been holding this in for the past few days."

"Sure. Ask away," Ira said, but hoped she had a change of heart.

Naomi sat on the edge of the bed, and looked Ira in the eyes. "How have you been? You know, since Nick has been gone?"

"I'm just taking it one day at a time Naomi. That's all I can do. I miss him like crazy," Ira said.

"I'm sure you do. I miss my ex-boyfriend and he is only in another county," she chuckled. "I admire you as a woman. I think you rock."

"Thank you, and are you referring to that nice guy you were dating a few years ago as your ex?"

She giggled, "Yes, we broke up a few months ago."

"I'm sorry to hear that. From what I saw you two were great together," Ira said holding on to the top of the blanket.

"Don't be sorry, he cheated on me with a friend of mine."

"Wow, well his loss."

"I know, I just don't understand why I feel like I am the one that experienced the loss," Naomi said.

She was looking at Ira as if she had answers for her, and Ira just wanted her to go to her given room until she put on some clothes.

"I guess if I had a penis I could solve my real problem," Naomi laughed, and then covered her mouth. "I am so sorry Ira. I am getting a little bit too comfortable. That will not happen again."

"Oh stop it. You're fine," Ira waved one hand, but kept the other in place. "I've heard much worse come out of my friend's mouth."

"I didn't mean to be a bother. I'm just wide awake and full of energy, but I'll leave you alone now. Sometimes I just need a listening ear," she giggled "but I see you're enjoying a nice book and a glass of wine, so I'll get out of your hair."

"You are not a bother, Naomi. I don't want you to feel like you're not wanted here," Ira said. She was trying not to be rude after the "listening ear" comment.

"Really?"

"Yes really," Ira smiled.

"So you don't mind if I do this," Naomi said.

She was up off the edge of the bed, and face to face with Ira before it registered to her what she was about to do. Naomi pressed her lips against Ira's than stuck her tongue into her mouth. Everything in Ira was saying "Stop it," but her lips had other plans. They seemed to have a mind of their own, and welcomed Naomi's thick and luscious lips without a problem, but Ira knew that what they were doing was wrong. Naomi ended their kiss and slightly pulled away from Ira.

Again she wanted to say, "Naomi what are you doing?," but nothing came out. Her heart was beating so fast and her kitty felt like it was doing some sort of dance in between her legs. Naomi placed both of her hands on Ira's which still had a tight grip on the blanket. She lowered Ira's hands revealing her breast as Ira sat frozen in place unable to speak.

"Hmm—those are nice," Naomi said as she leaned forward, and licked Ira's right nipple.

She gently nudged Ira's shoulders causing her to lie on her back then she climbed on top of her. Her tongue went right back to work exploring Ira mouth as her hands explored the side of Ira's body. She ran her hands up and down Ira's thigh until they found her goods. Naomi must have noticed that Ira tensed up a bit and pulled her hand away. She took her tongue and alternated between making circles on Ira's neck, and planting juicy kisses around her earlobe. Ira's pant became louder and louder as her juices began to flow. Naomi sat up on top of Ira, and circled her lips with two of her fingers. Ira could smell her own juices on Naomi's hand.

"You smell so sweet," Naomi said.

"We have to stop," Ira finally admitted.

"Don't worry I locked the door on the way in."

She pulled her black cami over her head than unsnapped her bra. Her breast fell from underneath, and Ira's eyes grew wide. She had never been with another female and actually never thought about it, but she has always longed for a pair of nice breasts to place in front of Nick when they made love. She was not sure what size bra Naomi wore, but she had more than enough breasts.

Naomi grabbed both of her own breasts and smashed them together. She took her tongue, and slid it across both nipples until they both hardened from the touch. As Ira lay there looking on in amazement Naomi reached down and grabbed a hold of both of Ira's hands. She placed each of them on a breast then placed her own hands on the back of her head. Ira wasn't sure what to do so she just squeezed them a little and massaged the sides. Now she knew what it was like for a teenage boy who had his first set of boobs in front of him. Naomi moaned and shook her tits from side to side. She placed her hands on the back of Ira's head and guided her toward her full breast. Ira sucked one of her nipples into her mouth and held on to it. Naomi moaned even louder than held her breast while Ira went to work.

"Oh—that feels so good," Naomi said.

Ira moved on to the next nipple and sucked even harder. Naomi's moans turned to groans, and her crying out in pleasure. Ira herself was now dripping wet. There were times that what was happening, and who it was happening with came to the forefront of her mind, and she wanted to stop but the pleasure would sneak up and completely wash away any apprehension she was experiencing.

Moving her tongue around Naomi's massive brown nipples, she tried her best to suck as much of it into her mouth as she could. Naomi's skin was sleek and smooth with a sweet and savory smell. Ira inhaled the cotton candy-scented lotion Naomi's body was smothered in, and pulled away. Reality had finally hit her. She was sucking on a woman and not just any woman, her children's nanny.

"What are we doing? I cannot do this. This is not me," Ira said. She reached down and covered herself back up with the comforter.

"I just think that you are so beautiful," Naomi said. She leaned closer to Ira, and was now inches away from her face. "I just want to make you feel good," she whispered.

"No, we can't. I can't," Ira said.

"You don't have to do anything buy lie there," Naomi leaned in and covered Ira's lips with hers.

Ira couldn't understand why her mouth said one thing, but her body would defy her and do another. Every time Naomi touched her she sent a surge through her body that always landed at the tip of her clitoris.

"I just want to taste you," Naomi whispered in between planting pecks on Ira's lips.

She held Ira's head in her hands and kissed her deeply. This time a moan escaped Ira's mouth. Despite the conflict that was taking place within her body she couldn't hide the fact that she was all the way turned on as she kissed Naomi back. Their tongues danced against each other as their moans met and they each explored the other's mouth.

Naomi ended the kiss and climbed off the bed. She stood up and looked at Ira with lustful eyes. "I want you to relax," she said as she removed the covers from Ira's body exposing her birthday suit.

She mounted Ira and started her venture at Ira's neck. Her hot and wet kisses against Ira's skin made her temperature rise, and her breathing became shallow. She maneuvered her way down Ira's caramel body. Licking and kissing every inch until she reached her destination. Naomi looked up at Ira and licked her lips before devouring the sweet juices that seeped from Ira's kitty. Taking her well-manicured fingers, she spread Ira's bare pussy causing her enlarged clitoris to come out of hiding. Immediately she took it into her mouth, and began twirling her tongue around. She stuck her tongue inside of Ira's goods and brushed it against her sugar walls. It took all Ira could do not to scream out in sheer, freaky, uninhibited bliss. As Naomi began sucking on Ira's erect clit she slowly inserted two fingers inside of her moist pussy. She repeatedly twisted and turned her fingers before curling them upward to explore one of the most erogenous zones on a woman's body. Once her fingers rubbed against the soft ripples she knew she had found Ira's g-spot, and was more than ready to taste what Ira had to offer. She simultaneously added pressure to her g-spot by pressing one hand on the top of her vagina while lightly tapping her g-spot with her two fingers. Ira began to bounce on Naomi's fingers further stimulating her g-spot and causing beads of sweat to form on her forehead.

Ira bounced, Naomi thrust, Ira bounced harder and Naomi's thrusts became more intense. She grabbed a hold of Ira's clit and sucked it into her mouth again. This time sucking with such force that it felt as if she was extracting Ira's orgasm from her body. Her entire body shook as clear fluid squirted from in between Naomi's fingers. Not missing a beat Naomi withdrew her fingers and tidied up the mess she had helped make. She took her tongue and licked every speck of cum from around Ira's kitty than cleaned her fingers in the same manner. Naomi decided she would take care of herself when she got to her room.

Ira lay still on her back watching Naomi as she dressed in front of her bed. There was an awkward silence lingering in the room and she did not know what to say. She was embarrassed, and more so ashamed that she had given into such temptation.

She was not interested in women, so how did this happen? Rightfully she was lonely, but she did not have to stoop to this.

She silently prayed and asked God for his forgiveness. She knew that the God she worshipped was a forgiving God and forgiving herself would be the hard part. Her head was spinning. She did not want to be there at that moment and she absolutely did not want to admit to herself that the orgasm that had just ripped through her body was the best feeling she had ever had the pleasure of experiencing.

"This cannot happen again," Ira whispered.

"Oh. Ok," Naomi said. She placed her cami over her head than over her shoulders.

"I can't believe I did this. I don't like women Naomi and I'm sorry if I gave you that impression."

"No, not at all, and I don't like women either. I mean, I don't date women, but I do like to play around with them if one catches my eye," she smiled playfully as if she didn't have a care in the world.

Ira sat up and placed her head on the headboard. Still in disbelief from what had just happened. She was too ashamed to even look Naomi in the eyes.

"Look, it was just fun. No harm done right?" Naomi asked.

"I guess, but this is not me. I do not do things like this."

"I know, I could have guessed that just by being in your presence," Naomi played with her finger nails as she spoke to Ira. "If you don't want to do it again we don't have to. I just thought I would bring you some pleasure. I'm sure you haven't been with anyone since—well you know, and I just wanted to make you feel good."

Now Ira was even more confused. Was she supposed to say "Thank you?" This was too much for her to deal with.

"Oh, well I'm going to get some rest," she managed to say.

"Okay, I'll see you in the morning," Naomi said as she made her way to the bedroom door. "I hope this doesn't change anything between us. I really didn't mean any harm Ira, I swear."

"It's okay," Ira replied and Naomi closed the bedroom door behind her. She just wanted Naomi out of her face, better yet, out of her life. How would she explain this to her friends? She wouldn't. She decided this was one secret she would keep between herself and Naomi. Normally she would never be able to keep a secret from the girls, but she has never had a secret like this before.

The blare of her alarm clock ricocheted off of her ear drums as she reached for the snooze button. Ira sat up in her bed and scanned her room and body still in disbelief of what happened the night before. Her mind raced as she looked down at her body, which still wore the silk night gown she put on after her shower then at the door which was still ajar as she usually kept it. Her book was lying next to her and the glass of champagne that sat on her night stand was still half full.

She closed her eyes and let out a deep sigh after realizing it was all a dream, a freaky and confusing dream that she couldn't believe her subconscious ever mustered up. She was not into women and would never do such a thing. Sure Naomi was a beautiful woman, but surely she was not a man. Her loneliness was conjuring up a heap of abnormal thoughts that she had to gain control of, but right now it was time for her to get out of bed and start her day.

Chapter Five

"What has gotten into you? This is not the man that I arrived with."

"Babe, it's almost six thirty. We have to get going before we're late," Trent yelled from the bottom of the stairs.

"Okay, I'm coming," Jade said. She made her way down the stairs after settling on a black cocktail dress to wear to the fundraiser. "We could have been on our way if you hadn't asked me to change," Jade rolled her eyes at Trent as he held open her coat for her to place her arms in.

"Jade it's a fundraiser, not a nightclub. You would have had every man in the room breaking their necks in the hopes of you having some sort of mishap with that last dress you had on," he locked the door behind them as they entered the garage.

"Whatever Trent."

"Look, there is nothing wrong with the dress you have on. I think you look beautiful," Trent said as they exited the garage.

"Of course you do, because you picked it out."

"Jade, I'm not doing this with you right now."

"Doing what," Jade said. She had her face broken down since she was already upset about the change of clothes.

"I'm not going to argue with you about some bullshit."

"Bullshit—you know what Trent, I don't know what your problem is today, but I'm just going to leave you alone," Jade said turning her head towards the passenger's side window.

"I don't have a problem. I just wish you wouldn't have taken your time getting dressed. You know how important it is for me to make a good impression with Mr. Davenport," Trent said. He was doing at least sixty in the forty-five miles per hour zone as he approached the entrance ramp to the highway.

"Whatever," Jade said.

She leaned forward to turn up the radio. Not caring what station it was set to she just wanted to drown out Trent. He had been in a bad mood the whole day, and she knew he was nervous because he kept pacing the floor in their home, and was now jumpier than a crack head. Instead of adding to his problems she decided to lay low and give him his space. He weaved in and out of traffic on the beltway until he reached his exit. Jade wished he would slow his ass down. She was in no hurry to join the rich and annoying.

When they pulled into the parking lot of the Ten Squares Ballroom, Jade noticed all the fancy entrepreneurs, CEO's, and investors dressed in their expensive clothes with diamonds dripping from the women necks, and all she could think about was all the other places she would rather be, but she was there to support her husband, and that was what she was going to do.

"Hello Madam," the valet said as he assisted Jade out of the truck.

"Thank you," Jade gave the young man a friendly smile.

Trent came around and placed his hand on the small of her back as they walked the red carpet toward the gold double doors. Once inside she would inconspicuously search for Elaine, the wife of Trent's business partner Sheldon. She was older than Jade and very quiet. Jade could tell that she was a bit of a doormat when it came to her husband. She was very obedient and seemed more like Sheldon's daughter than his wife, but oddly enough she gave the impression of being a happily married woman. The first time Jade met her she made it a point to let Trent know it was not going down like that in their marriage. Sure he was the man or the captain you could say, and where ever he lead she would follow, but she was the co-pilot and was more than ready to assume his duties if ever he needed her to do so.

"Hey, Trent isn't it?" A tall man asked as he approached the couple. He extended his hand and Trent reluctantly accepted.

"Yes it is," Trent said staring intently at the man. "I'm sorry, but do we know each other?"

"Oh no, where are my manners?" he chuckled. "I'm Ben Stanford. I loved the work you did on the Pressman's project. You know I heard that you overhauled the design after the disaster Forman created."

"Thank you, but I was just doing my job," Trent grinned.

"Well a great job it was, and who is this beauty you have on your arm?" he asked.

"This is my wife Jade."

"Hi, it's nice to meet you," Jade said.

"The pleasure is all mine," he said as he shook Jades hand. "My wife is around here somewhere. I'll catch up with her sooner or later," he laughed.

"Well sorry to just run off, but—"

"Oh, nonsense," he cut Trent off in midsentence. "You two go on. I have a big project coming up, and I will be on the hunt for a reliable architect," he said as he raised his eyebrows, and placed a huge smile on his face.

"Well, please do not hesitate to give us a call," Trent reached into his pocket and handed him a business card. He shook the man's hand one last time before they turned to walk away. "These always come in handy," Trent said to Jade, referring to his business cards. He nodded his head, and waved in few different directions as they navigated through the crowd then stopped abruptly.

"Jade, please do not act salty towards these people," Trent said. He was standing inches away from Jade, staring at her with a straight face.

"What people?" Jade asked.

"Those people," he said.

He looked towards an older man who was standing near the tall windows with an older blonde-haired woman and a dark-skinned young lady. She figured the young woman was Ms. Darkskn21, and the other two were Mr. Davenport and possibly his wife. She instantly became a little agitated.

"Do I have a reason to act salty with those people Trent?"

"Jade I'm serious. Do not mess this up for me."

"I am not a child Trent so therefore I do not need a lecture."

"Good," Trent said. He grabbed a hold of his wife's hand and walked over to Mr. Davenport.

"Trent DeVoe," Mr. Davenport said in a husky voice as Trent went in for a hand shake, but Mr. Davenport went in for a hug. "Just the man I have been waiting to see," he embraced Trent.

"Sorry we were late. Traffic was a bit congested," Trent lied.

"Don't mention it. You must be the Mrs.," Mr. Davenport embraced Jade.

"Yes this is my wife Jade. Jade, this is Mr. and Mrs. Davenport."

"Hi," Jade said. She embraced the both of them and eyed Ms. Darkskn21 over Mr. Davenport's shoulder.

"Oh, and this is my secretary Tamra," Mr. Davenport said. He gently pushed her towards Jade.

"Hi, it's nice to meet you," Tamra said. She looked at Jade for a split second then dropped her head. Her voice was so soft and innocent.

It's her, Jade thought to herself. The woman from the bakery with the oval-shaped birthmark was Darkskn21. Why the hell was she constantly hanging around her bakery? She stared at the woman and managed to say, "Likewise."

She eyed the woman standing before her from head to toe. She was beautiful with round doe-like eyes that were brown. Her lips were covered in bright red lipstick that matched her red strapless dress which was similar to the one Jade was going to wear except hers was blue.

"Trent, I would like to talk to you if you have a minute," Mr. Davenport said. He was motioning towards a table in front of the floor length window, with Trent's partners occupying two of the chairs. "Excuse us ladies."

Mrs. Davenport did not take heed to her husband's words, because she surely walked off with the guys. Jade was ready to indulge in a nice conversation with Tamra until she felt a tap on her shoulder.

"Jade," Elaine squealed.

"Hi, Elaine," Jade said.

"Mr. Davenport stole my husband away from me," she giggled. "They reserved a table for us if you want to come over."

"You lead the way," Jade said and followed Elaine across the room. Not long after taking a seat did a cocktail waiter approach the table.

"Hi, would you ladies like anything from the bar?" the red-headed waiter asked.

"No, thank you," they both replied.

"So, how have you been?" Elaine asked.

"Pretty good, how about yourself?"

"I've been good. You know I have been thinking about getting a part time job just something that will get me out of that house for a while, you know."

"You know I know," Jade laughed.

"Hey, if you need any help at the bakery let me know."

"Yeah sure," Jade replied. It didn't matter what her response was. She knew Elaine was not leaving her home unless her husband gave her permission.

As Elaine sat across the table rambling Jade couldn't help but notice Ms. Darkskn21 eyeballing her on and off as she moved about the room. Whenever Jade would meet her gaze, she would turn away. The more that Jade looked at the woman, the more youthful she appeared. She seemed so innocent and shy which made it hard for Jade to shun her as she had planned after reading those instant messages, but the fact that she visited her bakery asking questions didn't sit well with her at all, and she wanted answers, but didn't want to make a scene and ruin Trent's night.

Her gaze followed the young woman as she spoke to various people throughout the building. After greeting everyone she took a seat at an empty table, and sipped on a glass of water the waiter poured. Jade could tell from a distance that the woman didn't want to be there anymore than she did. She noticed Jade's glare, and quickly turned her head in the opposite direction.

"Are you listening?" Elaine asked.

"Oh, I'm sorry Elaine."

"That's okay. Do you know her?"

"Do I know who?"

"Mr. Davenport's secretary over there. I noticed you keep looking at her. She seems like a nice young lady."

"So, how is the baby making process going?" Jade asked trying to change the subject. She knew that Elaine and her husband has been to trying to conceive for quite some time now.

"It's going," she said, and dropped her head. "It's taking a lot longer than we expected, but we are not going to give up," she continued.

Jade instantly felt bad for asking. "You will be a mommy before you know it." She gave Elaine a comforting smile. "Look at it this way. You get to do a lot of practicing, which is the fun part." Jade raised her eyebrows, and Elaine laughed, but Jade was serious.

"Hi, I see you two did not receive your envelopes," Tamra said as she approached the table. She caught them both off guard since they did not see her coming. She placed a white envelope in front of Jade and one in front of Elaine. "These have your auction numbers in them, and an envelope for your donations. A portion of all proceeds will be donated to the Children's Hospital. Enjoy your night," she added before she quickly turned and abruptly walked away, but Jade wasn't having it.

"Excuse me," Jade said and Tamra turned around. "Do I know you?" She asked.

"No," Tamra said shyly.

"I'm pretty sure I've seen you before at my bakery."

Tamra let out a nervous giggle, "I get that a lot, I must have a twin or something," Tamra said as she turned and rushed away.

"Okay, that was rather quick talking," Elaine said. She opened her envelope and emptied the contents.

"What kind of auction are they having?" Jade asked brushing the woman off. She wasn't crazy, that birthmark was a dead giveaway, but she had to mind her manners tonight.

"I think it's a charity dating auction."

"Well, I will not need this," Jade said as she sat her envelope aside, "and Trent can make the donation. I am ready to go."

"Yeah, I'm with you on that one."

"Hello ladies," Sheldon said as he pulled a chair from underneath the table. Jade looked around and noticed Trent and

Greg walking in their direction.

"Hello fellas," Jade said as they took a seat. She noticed
they were all beaming from ear to ear, and couldn't wait until
they got in the car to juice Trent for answers. He moved his chair
closer to Jade's before getting comfortable and placed his arm
around her shoulders.

"Did you order your food yet?" Trent asked. Jade looked
at her husband and took in his handsome face. The way he kept
his short, boxed beard neatly trimmed and defined made her want
to jump his bones. It's amazing how the ones you love have the
ability to get under your skin and antagonize you, then
effortlessly access your good graces without you granting them
permission.

"No, we were waiting for you all," Jade said.

She pulled the menu from under her purse, and shared it
with her husband, although he had his own. Trent leaned closer
to his wife and kissed the side of her neck. She jumped and
tapped him lightly on the leg. He knew that was her spot, and this
was not the place for her to get all excited.

"I think I just want to eat you instead," he whispered in
her ear.

Jade looked around the table at everyone, and they
seemed to be preoccupied with either their menus or each other.
"What has gotten into you? This is not the man that I arrived
with," Jade spoke softly yet with a hint of attitude in Trent's
direction.

"We got the job," Trent said.

"Really," Jade smiled as Trent nodded his head. "I'm so
happy for you." She kissed her husband's puckered lips.

Everyone placed their orders and handed over their
menus to the waiter. Jade had to admit she was not as bored as
she was at the last gathering. Everyone seemed a lot more
talkative and laid back. It may very well have been the lucrative
deal they just landed. Trent has talked about how well Mr.
Davenport was willing to pay for this project for over a year
now. They have done work for him in the past, but not anything
of this magnitude. Mr. Davenport was a very rich man, and from
the stories Trent has told her he was very down to earth for a
man with such power. Thankfully their architectural firm was a

very reputable company, and came highly recommended.

As they sat around the table debating about who made a better parent, men or women, Jade could feel Trent's hand moving further up her thigh and closer to the goods. She placed her hand on top of his to stop it from moving.

"Behave yourself," Jade whispered trying not to bring attention to the two of them.

"Come on, just let me touch it through you panties," Trent said.

"No."

"Why not," Trent asked. His fingers were steady wiggling and trying to break free from her grasp.

"Because I don't have any on Trent," Jade looked at her husband as his face lit up. She knew what his next move was going to be, but this was not the place.

"Now you know you have to let me get in there," Trent said. He had the same sinister look on his face that he gets whenever he's feeling freaky.

"No," Jade said.

"Please," he frowned.

"No, now be quiet."

"Trent, you with me man?" Greg asked from across the table. All eyes were on Trent as they awaited his input.

"What's that?" Trent asked.

Jade chuckled under her breath. Trent didn't have a clue what they were talking about, as he was too busy trying to put his fingers to work.

"Forget it, just know that our way is the best way," Greg said, and everyone laughed.

Trent's fingers went back to work once the conversation resumed. Jade decided to let him have a little fun. She opened her legs wider, and that grin appeared on Trent's face again. He let his fingers follow the heat trail until he found Jade's wetness. Keeping his eyes on everyone at the table, he slowly dipped his fingers in and out. Jade slid her hips forward giving Trent a little more access. She couldn't believe they were doing this in a public place, but she couldn't deny that it excited her. Trying to keep her composure Jade smiled and added an "Uh huh" every now and then to the conversation. She pulled the long white table cloth towards her hip to be sure their kinky behavior was completely hidden. Despite their limited movement, Trent still found her spot with those long fingers of his. He couldn't hit it the way he wanted to without attracting attention, but he did manage to hit it one good time causing Jade to quiver as a weak cry crept from her closed mouth.

"Are you okay Jade?" Elaine asked. Sincere concern covered her face as she prepared to tend to Jade.

"Yes I have a bit of an upset stomach, but I'm okay Elaine. Thank you," Jade said as she sat up and properly placed her back against the chair.

"The steak and potatoes," the waitress said as she placed Sheldon's plate on the table.

Jade looked over at Trent as the ballroom staff distributed their meals. He looked Jade in the eyes then brought his fingers up to his mouth, and treated himself to a quick appetizer as he licked her juices from his fingers.

"Trent you must be hungry over there since you're licking your fingers already." Greg said.

"Starving," Trent replied as he and Jade shared an inside laugh.

As they all prepared to eat Jade looked across the table and observed Elaine cutting Sheldon's steak. Her mouth did everything but stay closed.

"I'm sorry, but is there something wrong with your hands Sheldon?"

"Oh Jade, I don't mind doing things like this for my husband. I do it all the time," Elaine said.

Jade wanted to reach across the table and smack that steak knife out of her hand, but instead she just turned her attention to her own food. Soon after she looked to her right and Trent was sliding his plate towards Jade. He laughed when he saw the look on her face. There was no way she was going to chop his food up while he sat there watching. He was thirty-four years old, not four. In her opinion, Sheldon needed to be examined by some sort of doctor, or preferably by her to see if he still had a hefty set of balls dangling between his legs, because he could have fooled her.

She watched as Elaine seasoned his food with salt and pepper then placed his plate in front of him. Jade wanted to barf all over the table. Sheldon was officially not a man in her book, and she made sure that he felt her displeasure by rolling her eyes at him every chance she got. Knowingly it was not her place to judge or stick her nose in someone else's business, but the foolishness that was going on at the table was unheard of. Now Jade knew why they were not conceiving, because Elaine was married to a damn woman. Sheldon was clearly taking advantage of Elaine's kind nature, but is he all to blame? Elaine didn't see a problem with her marriage so Jade should just mind her own business.

The rest of the night went on without incident. The auction was a success due to all the older wealthy women in attendance. Hoping Trent would catch the hint, Jade starting to do her normal routine for when she was ready to go. She picked up the white envelope she was given, and started her bogus yawning. She knew that Trent was enjoying himself, but she had to be up and at it early in the morning, unlike him who could sleep in if he wanted. Her performance was in vain for Mr. and Mrs. Davenport took the stage to express their gratitude, and inform every one of their upcoming events. Not long after, everyone started to evacuate the building, and Jade made sure she and Trent were the first in line for their vehicle.

Trent was ecstatic the whole ride to her mother's house to get the children. She knew how hard he had worked for this job, and if anyone deserved it Trent did. That smile will most likely be plastered on his face the rest of the evening.

On nights like this, Jade did their quick routine. Two quick showers, one quick bed time story for the both of them, and then off to bed. Thankfully her mother had them fed and ready for bed before they picked them up, so Jade's job would be fairly easy tonight if everyone complied, and she didn't have to fight with them to get into their pajamas. Her concerns were laid to rest when both kids fell asleep without a putting up a fight.

She shook her head as she reached the bottom of the stairs and heard the sound of a game coming from the basement. Trent turned a part of the basement into his very own man cave a few months after they bought their home. It was fully equipped with a seventy-five inch flat screen television, surround sound throughout, brown leather recliners, and what had to be his favorite possession: his pool table. Initially he implemented a "No kids allowed" rule, but that rule was quickly broken due to Trent Jr. wanting to be around his father at all times, and that's where he spent most of his time when he was at home.

Jade made the decision to let him have his alone time while she tackled the kitchen before heading to bed. She opened the dish washer and began to place the dishes back into the cabinet. Humming the tune that was stuck in her head she swayed back and forth as if there were music playing from a radio. She grabbed the broom and swept the scattered crumbs from this morning's breakfast into a pile then onto the dust pan. After wiping the counters down, she turned her attention to the kitchen table. As usual it was covered with coloring books, crayons, and old mail that the kids decided to use as drawing paper. Jade placed the coloring books into a neat pile, and opened the chicken scratched covered mail. She had a habit of opening mail and tearing it into shreds of paper before disposing of it. Although they had a shredder in their office she never used it.

Before tossing the envelope she received at the fundraiser into the trash can, she opened it and pulled the auction paddle out with the number 230 sprawled across both sides. She sat it on the table and began to pull out the donation form and flyers when something fell from the envelope onto the table. Jade picked up the tiny devise and gazed at it curiously. She wondered why the device was in her envelope, and whether everyone in attendance received one. It appeared to be some sort of flash drive, but why give away flash drives. She thought about Mr. Davenport and how flashy rich folks can be at times, and figured the flash drive was filled with Mr. Davenport's past and upcoming endeavors. Jade knew how things worked in the world of the "You can never have enough wealthy folks." They take your pennies and turn them into dollars which goes straight into their pockets. The only difference between this wealthy man and all the others was he was about to put money in her family's pocket so the least she could do was view the contents on the flash drive.

Content with the tidiness of the kitchen, Jade poured

herself a glass of orange juice, and made her way to their home office. She walked past the great room to the short hallway, and entered the office. As usual the computer was already powered up because she never turned it off. Before waiting to see her screen saver she inserted the flash drive into the USB port, and took a sip of her juice. A few seconds later, a small box appeared on the screen with seven files arranged one after the other, but in no specific order. She scratched her head after reading the titles that seemed to be a little more on the romantic side. She clicked on the first file entitled "True Love" and waited for the hour glass symbol to disappear. When the file was fully loaded a video began to play, but not an advertising video like she expected.

A bedroom appeared on the screen, and Jade looked puzzled as she scanned the room. She watched the video and took in the bright, pink colored comforter and pillow cases. Soon after the woman that was just introduced to her as Mr. Davenport's secretary came into view and moved closer to the camera. Jade couldn't help but think that somehow she had received the wrong envelope, but instead of detaching the flash drive she move closer to the screen and turned up the volume.

She listened intently as Tamra described the love of her life and how much of a factor he played in her life. She smiled proudly into the camera exposing a small gap between her two front teeth before letting out a giggle. She lifted her head and proceeded to talk:

"No other man can do the things that he does. The way he touches me, the way he kisses me, the way he loves me cannot be duplicated. He deserves the best, and that's what I am prepared to give him. I know if my mother heard me say this she would have a fit, but if he asked me to jump—I would say "How high?" I may be young, but I know a good thing when I see it. I have it in my hands and that is where it will stay."

Jade watched as Tamra spun from side to side in her swivel chair with a shy smile on her face. She tactically played with an ink pen, twirling it in and out of her fingers while Usher's "Confessions" played softly in the background. Her high pony tail swung with every movement she made as she hummed along to the song for a brief minute before turning her attention back to the web cam:

"It's like I'm the luckiest girl in the world and the only girl in the world when he's around. One of these days I am going to make a great wife. I'll be home ready and waiting for him every day. I'll have his dinner hot and ready with something sexy on to keep him interested. I know that'll come in due time. My only wish right now is that I can cuddle up and sleep in his strong arms every night, but..."

Tamra paused and let out a sigh:

"But he's worth the wait, and he knows I have my own place if ever he needs some where to lay his head. Although my one bedroom apartment could probably fit inside of his entire home, and still have lots of room left, it's still full of love."

Jade sat thinking about how she was invading this young woman's privacy. She clearly received the wrong envelope, and the right thing to do was to return it to its rightful owner, but she could not turn away. She sipped her orange juice while in deep cogitation. Everything in her told her to remove the flash drive, but of course, her curiosity was getting the best of her. Just when she was about to reach for the device, a man appeared on camera. He walked through the bedroom door startling Tamra, but catching Jade's attention. She scooted closer to the screen again, then was startled by the sound of the basement door knob jiggling, which needed to be fixed. She hurried to turn the volume down and minimize the screen before Trent walked in.

"Babe I'm watching the Chicago Bulls/Boston Celtics 1984 championship game," Trent yelled from the kitchen. Jade could hear him fumbling through the cabinet.

"Oh really, I haven't been a fan that long so that probably wouldn't interest me," Jade said trying not to sound suspicious.

"Well it was a damn good series. You should watch it with me," he said. "Hey what do we have to snack on in here?"

"I'm not sure you'll have to sift through the kids snack cabinet."

"That's alright, I'll just eat the rest of these chips," he said before heading back down the stairs.

Jade restored her screen, and clicked the rewind button to review what she had missed. Tamra turned around and smiled as the guy wrapped his arms around her shoulders, and Jade turned the volume back up.

Male: "Are you talking about me in here?"
Tamra: "Maybe, (giggles) what are you doing here?"
Male: "I wanted to see my favorite girl in the world."
Tamra: "Aww, you're too sweet."
Male: "Yes I am, but only for you, and maybe a few other females (he smiles). You want to do something tonight?"
Tamra: "Sure."

Tamra reaches for the computer:

Male: "Oh so because I'm here now you're done spitting sweet nothings to the camera."
Tamra: "Oh stop it, you of all people should know how shy I am."
Male: "You're shy, huh?"

Tamra stopped the video as the young man began to tickle her. Jade thought they made a cute couple. He was a tall slender man with a wannabe thug appearance. He wore a pair of baggy jeans, and an oversized red and white shirt that was inches away from touching his knees. His facial hair looked as if it were just starting to grow in because of the isolated patches of hair strewn about his face, and for whatever reason he wore his hair in two puff balls on both sides of his head with one too many sweatbands.

Jade closed that file and previewed the others before deciding on the next one to open. She clicked on the fourth file entitled "Moving Forward." Tamra appeared again as soon as the video began to play. Her hair was pulled back into a bun, and she wore a set of large silver and white pearls around her neck with a gray blazer. An excited expression covered her face as she began to speak:

"So I am very excited today, because me and my boo made plans to move in together. We went house hunting in Crofton, Maryland since we both agreed that it would be best to move away from where we reside at the moment. Of course it was only through the internet that we looked at houses, but we are working our way up. It's going to be quite a ride to work every day, but it'll only be temporary until we relocate out of state where we can officially start our new life, so ciao until next time."

Jade actually felt a hint of compassion for the young couple. Although her first impression of Tamra also known as Ms. Darkskn21 was not the best, she had to admit that she seemed to be a nice young lady, and more importantly she was in love with her own man and not Jade's. Tamra's video diaries reminded Jade of herself when she was head over heels in love with this charming young man who ultimately became her husband. Her love-smitten memories warmed her heart, and she thought about how far she and Trent had come over the years. As soon as Jade got a chance she would return the flash drive to Tamra personally. She wished she could pass along her well wishes while they were face to face, but that would only reveal her guilt. A guilt that she was about to add to as she clicked on the file entitled, "Love Love Love."

Tamra's appearance this time was a little different from the last videos. It was apparent that she was in bed with the laptop sitting on her lap. Her hair was messy and there was a puffiness around her eyes that was above and below her eyelids. Tamra's stretch and yawn turned into a huge grin that covered her face. She spoke softly into the camera:

"I just want to say good morning to myself. Today will be a great day for me no matter what actions take place because... I actually woke up next to the love of my life. Yes it is only 3:26 am, but this is still a monumental moment for me. In the few

months that we have been together, I have never awakened to his warm body nestled next to me."

Tamra became quiet when her boyfriend began to squirm under the covers. She looked at the camera, and smiled as she placed her finger over her lips to silence herself.

"I love this man."

She whispered into the camera, and Jade smiled feeling happy for someone else's genuine love for their spouse. She gulped down the rest of her orange juice as she continued to watch:

Male: "Who do you love?"

Jade froze as she stared at the screen.

Tamra: "You're silly, sorry I woke you."

Tamra's boyfriend came into view, half asleep, as he planted kisses on Tamra's neck. The only thing that appeared out of the ordinary was instead of seeing Tamra's scrawny boyfriend, Jade was looking at a familiar face as he hugged and kissed on another woman.

Jade's insides became a four-alarm fire within a matter of seconds. On a scale of one to ten, her anger was a one hundred and one. Her chest lifted and fell as she damn near turned to stone staring at the computer. She listened as her husband confessed his love for this woman who was not her. He even went on to talk about his plans to leave her for Tamra. Jade couldn't believe what she was seeing or hearing. Trent would not do this to her, would he? Could there possibly be a man that resembles her husband, and bears a similar voice as well?

Unfortunately her questions were answered when the blanket fell from Trent's shoulder and the tattoo of Jade's name on his forearm came into view. There was no way to describe the anger she felt at that moment. The disgust and utter betrayal was gripping. Tears silently fell from her eyes as she watched her husband playfully tickle his mistress before Tamra blew a kiss to the camera and the screen went blank.

Jade didn't move. She couldn't. Her emotions had temporarily immobilized her. She sat still in front of the computer, and allowed her tears to fall. When did this happen? Why did this happen? Her head was spinning. In her mind, her marriage was a happy one. Of course they had their ups and downs like every other relationship, but nothing that would make either of them seek refuge outside of their union. She would never step outside of her marriage, or even think twice about it. No amount of dick was worth her family and her children's happiness. Yes, temptation was a motherfucker, but giving in would be detrimental to their lives, and all the hard work they put in over the years to get to where they were now.

Her tears had now turned to animosity. The image of Trent lying in another woman's bed flashed in Jade's head. She stood from her chair, and wiped her face with the back of her hands. Her breathing was heavy and she could feel her heart pounding in her throat. She made her way towards the basement door to confront her cheating husband. Blinded by anger she swung the door open causing it to slam against the wall. She didn't flinch as she marched down the stairs. At that moment she hated her husband. There was no way he loved her as much as she loved him, or else this Tamra woman would solely be the secretary she is.

The thought of Tamra enraged her even more. She would deal with her later. Right now she had a problem in her home that had to be dealt with, but the whore would not get off that easily.

The game was still playing on the flat screen as Jade stood over her husband. He was sound asleep in one of his recliners as Jade contemplated her next move. She couldn't make out one clear thought as her mind was going haywire. She wanted him to hurt like she hurt. She wanted to physically inflict pain upon him until he cried out in agony, but instead she turned around and picked up his framed autographed Lawrence "L.T." Taylor jersey and smashed it against his beloved seventy five inch TV. Glass shattered from the frame as colorful lines covered the television screen. The clash woke Trent from his sleep. He sat up in the chair with wide eyes looking at the damage.

"What the fuck did you do?" he screamed.

Jade walked over to Trent and glared at him, with specks of blood rolling down her face from the glass. "Get out." She said in a low tone.

"What?"

"GET OUT," she screamed at the top of her lungs. Her hands were shaking as beads of sweat began to roll down her face and landed in her eyes.

"Get out for what? Why the fuck did you do that to my TV? You know how much money that thing cost me?"

Trent never saw it coming. He was too busy bitching about his TV. Jade swung again, and again, and again until he finally subdued her, and pinned her to the floor. She squirmed and tried her best to kick her legs, but she was no match for her two hundred and twenty pound husband.

"What the fuck is your problem?" Trent asked out of breath.

Jade was lying on her back staring up at the man she loved. Red scratches were surfacing on his face as he looked down at Jade angrily. She never hit her husband before, but as angry as she was she wanted to do it again. The sight of him made her angry and sad all at the same time. She wiggled again in an attempt to free herself, but nothing happened.

"I want you out of my house Trent, right now," she mustered.

"Why?"

"Because I hate you," she stated as her tears rushed from her eyes.

"Baby, you have to talk to me. I don't understand what's going on."

"Just get out," Jade said.

She looked at her husband through her tears. He had a look of confusion on his face. "Go stay with the whore you are supposed to leave me for."

All of the color left Trent's face. He was as pale as Casper the friendly ghost.

"Get out," Jade repeated.

"I don't know what you're talking about."

"Of course you don't, because I wasn't supposed to find out. Now get out," Jade said.

Once again she tried to free her hands that Trent had a firm grasp on to no avail.

"You know I love you and would never do anything to hurt you."

Jade burst into laughter. Her tears continued to fall towards her ears. "You have me all the way fucked up Trent, and you have two seconds to get off of me. I have to check on my children."

"I'm going to let you up, but you need to keep your hands to yourself, and talk to me like an adult," Trent said as he came to a stance. He quickly backed away from Jade as she sat up and came to her feet.

"Now talk to me," Trent said.

"I have nothing to say to you Trent besides I want you out."

"Hell no, I'm not leaving until you tell me where the fuck all of this coming from."

"Your girlfriend," Jade paused, "she snitched on you." She laughed that demented laugh again.

"I don't have a girlfriend," Trent said raising his voice.

"Sure you do, and her name is Tamra. Now get the fuck out of my house until I find a place for me and my kids to live. Do not come back until I am long gone," Jade made her way up the stairs.

"Baby I can explain that," Trent yelled from behind Jade.

"Really Trent," Jade stopped dead in her tracks. "You can explain to me why I just watched a video that was given to me with my husband in bed with another woman? You can explain that to me?"

"I'm sorry," Trent said as he dropped his head.

"You damn right you are. Now get out."

"I don't want to lose my family, Jade. Please don't do this."

Jade slammed the door in response to his plea. He ran up the stairs behind her not ready to give up just yet.

"I was never going to leave you, I swear. That whole thing was a mistake that will never happen again."

"Well that mistake has cost you your family, so I hope it was worth it. Now I will not argue with you right here. It's too close to my children, and I don't want them to know anything about this. I'm going upstairs, and I would really appreciate it if you would get your shit and leave," Jade tried to turn around before the tears began to fall, but it was too late.

She walked up to her bedroom as Trent stood at the bottom of the stairs watching his wife walk away. As soon as she reached her bed she broke down, and buried her face in a pillow. Her life as she knew it was now over. The only man she has ever loved was in love with someone else. She felt so foolish, and never suspected her husband of being a cheater. How would she break the news to her children when they asked where daddy was? She hated that her children were going to be products of a broken home. That was something she always said she would never let happen, but hearing him make plans about leaving her hurt like hell, and to think that bitch Tamra had the nerve to break it to her the way she did. Now it all made sense, that's why she vandalized her vehicle and kept hanging around her bakery. Although Jade knew who had the last say, and she knew that two wrongs didn't make a right, no one could stop her from getting to Tamra. She was going to hear from Jade in person one way or the other.

Jade crawled under her covers with her clothes on, and continued to cry. She was not looking forward to tomorrow or the rest of life for that matter. She prayed for God to give her strength. Before dosing off to sleep she heard the alarm beep twice and shortly after the front door shut. Her husband was gone.

Chapter Six

"I try so hard to be a good person."

Courtni pressed the send button on the group text message she wrote to the girls. It's been well over a month since the party, and also since the last time she has spoken to her friends. Finally taking responsibility for her own actions, she decided to send them a text apologizing. She hoped they weren't ignoring her even though she knew they had every right to be upset with her. After the party they called her everyday all day and even stopped by, but she needed time to process what had happened. Admittedly she placed most of the blame on her friends for not taking care of her like she has done for them so many times over the years, but she was an adult and they were not responsible for her actions.

She leaned over to pull a tissue from the box to blow her nose. Her allergies were doing a number on her. She's been suffering for about two weeks straight. Between the sneezing, watery eyes, stuffy nose, and upset stomach, she was a miserable mess. Her doctor's appointment was only about an hour away, and she prayed he would prescribe her something that would knock every harassing symptom from her body. Due to her illness, she would miss her sessions today, which really bothered her. She loved her job, and would have to make it up to the kids when she felt a little better.

Dragging her feet as she walked into the bathroom, she wondered how long her bathroom has been so far from the bed.

After catching a glimpse of herself in the mirror she turned away, and reached inside of the shower for the hot water nuzzle. She stood still as saliva began to form in her mouth. Her stomach rumbled as she thought about how long it had been since she'd ate a meal, or anything for that matter. Her eyelids became heavy, and her skin became feverish before she dropped to her knees in front of the toilet. Clear fluids mixed with mucus escaped from her body as she gripped the sides of the toilet. She couldn't make it to her doctor's office quick enough.

After a quick shower she brushed her teeth, and ran her herbal hair oil through her thick hair. The wide tooth comb fluffed her naturally curly hair and she accented her look with a beaded, blue headband before throwing on a pair of sweat pants and a hoody. Her attire did not reflect the bright sun and chirping birds outside of her window, but she could care less as long as her hair was decent.

Once on the road, she listened to her gospel CD, and munched on saltine crackers and ginger ale. The last thing she wanted was to have an accident at the doctor's office. Her phone rang and she smiled when she saw her grandmother's number display across the screen.

"Hey Granny," she said after accepting the call.

"Hey baby, how are you feeling?" her grandmother asked lovingly.

"Still the same Granny," she spoke quietly.

"Well, are you able to hold anything down?"

"I'm eating crackers right now, and so far so good. I'm headed to the doctor's office as we speak."

"Good, that sounds like the flu to me, and don't think you're in the clear because it's no longer flu season. Germs can linger for some time."

"I know that's why I figured it was time to seek medical attention."

"Okay, if you're feeling up to it, stop by my house and pick up this chicken noodle soup I made for you."

"Thank you, I'll be there shortly."

"Okay, see you later."

Courtni disconnected the call, and thought about her grandmother's homemade chicken noodle soup that has been her favorite since she was a kid. The only difference this time around is the thought of it made her queasy. She grabbed her bottle of water quickly trying to prevent the eruption, and to her surprise, it worked.

After sitting in her truck trying to get herself together, she got out and entered her doctor's office. The room was full of women of all ages that were either reading, or watching the muted television that sat on a shelf in the corner of the room. If she was lucky or if they had any sympathy for a rather feeble woman, she would be in and out in a matter of minutes. Doubtful, she placed her dark shades over her eyes, and leaned her head back on the papered wall. She told herself she would be back in her bed in no time.

One hour later, Courtni emerged from the brick building, and slammed the car door once inside. Her fingers moved hastily across her phones keyboard as she urgently texted her friends. Lani and Ira replied quickly and agreed to meet her at her home since they all worked nearby. She dialed Jade's business number when she did not reply in time.

"Thank you for calling Sweet Treats. This is Arnie, how may I help you?"

"Hi, is Jade available?" Courtni asked trying to compose herself.

"May I ask whose calling?" Arnie asked.

"Tell her it's Courtni, and she need to get to the phone right now."

"Whoa honey, hold on a second. Is everybody having a bad day today? Dang," Arnie said, and soon after Jade's voice filled her speaker.

"Hey Court, I got your text, but I don't think I'm going to make it. I have a lot to do here, and I'm really not in the mood," Jade said in a mellow tone.

"Jade, I really don't care what kind of mood you are in. I need you to be at my place in thirty minutes," Courtni snapped.

"Whatever Courtni, I see you still have a stick up your ass, and I don't have time for it. I have my own shit going on, so bye."

"It will only take a second then you can go on with your life, and for the record I'm not feeling well either, but I need my friends right now," Courtni said, trying to keep her anger caged.

Jade let out a deep sigh. "Fine, but only for a minute."

"Bye," Courtni disconnected the call and headed for the busy downtown area. Her thoughts were all over the place, so she started to pray out loud. She was lost. As soon as she began to get herself together, something comes along and knocks her back a couple of feet. The tears started again. She was so tired of crying. This is why she has always stayed on the straight and narrow, because things like this tend to happen and it happens all too often.

"Lord, please keep me near your cross," she cried out. "I need you right now." She cried as she sat in her truck outside of her home. Not sure if she even wanted to go inside, she stared through her windshield with tears rolling down her face. To her surprise, Lani was pulling up behind her so she wiped her face with her shirt and hopped out.

"Hey Court, what's up?" Lani said as Courtni brushed past her to unlock the door.

"Is Ira on the way?" Courtni asked.

"I don't know, Courtni what's going on?" Lani asked concerned as she walked inside behind Courtni.

Courtni looked at Lani, but couldn't speak. She wanted to cry again and again until the humiliating feeling was gone.

"Courtni, you are scaring me." Lani said as she sat next to Courtni on the couch.

"Who is scared of what?" Jade asked as she barged into Courtni's home

"What the hell is wrong with you? Why are your eyes so puffy and why are there little scabs on your face?" Lani asked Jade.

"Issues," Jade said. "and for the record you two don't look too rejuvenated yourselves."

"What's going on?" Ira asked, as she walked in and took a seat next to Jade.

"I need you all to tell me everything that happened at that party," Courtni said.

"Oh gosh, here we go again. Will you let that shit go please?" Jade barked.

"No, Jade I cannot let the shit go. Now start talking," Courtni insisted.

"We don't know Courtni. We told you that. Everybody was doing their own thing," Ira said.

"Well somebody better say something. Tell me something, anything," Courtni screamed.

"Calm down, why are you doing this to yourself?" Lani asked.

Courtni dropped her head and burst into tears "I try so hard to be a good person, and I just cannot catch a break. All I want is to wake up the morning before that party, and make completely different choices," she managed to speak through her tears, as all the girls looked on. "I'm pregnant."

"What?" Lani said while Ira and Jade looked on in shock.

"With a baby that I made with a complete stranger, what am I going to do?" she sobbed. "I just need my friends to help me, and to be there for me like I have been for you all on so many occasions," Courtni sobbed.

"Oh, I'm so sorry Courtni. This is all my fault. I shouldn't have left you there alone. I'm so sorry." Jade said as they all gathered around their friend to embrace her.

"You know what Jade as much as I wanted to blame everyone else for what happened, it's no one else's fault but my own. I am an adult and I knew better," Courtni said.

"Well, just tell me what I can do to help," Jade said.

"You know we will support whatever decision you make," Lani said.

"I just can't fathom the fact that I have a stranger's baby inside of me. I can't," Courtni continued to sob. "I can't fathom the fact that I have a baby inside of me period, and no man, no recollection of sex, and no answers as to who the hell put this baby inside of me. This is too much."

"Well I don't want to sound insensitive, but what are you going to do?" Lani asked.

"I don't know, but I can't kill a baby."

"Well how do you want to proceed? Are you willing to do this on your own? I mean with our help, but what about the father?" Lani asked.

"How are we supposed to find him, if no one knows who he is? We all know this will solely be on me."

"Oh, someone knows him if he was at that party," Jade said.

"That's right. I'll talk to Deidra," Lani said.

"That's a good idea," said Ira.

"Thanks guys, but it's no use. Even if I do find him what do I say? 'Hey, I know you don't know me, but I'm pregnant with your baby?'" Courtni said, and the girls didn't respond.

"It'll be okay, and if we have to do this together then we will," Ira said.

"Please don't tell anyone about this. I'm still not positive as to what I'm going to do. I mean I know an abortion is out of the question, but there are other outlets, right?" Courtni asked looking to her friends for reassurance.

"Yeah, if that's what you want to do. There are plenty of good people who would love a blessing like the one you're carrying," Ira said.

"I'll talk to you ladies later. I know you have to get back to work," Courtni said.

"No, I'm going to stay right here with you. Arnie will call me if he needs me," Jade said.

"Yeah and I didn't plan on going back to work today," Lani said.

"I can stay as long as you need me to," Ira added.

"I guess I'll grab the ice cream," Jade said as she headed for the kitchen.

"I'll grab the spoons and bowls," Ira said.

"I'm so upset with myself right now," Courtni said to Lani.

"Don't beat yourself up. We all make mistakes Courtni," Lani said.

"What am I going to do?"

"Well, first we have to get you some prenatal vitamins because you have to take care of yourself and that baby." Jade said as she and Ira placed the bowls on the table and began to fill them with ice cream.

Courtni loved that her friends would drop everything they were doing to be by her side and to comfort her in her time of need. She sat on the couch and observed her friends that were more like her sisters as they surrounded her offering as many comforting words as they could, but she knew there was not much they could say. Nothing was going to change her current situation, but she took comfort in their presence.

"I love you ladies so much," Courtni said as she leaned forward and placed her bowl of uneaten ice cream on the coffee table.

"We love you too, and we're going to get through this together," Ira said.

"I'm going to talk to Deidra as soon as I leave here, and

"You mean if you get any information out of her," Courtni said.

"Girl please, Deidra needs to be liked by everyone. As soon as she thinks for a second that I'm upset with her, she'll sing like a canary," Lani said.

"I'll keep my fingers crossed," Courtni said.

This is what happens when you steer too far away from His cross. Her grandmother always told her, "He who walks with the Lord will always get to his destination." She had put her desires before her faith, and wants before her God. Now she was another one of his lost children who needed to find her way back home. Thinking about how disappointed her grandmother would be caused her heart to ache once more. She has been her biggest cheerleader Courtni's entire life. Constantly bragging to her friends about her well-mannered, well achieved, well-established granddaughter, who was destined to be someone spectacular. Right then and there she made the decision not to tell her grandmother the truth. It would crush her to know that her precious Courtni could be so irresponsible.

After a few hours with the girls, she told them she wanted to take a nap, and they all respectfully left her alone. She tried her hardest to remember anything she could from the party. The only male that came to mind was Uncle Marty, and thank the Lord he was not the culprit. In the vague thoughts that cascaded through her mind, there were only blurred and unfamiliar faces that came into view. No memory of her descending the stairs entered her thoughts. It was as if she sat at the bar in the kitchen, fell asleep and woke up on Lani's couch. Although her friends attest that there were no signs of foul play, she was not convinced. Not even the clean drug test she received two days after eliminated her doubt. There had to be some sort of drug that cannot be traced or something. No way would she comply with a stranger's advances and have no memory of it what so ever. The only good thing to come out of this was the negative HIV and STD screening she received. She thanked the Lord, because although things were not going the way she would have liked for them to they could have always gone much worst. Her life was spared, and that in itself was enough to shout about.

Closing her eyes, she tried to go to a happy place. A place in her mind that she could escape to since her reality was a nightmare at the moment.

The heavy knocking at her door caused her dog to bark. She jolted out of her sleep and looked at the clock that hung on the wall. She had slept the day away, and that was more than fine with her. She coughed and sneezed as she made her way to the door. After looking through the peephole, she saw Lani on the other side and unlocked the door.

"Why aren't you answering your phone?" Lani asked, as she walked around Courtni into the house.

"I fell asleep."

"Well I talked with Deidra, and although it wasn't easy, she did give me a name," Lani said. She pulled a chair from the dinette table and took a seat.

"Really, just like that? How do you know if she's telling you the truth? Why would she willingly give up information about one of her friends?"

"That's why I said it wasn't easy. At first I think I addressed the situation completely wrong. I got right to the point and asked her if there was a guy asleep in her bed the night after the party, and how do I get in contact with him. She played dumb, but then I told her that one of my friends hooked up with him and she wanted to see him again." Lani placed her phone on the table, before she grabbed a banana from the fruit basket.

"And?" Courtni asked.

"And after she finished lecturing me about how rude she thought it was that you all used their bed to get busy, and apologizing on your behalf," she gave Courtni the side eye, "she did like I told you she would do. She sang like a canary. She's not sure about his phone number, but she says he is a business partner of Laurence and his name is Bo."

"Wow, so I gave my precious purity to a drug dealer named Bo."

"Drug dealer?" Lani asked.

"Well, you even said it yourself that you don't know what type of business Deidra's fiancé has his hands in, so I'm sure his "business partner's" hands are in the same pot. I don't want to know who he is anymore. That was more than enough. I'm going to pray on this and try my best to move on with my life."

"Okay, first of all, just because you don't know his occupation doesn't mean he's a hustler and if you never meet him for yourself I don't think you'll ever have closure. You never know, maybe he has the answers to all those unanswered questions you have." Lani said.

That last sentence made the wheels in Courtni's head turn. Did she really want to move on and never know what happened, or did she want to get some type of answers so that she could move on with her life? A huge part of her wanted to meet the sorry ass that had his way with her knowing she was inebriated, and was not capable of making rational decisions so she could tell him what she really thought of him. He was sure to be some low life that couldn't get a woman to pay him any attention if he had all the riches in the world. According to her friends he was good looking, but that doesn't mean he's a good person, besides their opinions of "good looking" is entirely different from hers. Every man they have ever pointed out as being "cute" or "fine" was okay in her opinion. Nothing impressive, but she could care less about his looks. She just wanted to speak her peace.

"So how are we supposed to get in contact with him?" Courtni asked.

"Tomorrow evening he's going to be over Deidra's house, and so will we."

"What? No. Not tomorrow." Courtni said, already getting cold feet.

"Yes tomorrow."

"I still have to tell him the truth as to why I wanted to meet up with him, since you didn't let the cat out of the bag. What if he doesn't want to see me because he knows he was wrong?"

"I don't know Court, but that man was intoxicated as well so I doubt that he feels he has done anything wrong. Just know that you don't have to do anything you don't want to do."

Courtni sat in silence across the table from Lani. She sniffled in between thoughts, and noticed Lani's phone continuously vibrating along the black tabletop, but Lani ignored every call. She wasn't sure who was on the other end and didn't bother asking, but she made the decision to move forward with her own situation.

"What time tomorrow?" Courtni asked.

"She said he'll be there around seven."

"Ok, I'll be ready. Thank you for coming by. I know you're more than ready to get home instead of sitting here with me and my problems, so call me when you get there."

"Not really looking forward to being there either, but I'll leave you alone," Lani said, as she stood from the table.

Courtni wanted to ask if everything was okay between her and Jackson, but decided against it. She knew Lani, and if she wanted to talk, she would.

"Call me," Courtni added.

"Okay," Lani said.

Courtni watched as Lani walked to her vehicle, and pulled away. Her thoughts were now on her big day tomorrow. She wanted to make sure she said everything she wanted to say to this fool, because she may never get a second chance to tell him how much he has ruined her life. Hopefully, she could scare him straight, and he'll get his life together.

Putting her thoughts aside, she went into the kitchen to heat up a can of soup instead of her grandmother's homemade soup she missed out on. Right now she needed to mend her health, so that she could make it out of bed and in to work in the morning. If her home remedies failed she would simply call and cancel her appointments, which she dreaded, but she didn't want to risk spreading her bad attitude. She had to take care of herself before she could think about taking care of anyone else.

Chapter Seven

"Bye Jackson."

It has been four long weeks since Lani's confrontation with Jackson's wife. She was proud to say that she has finally gotten to the point where she didn't shed tears at the mere mention of his name. The hardest thing she had ever had to do was put on a brave face for her friends and coworkers. None of her friends knew of her problems with Jackson, and as far as she was concerned that was more than fine with her. Her friends would only try to convince her that she didn't need him, and she was better off without Jackson, the liar, but the truth was, she wasn't better off without him. She loved him and the way he treated her like a lady, and not just a piece of meat. She missed his voice, his face, his scent, his lovin', and most of all his promises of their divine future.

She thought about her future without Jackson as she drove down Route 1 to her home. It still hurt like hell to think about how Jackson used her, and basically made her his side chick. That in itself was enough to make her want to go upside his head. Before Jackson, Lani would have never been anyone's side piece. As a matter of fact she made thirsty men her side piece. She would be lying if she said she never thought about looking back. If Jackson would have had a girlfriend and not a wife, she was positive that she wouldn't have gone out without a fight. Of course, not a physical fight, because ladies fight with their intellect, while girls fight with their hands. Jackson was one of a kind and she would have had no problem abolishing her competition.

Her friends wouldn't agree and, in fact, didn't think any man was worth any type of fight from a woman, but Lani would disagree. She could not get over the fact that he had a wife. The kids were one thing, but married men were off limits. She was a firm believer in karma, and she didn't want her to come hunting her down when she finally found Mr. Right. As much as she missed Jackson, and her heart ached for him she had to let him go. He called her constantly, emailed her constantly, text her constantly, and made a few appearances at her job, but she had her co-workers lie for her and tell him that she no longer worked there. She never answered any of his attempts to contact her, so she still have not received any explanation but she could imagine what he would say, "I'm sorry," "I'm not happy with her," or "I'm getting a divorce." She would spare herself the dreadful lies.

Backing into her driveway she looked into her side mirrors to ensure that she didn't hit any of the stones that lined the edge of her yard on both sides. After exiting her vehicle, she locked the doors and headed up the walkway.

"Lani?" She heard a familiar voice call from behind her. She turned to see Jackson walking across her lawn. She was so preoccupied with her thoughts that she hadn't noticed his car parked across the street from her house. Lani turned back around and continued to her door.

"Lani please, just let me explain," Jackson begged as he began to pick up speed towards Lani.

She never looked back at him, as she placed her key in the door and turned the lock.

"Please baby, I just want to talk to you."

"Don't call me that," Lani said as she finally turned to face him.

The sight of him actually calmed her nerves. As he stood inches away from her she couldn't control the sudden stream of tears that raced down her cheeks. He looked a little different from the last time she had seen him. She could tell he hadn't shaved in while, but he smelled as good as she remembered.

"I love you Lani," he whispered.

"You can't love me and your wife Jackson." She waited for him to disagree, and when all she got was silence she opened her door.

"Bye Jackson, and please don't come here again."

"No, wait, wait, wait," he pleaded. "Can I please come in just to talk, that's it. I figured I would give you some time before I came by since you weren't answering my calls," he paused. "Look, I think you deserve an explanation from me, and as a man I need to give you that. Whether you forgive me or not is completely up to you, but please do not shut me out of your life without giving me that chance."

Lani stood in place for a few seconds pondering her choices. She could let him come in and risk possibly dragging her back to square one of her grieving, or she could stand strong, and do without the explanations and continue to heal day by day. Her common sense slowly began to kick in, but her body pushed the heavy wooden door open so that Jackson could enter. Curiosity won that battle.

He never took his eyes off of Lani as he walked past her into her home. She looked across the street and noticed nosey Mrs. Steinberg shamelessly standing in her doorway staring directly back at her before she shut the door. Not really sure of what to do next, she sat her purse on the table in the corner then held on to the banister as she removed her white clogs from her aching feet.

Jackson stood near the couch looking more nervous than a whore in church. She has never seen him this way. Jackson has always come across as being very confident and assertive, but the man that stood before her looked as if he could use a hug or two, and was waiting for permission to speak.

"So are you going to talk or just stand there?" Lani asked. She sat on the second step and gave Jackson her undivided attention.

He cleared his throat and played round with the items in his pockets. "Well, I don't really know where to start."

Lani didn't move a muscle as she sat unaffected by his despondent appearance. She waited for him to think of something silly to say, so she could tear every lie apart. When the silence lingered too long she asked, "Why don't you start with why you decided to pursue me knowing you had a wife at home?"

"Because I thought you were beautiful," he said without hesitation.

"It doesn't matter," she yelled. "When you are married, you cannot chase other women and lead them on Jackson. What you did to me was not fair. While you got to go home to your wife, I had the honors of coming home to my lonely house with a million questions racing through my head like, "What the hell just happened?" Do you know what happened? Do you know I walked into your apartment unaware that there was a disgruntled wife waiting to meet me? Do you realize the position you put me in? She could have done anything to me."

"She would never harm you," he said solemnly.

"Are you serious Jackson? I don't give a fuck about your wife or how tough the bitch is. All I'm saying is you put me in harm's way, and if you really cared like you said, you wouldn't have continued to lie to me for two years."

"I didn't intend for things to happen this way. Yes, of course when I first met you I wanted you, and that was all. I didn't know I was going to grow to love you and to care for you, and the next thing I knew I was in love. I didn't want to be without you, and I still don't."

"You should have told me from the start."

"Then what? Would you have still given me a chance?" Jackson asked.

"No, but that should have been my choice."

"I understand, and I realize that the decisions I made were selfish of me, but I didn't lie when I told you that I loved you."

"Do you love your wife?" Lani asked, and Jackson dropped his head. "You do, don't you?"

Jackson never answered her question. Instead he leaned against the back of the couch and folded his arms. He didn't answer her, but she already knew the answer to her own question. She swallowed the lump that was forming in her throat and held back her tears.

"You can't be in love with two people Jackson—you just can't, and because she has the ring, the kids, the papers, and the man I'm going to assume that she's the winner," Lani said.

"You have a ring also." Jackson said. He looked her dead in the eyes, and walked over towards her then dropped down onto one knee.

Lani looked at him baffled.

"I know that I have done you wrong, but I'm willing to spend the rest of my life making it up to you. Baby please accept this ring as a sign of our love for one another."

"What the hell is this?" Lani said. Her face gave the impression that she was absolutely confused. "Did you not hear a word that I have said to you? I met your wife. I know that you are already married. What are you doing? You know what? Just go Jackson. Get up off the floor and go, because you apparently take me for some type of fool."

"No I don't, listen," he said. He came to a stance and placed the white gold ring with a huge rock atop, and princess cut diamonds along the band back in his pocket. "My wife understands, and she wants to meet with you—with us."

"For what and what do you mean she understands?" Lani asked.

"We have been talking a lot since you guys met, and I told her that I love you, and yes I love her too. I love my children. I love my home, but I love you too Lani."

"So your wife accepts that her husband is a cheater? Is that what you're trying to tell me?"

"No, what I'm trying to tell you is she loves me as well, and doesn't want to lose me, so she says she would be open to actually getting to know you, and us going from there."

"Us going from where? What the fuck are talking about Jackson? Your wife would like to interview me for the side piece opening?" Lani asked. "I thought you would have known me better than this by now Jackson. Why do you think I would settle for being second best when I could easily find another man just as good as you without a problem," she said boldly, but didn't believe her own statement.

"I know you can and that's why I don't want to let you go. I know that legally we cannot marry right now, but I can make a commitment to you. We can even do it in front of your family and friends if you like."

Lani couldn't believe what she was hearing. She would have given her left kidney to hear Jackson propose to her, but never in a million years would she have thought it would be under those circumstances. She was at a loss for words.

"I hear there is talk about legalizing polygamy in the state of Maryland, and as soon as that happens, we will be the first family at the courthouse," Jackson said.

Now she was a part of the family. This is crazy, she thought, and the more Jackson elaborated, the more her head spun.

He came closer to Lani and kneeled down in front of her. "I know you miss me just as much as I miss you Lani. Tell me you don't. Tell me you don't love me anymore," he said in a voice just above a whisper. "I just want to make things as right as I can, and I will love you the way I have been for two years now. I am the same person you met at the hospital that beautiful day, and I know I didn't announce my wife but trust me, she is on board. The only reason she was so upset is because I had a relationship behind her back instead of letting her know what was going on. My wife loves me and would do anything for me."

To hear him say 'my wife' over and over again caused a mini rage inside of her. "Bye Jackson," she said as she stood from the step and walked over to the door. She held the door open for him.

"I know this is a lot to take in, but just know that nothing will change. I promise you'll love me if not the same, more than you loved me before this all happened," Jackson stepped down and out of the doorway. "This ring is all yours Lani and I'm not giving up on us just yet," he continued.

Lani closed her door in his face, but watched him get inside of his car, and pull away from her living room window. It was hard for her to comprehend what had just happened. Could Jackson have actually been telling the truth? Was his wife really okay with sharing her very handsome, very successful husband with another woman and if so, why? If that woman had any sense at all she would go above and beyond her wifely duties to make him forget about other women. It seemed that she loved Jackson more than she loved herself.

Hell yeah, Lani would miss him and all that he had to offer, but how was she supposed to act as if she was the only one. Whenever he was not with her Lani could only imagine the thoughts that would circulate throughout her mind. Him playing with his children, loving on his wife, caressing her, kissing her, and being the husband and father he is supposed to be to them, while she sat at her table eating a TV dinner watching reruns. That was not the life she looked forward to, although it caused her spirits to rise a bit just to know that he wanted her so badly.

She stripped off her clothes at the top of the stairs, and tossed her scrubs in the hamper. After a quick shower she went into her closet and reached for her goodie box. She removed the lid and pulled out Big Brown, her ten-inch pussy buster and strawberry-flavored lube from the box. She had some aggression she needed to unleash, and Big Brown was her outlet of choice.

On her knees, Lani pushed the wooden table that sat at the foot of her bed against the empty wall. She then slammed Big Brown's suction end against the side of the table, and nudged it on both sides. Satisfied with her work she poured lube on top of it, and massaged the shaft up and down. Circling Big Brown's head with the palm of her hand she could feel the tension slowly starting to make its way out of her body. She closed her eyes and enjoyed the realistic feel of Big Brown then took her lube filled hand and ran it over her moist goods. Before giving Big Brown the ride of his life she took her tongue and circled his head. The taste of strawberry danced across her taste buds as she stroked Big Brown up and down as if he could erupt in pleasure like a real man. She turned around and backed her ass up until it met Big Brown's head. Lani couldn't remember how she discovered the table was the perfect height for her freaky mischief, but she was thankful that she had. She eased Big Brown inside of her and allowed him to stretch her anxious kitty. Her next move was her best move. Without thinking twice she backed her ass up with force onto Big Brown. She moaned out loud from the pain and pleasure that shot through her body. Never stopping her stroke she bounced back and forth on Big Brown, and played with her breast with one hand until she felt her temperature rise. She slowed it down and rolled her hips in circles while now playing with her clit. She began to bounce against Big Brown again this time with her fingers moving lightning fast against her clit. Her kitty proceeded to throb and her pace slowed down as her fingers curled against the cream colored carpet. Pulling strands from its base, she cried out loud before falling to her stomach and lolling in her orgasm.

After cleaning Big Brown and placing him back where he belong, Lani cleaned herself up and watched TV. She tried not to think about Jackson because there was no need. He could not do for her what she needed her man to do. She did not want to share him no matter how much she wanted to be with him. Big Brown was not a real man, and could only do so much, but he would have to do for now.

Chapter Eight

"Excuse me if I'm a little lost as to why this has come about."

Ira was glad that her friends seemed to be too wrapped up in their own lives to inquire about hers. Things have been a little crazy in her world. Jonathan continued to unveil his fondness for her, but not in a disrespectful way. Her restaurant was as busy as ever, and her boys were doing great with Naomi. She was a big help and Ira greatly appreciated her hard work. After her raunchy dream about Naomi, it was hard for Ira to face her the next day. It felt as if Naomi could see straight through her to her nasty thoughts when in fact she was not worried about Ira.

She closed the window of her email account after emailing Nick's mother. She made sure to keep in touch with her in-laws, so her boys would always have a piece of their father in their lives. Besides she loved her in-laws. They have always been so helpful and supportive, even after Nick passed. In fact before she hired Naomi, they did all of the babysitting for her, but between the boys school and extracurricular activities and Ira's schedule it became too much for Nick's working class family.

Whenever she viewed her daily planner she thought about how Naomi was a breath of fresh air. There was just that enormous elephant in the room that only Ira knew of no matter how much she tried to avoid it; it always made an appearance. She figured things would get better and her thoughts would become a little less vivid as time went by. The number of times she masturbated has gone up tremendously since her freaky dream. Despite the battle she fought inside every day.

She wondered if she would ever fully recover from losing her husband. If she would ever be able to move on with her life and not feel like she was leaving Nick behind. Truthfully, over the past two years she stayed where she was because she didn't want to leave. She wanted to stay close to Nick, close to the life they shared together and oddly enough that was rather soothing to her. She still felt close to Nick and wished like hell that she could feel him, or see him even if just for one day. She was slowly beginning to understand that would never happen, but took comfort in knowing that she could always look at the two gifts he left behind. Their boys were Nick all over again, as his mother would say and she hoped things stayed that way.

Ira picked up her home office phone and dialed the restaurant.

"Hick's by the Docks," a deep exotic voice sang through the phone, and she could tell it was Jonathan.

"Hey there Jonathan, how is everything going?" Ira asked.

"Oh, everything is great. We met our goal about an hour ago."

"Wow, that was rather soon. Were people beating down the door this morning? What did I miss?"

Jonathan laughed, "Well we actually had a bus load of people come in today. We weren't on their agenda, but they stopped by anyway. You have got to love tourists."

"Well I'm not mad at them."

"That makes two of us."

"Call me if you need me. I have a few errands to run today, but you know I'm only a phone call away," Ira said.

"Yes, I know. You be careful out there," Jonathan added.

"Ok, and thank you Jonathan."

"Not a problem my Queen, good day."

Ira went into her oldest son's room with a set of folded super hero sheets. After placing them on his bed she made her way to her youngest son's room and repeated the act. Next she had to tackle her own room. That was pretty much the only thing she had to do around the house since Naomi had everything else covered. She cooked, cleaned, and even had a distinguishing way of helping the boys with their work. Although Tij's work consisted of coloring letters and animals, Ira usually had to fight with him to keep him interested, and to get the job done, but not Naomi. She would sing to him, do little hand gestures, play games, and manage to get the job done within a matter of minutes. Ira was very careful with whom she had around her children. They were all she had. Her biggest accomplishment was becoming a mom, and their safety and needs will always come before her own.

She finished making her bed and placed the decorative pillows near the headboard. Naomi was out of the house but would return soon, and she had about an hour in a half before the boy's school bus was to arrive outside, and she had plans on surprising them with a trip to the Jump Zone. They loved that place and so did she. The looks on their little faces when they enter that building were priceless. She and Nick used to run through the maze along with Jr., and slide down the slides as if they were children as well.

She missed her family, and asked God daily to keep her memories of her husband fresh in her mind, even in her old age. She never wanted to let him go. Everyone constantly commended her on her strength, and praised her for getting up and moving on with her life, but what was she supposed to do? Life is what you make it, and she made plans when Nick was here with her, and she planned on fulfilling those plans, although he was supposed to be a part of things she had to keep going. What everyone didn't know was she cried herself to sleep every night, she cried in her office at work, she cried in the shower, and anywhere else she could managed to let it out without drawing anyone's attention.

Ira jogged across the bedroom to grab the home phone that was on its third ring before she decided to answer it.

"Meadows residence," she spoke into the receiver since she didn't recognize the number right off hand.

"Hello, may I speak with Mrs. Ira Meadows?" The gentlemen on the other end replied.

"This is she," Ira said, and pulled the phone away from her ear to view the number on the caller ID again. This time she recognized it as her lawyer's office.

"Hi, I'm Dave LaPaul calling on behalf of my father Tim LaPaul, and LaPaul and Associations. How are you doing today?"

"I'm pretty good and yourself?" Ira asked, but wanted him to spit out what he was calling her for.

"That's good to hear and I am well. I'm calling in regards to your late husband Nicholas Meadows estate, which rightfully so is now yours and your children's estate," he paused and waited for a response from Ira.

"Okay," was all that came out of Ira's mouth.

"Yes, well, we received a claim against his estate today."

"What? Why, I don't understand. I thought your father took care of all of this about a year ago, or at least that is what I was told. I received a copy of the court documents, and receipts for all of the legal fees, so excuse me if I'm a little lost as to why this has come about."

"I understand Mrs. Meadows, but this document was filed only three days ago, so this is a new case that has been bought against him."

"You mean me," she sighed.

Here was another headache she would have to endure for God knows how long. When you get married no one ever discloses to you that "til death do us part" doesn't always apply. All of Nick's burdens, and bills fell on her after his death, so she had to stand tall once again.

Nick sold his plumbing business when he learned that he was being deployed. He did so while business was booming so he walked away with a pretty good chunk of money. When he passed away Ira made plans to split the money between their boys, and place it in a trust fund for them to have once they reached the age of twenty one. Between Nick's estate, his life insurance, and his death gratuity from the military she took great comfort in knowing her boys would be financially stable to start their adult hood. Now the only thing she had to do was pray that they would act responsibly with their funds.

"I know, and I'm sorry this is happening to you again, but we will do our best to handle this matter in a timely manner. You have my word."

"So, what's next, and to whom will I be paying? I don't think you mentioned who filed the claim." Ira said.

He cleared his throat, and took a few seconds before hesitantly responding.

"Um, well Mrs. Meadows it was filed by the Child Support Enforcement Agency."

Surprisingly Ira let out a laugh, and took a deep sigh. "Gosh Dave, you had me all worried for nothing. This is obviously some sort of mistake. My husband and I only have two children, and I would not file a claim against my deceased husband," Ira chuckled.

"Yes, I'm aware of that," he said earnestly.

"Well then, there you go," Ira giggled.

"Mrs. Meadows, although I do not have all of the information on this case, just yet, I was hoping that you could shed a little light on the situation," he paused again, and was met with silence on Ira's end so he continued, "but if you are unaware as to the facts and what this is all about I will make a few phone calls to get you some answers."

"Yes, please do, but I assure you they have the wrong Nicholas Meadows," Ira said positively.

"Ok, well I'm going to get right on this, and if you do not hear back from me today please feel free to give me a call tomorrow. At some point I will need you to come down to the office, but I'll let you know when," he stated.

"Not a problem, I'll be in touch," Ira said and ended the phone call.

There was no way her husband could be listed at the Child Support Agency. He was a great father, and did any and every thing for his children including giving his life in an attempt to ensure their safety. No sir, not Nicholas Meadows. He was a real man, and stand-up guy. She would be sure to follow up on this in the morning because no one was going to slander her husband's name. He was not here to defend himself, but she was alive and well, and would handle this situation with poise just as she has all the others. Sure it was hard and mentally draining to carry such burdens, but she didn't think it would be fair to dump them on her friends. They didn't deserve the trouble just as she didn't, but the good Lord will not put more on you than you can bear. She was living proof of that. Her world crumbled two years ago, and she emerged shaken, but mighty. The loneliness is rough at times. Not wanting to bother her friends late at night, she always thought about Nick. Time was healing her wounds, but they were still open enough to cause a slight bit of pain.

She checked the time and still had an hour before the boys would be home, so she walked into her bathroom, turned the shower on, and hopped in before the water begin to warm up. It was time for her to put the drama aside, and spend time with her boys on her day off.

Chapter Nine

"Damn, I picked the wrong day to wear these tight ass pants."

"So what you gon' do?" Arnie asked, after Jade finally gave him the low down on her current situation with Trent.

"I'm going to move on with my life. That's what I'm going to do," she took a sip of her virgin daiquiri. "Right after I pay that hussy a visit."

"Where is your husband?" he asked.

"Probably with his bitch," Jade stated, but she knew he was staying at his mother's since she called every other day trying to force reconciliation.

"Well, I know you didn't ask for my advice but I'm gonna give it to you any way honey. Shit, you just may be the first person my advice actually helps," he pressed his lips together, and they made a popping sound when they separated.

"You need to go find your husband, hear him out, work that shit out, and then let me send my girls to pay the whore a visit, 'cause you mess around and get locked up, and I'll mess around and not get paid," Arnie laughed and Jade smiled.

"There is no working it out with him, Arnie. I actually heard this man with my own ears say he was leaving me, and saw with my own two eyes him snuggled up with another woman," she shook her head. "I can't believe I was so naïve and blind to his bullshit." She took another gulp of her drink.

"Ok, first of all stop sipping on that drink all slow like it has alcohol in it, and you gettin' a buzz, cause you're not," Arnie said, removing the drink from Jade's hand and bringing it closer to him. "Second of all, he was still with you, in yo bed every night, under yo roof every night, laying up under yo big ass booty every night, so obviously he had no plans on leaving." He put his hands up to silence Jade as soon as her lips began to part. "I know, I know it doesn't excuse the cheating. Trust me I know, but look at all that you have to lose. I mean," he paused again and did that lip popping thing he does with his lips, "You don't even know how long ago that happened. Are you really gonna walk away from everything without getting answers? Oh, and you know he's not gonna stop calling and coming by the bakery."

"I don't care what he does," Jade said plainly. As much as she tried to sound tough, pain and sadness rippled through her statement and won the battle.

"Oh, honey," Arnie said. He rose from his seat, and wrapped his arms around Jade which sparked the tears.

It's been an entire month since she's had her husband at home. He came to get the kids last weekend, and calls all day every day. He pleaded with Jade not to hang up on him, to let him in the house to talk to her, or to be with his kids. If he wasn't bugging her at home he was bugging her at the bakery. There was nothing he could say to her that would make her forget the betrayal she experienced. She didn't bother viewing the last of the video files on the flash drive. The damage was already done. Over the past few weeks she thought about Ms. Darkskn21 every single day, and wanted nothing more than to rip her ass apart, but couldn't approach her in the fragile state she was in. She just couldn't shake the bitter mood that constantly consumed her.

"I better get going it's almost seven, and I need to make a market run," Jade said.

"Let me tell you somethin' honey," Arnie brought his hands up to Jade's face and forced her to look at him, "if you need me for anything, and I mean anything at all please call me. If you want to ride on that whore, let's ride. You hear me?" He said while rolling his neck.

"Loud and clear," Jade said with red eyes and a smile on her face.

She stood from her stool and placed a twenty dollar bill on the table, and they began to walk towards the exit, but stopped short of the door when Trent entered. His eyes darted around the room, and landed on Jade.

"Damn, I picked the wrong day to wear these tight ass pants," Arnie said referring to the black skinny jeans he wore. "We may have to tag team his ass if he gets outta line," he said in a low tone of voice, but loud enough for Jade to hear. "Hey Trent," Arnie sang out loud in Jade's ear.

She turned to look at him.

"What? Girl, he kinda thick. I got these tight ass pants on, and I aint got my mace," he rolled his eyes and his neck

"Bye Arnie," Jade said.

"I'm not leavin' you here by yo' self. I told you I got yo' back," he said pointing his finger.

"You know I wouldn't hurt my wife, Arnie," Trent finally spoke up.

"Uh uh, see, I thought I knew you, but I don't," he said shaking his head again.

"Can I talk to my wife, please?" Trent asked, then turned his attention to Jade, "Please don't walk away. Just give me five minutes."

"Two," Jade fired back with her arms folded.

"Ok, two," Trent accepted.

"Imma be outside Boss lady," Arnie said and exited the bar.

Jade took a step back to take in her husband from head to toe. He looked and smelled edible in his black Korean style casual suit. His close, shaved beard connected with his sideburns, and his green eyes seemed to jump out at her. He stood nervously fumbling with his car keys.

"Ok, start lying," Jade said scurrilously.

"I'm not going to lie to you Jade."

"You have a minute in a half," she said looking at her watch.

"Look, baby I love you. I miss you, and I need you. I—"

"Do you love her?" Jade cut his plea short.

"No," he quickly replied.

"Are you in love with her?"

"No, I'm in love with you."

"You expect for me to believe that Trent?" Jade said a little louder than she should have. The few people that were sitting at the bar enjoying happy hour turned to see what the fuss was all about.

"Yes I do, because you know me better than anyone else. You know how much I love you Jade."

"No, I thought I knew you Trent. Just like I thought my marriage was safe, and happy," Jade walked around her husband to the door, but he gently grabbed her arm and continued talking.

"I'm headed to a meeting. I talked to your mother today when I called the kids, and she said she's keeping them for the weekend," he stared at his wife.

"So," Jade said bluntly.

"So, I was wondering if I could come by the house today, and talk to you a little more."

"No you cannot Trent and your two minutes are up," she said and pushed the door open.

She proceeded towards her truck with her husband following close behind.

"Are you having company or something tonight?" he asked and Jade stopped and swung her head around.

"Are you fucking kidding me?" She walked closer to him and stood looking upward at his face. "You know some folks actually respect themselves, their homes, their families, their vows," she paused and poked him in his chest as she spoke, "I loved you Trent I would never ever do anything to jeopardize our marriage." Her eyes begin to water as she angrily looked her husband in the eyes.

"I'm sorry."

"Don't touch me," she snatched her arm away as soon as Trent tried to console her, and continued to her car. All of the ill feelings she felt that night came rushing back, and the last thing she wanted to do was cause a scene at someone else's place of business.

She got into her truck while Trent stood on the sidewalk in front of her vehicle, bearing a languishing look. Jade momentarily fell for his pathetic display, and actually felt a little tug at the heartstring. What the hell was her problem? She had so many emotions running through her body she didn't know how to feel. Reality set in quickly as Trent made his way over to her driver's side window.

"I only want to make things right Jade. I'm still your husband," he spoke from the other side of the glass.

She cracked her window and said, "Not for long." Just to take one last jab at him before she turned and looked through the passenger's side window and waved goodbye to Arnie who was still sitting in his car.

"Don't say that, Jade," she heard Trent say as she placed her truck in reverse, and began to back out of the parking spot.

Some weekend this would be for her and it was only Friday. She has spent her whole adulthood up until now with her husband. If she wasn't busy with her children she was being courted by her husband, or hanging with the girls and that was the last thing she wanted to do. Courtni's problems were a lot deeper than hers, and she deserved to have their undivided attention. The only thing is Jade didn't feel that she could give her that at the moment. Her life was in total disarray.

After purchasing a few things from the market she drove the rest of the distance in thought. Her cell phone rang off and on the entire ride, and each time it was her husband. A part of her wanted to hear what he had to say for himself, but her trust had been violated, and there was no excuse for cheating. If he didn't want to be with her anymore all he had to do was simply tell her. Cheating was the cowardly way of getting what you want without doing the hard work first, which in his case would've been walking away from his family, and into the arms of his carefree mistress. He had a lot to lose, and allowed temptation to win, but you see she was a different story. Granted she knew of his wife and children, but she had no reason to be loyal to Jade. If she had any morals or values the thought of involving herself with a married man would have never crossed the threshold into her simple ass mind.

The thought of Ms. Darkskn21 took her thoughts to another place. She imagined her living her life with a dignified smile on her face. Proud of what she has accomplished, and relishing in her premeditated malevolence as if the score was tied or maybe even feeling victorious. Well, she has interrupted the wrong lives, Jade thought. Not only has she ruined her marriage, she interrupted her children's lives. Jade was the one that had to answer the same questions every single night. Where is Daddy? Why is he not here? When is he coming home? She shook her head thinking about the sad faces her children went to bed with every night when they only got to talk to their dad on the phone, and not hug or kiss him good night.

Once at the intersection, she normally made a right turn on to the long stretch of road her home was located on, but this time she went straight through the light. She pulled into the Exxon gas station, but not to gas up. Instead she picked up her cell phone and searched for Davenport Corporation. She had laid low long enough. It was time for her to give Ms. Darkskn21 a piece, no, a chunk of her mind. Her fingers glided across the key pad until her search was complete. She clicked the tab that read "Get directions" and hauled ass in the direction of the blue flashing arrow.

She hoped she didn't miss her by the time she arrived. With no plan set aside she thought about what she would say when she was finally standing face to face with her husband's mistress again. At the fundraiser, Jade knew something was up with her. The way she kept staring at Jade from across the room, and that half ass speech she gave to her and Elaine when she handed them their fundraiser package. If she had any real balls, she would have disclosed that information right in Jade's face. Thankfully she actually took the package home, and didn't discard it at the fundraiser like most in attendance most likely did.

The incoming call from her phone caused the navigation system to pause, but she kept driving after taking note of her upcoming exit.

"Hey Lani," Jade spoke out loud, with her phone on speaker.

"Hey, what are you doing?"

"Driving,"

"Where to?" Lani asked.

Jade took a deep breath, and blurted out the answer, "I'm going to Trent's mistress's job to see what the hell she has to say, with her nasty ass."

"Trent's what? Jade, what is going on?" Lani questioned.

"I don't really have time to explain. I need to hear the navigation from my phone, and you're interrupting that."

"Hello, use the navigation in your truck. Now, what the hell is going on?"

"Lani, I promise I will tell you later, right now I need directions so I'll call you back."

"No, don't you hang—," Lani said as Jade disconnected the call just in time for the next set of instructions.

She sat at the light waiting to turn left, and could see the four-story office building through the short trees lining the sidewalk. Her heart was racing and adrenaline pumping. Her fingers tapped the steering wheel as she nervously nibbled on her bottom lip. No level of nervousness would stop her from seeing this woman or girl or whatever she wanted to call herself. She didn't understand why she was feeling queasy with butterflies in her stomach. Maybe it was because she would hear some things she didn't really want to hear or learn some things she didn't want to learn from Ms. Darkskn21 about her husband. Things that could be even more damaging. Jade has always feared the unknown, but this was one time she was going to march forward and get answers. Whether they were the answers she wanted or not, the bitch was going to give her some sort of answers as to why she decided to disturb her world.

As the light turned green and she pulled into the parking lot. Ira's soft and mellow voice popped into her head reciting one of her many scriptures that were always on point, "Do not take revenge my dear friends, but leave room for God's wrath, for it is written. It is mine to avenge." At that point she should have turned around and drove back home, but Jade did not. She backed into a parking spot in between two compact cars. The lot was scattered with a few vehicles here and there, and there was a group of four women joined in a circle talking and laughing in front of the door. She wondered if one of them knew Ms. Darkskn21, and debated about asking but decided against it. The ladies meeting adjourned as they walked around the corner and stood there for a little while. Jade watched as they all disappeared and soon after four cars drove out of the parking lot.

She sat there trying to convince herself that what she was doing was foolish, that she was wasting her time and could be at home watching a movie or doing something constructive with her time. After all, Ms. Darkskn21 may be long gone, but her animosity would not let her leave. She just had to see the girl so she could bring closure to the situation.

That's it, she thought.

All she wanted was closure. She wanted to know why. Why Trent? Why her family? Why now? Her husband held the answer to each one of those questions but she wanted to hear it from her, from a so called woman. Yes, the dick was good, but was it so good that she felt the need to destroy a family, and take a man away from his children. Were the pickings that slim nowadays that she couldn't go out and find her own man? A man that wasn't attached to a family, or did she simply not care?

"Lord, I really just want to be done with this. I want the hurt to end, and I want to be happy again. I don't want to care about this anymore" Jade spoke out loud. She knew the power of prayer was a mighty weapon, but she also knew that it was up to her to move her feet in the direction of his voice.

The afternoon sun was fully hidden behind the horizon, but the sky was still well lit casting a tad bit of light upon the busy commuters. She was just about to chalk her visit up as a lost when Ms. Darkskn21 appeared before her very eyes. She exited the building wearing a white pants suit, and cradling a stack of folders in her arm as she felt for her keys in her purse with her free hand.

Jade's heart started racing again, as her chest heaved in and out. The solemn mood she was in erupted into hatred. She turned her truck off, pulled her keys from the ignition and stepped out. She walked a few steps and leaned against the side of her truck's fender with her arms folded.

"Well if it isn't Ms. Darkskn21," she paused, "in the flesh," Jade continued.

Tamra stopped and stared in Jade's direction. A look of fear and confusion covered her face as she made her move. She tried to make a b-line for her car which just so happened to be one of the cars Jade parked beside.

"Don't run now, we're just getting started, home wrecker," Jade spewed at her, as she slid over in front of Tamra blocking her from her car.

"I...I..."

"Oh now you don't have anything to say, huh?" Jade's face wore an evil gaze.

"I don't have anything to say to you," Tamra's voice quivered, as she shuffled to the left then shuffled to right in an attempt to get around Jade. "I don't owe you anything. You have what you want. You won alright, so why are you here?"

"I won," Jade sad angrily. "You think this is a fuckin' game?" Jade shouted.

Scampering in her kitten heels caused Tamra's ankle to buckle, and she fell to her knees along with the files she was carrying. Before she could get up Jade was hovering over her like a hawk. She stood tall and statuesque as she glared down at Tamra. Her kinky shoulder length hair dangled down past her face as she shifted her position and bent down closer to Tamra.

"Did you really think you was just going to fuck my husband, and wouldn't have to deal with me?" Jade yelled down at Tamra who was now crying, and shielding her face. "Do you know what the fuck you have done to my life? To my kid's lives?" she paused, "I ought to rip your fucking face off, you fucking coward." Jade screamed and smacked the folder Tamra was using to cover her face.

"I hate you," Tamra shouted through her tears. "Trent should be with me," she said and spit in Jade's face.

"You little bitch," Jade said as she grabbed a hold of Tamra's hair. Her fist met Tamra's face multiple times before she yanked her by the hair and drug her across the concrete. "You should've fucked someone else's husband, you whore."

Tamra swung her legs around and kicked Jade dead in the stomach. She stumbled backwards as Tamra came to her feet.

"Who's talking shit now," Tamra said as she gained a little more courage and cockiness. She approached Jade ready to swing, but Jade grabbed her wrist and yanked her to the ground ready to shut this shit down so she could take her ass home.

She climbed on top of Tamra, and used her legs to pin Tamra's arms down. That crazed laugh returned as she looked down at Tamra who was trying her best to break free. "Oh you had a lot of balls between those scrawny ass legs when you gave me that envelope, but your ass can't back it up." Jade laughed and grabbed a handful of Tamra's hair and slammed her head into the concrete. "I promise you bitch you don't have enough experience under your belt to fuck with me, so you better stay your little young ass in a child's place and stay the fuck away from my family or else," Jade said.

"Jonesy, Jonesy help me," Tamra delivered a piercing plea as she looked towards the office building.

"Look at me bitch," Jade gripped Tamra's face and forcefully turned it in her direction. She had completely lost her mind, and was out of control. She couldn't handle the amount of adrenaline that was running rampant through her veins. "You fucked with the wrong bitch, and from this point on as long as I'm hurting bitch you will too. I will make it my business to haunt your fucking dreams, you hear me," she screamed in Tamra's face.

"Tamra, are you okay?" Jade turned to see the tall skinny figure right before he tackled her to the ground. She fell on top of Tamra, and she screamed as the weight of the two of them came down on her.

"I'm security ma'am. Put your hands behind your back," he demanded of Jade.

"Get her Jonesy," Tamra screamed.

"I got her," the security guard said as he tussled with Jade.

Jade wiggled her shoulders as she tried to free herself from his grasp, and stop Tamra from getting away. She wiggled underneath Jade and eventually freed herself once the puny security guard thought he had subdued Jade. Tamra crawled backwards to get away from the mayhem. Her makeup was smeared and she was visibly shaken and holding her head. Jade glared her way and noticed she only had on one shoe. The other one must have been underneath her, but she didn't feel it as angry as she was.

"I don't know who you are miss, but you are messing with the right one now. You want trouble, well you got it." The security guard said, trying to sound tough as Jade continued fidgeting.

As he fumbled for a pair of flex cuffs on his hip Jade gathered the strength to lift her body and the security guard toppled over. Tamra screamed and hauled ass to the opposite side of her car with bloody hands while Jade tussled with the guard. He grabbed a handful of Jade's hair as she clawed at his face.

"Let me go," Jade demanded.

"Ahhh," he screeched like a girl.

"Just get off of me," Jade said out of breath. "She's not worth all of this trouble."

Between his screaming and Tamra's she didn't know who was more annoying, and before she knew it she grabbed his Taser from his waist, stood up with her hair still in his hands, and released 50,000 volts of electricity into his side. His body jolted and squirmed and soon after a dark stain begin to emerge on the front of his pants.

Jade dropped the taser, and cover her mouth, "Oh shit," she said into the palm of her hand as Tamra stood screaming from behind her car.

"Oh dear Lord, are you okay?" Jade said as she kneeled down to assist the guard. She then noticed the guard was the same scrawny young man she saw on one of the videos she watched. Her rage had caused her to do the unthinkable. It was not her intention to harm anyone, and she wished like hell she had never come to this place.

Tamra stood in place still screaming, crying and barking in between. She screamed as if she was auditioning for the leading role in a horror film then she'd go into a mini cough attack before screaming again, and looking at her bloody hands in between holding the back of her head.

"Will you shut the hell up, before you cough up a lung, damn," Jade yelled in Tamra's direction as she turned her attention back to the guard who was rolling around and crying himself.

"You made me piss myself," he cried.

"I'm sorry," Jade said. "I didn't mean to do that I swear." Jade tried to assure him as he continued to sob.

"Damn, that hurt," he said.

The red and blue flashing lights startled Jade, and she jumped to her feet.

"Everyone put your hands in the air." The two officers stood behind their opened car doors and barked orders. "Lie down on the ground and place your hands behind your head."

Jade and Tamra did as told, and the guard tried to but couldn't stop the mini convulsions and tears. She couldn't believe what was happening. There was no way she was being arrested. She was no criminal, but the feel of the metal handcuffs fastening around her wrist confirmed her fears. She would not be sleeping in her own bed tonight.

Chapter Ten

"This is your chance to ruin someone's life."

Courtni paced the floor of her home while waiting for Lani to pick her up. She regret asking Lani to drive, since she was always late, but with her being nervous about meeting the pervert that had his way with her, she couldn't get too upset. She wanted her to be there with her. There was no telling what was going to happen today, but she had a feeling it wasn't going to be good. She replayed the scenario over and over in her head. Surely, he would deny playing a role in the act. Surely, he would be defensive, and she was almost certain that he would be a heathen of some sort. Someone she wanted nothing to do with or the baby. Just the thought of him touching her and doing as he pleased with her while she was incapacitated made her sick to her stomach, and not to mention it was unprotected and he planted a seed inside of her body. There was no way he was an upstanding citizen that could be trusted.

She had a few reasons why she wanted to meet him. After praying on it throughout the night, she decided he deserved to know that he would be a father, but more so she wanted to give him an earful. Maybe she could get him on the right path, and force him to see that the life he lives is not one of a man. If she could help the next young woman then her job was done.

Courtni picked up her phone and dialed her brother's number in the hopes of him calming her nerves. She made him promise not to tell their grandmother about her pregnancy and she was sure that he wouldn't. Their sibling bond seemed to be all they had at one point in time.

"Hey Randy," she said once he answered the phone.

"What's up baby sis? How are you feeling?"

"Nervous, I'm waiting for Lani so I can meet this fool."

"Do you think I should go with you instead?" he asked.

"No, I'll be alright. I just want to get it over with so I can move on to the next step." Courtni said as she played with the string that hung from the blinds.

"Well I hope you make the right the decision. That is an innocent baby you are carrying Courtni."

"I know that Randy, but it's just too much for me right now," Courtni said. "I have already decided not to abort the pregnancy since I would never do that, so either way I'll be making the right decision."

"Not really sis," Randy replied. "Imagine getting a phone call from a young adult eighteen years from now asking you why did you give them away?"

Courtni closed her eyes as if it would prevent her from hearing what her brother said. "I can't do this right now Randy," she said teary eyed.

"You know we are here for you. I just don't want you to live the rest of your life with regret. You made a mistake and now you have to deal with the consequences, which is nothing for a trooper like you."

"I know, I have to go Lani is here," Courtni said.

"Let me know how things work out, and the next party y'all go to let a brother know something," Randy laughed.

"Ha ha Randy. Love you," Courtni ended the call.

She grabbed her purse when she saw Lani pull up in front of her house. It was time to get this done and over with.

"Hey Boo," Lani said while looking at her phone.

"Hey, and what's up with the shades? The sun is not out anymore," Courtni said.

"Don't you have bigger problems to worry about other than my shades?" Lani laughed, and removed her sunglasses.

"Thank you," Courtni said. "I'm not sure if I even want to do this."

"This is your chance to ruin someone's life," Lani laughed at her own joke.

"Lani, if you're going to crack jokes all night you can turn back around and take me home."

"Ok, no more jokes. I just figured we all could use a laugh with everything that's been going on."

"I've been meaning to ask you about that. Is everything all right with you and Jackson?"

"We broke up last month," Lani said. "His wife met me at

his apartment, and that was that," she said, popping a potato chip in her mouth.

"What do you mean his wife?" Courtni asked.

"His wife Court, and she comes fully equipped with two kids."

"Oh no, I'm so sorry Lani. Men are disgusting. Disgusting dogs and this is why I'm single," she said, and Lani laughed. "I'm serious."

"Every time a guy does anything, you say that's why you are single. When in reality you, my dear, are single because you're afraid of men," Lani said still eating her chips.

"I'm not afraid of men. I want more than these boys are willing to offer. Besides, it's not my fault I don't get approached by men. They're afraid of me, of my confidence, of my success, my voluptuousness, and my beautiful natural coils. Guys these days don't know what to do with a real woman," Courtni said while enjoying Lani's chips.

"Yeah well, I give up on love. Jackson was my one true love."

"That's what you may think, but God has so much more in store for you," Courtni assured her friend.

"I don't want you to worry about me. Just focus on that little bun in the oven," she reached over to rubbed Courtni's stomach, but she pushed her hand away.

"Don't do that, please," Courtni said softly. "It makes it...real," she dropped her head.

There was so much she needed to do, but didn't know where to start. For starters she had to make a decision as to whether she would keep her baby. Only God knows how badly she wants children, but not this way. How would she tell her child where the father was when she didn't know? If she did decided to keep her baby there was also a chance that she would have to deal with a man that probably had no job, lives with his momma, and she did not want to spend eighteen years running back and forth to the Child Support Agency. There are lots of good hearted people that dream of being parents, and she could help fulfill that dream for one lucky couple.

"Look familiar?" Lani asked as they pulled up to the security gate.

Courtni let out a sigh, and reached into her wallet for her license. Lani handed it to the woman in the small booth, and they pulled away once she gave it back. Her nerves decided to reappear once more. She pulled her lip gloss from her purse and glazed it over her full lips then pulled out a bottle of Chanel No.5 and sprayed it around her neck, and on her wrist.

"Am I missing something?" Lani asked as she parked her car at the edge of Deidra's driveway. "Are you trying to snag this man or what?" Lani asked.

"No, I want nothing to do with that buffoon. I just want to look and smell good while I'm teaching him a lesson," Courtni said. She had her thick hair pulled up into a pineapple pony on top of her head, accentuated with a teal head wrap that matched her teal and brown maxi dress.

They got out of the car and Courtni didn't move. She was having second thoughts as she noticed the group of men working in the garage.

"I don't want to do this," she blurted out.

"Courtni, we're here now. Just relax, speak your peace and we can leave," Lani said.

"Ok, ok I can do this," she told herself as they walked towards the house. Deidra spotted them and came down off the porch.

"Hey ladies," she said loudly as if they weren't within earshot. She hugged them both and beamed with joy as if they came bearing gifts.

"Can I first say that I am so very sorry for my behavior that night?" Courtni said.

"Don't worry about it. I'm glad you were ok, and nothing terrible happened to you," Deidra smiled, and Lani made a face that said "Not quite." "Well come on girls, Bo is right over here," she said walking towards the huge garage. "He is a piece of work, you know," she giggled.

"Yeah, I bet with a name like Bo," Courtni said snidely, and Deidra gave her a look out of the corner of her eye.

"That's him right over there," Deidra said pointing in the direction of an old refurbished 1972 Monte Carlo.

"Oh hell no," Courtni said after seeing the big-bellied older guy that stood next to the car wiping it down with his oily shirt.

"No, not him," Lani laughed. "Him," she said with one eyebrow raised, and a look on her face that said, "Damn."

Bo slid from underneath the car on a mechanic's creeper, and stood up looking like a chocolate playground. His long dreads were pulled back into a ponytail, and his once white t-shirt was now stained with oil and grease spots. The short sleeves were no match for his bulging muscles that pushed the cotton material to its limit. He stood pointing to the car and in deep conversation with the older guy.

"Sweet baby Jesus," Courtni said with wide eyes.

"Bo, could I talk to you for a minute?" Deidra asked.

"Come on Babe, we're working out here," Laurence said from underneath another car.

"I know baby, but someone wants to meet him."

"Actually it's a little more than that," Lani said.

"It's ok I could use a break," Bo said in a deep potent voice.

Courtni's mouth was still open as Bo wiped his hands with a towel, and came closer to the girls. "This can't be him," she whispered to herself, but Lani overheard her.

"Oh it is, and if you don't want him, chick send him my way," she whispered back at Courtni, but kept her eyes on Bo.

"Courtni this is Bo, Bo this is Courtni," Deidra introduced them, and he extended his hand. "She's the one that you were with at the party that night, in my bed," Deidra said playfully but there was a serious under tone.

"Oh, I'm sorry about that," he said. "What can I help you with?"

Courtni looked around the garage. Everyone had stopped what they were doing and had all eyes and ears on the two of them. She cleared her throat, swallowed the lump and let it out, "You took advantage of me that night in my impaired state and you impregnated me," Courtni rattled off in one breath. She heard a few gasps and a "oh shit" from one of the guys.

"Whoa, whoa, whoa, I have never taken advantage of anyone in my life," Bo said.

"Well, I must have been number one."

"Bullshit," he said.

"Do not curse at me," Courtni said.

"Maybe we should give them some privacy," Deidra said. "Come on guys, let's go in the house."

Courtni watched as they all emptied the garage, and she gave Lani a nod to let her know it was ok to leave with the others.

Once the door was closed Courtni continued, "I don't really care what you have to say, I just wanted to inform you of what you have done, just in case no one else does."

He folded his arms and leaned against the car Laurence was working on. "How do you expect for me to believe that you are carrying my child, and I don't even remember the act, and I don't know you?"

"I don't care what you believe. I just want you to know that you cannot continue to live your life this way. You are going to leave a trail of fatherless children, and scorned women. Let this be your lesson," she said sternly and he chuckled.

"How do you know how I live my life?" he asked.

"Well, I don't," she said, looking around the garage at all the shiny new car parts, "but I can take a guess, and I imagine you already have children as well."

"You imagine wrong, and I'm pretty sure your guess is as well," he smirked.

"I'm done here," Courtni said, and headed towards the door to the house that everyone went through. She had enough of his smug attitude.

"Wait, and what about the baby?" he asked.

"That's not your issue," she said.

"If that's my baby like you claim it is, than it is my issue."

"Like I claim it is?" Courtni barked back at him. "Let me tell you something, I was a virgin before I crossed paths with you, and I would have remained one until I met a real man, not some low life hustler."

"If you say so," he brushed her off.

"I do say so, now good bye. Go back to your illegal activity," she said, and opened the door.

"So, I guess in about eight to nine months I should be expecting another visit, and you informing me that I have to pay child support for my alleged child, since that's all you want right, money?" he said.

"Go to hell," she slammed the door.

She didn't care how fine he was. He was not going to stand there and insult her. She spoke her mind and said everything she wanted to say, so today was a success. She didn't expect for him to be that fine, but fine didn't mean mature. Now her next task was to pray every day about whether to take on the task of being a mother or bless someone else with the title.

Once at home she showered and curled up on the couch to watch a movie. She knew to expect nausea half the day tomorrow, so she had to pig out at night. Strawberry pie, vanilla ice cream, and chocolate chip cookies were on deck. She tried her best not to think about her pregnancy. Every time she did she wanted to cry. Her disappointment in herself was tremendous, and her worry was even greater. She knew she didn't remember the baby going in, but she would surely remember it coming out.

Courtni flipped through the movie channels and stopped at *Steel Magnolias*. That movie was a classic and one of her favorite movies. With her cozy fleece pajamas, fleece blanket, and snacks lined up across the table she was ready to enjoy her night.

There was a knock at the door and she looked at the clock to see what time it was. The clock displayed 10:00 pm, so why was anyone knocking at her door? After the second knock she walked over and peeped through the peephole.

"What the heck," she said surprised. Colby barked at the door and ran circles around her legs as she tried to calm her nerves. She instantly recognized the face that was all up in the peephole trying to look in. The question was how did he know where she lived? She ran up the stairs in search of her robe to cover up her not so sexy pajamas. Then went into the bathroom, snatched the head scarf off of her head, fluffed her curls, and flew back down the stairs.

"What the hell am I doing?" she asked herself, before opening the door slowly as if she didn't just run around the house like a mad woman.

"Hey," Bo said.

She immediately wanted to kick herself in the ass when she saw him standing in front of her in a plain dark blue shirt, and a pair of distressed jeans. The tongue from his Conquest POLO boots stuck out from under his left pants leg, and his locks were loose and hang down next to his chest.

"I'm sorry, let me repeat that, hello Ms. Courtni," he said when she didn't respond.

He didn't realize her kitty said hello as soon she laid eyes on him. "How did you know where I live?" Courtni asked.

"Can I come in?" he replied.

"No, I don't know you."

He threw his hands up, "Understandable."

"Now can you answer my question?" Courtni asked.

"I asked Deidra, Deidra called your friend Lani, and now I'm here," he said.

"Hold on," Courtni shut the door, and grabbed her cell phone from the end table then dialed Lani's number.

"Hello," Lani answered.

"Why did you give out my address to this fool? Do you know how dangerous that is?"

"That is your child's father. Y'all better work it out sister," Lani giggled.

"I'll deal with you later. Bye." she hung up the phone, and went back to the door.

She stepped outside just in case he felt like acting crazy her nosey neighbors would bear witness.

"All right, what do you want?" Courtni said.

Bo was now sitting at the top of her eight step staircase. "I wanted to apologize about earlier," he said. "My father would kill me if he heard me talk to you that way."

"All is forgiven. I know you were taken by surprise, and if I were in your shoes I'd be skeptical as well," she let out a nervous laugh.

He sat looking at her like he was taking a mental picture, with her fluffy robe and colorful socks. His gaze made her even more nervous, and his gorgeous face made her pussy pucker up. She didn't know whether to hate this man or lie down and let him do whatever it was he did to her that night all over again.

"I really don't remember much about that night," he said, rubbing the hair on his chin. "I'm not a drinker, but I figured hey, I'm staying with friends, it'll be ok, then Uncle Marty made me some drink called a Slow Death and—"

"He made you that too?" Courtni asked. She came closer, and took a seat next to him on the step, shocking herself.

"Wait, you had a Slow Death?" he asked. "So, you were a virgin that drinks hard liquor?"

"No I didn't drink hard liquor before then, and yes I was a virgin. Whether you believe me or not, is not my problem. Having a drink doesn't mean a woman is looking to have sex."

"Under the circumstances you can't blame me for being doubtful," he said.

"What do you remember?" Courtni asked, changing the subject.

"Everything up until the drink, but apparently I went up the stairs to lie down. At least that's what Laurence told me. The next day I woke up in their bed, half naked, and smelling like that perfume you wore earlier today," he looked over at Courtni. "What do you remember?"

"Everything before the drink, and then waking up at my friend's house the next morning," Courtni said, and there was a silence that lingered for a while.

"So, where do we go from here?" he asked.

"I'm going to do some research on adoption agencies, and pray, and go from there."

He stared intently at Courtni. "You're going to give your first child up for adoption?" he asked.

"It's not as uncommon as you may think."

"I don't think it's uncommon. I'm just wondering why you're doing it. You have this nice big house so I'm sure you're doing well for yourself, and I know this is your place and not some guy's."

"How do you know that?" Courtni asked.

"Your friend told Deidra and—"

"I know, Deidra told you. I'm going to kill Lani," Courtni

said.

Silence fell upon them once again, and they both sat looking straight ahead. She figured he was trying to guess what it was she was thinking just as she was him. There was no way of knowing how he really felt about the situation. Understandably he was upset, but he didn't come across that way. No one wants a child with a stranger, and no one wants to go through the motions of not knowing whether a child is theirs or not. She knew that she was struggling with the issue, but he was a man. He could stand up, walk away and never look back. His life would never change.

"Look," Courtni broke their silence. "I'm sincerely sorry for this whole mess. I know we were both at fault, but somehow I just feel like an apology is due," she said.

"Why, did you rape me?" he laughed.

"Actually, I think I did," Courtni admitted to herself, and he laughed even harder.

Courtni sat next to him with a serious face. "I'm serious my friends told me they found me on top of you."

"I know," he said. He was trying to stop himself from laughing. "I was told by a friend of mine that they saw two girls dragging one girl down the stairs, and out the door, but I seriously doubt that you raped me. I can be persuasive when I'm sober so imagine the work I can do when I'm intoxicated," he said proudly.

"Well don't flatter yourself because I don't think you're that persuasive, and you're not my type, sorry."

"Oh really, well what is your type?" he asked.

"Not that it's any of your business, but I prefer business men."

He smiled, "Well good for you," he paused, and stood up. "I guess I'll keep in touch. I would really appreciate it if you would keep me posted on your choice," he said.

"Why?" Courtni asked.

"If or when I should say, I get a DNA test and that is my child, if you decide you want to put him or her up for adoption, me being the father, I would have the choice to raise my child."

"I'm sorry, but I don't think it's a good idea to raise a

child around hustlers and drug dealers," she said with her nose turned up.

"Hold up," he said standing at the bottom of the stairs. "I ignored your 'illegal activity' comment earlier, but you are not going to call me a drug dealer. I work hard for everything I have," he stated.

"If you say so," she hit him with his own line, as she stood up and headed for her door.

Once inside she locked her door and watched him walk to his car from the window. He opened the door to a silver Porsche Boxster and hopped in.

"Work hard my behind," she said from behind the blinds.

She went over to the couch to resume her movie and snacks except her ice cream was melted, and she had Bo on the brain. His brilliant face, and succulent lips were hard to miss along with the rest of his titillating presence. She surprised herself since normally she was attracted to well groomed, well spoken, well dressed, educated men. Although he was pretty well put together, dreads were not her thing, and his lack of legitimate work would not suffice, so the quicker she got him out of her life the better.

The sound of paper ruffling caught her attention, and she turned towards the door. Colby went over to sniff, then immediately started barking. She went over to the door and noticed a folded piece of paper made its way into her home. She peeped through the peephole, and Bo was halfway down the steps as he looked back at her home then continued to his car. She picked the paper up, and read its content. An enormous smile covered her face, but she quickly erased it. Why was she acting as if she had a school girl crush when in fact he was not what she wanted, and surely he wouldn't want her? Guys like that always wanted the superficial girls that looked good, but couldn't hold a conversation outside of sex and reality shows. She looked at the phone number in her hand once again before sticking it in the junk drawer in her kitchen.

With a hand full of snacks and melted ice cream she tossed everything in the trash. The cravings were long gone so she opted for a popsicle instead. The direction her thoughts were going in was reminiscent of the old Courtni, before the party, before the incident, and before her dilemma. The Courtni that, yearned for male loving, and fantasized about it constantly was back.

"Let's try this again," she said, as she flopped back down in front of the television.

This time around she went straight to the HGTV channel, and watched as a young couple searched for their first home. Her interest didn't last long as her thoughts shifted right back to Bo. She thought about how thoughtful it was of him to leave a contact number. Then she thought about how thoughtful it would be of him to take both of her breasts into his mouth and suck all of the frustration out of her.

She skillfully unbuttoned her top with the popsicle still in hand, and released the girls. Her ample breast freely escaped the soft fabric, and sat looking rounded and divine. Ready to be caressed, she sucked the top of the popsicle then placed it between her breast. She slowly traced it around her wondrous mahogany nipples. The coolness on her warm body made her nipples stand at attention, and small goose bumps emerge all over her body. Her nipples has been extra sensitive as of lately, and tonight her raging hormones came in handy. She repeated the same thing on the other nipple then took it into her mouth and sucked every speck of the sweet juice from it. The melting popsicle begin to drip onto her thighs and each drop was more tantalizing than the other. She placed the cool popsicle on her now enlarged clitoris and moaned as the cold ice sent a charge through her juicy goods. After placing the popsicle on its wrapper she finished the job, all along thinking about Bo between her legs pleasing and teasing her until she saw the black and white checkered flag waving in the air.

Surely Mr. Bo would move on with his life, and she had to follow suit.

Chapter Eleven

"Please make no mistake…I run this shit."

Curiosity killed the cat, but satisfaction brought it back. Someday Lani would learn to just walk away from certain situations, but today was not that day. She was up early on a Saturday morning, already leaving one appointment and headed to the next. Her rebellious nature wouldn't allow her to simply wave her hand at the offer, although she did get a nice laugh out of it, she still had to see this for herself.

Driving with her windows down, her freshly blown out hair blew about as she used her Chanel shades to shield her face from her shiny black hair. She smiled thinking about what she was getting herself into, but it was the weekend and she had nothing else to do. Besides, there was no way she was going to miss out on this opportunity. This had to be some sort of joke, but she had a sense of humor and loved to laugh so why not. Life was all about getting out there, throwing caution to the wind, being brave, and having fun. One thing was for sure, she would be having a drink as soon as she stepped into the restaurant although it was only twelve in the afternoon. Usually on a Saturday she would still be in bed, but today she had a lunch date, or dates would be more fitting.

"Thank you," Lani said to the valet, as she stepped out of her car wearing a red pencil skirt, and white chiffon blouse. She decided against wearing heels just in case things went south.

"Welcome to Delamore's Seafood Room," the hostess greeted Lani.

"Thank you, I'm here to meet Dr. Andrews," Lani said.

"Oh yes, right this way," the hostess said, and proceeded in the direction of their table.

Jackson came to a stance as soon as he spotted Lani. He smiled from ear to ear, but Lani couldn't believe this was really happening.

"You look beautiful," he said as he hugged Lani, but she didn't hug him back.

"Thank you," she said hesitantly.

"Well, let me properly introduce you two," he said, "Lani this is my wife Maya, and Maya this is Lani," Jackson continued as his wife stood up and shook Lani's hand. She had a forced smile on her face, and Lani couldn't help but smirk.

This is going to be good, she thought to herself.

They all took a seat and Lani ordered a glass of Moscato to join in on the drinking since Jackson and Maya started without her. She kept her eyes on Maya trying to read her, but she couldn't. She was far from the angry woman she had encountered at Jacksons house. This time she sat calmly sipping her wine with a look of contentment on her youthful face. Jackson, on the other hand, was a nervous wreck. He was already on his second glass of wine, and kept clearing his throat. After the waitress left, there was nothing but silence between the three of them, and Lani was not going to be the one to break it. She was there to listen and that's what she going to do.

"So, how have you been?" Jackson asked.

"Surviving," Lani answered.

He cleared his throat again. "Well, you look great," he said.

"Thank you, again," Lani said.

Jackson took a sip of his wine. "How is work coming along?" he asked.

"I don't mean to be rude, but cut the bullshit Jackson and get to the point," Lani barked.

He cleared his throat once again, and this time Maya spoke up, "I guess I could start things off," she said, and Lani looked in her direction. "I absolutely love and adore my husband, and I took my vows very seriously when I recited them in front our closest family and friends. I would do anything for him, and first I would just like to apologize for the way I came off at you that day. I acted on emotions and I was out of line," Maya said and Lani just stared at her.

She had to be kidding. If the shoe were on the other foot Lani would have done far worse than Maya had. Jackson was a worthy catch, and she had every reason to be heated about him having an affair with another woman.

"I understand," was all Lani could come back with.

"We have been talking about this pretty much every day for the past few weeks. At first I was upset to find out that my husband was in love with someone else, but now I can accept that and you," she said.

Lani would be lying if she said her pussy didn't twitch with that last sentence. She automatically thought about Jackson between her legs again, putting it down and dining at the Y like there was no tomorrow, but those thoughts were quickly dismissed once she picked her mind up out of the gutter.

"I don't think I'm following you," Lani said, as she leaned forward in her chair.

"I'm saying that my husband loves you. He has expressed that to me more than once, and I love my husband and want him to be happy, so if that includes you then I can accept that. All I wish is to be included in my husband's life. He has always shared everything with me except this," she said moving her hand back and forth between Lani and Jackson. She tucked her relaxed, shoulder length hair behind her ears, and continued talking. "I have nothing against you. I now know that you had no clue about me, so I do apologize about that. If you are willing to share Jackson with me, then the offer is on the table."

Lani laughed, "So let me get this straight. You're going to allow your husband to have a girlfriend basically, and continue to live a double life as if you don't even exist," Lani asked.

"No, I will and I do exist. I would like for the three of us to get to know each other a little better, and continue from there," Maya said.

"What?" Lani said confused.

"You will still reap all the benefits you have been reaping for the past two years, and let's be honest I know he made you very happy. I know about the house, and the car, and the credit cards. Now tell me you want to give all of that up when you can still have it all, and the man."

Lani sat blinking, and thinking. She was better than this. She could have any man she wanted, and didn't have to share a man for the sake of bragging rights or expensive things, but on the other hand she missed Jackson like hell and wanted him back badly.

"So, what roll would you play when he's with me?" Lani asked.

"Well, I would like to come along sometimes, and sometimes you guys could have your own time together. I think I could do that, as long as you aren't rude or condescending and we all can get along."

"Can I get another, please?" Lani asked the waiter as she held her glass up in the air. "What would we all do together?" Lani asked.

"Whatever you ladies want," Jackson chimed in, and Lani shot him a look because she knew what he was thinking.

"I don't know what ever comes about," Maya said. "I just want to be included since we plan on including you into our union."

Lani looked back and forth between the two of them not knowing what else to say. She watched as Jackson stood from his chair and got down on one knee. Lani's eyes automatically went straight over to Maya, and she smiled an approving smile with her chin resting comfortably on her clasped fingers. This cannot be happening.

"Lani, I know this is not the way you envisioned things between you and I, and I know that we cannot legally marry, but I can and will commit to you. I love you, and I don't want another day to go by that I do not see you, or hear from you. I promise to love you as I always have. Please take this ring Lani. Join me and my wife, and we can continue on with our lives together."

Lani looked around the restaurant and no one seemed to be paying them any attention. She looked at his wife who seemed to be waiting for an answer.

"Ok, this has gone on long enough," Lani said. "Jackson you can get up off of the floor now. Are you two done having fun, and exactly why are you trying to hurt me?" Lani said, looking at Jackson. "I did nothing to you. Why are you playing these games with me?" Lani asked, and they both remained quiet.

"Lani baby," he paused. "We're serious."

No way. Folks didn't do things like this, well not the

folks that she knew. "So basically this would be like a plural marriage kind of thing?" Lani asked.

Jackson pulled his chair closer to Lani, and took her hand in his, "Yes, but if you're not comfortable putting a label on things, then don't."

"Things will go smoothly I'm sure. I love him and so do you. The only thing is we both know about each other, and choose to be happy living our lives openly," Maya said. "You guys have been together almost as long as we have been married, and I am willing to give this arrangement a try because I know how much it means to my husband," Maya said.

"Just give it a try." Jackson said as he slid the three in a half carat ring on Lani's finger. "I'll be right back," Jackson said, and hurried towards the sign that read "Restrooms."

Lani sat across from Maya again trying to read her face and posture, but got nothing in return. "Now that he is gone, you can tell me the truth," Lani said with a little bit of an attitude. "Do you want to do this? Is this some sort of game he wants to play to get back at me for leaving him alone or is this your little strategy to get back at me for being with your husband?"

"This is my way of keeping my family together, and to continue to live the life I have become accustomed to," Maya said. She leaned forward in her chair and looked Lani dead in the eyes as her entire demeanor changed. "Please make no mistake Ms. Lani, I run this shit. The only reason I haven't left Jackson and collected my alimony and child support is because I know better than that. I presume I would collect alimony for about five years tops then I'll have to live off of child support or go back to work, and let's be honest there isn't much room in the modeling world for an ex model over the age of twenty-five, no matter how good she looks."

Lani let out a loud laugh as she tried to regain her composure. Maya had to be kidding. No one was better than Lani at playing the bitch roll. "Oh sweetheart, you can save your attempts of trying to intimidate me because that will get you absolutely nowhere."

"I am trying to play nice with you," Maya said and Lani could tell she was forcing herself to speak those words. "I asked Jackson to be honest with me, and to tell me how he really feels about you and the affair the two of you had, and he said to me, 'I love her Maya, but I love you and my kids as well. I don't want to lose either of you.' What's a girl to do?" she said.

"I don't know, but there is no way this is going to work," Lani said.

"Look, I don't want his money. I want him," Maya said. "As do you, I can tell by the way you look at him. You may say something sarcastic but your eyes say something different. You've had the dick so there's no need for me to elaborate," Maya said.

She damn sure did have the dick, and it was damn good, but was it so good that she was willing to play along with their little game?

"What if I get pregnant?" Lani blurted out.

Maya took a deep breath, "Than we'll have to deal with it. Are you using any contraceptives?"

"Nope" Lani said, and folded her arms. Of course she was on birth control.

"Ok, we can cross that bridge if we ever come to it," she said.

Lani could tell that thought never crossed her mind. Her feathers were ruffled, and she had something else to think about.

"Look, either way I'm jumping head first into this. It's what my husband wants and what he shall receive. That is if you are willing to step outside of the box," Maya said.

"I have no need to. I have plenty of other options besides Jackson."

"I'm sure you do you're a beautiful woman," Maya said, "but I know there is only one man you really want," she added.

She sat confidently sipping her wine with a smirk on her face. The small beauty mark on her cheek disappeared into her dimple whenever she smiled. Lani could tell by her arms that she was fit, and in really good shape. Jackson obviously had a preference when it came to women and it seemed to be light skinned sistas, although Maya was a little lighter than Lani.

"Getting to know each other a little better?" Jackson asked upon his return.

"I have to go," Lani said.

Her head was up in the clouds, and she couldn't make out

one clear thought. She stood up and grabbed her purse.

"You're leaving?" Jackson asked. He stood up as well, and Maya followed. "I booked us a room upstairs, so we could, you know, celebrate," he said. Lani forgot there was a luxury hotel attached to the restaurant. She has never been there, but heard it was nice.

"Celebrate what?" Lani asked.

"Us, no drama, no problems, and unity," Maya said.

Lani eyed Maya's confused ass. She was this mellow woman in front of Jackson, but a wannabe bull dog behind his back. Lani knew she was trying to please Jackson and didn't want to ruin anything, but at the same time she wanted Lani to know that she was not on her level. Lani's devious side wanted to play hardball with Maya just to show her how it was really done.

"Come on just for a little while," Jackson smiled, and Lani's attitude dwindled.

"I really need to go," Lani said trying to convince herself, but curiosity crept up on her. She wanted to know what would happen when they were upstairs. Exactly what were they going to do?

Jackson grabbed his wife's hand then went over to whisper in Lani's ear. "I haven't had a taste of that sweet ass pussy in almost two months. Are you going to deprive me of what is mine?" Jackson said, and Lani's pussy was officially awake.

"Come on," he said, nodding his head towards a set of glass double doors in the corner, and grabbing Lani's hand.

They walked down a long hallway hand in hand. Jackson had his wife on one side and Lani on the other. Everyone that walked by them did a double take, and one man gave Jackson two thumbs up. Lani thoughts were all the way in the gutter. She didn't care about what anyone thought at that moment. For all she cared, when they got to the room his wife could sit in the corner while Jackson dicked her down and licked the pink out of her pussy.

They stepped inside of the empty elevator, and both Lani and Maya leaned against the rails while Jackson pressed the button for the 11th floor. He came back and slid in between the two ladies.

"Thank you," he said to his wife, and gave her a deep kiss.

Lani watched as Jackson kissed his wife, and felt a little out of place, but there was no turning back now. Her goody box was speaking to her, and she had the answer to silence it standing right next to her.

"Thank you too baby," Jackson said, and went in for a kiss. Lani hesitated, but not for long. The moment Jackson's tongue entered her mouth, he awoke all those intimate feelings she had suppressed. For her it was easy to remove her emotions from sex, but not with Jackson. She didn't want to feel this way anymore. She wanted to move on, and forget about him but instead she had just taken one giant leap backwards.

That's ok, she thought, she'll use him for what he's worth, and move on when she was ready.

They exited the elevator and Jackson lead the way down the hall to room 1107. Lani watched as Maya walked behind her husband, and made a mental note to hit the gym a little harder from now on. Maya's body was tight. She wore a fitted sleeveless purple dress. Her body casted the perfect silhouette on the wall as they stood in front of the door waiting for Jackson to open it. Lani took in Maya's toned calves and bubble butt. She had to give it to her she looked great after having two kids.

"After you ladies," Jackson said, standing aside while holding the door open. Lani walked into the room and her jaw dropped. The room was all white with rose pedals everywhere, and two bottles of champagne on chill. She noticed the two small gift boxes that sat on the bed the same time as Maya. They both smiled and went over to grab a box. Lani's face lit up, and her eyes sparkled at the princess cut black diamond stud earrings she held in her hand. Maya's face greatly resembled Lani's, and they both let out a squeal, and high fived each other.

"Thank you Doctor," Lani said, and Jackson looked up from the hot tub he was filling and grinned as they shared a little inside joke.

"You want to go see the rest of the room?" Maya asked Lani.

"Sure," Lani said.

She sat her purse on the white love seat a few feet away from the bed. She still couldn't fathom where she was and whom she was with. The two of them walked through a set of white double doors and entered a room that resembled her living room except a little more expensive, and colorless. The suite was amazing, and Lani would keep in mind how beautiful it was just in case she needed to get away for a little while on her own. Maya went over to the large wall-to-wall windows, and pulled the string to allow the drapes to open. The afternoon sun lit the snow white suite up, and reflected off of the shiny silver chandelier.

"This suite is amazing," Maya said.

"Yes it is. Is this your first time here?" Lani asked.

"Yes, a friend of mind used to work here so I figured we could check it out."

"Cool," Lani said, then decided to pick her brain a little more. "So, what do you think Jackson has planned for us or do you know what Jackson has planned for us?"

"I'm assuming he wants the two women he loves together," Maya said. She sat on the edge of the sofa and crossed her legs.

"Well he had that downstairs at the restaurant," Lani said, still probing. She wanted to hear her say the word "fuck" just for the hell of it, but Maya just sat there smiling. She could tell that she was a very conservative woman, and very well put together. Lani imagined she didn't like to be put on the spot, and felt uncomfortable. She was sure Maya had to dig deep for the confidence she wore earlier, but now that they were in the hotel room she was a bit nervous.

"Be honest with me Maya. I can call you that right?" Lani asked.

"Of course," she said.

"Are you sure you want to see Jackson fucking me, sucking me, kissing me, and me doing the same to him? I mean can you honestly handle that?"

"Can you handle him doing the same to me?" Maya replied.

"I'm not sure, but I guess we'll see," Lani said. She was really enjoying the moment. She would have never thought she would be doing such a thing, but here she was ready to get busy with a man in front of his wife then watch him do the same to her.

"I'm here for my husband," Maya said.

"So let me get this straight, basically you need me to keep your husband happy and content so that he doesn't run out on you again," Lani said. This time she wore the smirk with her arms crossed.

"Please don't think for one second that I cannot keep my husband happy, and no I do not need you but apparently he does. Had I known he was even thinking about anyone else I would have been all over it, and you wouldn't exist in our lives. At one point, I was a very busy woman and that is where you crept in," Maya said.

"Is that right," Lani replied.

"I just want everything out in the open, and to rid myself of that awful feeling of uncertainty. This is not what I want, but being the good wife that I am I'm willing to accept it and remain respectful towards you as long as you show me the same in return. Deal," Maya held her hand out for Lani and they shook on their arrangement.

"You need a drink?" Lani asked Maya.

"I guess I could go for another," she replied and they walked back into the room with Jackson.

"I see you didn't kill each other in there," Jackson said.

He was over by the bar pouring three glasses of champagne. When he finished, he pulled his shirt over his head, and slipped out of his shoes. Lani stared him down, and inadvertently licked her lips. She's been bouncing all over Big Brown for the last month in a half, but Big Brown couldn't put it down like the real deal, and she was long overdue.

Lani looked to her left and Maya was pulling her shirt over her head as well. Soon after, Lani was staring at her clearly visible abs. This woman was bad, and must work out and eat healthy every day to maintain such a physique.

"Wow," Lani said, trying to compose herself. "I have to give it to you girl, you look great," Lani said, and Maya smiled.

"Thank you. Do you work out?" Maya asked.

"Yes, but obviously not enough," Lani laughed.

"Don't be ridiculous, maybe we can work out together some time."

"Sure," Lani said. She watched as Jackson walked over to his wife and kissed her before slowly stepping into the hot tub.

"Babe, bring the bottle over with you," Jackson said, and both women reached for the bottle of champagne.

"Ok, first awkward moment," Lani said, and Maya let go of the bottle.

"Sorry I guess I have to come up with new nicknames," Jackson said.

Both ladies grabbed a glass, and headed over to join Jackson. Lani sat her glass down, and stripped off of her clothes as Maya unfastened her bra exposing her firm, round breasts. They were average size, maybe a B cup but very cute and shapely. Jackson stood up and helped his wife into the hot tub, then waited patiently for Lani to expose the goods, and expose the goods she did. She revealed her newly pierced nipples, and newly pierced kitty. Jackson leaned forward and seductively flicked her nipple with his tongue.

"I love your crazy behind, you know that?" Jackson said as he helped Lani step into the warm bubbly water. He casually floated over to the opposite side of the hot tub, leaving Lani and Maya side by side. "Damn, I'm a lucky man." Jackson said. He sipped his champagne, and smiled. "I promise to love you two like you've never been loved before. Thank you for choosing me," he said.

Lani glanced over at Maya who was smiling lovingly at her husband, but Lani had already downed her glass of champagne and was ready to get busy. Enough with the small talk, her pierced nipples stood pointed at Jackson like aimed missiles, and her pussy was throbbing just thinking about what he was about to do to her. He must have read Lani's mind because he put his glass down and came closer to the two of them. He pushed them both closer together until their arms touched, then guided his hands between both of their legs and simultaneously played with both of his pussies. Lani moaned out loud from his touch, as Jackson dove deeper while kissing and sucking erotically on Maya's neck. He made his way over to Lani, and skillfully maneuvered his tongue in and around her earlobe. Lani turned her head, and slipped her tongue in his mouth. She wanted to feel him inside of her so bad at that moment. Jackson pulled his hand out of the water and placed it behind Lani's head, while still fingering Maya. Lani reached for the dick which was already hard and ready for pouncing. She slid her hand up and down his shaft until she felt him throb with every stroke. In mid stroke, she felt Maya's hand reaching for his goods as well, but she continued to move down to his balls. Jackson was in freak-nasty ecstasy. Maya placed her hand on top of Lani's, and the stroking became a group effort. They both decided to take to his neck, licking and sucking until Jackson pulled away.

"I see how you two are playing this," Jackson said.

He stood up and grabbed one of the neatly rolled towels from the side of the hot tub, and quickly dried himself off then walked over to the floor length windows with his Johnson swinging. He opened the large drapes just as Maya had done in the other room. The sun lit up the room, and the harbor's water was all Lani could see from the hot tub. Jackson unlocked the sliding glass doors to allow the warm breeze to enter the room, while Lani and Maya dried themselves off.

Jackson positioned himself on his back in the middle of the king size bed, and Lani was more than ready to give him what he wanted.

"Mmm," Lani said. "You want to start at the top or the bottom?" She asked Maya.

"I'll take the top," Maya said.

They both climbed onto the bed and Lani wasted no time going down on Jackson, and planting kisses all over his stomach and thighs. Maya straddled Jackson's face backwards and watched Lani go to work. Jackson moaned from under Maya, and he tucked his hips trying to get away from Lani relentless suction. Lani giggled, knowing he was trying not to end things before it even started.

"Your husband's juices taste so sweet," Lani said, looking up at Maya and licking her lips. "Now I just want to feel him inside of me," Lani said, before taking one long hard suck from the tip of Jackson's dick. He let out a loud grunt. "Can I ride your husband's dick until my pussy explodes?" Lani spoke the raunchy words in an innocent-like voice while batting her eyelashes.

"Mmm, please do," Maya said. She never missed a beat from riding Jackson's face. "It's your dick as well," she opened her eyes and smiled at Lani.

Lani rubbed Jackson's head on her erect clit, then slid down on it without warning. The sensation caused her and Jackson to shiver as she played with her piercing. Lani and Maya's rhythm were in unison as they both rocked back and forth, one on his face and one riding his swollen manhood. All three were in an erogenous zone with the wind blowing, and the sound of the nearby harbor traffic wayfaring throughout the room. Maya reached out to caress Lani's smooth breast, and Lani welcomed the gesture. She didn't really expect for the two of them to play around, but hey, if that would heighten her orgasm she was all for it.

They made eye contact, and shared a warm French kiss. Maya moaned with her tongue in Lani's mouth as they both kept their pace, and Lani sucked the last remnants of champagne from Maya's tongue before she pulled back as Jackson began to slap her ass. She threw her head back with her eyes closed, and Lani picked up her pace. She begin to bounce on Jackson's throbbing dick as Maya's cry grew into a loud "YES," and Lani's eyes rolled back into her head. They both reached their climax at the same damn time.

Lani fell over on one side of the bed and Maya on the other, as Jackson came to his knees ready to release his own frenzy. Maya wrapped her lips around Jackson's dick before Lani even realized they were still going, so she joined in and ran her tongue over Jackson's prized jewels then sucked them both into her mouth. Within seconds, Jackson's cream was spilling out into Maya's mouth.

"This is why I love you both," Jackson said out of breath. "I swear I do."

"You better," Maya said as she wiped her face with a towel.

The three of them lay on the bed sharing small talk, and jokes about what just went down. Lani's body was weak, but thoroughly fulfilled. She didn't know where things would go from here, but at least she busted one hell of a nut that should hold her over for a few days.

"Let me get up, and get myself together," Lani said while lying on her back.

"Why, where do you have to go?" Jackson asked, and Maya lifted her head from his chest.

"I'm supposed to take my car to the dealership to have the tire pressure sensor replaced. I can't believe something has malfunctioned on it already."

"Do you need me to take care of it?" Jackson asked, and Lani glanced at Maya again, but she still seemed to be unfazed by the whole situation which Lani knew was a front.

"No, they are replacing it for free. I think I have a fan over there," Lani winked.

"Is that right?" Jackson had a serious look on his face.

"Well you may need to take it somewhere else since you've just committed yourself to us," Maya said. "We'll take care of the fees. You can't stray away already," Maya smiled.

Lani started to make up a price and take their money, but she really didn't need it. "I'll be good," Lani said as she sat up in the bed ready to leave, but Jackson stopped her.

"Who said I was done with you?" Jackson said. He playfully pulled her to the edge of the bed, and got down on his knees. "You haven't shown me how this thing works yet?" He said referring to her piercing. He spread her outer lips and used his tongue to fiddle with the small barbell.

Lani rested her head on the bed, and closed her eyes, as Maya cheered her husband on. Her life was like a scene straight out of one of her many porn flicks. It was safe to say she would miss her appointment today, but tomorrow was a new day. Right now all she wanted was to lie there and receive the joy that comes along with Dr. Jackson Andrews.

Chapter Twelve

"Just take the pain away."

Ira scurried around the restaurant tiding up and giving her employees a little pep talk before the doors opened. Sunday afternoons were always busy days for her crew, and she looked forward to business running smoothly until it slowed down during the evening. She stood in the front of the restaurant looking out at the parking lot. There were a few customers waiting for the doors to open as she watched the remaining minutes to tick away, and the clock to strike eleven thirty.

"Are you ready to start your day, Mrs. Meadows?" Jonathan asked, as he stood next to her.

"I sure am, how about you?" Ira asked.

"As ready as I'll ever be," he smiled.

"Did you find someone to cover the second shift?"

"Yes I did. Royce will be in at three," Jonathan said.

Ira stood next to him a bit speechless. He was always two steps ahead of her and made things a whole lot easier for Ira. She would have to do something nice for him soon. He was such a good person and asked for nothing in return. He smiled as Ira stood absorbing his deep set eyes, dark skin, and bold head. The lightest thing on his body had to be his full appetizing lips that drove all the single ladies, and some married women crazy as well. It has been brought to Ira's attention many times over the years that Jonathan was a hot commodity amongst the customers and employees, but he always respectfully declined their advances.

"What," Jonathan asked. "Did I miss something?"

"Not at all," Ira said, and smiled before walking over and unlocking the doors. "We are officially open for business on this beautiful Sunday morning,"

She smoothed over the young hostess's uniform, and tightened her black, standard-issued tie. The customers that didn't frequent her restaurant were always surprised to meet the owner, but Ira was very hands on, even with a staff full of business savvy managers, supervisors, and a few employees.

Most of them were students, and she would love to see them go from employees to employers.

"Mrs. Meadows, I really need to speak with you when you get a chance," Jonathan said.

"Well everything seems to be in order here. We can go to the office now if you'd like."

"You lead the way," Jonathan smiled.

Ira proceeded towards the office, and waved her hand at the shift supervisor then towards the office. She knew that was a signal to watch over things instead of her yelling across the room.

"So what's on your mind, Jonathan?" Ira asked as she took a seat behind her desk. "Is it the inventory sheets? I think I finally found a more accessible routine, something that would be a lot less—"

"Dreadful?" Jonathan said.

"Yes, dreadful," Ira laughed.

"Well that's good to hear, but that is not why I wanted to speak to you," he cleared his throat, "I have been working on a project, a dream of mine and, um, as much as I'm going to miss you all I have to get out there and go after my dream. I'm not getting any younger," he said, and Ira just sat there with a lump in her throat. "I can stay as long as you need me," Jonathan continued when Ira didn't speak up. "There's no need to worry. I've been training Lara for my position without her knowing it," he laughed.

"Ok," Ira said. She took a deep breath. This news was unexpected, and she actually felt as if she was being dumped. "By all means, you should follow your dreams. Please forgive me for my silence it's just that you surprised me a bit," Ira said, and tried to muster up a laugh.

"I'm sorry, if I could manage both I would."

"No no, you go out there and excel, and if there is anything you need, do not hesitate to ask," Ira said.

"Likewise," Jonathan said.

They sat across from each other with locked eyes. Ira was truly sad to see him go. Although she knew she had a few more weeks with him. The place wouldn't be the same without him.

"So, when exactly are you leaving me?" Ira laughed.

"You tell me. I already have my father and brother working on the place so I'm all yours," Jonathan said. His statement had a sentimental undertone to it, and Ira caught it.

"May I ask, or pry I should say," Ira smiled, "What are you venturing off to do?"

"I'm opening a restaurant that sells Nigerian cuisines. I would love it if you could stop by when I'm up and running."

"I will be there with bells on," Ira said.

"It's a small spot. I can only add about eight to ten tables so I guess it will be more of a carryout," Jonathan said.

"A carryout that will grow into a restaurant," Ira said.

"I hope so."

Ira stood, "I'm sad to see you go, but very proud of you Jonathan."

Ira came around the desk as Jonathan stood and hugged him tight. She felt the tears rolling in, and pulled away. Gosh, he smelled delectable. Did he always smell this good? She thought.

"I owe everything to you," Jonathan said. "I've learned a lot from you over the years."

Ira smiled, "Come on let's make sure the place is still in one piece."

They entered the dining area just in time for the hostess to point a young woman in Ira's direction. She was holding a little girl by the hand, and walked hastily toward Ira with a worried look on her face. Ira surveyed the woman from head to toe, but did not recognize her as someone she had ever come in contact with.

"Hello, how may I help you?" Ira asked.

The girl stood face to face with Ira, soundless. Her compassionate eyes peered through Ira, and gave her chills. She watched the woman blink away tears before speaking.

"Are you Ira Meadows?" the woman asked.

"Yes," Ira replied.

"The wife of Nicholas Meadows?" she asked.

"Yes," Ira replied confused.

"Well, this is his daughter, and I can't take care of her anymore," she said while pushing the little girl towards Ira. "Her mother was my sister and she's dead. My mother has been raising her, and she is being transported to a nursing home as we speak and I cannot do this," she cried, "I shouldn't have to. I'm only twenty years old, and this is not my responsibility," she pronounced hurriedly.

"Now wait a minute," Ira raised her voiced, "This is not my late husband's child. I'm sorry about what you are going through, but you have the wrong person. I promise you."

The woman dug through the child's book bag that hung from her small shoulders, and pulled out a piece of paper. She unfolded the paper and handed it to Ira.

Her heart stopped as she read the contents of the Maryland state issued birth certificate. Her husband's name, date of birth, and age was listed under the father's information. This time it was Ira who tried to blink away the falling tears. She recalled the incredulous phone call she received from her lawyer's office just days before, and slowly everything began to click.

"This can't be," Ira mumbled.

"I'm sorry, but I have to go," the woman said. She turned around and tried to leave but Ira stopped her.

"You will not leave this child with me. She is not my responsibility regardless of what Nick did," Ira shouted in the woman's face. "Get this child out of my restaurant right now or I'm calling CPS."

The woman's tears begin to fall once more, but she didn't back down, "She deserves a home just like your children. She deserves to eat well every night just like your children, and clothes that fit her just like your children. Your husband took care of her. I'm sure this is what he would have wanted for his child."

"I don't give a damn," Ira said through her tears. They were so close to each other that Ira could see the tiny beads of sweat on the bridge of the woman's nose, and so close that Jonathan felt uncomfortable enough to step in, and pull Ira away.

"Let's all calm down, and you two can go in the back and talk away from the crowd," Jonathan said, and Ira looked around to see some of her employees, and a few customers glaring in their direction.

"Get her out of here," Ira said to the woman.

She shook her head at Ira's demand, "I can't," she said. "My ride is outside," the woman said before jogging towards the door and jumping into an awaiting vehicle.

Ira chased behind her with no luck. She stood in front of her restaurant dumbfounded. Not Nick. There was no way he would do this to her. He was her husband, her wonderful, supportive husband that worshipped his wife and children. Everything he did, he did it for the four of them. Their boys were his world, and they often talked about having a daughter. Ira knew how badly Nick wanted to add a baby girl to their growing family, so there was no way he would do such a thing with another woman. Ira was appalled, and couldn't grasp what was happening to her.

She felt Jonathan's arms wrap around her, and she turned around to bury her face in his chest. Her tears quickly invaded the cotton fabric of his shirt as she sobbed uncontrollably.

"Come on, let's take a walk," Jonathan said.

He walked with Ira around the side of the restaurant and down to the end of the dock to shield her from the poignant onlookers. Ira sat next to Jonathan with her head resting on his shoulder. Her thoughts were foggy, and her heart had cracked, crumbled, and all but dissipated. She now had a new wound that would take years to heal thanks to Nick. This couldn't be her reality.

"I think you should go home and get some rest. I'll take care of the restaurant," Jonathan said.

Ira didn't speak, she didn't move, she just sat there staring out at the water. Her thoughts were so scattered she couldn't even form a sentence.

"You know it may not seem like it right now, but this could be a blessing in disguise," Jonathan said.

Ira huffed.

"You're a spiritual woman, and you know the Lord works in mysterious ways," Jonathan said.

"My faith is what I'm going to lean on right now, but I haven't exactly been the best child or the most deserving," Ira said.

"He knows your heart."

"What am I going to do with that little girl?" Ira asked.

"What does your heart tell you to do?"

"Run," Ira said, and Jonathan chuckled.

"Do you want to go back in or would you like for me to bring your things out for an easy getaway?"

"I guess I have to face the music," Ira said. "Everyone knows my deceased husband had an affair and produced a child with someone else." Her heart palpitated when she confessed out loud.

"Well, there are outlets that you can look into to determine whether that is in fact true," Jonathan said.

"Maybe I can look in to that," Ira nodded her head. "How could he do this to me?"

"I don't know, and I couldn't imagine why he would want to. There are men out here that would cherish every moment they had with you. Trust me I know," Jonathan said. He stood up, and grabbed Ira's hand as they headed towards the restaurant. "Put your game face on," Jonathan said before opening the door.

Ira walked in behind Jonathan prepared for the stares and glares of all the eye witnesses, but everyone was too busy working and eating. Her eyes came to rest on the little girl the woman left behind. She sat holding a doll baby, and brushing its knotted hair with her hand. It was then that Ira noticed the two grocery store bags the woman must have left behind as well. The bags were packed with clothes and a pair of shoes. She looked up from her doll and her eyes evoked an array of tears that Ira thought she had shed outside. Silent tears fell as she looked into what seemed to be a familiar set of eyes. The little girl possessed the same dark eyes, and thick eyelashes as her late husband and her oldest son.

"I can't do this," Ira whispered.

"Yes you can, my Queen," Jonathan said. "You need to find out as much information as you can about her, and go from there. Look at her, she's a child, and she needs someone."

"That's what Child Protective Services is for," Ira said to Jonathan, but her eyes never left the thick-haired little girl.

"It's your call," Jonathan said.

Ira walked over to the bench across from the child, and stared at her from a distance. She couldn't make out the jumbled mix of emotions that barreled through her body. A part of her wanted to call the police and have them deal with it, but another part of her didn't want to live with the guilt of placing a child in the system to bounce around for the rest of her childhood or possibly land in a home with a heinous couple. Maybe she could find a family member that would be willing to take her in. Her boys crossed her mind. How would she explain this to them? How would she explain this to her family and friends? She instantly became embarrassed. As much as she boasted about her wonderful husband, all the while he was not happy with her, and they were living a lie.

"Jonathan can you grab my purse for me please?" Ira asked in a somber tone.

Jonathan hurried towards the office and returned while Ira gathered the girl's belongings. She was afraid to be alone with the child, afraid of what she would reveal, and afraid to move forward. She had to remind herself that she was just a child, and didn't asked to be in this situation, and most certainly didn't create it, but that didn't stop Ira from wishing this was all just a dream and she would wake up and her faith in her husband would have been restored.

"You're coming with me, ok?" Ira said to the little girl. She tried not to sound so bothered, but the events that were transpiring were still sinking in, and her nerves were rattled.

The little girl nodded her head yes and followed Ira out of the restaurant. She climbed into the truck and buckled herself in. As she drove down the road she looked at the quiet little girl in the rear view mirror. She resembled Nick so much, and as much as Ira wanted to hold out hope that there was a chance she was not Nick's child, she knew the chances were slim. Between her looks, the information the woman had, and the child's birth certificate, Ira would be a fool to remain in denial. She would call her lawyer first thing in the morning since he didn't call her back on Friday. There was a lot she needed to take care of, but the first thing she needed to do was clear her head.

Ira pulled in front of Courtni's house and parked her car.

There was no way she could take the child to her house, and she knew Courtni was great with children.

"Grab your things," Ira said to the little girl, and they walked up the long stair case to Courtni's door. Ira knocked twice and Courtni came to the door dressed in her Sunday's best.

"Hey Ira," Courtni said. She looked down at the child and her eyebrows moved towards each other as a confused look covered her face.

"Ms. Jeffries," the little girl screamed and hugged Courtni's legs.

"Nicah, what are you doing here?" Courtni asked.

"You know her?" Ira asked just as confused as Courtni.

"Yes, she's one of my clients," Courtni replied.

"I came to live with my new mommy," Nicah said.

Ira wanted to tell her she was not her mother, and never would be, but reframed from doing so.

"What?" Courtni asked, and looked at Ira for an answer.

"Her aunt dropped her off today at my restaurant. She said Nick is her father and she can no longer take care of her," Ira said. The tears were well on their way.

"Nicah, why don't you go play with Colby," Courtni said, and Nicah ran pass Courtni into the house. She dropped her book bag in the center of the floor and picked up the dogs chew toy.

"Now, what happened?" Courtni asked.

"I just need you to keep her overnight. I need some time to get myself together, and talk to my lawyer, and the kids, and—

"It all makes sense now," Courtni cut Ira off. "Her grandmother. Where is she?"

"In a nursing home, according to her aunt."

"Wow, this is unbelievable."

"Can you keep her?" Ira asked.

"Yes, but there is no way I'm missing service today. Lord knows that's the last thing I need to do, so I guess she's coming with me."

"Thank you, I'll call you later," Ira said and headed for her vehicle although she wanted to sprint and never look back.

"Ira wait," Courtni said, hot on Ira's heels "Are you alright? How do you feel?" she asked.

"Just pray for me," Ira said and shut the door.

She knew Courtni meant well, but she was not up for a psychiatric evaluation. All she wanted to do was crawl under a rock and pray no one tried to find her. Anger was slowly creeping up on her. How could the man she has dedicated so much of her time and love to do such a thing? She has always held him down even in death.

How many lies did he tell her? Why was he with her if he wanted someone else? How could he look her in the face knowing he had this big secret? Was she ever supposed to find out? A million questions raced through her mind, and she wanted answers. Her heart ached knowing that these were scars she was going to have to live with because dead men don't talk.

"Lord, I don't know what to do," she spoke out loud through her tears. "I can't do this anymore. How much more will I have to endure? I know I've done wrong, but I've done so much right," she cried, "I'm not as strong as everyone believes, and I just can't do this. I can't."

She sat in her truck for a minute to gather her thoughts before heading in the house. Once inside she filled Naomi in on the news, and poured herself a glass of wine. She watched her boys play in the back yard from the kitchen window. Their little lives were about to be interrupted, but as their mother it was her job to soften the blow.

"They will be just fine," Naomi said from the bar stool. "Children are a lot more accepting than us adults."

"You think so?" Ira asked.

"Oh yes, I'm sure they will have plenty of questions, but in the end they will adjust nicely."

"I just need a break away from all of this mess," Ira said.

"Well, lady luck is on your side, just a little bit," Naomi said as she stood up. "If you don't mind the boys and I are going to my parents for dinner. You are more than welcome to come with us."

"No thank you, but I would appreciate a nice warm bath and the rest of this bottle of wine," Ira laughed.

"Well enjoy," Naomi said. She gathered the boys and left Ira alone with her depressing thoughts.

She ran a warm bath and soaked until the water was cold, and her teeth began to chatter. Her gospel music was soothing to her soul, and gave her just the amount of warmth she needed to maneuver her way around the cool bathroom gathering her moisturizers. She paused when she thought she heard the sound of her door bell, and a second ring confirmed the notion. Wrapping herself in a silk bath robe, she rushed to the door wondering who it could be. While she was in the tub she received a text from Naomi saying she would have the boys back by eight, and it was only three in the afternoon so she knew it was not them, besides Naomi had a key.

She looked through the glass side panels along the door, and was surprised to see Jonathan on the other side. After tightening the belt around her waist she opened the door.

"Hey Jonathan is everything ok at the restaurant?"

"Yes, I just came to check on you before heading home," he said.

"I'm living," Ira said. She stepped aside and invited him in. "Would you like something to drink?"

"Water would be good," Jonathan replied.

He followed Ira into the kitchen and took a seat at the table. "I see you have already started your evening," he said referring to the bottle of wine sitting on the counter.

"Yeah well, the plan was to finish it off, but I'm a mother so that will have to wait," Ira said.

"Is that the reason or is it because you are not a drinker," Jonathan laughed.

"You think you know me, huh?" Ira joined in. She took a seat at the table with him.

"Where are the boys anyway?" Jonathan asked after taking a sip of his bottled water.

"They are out having dinner with the nanny and her family."

"And the girl?"

"She's with my friend. Is everything really ok at the restaurant?" Ira asked changing the subject.

"Yes it is," Jonathan chuckled. "Do you ever stop thinking about the restaurant, and just tend to your home life?" he asked trying to tame his thick accent.

"Have you forgotten what's going on with my home life?" Ira asked. "My husband has left me with yet another problem to mend, another load to carry," she paused, "Well, I'm all tuckered out Jonathan. I don't have anything left to give, so someone else will have to mend this situation," Ira said. She dropped her head, and fiddled with a tiny piece of paper in the center of the table.

"Are you sure about that?" Jonathan asked, but Ira didn't answer. "You know, although I have the authority to terminate someone at work I always come to you first, do you know why?"

Ira looked up from the table, awaiting Jonathans answer.

"I do it because you see things differently from the average person. Your heart, it's different. You love different, you see different, you hear different from me and others. You are a special person Ira, and I've seen you weather a storm like no other. This is nothing for someone with your level of strength."

Now the flood gates were open and Ira's clutch on her tears was no longer intact.

"No, no, no, no tears," Jonathan said. He got up from his seat and stooped down in front of her. "You are too beautiful for all of this frowning," he said.

"I can't do this Jonathan, you don't understand," Ira tried wiping her tears but they kept falling. "Put anything else in front of me, anything, and I will work it out, but not this. I cannot take in my husband's illegitimate child as if I approve, because I don't." She cried. Her heart ached, and she thought about how she had no one to make it better. "All I ever did was love him, and now to find out that our marriage was a lie, it hurts like heck."

Jonathan laughed, and Ira eyed him through her teary eyes. "Even in the mist of letting off steam you still cannot curse," he smiled. "That is what I was trying to stress to you. You are an extraordinary woman, and you blow my mind just watching you forgive, and love those that may not deserve it, but you give anyway because you have such a huge heart."

He stood up and pulled a paper towel from the holder, and wiped Ira's tears. "You know when we make decisions with an open heart we tend to make the right decision."

Ira sat looking at Jonathan through her tears. Everything he said made sense, and in retrospect was the reason for her tears. She knew that this was all on her, and that she now held an innocent little girl's life and stability in her hands. The unknown part of the story weighed heavy on her mind as well, but what she wanted most was for it all to go away. She wanted someone to stand in front of her and take the hit for once since she was already damaged.

"I want to make the right decision, and I want...," her voice drifted off as the tears reappeared.

"What, what do you want?" Jonathan asked.

Ira looked him in the eyes, "I want you to make me forget about all of this, even if it's just temporary."

"Just tell me what you want me to do," Jonathan said. His eyes pleaded with Ira, ready to jump on command.

"Just take the pain away," she whimpered, "and touch me."

"I can't do that my Queen."

"Why?"

"Because you deserve better than that. You deserve for a man to place you up on a pedestal where you belong, and treat you like the queen that you are," he said, and that didn't help matters any. It only made Ira want him more.

"I know what I want, and right now, that's you," Ira said.

"Yes, but will you be able to face me tomorrow or better yet yourself?"

Ira moved closer to him to make sure he understood her loud and clear. "Yes," she said, and with that he scooped her up into his arms and laid her on the kitchen table. He gave Ira another minute to decide whether this was what she wanted as he stood over her peering down into her red eyes. She gave him a faint smile before his head disappeared between her legs. The feel of his full rotund lips on her goods ignited her body, and awoke her senses. She wept on top of the table as her body enjoyed the stimulation, and her mind fought to release her pain. Her hips revolved slowly as she planted her hands on the back of his smooth head. She had never been with a man that wore a bald head before, and the feel was different but welcomed. He maneuvered his tongue around her pearl, and she pulled him closer to her while arching her back an allowing her tears to fall off to the sides of her face. With her eyes closed she reveled in the steamy moment, submitting herself to him. This is what she wanted. In that moment she felt no pain, no worry, no anguish, just pure pleasure, and she wanted more.

"I have to get some protection," Ira mumbled through her moaning.

"You want me to stop?" Jonathan asked.

"No, I want more. Just give me one minute," she swung her leg over his head and hopped down off the table. "I think I may have a few condoms upstairs."

She rushed towards the steps and made a mad dash for her bedroom. Before Nick passed away they were using protection before he was deployed. Back then she was afraid to end up with "Irish twins" and an absent husband. She was sure the condoms were expired by now, but they were her only hope. She jogged down the hallway pass the boy's bedroom and into her own. After opening the drawer to her night stand she fumbled through the papers and miscellaneous items until she reached the bottom. The edge of the gold wrapper emerged and she pulled it from the pile and headed for the pleasure that awaited her in her kitchen. She took two steps towards the bedroom door when the sound of a male's voice singing, "Yield Not to Temptation" stopped her in her tracks. It was as if a switch had been flipped and she was now thinking logically. She was in such a hurry to get to the door that she forgot to turn off her gospel music.

"Dangit," she said as she tossed the condom back into the drawer. "I get it Lord," she spoke out loud.

There was no way she could get it on now with that song stuck in her head. Today was not her day, and now she had to go down the stairs and explain to Jonathan that she had an epiphany midway into her freaky thoughts. She knew right from wrong, and she knew that her thoughts and behavior were not Christian like. She was fighting temptations every day, and the weaker she became from her troubles, the harder the temptations were to defeat. In the midst of her troubles she lost her way, and this was the wakeup call she needed. The instant fix would only be temporary, and a part of her still wanted to take that chance but then what?

Jonathan would have to understand, and hopefully forgive her for today. There would be no rocking of her boat, no working the middle, and no changing of positions. She had to learn how to work her problems out on her own.

Chapter Thirteen

"You can take the girl out of the hood, but you can't take the hood out of the girl."

Jade sat on the bottom bunk in the tiny cell watching her cellmate knock out sets of push-ups as if she was running on pure adrenaline. Oddly enough the woman was rather short and was the owner of the squeakiest voice Jade had ever heard. As soon as they placed her in the cell she instantly missed the holding cell she spent the first twenty four hours in. Every time she thought about where she was she had to suppress the oncoming anxiety attack. It was only Monday and it felt like she hadn't seen the light of day in years. She made sure her first and only phone call was to her mother, and had her mother call Arnie once they told her she would not be getting out the same night due to the commissioner's availability. She was starving and sitting in the same pair of underwear she was arrested in. Needless to say there was no sleeping in jail until you became accustomed to all of the noise, and constant complaining.

"I can't believe this," Jade said to herself as she watched two guards tussle with an inmate.

"Well, believe it sister," her cellmate said, "When you gettin' out of here anyway?" she asked in between counting her reps.

"I shouldn't be in here at all. All I wanted to do was ask the girl a few questions. I didn't mean for all of this to happen," Jade's voice diminished as she told her story. She wanted to be home with her children not entertaining some inmate. This was not the life she lived or was equipped to live.

"Looka here," the woman said. "Ain't no need in crying now. The only thing you did wrong was you forgot to tase the chick."

"I didn't want to tase anyone."

"Then why you bring a taser gun with you?"

"I didn't bring a taser gun with me," Jade said.

"Then where you get the taser gun from?"

Jade took a deep breath, "I took it from the guard."

"Oh hell yeah," the inmate said with her hand in the air waiting for Jade to give her a high five. "That's some slick shit right there."

"I just want to go home," Jade said.

"Don't start that crying shit again," the inmate barked.

"I can't help it," Jade said sniffling.

She got up off her knees and draped her arm over Jade's shoulder. "You see all these people, all of them over there?" She said pointing across the block to the other inmates. "They waiting to see you cry. They want to see you fall, and see you weak so they can attack, you see them?"

Jade looked across the block at the inmates only to see them minding their own business either reading or watching their tiny TV's.

"I'm almost positive they are not worried about me."

"That's what they want you to think," she said.

Jade wanted her to get out of her ear with that annoying voice of hers. She was clearly paranoid because not a soul in there was worried about her.

"What are you in here for?" Jade couldn't believe she was asking the age old jail house question.

"Routine traffic stop," she stated.

"What?" Jade asked.

"Rou-tine tra-ffic stop," she broke it down.

"I don't understand. What happened during that routine traffic stop?"

"Some events may have transpired," she said.

"Did you have a warrant or something?"

"No," she said. She sat back down on the floor and proceeded to do sit ups. "I got out of the car and I ran," she said.

"But your legs," Jade said.

"What about my legs?" she stopped.

"They're short," Jade said.

"I know that." She picked up her reps where she left off.

"It's just that, it wasn't a good idea," Jade said.

"Don't you think I know that now?" she asked. "I just didn't want to go back to prison, ok?"

"So you ran from the cops?"

"Look can we just drop it?" she yelled.

"I'm just saying running from the cops is a sure way to get you arrested."

"Jade DeVoe come with us. You are going to see the commissioner," a guard announced as she unlocked the cell door.

She reached under the thin mattress and retrieved the papers she was given.

"Turn around and place your hands behind your back," the other guard said.

"Am I going home?" Jade asked.

"Do I look like the commissioner?" the guard shot back.

Jade wanted to bark back, but that wouldn't be a good idea due to her helplessness at the moment. She did as told and prayed the entire way through the large blue metal doors, and down the flight of stairs to a metal bench she was instructed to sit on. Her nerves were going haywire and she thought about Trent and how much she missed her husband. This was the first incident she's ever been in that her husband couldn't take care of. Before the cheating came to light she thought they made a great team, and she knew he more than likely hounded her mother about her whereabouts by now. She imagined him going crazy trying to figure out a way to get her out. As much as she wanted to use her one phone call to cry to him she didn't, she called her mother who had her children. The disappointment in her mother's voice only added to her disappointment in herself. She was sweating bullets in the plain orange jump suit she was issued, and couldn't do a damn thing about it with her hands restrained behind her back. She felt the disgusting food the inmates called "sweaty meat" she forced down trying to make its way back up through her esophagus.

"I have to vomit," Jade said to the guards.

"No you don't. It's just your nerves," the smaller one replied.

"No it's that shit y'all fed me yesterday."

The guards laughed as Jade continuously swallowed the saliva that formed in her mouth. She watched as two other guards approached the blue door with the number three on it, and placed handcuffs on an inmate that wore a huge smile on her face. She assumed the woman was on her way home, and she hoped to have the same exit.

"Come on," the bigger guard yanked Jade up by her arm and escorted her into the room. She released Jade's wrist from the cuffs then cuffed them in front of her, and gave her a light shove into the room.

"Lord if you get me out of this I promise to take Courtni and Ira up on their offer of attending church regularly," Jade said a silent player as the door closed behind her.

"Have a seat," the commissioner said without looking up from the file that lay on his desk. He scribbled carelessly on the stack of papers inside the file, although Jade could barely see him through the filthy glass.

She took a seat on the dented metal stool, and looked around the small booth to examine the substantial amount of graffiti that covered the dingy walls then slid the paper in her hand through the slot. As much as she would have liked to come across as the stylish, mild mannered and respectful woman she was in her daily life, she knew that her appearance said otherwise. Her orange jumpsuit was two sizes too big, and her hair was strewed about atop her head resembling an intricate bird's nest.

"Hello sir," Jade said into the speaker in the middle of the glass, and the elderly man looked above the brim of his glasses as if annoyed at her gesture.

"Hi," he said in a cynical tone.

Jade sat nervously with a stomach full of bubble guts. Her insides rumbled and her legs bounced swiftly as she tried her best to control her emotions.

"Jade Serean DeVoe, you are charged with aggravated assault and battery. Bail will be set at $4,500. You will be allowed to contact a bail bondsmen or family when this meeting is over. If bail cannot be posted within twenty four hours you will be held in custody until your hearing date," the commissioner stated without ever looking up at Jade. "Do you have any questions?" He asked as he slid two documents under the glass through the narrow slot.

"No," Jade replied, still stunned at her current environment.

"Sign both documents next to the "X" please, and you will be escorted out of the room as soon as the guards make their way back to you. Do you understand?"

"Yes," Jade replied as she signed her signature with the chained ink pen attached to the counter.

The commissioner retrieved the documents and handed her a copy. He gathered his papers and files and exited the room through a door in the back.

"Thank you Jesus." Jade sat waiting for her next set of instructions, clinching the signed piece of paper in her cuffed hands.

Her next move was to decide who to call. It was Monday morning so everyone was sure to be occupied with work, but she knew her friends would never leave her to rot in a jail cell. One call she was not going to make was to Trent. The first step she would take once released was a step away from Trent, and the whole situation that has engulfed her life, but more importantly she wanted out of the hell hole she landed herself in, and to take her first breath of fresh air once outside of the barbwire fence. This disastrous experience was an eye opener for her, and a lesson learned.

Forty five minutes later, the sound of keys unlocking the large door sounded throughout the tiny room. Jade came to a stance ready to move forward and make her phone calls, after being locked in what seemed like a cage for nearly an hour.

"Let's go DeVoe," the large guard said. She grabbed a hold of Jade's left arm while the smaller guard held on to the right.

"Looks like you lucked up," the smaller guard said.

"What took you all so long to come and get me? My back is killing me," Jade said.

"You think you the only fuck up in here? We have a job to do and you are only one of many inmates we have to transport. You don't get any privileges in here Ms. High and Mighty." The smaller guard stated as they escorted her down the hall and up to her cell block.

"Damn girl, where the hell you been?" her cellmate asked as she entered the cell. "They left me in that booth for almost an hour." Jade said as she tucked her head close to her neck while taking a seat on the bottom bunk.

"That sounds about right," she said as she walked over to the bars and began to hang a sheet.

Up until that moment Jade's prison experience was going smoothly considering the circumstances. Her worst prison fear was coming true, but there was no way Jade was going to let anyone violate her without putting up a fight. Although her cellmate was pretty fit, Jade was ready to try her luck.

"What are you doing?" Jade asked.

Her cellmate walked over to Jade, and stooped down in front of her as she lowered her voice, "I'm about to have me some fun, so…"

"Whoa, now you have completely lost your mind," Jade snapped, putting emphasis on the word completely. "Do you really think I'm just going to sit here and allow you to do as you please with my goods? You are sadly mistaken."

"Girl ain't nobody worried about you," her cell mate deflated Jade's ego as she stood up and walked the three paces to the sink. "You big booty hoes always think somebody want y'all." She said and turned around to roll her eyes at Jade, "I mean you cute and all, but someone owes me a favor and I plan on redeeming that favor today."

Jade found it hard to believe that anyone would be intimidated by the squeaky voice character that stood inches away from her.

"Well, what is about to happen?" Jade asked.

"I'm about to have to some company as soon the coast is clear, and you can either stay or get lost, don't make me no difference," she said.

"What's going on in here?" a guard startled Jade as she pulled the sheet aside and looked inside.

"I'm about to take a shit, damn can I get some privacy?" her cellmate yelled.

"Make it quick Barker," the guard said and walked away.

That was the closest to a name Jade had for her cellmate. When they first transferred her to her cell the cellmate referred to her as newbie and Jade never asked her name.

"Don't you have a phone call to make or did they make yo ass stay here?" she asked Jade.

"Oh yeah, but there's a line to get to the phones."

"Well suit yourself," she said and just then a young petite Latina woman slid into the tiny cell with the two of them.

"Hey is the coast clear?" her cellmate asked the woman.

"Yup, and I got Tina on the lookout."

"Cool, Amber this is Newbie, Newbie this Amber."

"Hi," Jade said and the woman returned the gesture.

"Hey I need you to do me another favor," the woman said in a heavy Latina accent.

"What you need?"

The Latina woman leaned forward and whispered in her cellmate's ear.

"Ok you got that," the cellmate said. "I can have that to you by Wednesday." The woman smiled and began to quickly undress. That was Jade's cue to leave the cell and wait on a phone to free up. She sped up her pace when she noticed both phones were free, and dialed Lani's number. Jade followed the directions of the automated system and waited for the beep to say her name. A few seconds later the phone was ringing and Jade hoped Lani was not with a patient at the moment.

"Hello," Jade spoke into the phone.

"What the fuck is going on?" Lani whispered.

"I got arrested Friday and I need you to bail me out."

"It's Monday," Lani stated as if Jade lost track of her days.

"I know what damn day it is Lani. I've been here for three days now. Just get me out of here."

"What happened?"

"Lani!"

"Ok, ok, what do I have to do?"

"Stop acting like you don't know what to do. You have dealt with enough convicts in the past to know."

"You are not acting like someone who needs help right now," Lani said.

"Lani, if you don't get me out of here or contact someone that will—"

"Calm down, are you in the city?"

"No, the Baltimore County facility."

"Ok, I'm on it. How much is your bail?"

"$4,500," Jade said.

"Oh, you have to tell me what you did. See you in a few."

Jade heard Lani's car door sensor beeping before hanging up the phone, and she tried to mask her excitement. She did everything, but skip back to her cell in total elation, and break into an elaborate end zone dance upon arrival. Her excitement turned to astonishment then utter shock once she pulled the sheet back and entered the cell.

"Well, come in don't just stand there with the curtain open," her cell mate said and Jade wanted to correct her and inform her that it was in fact a sheet, but she was more focused on what was unfolding in front of her. She allowed the sheet to close as she crashed the duo's fruit party.

"Go ahead and get up on your bunk," her cell mate said over top of the television.

"No thank you," Jade said, never taking her eyes off of the odd scene.

"She likes this shit. Don't you?" her cellmate asked the woman whose lips were pressed tightly together trying to silence herself.

Jade watched as her cell mate increasingly plunged in and out of the woman's hairy cooch with a spotted ripened banana. The woman set up on her elbows and watched as her cellmate toyed with the banana, and Jade stood with eyes wide. She wanted to turn around and leave, but her feet were planted and her mind was blown. The woman didn't seem too pleased, so Jade figured this was her cellmate's idea and the owed favor from the woman. She removed the banana and brought it up to the woman's mouth.

"You know what to do," her cellmate said, and the young woman stuck her tongue out. "Hurry up," the cell mate squealed with that non-threatening voice.

The woman opened wide and tilted her head back as the cellmate slowly slid the banana down her throat. Jade cringed as the stained piece of fruit slid halfway down the woman's throat, and was forced the rest of the way. She eyed her cellmate who had one hand on the fruit and the other hand inside of her jumpsuit indulging in a little self-satisfaction.

"Swallow it," the cellmate demanded as she forced as

much of the fruit down the woman's throat and she began to gag. Her cellmate removed her own hand from in between her legs and placed it behind the woman's head as she jammed the banana in and out of the woman's mouth.

The loud sound of a wolf whistle penetrated the tiny cell, and impelled the women to scatter. Jade never moved a muscle as the petite visitor quickly dressed, and her cellmate hid the tainted piece of fruit. The woman sat on the floor in front of the bottom bunk while her cell mate positioned herself in front of the tiny sink.

"Come do my hair," the woman said to Jade.

"Hell no, I want no parts of this," Jade stated and folded her arms.

"Come on *chica*, I can't afford to get in trouble again, *complacer prisa*."

Jade huffed, but complied after hearing the urgency in her voice, and seeing her face bound with worry. She took a seat behind the woman and began to part her hair with her fingers just in the nick of time.

"I thought I told you to make it quick Barker," the same guard tugged at the makeshift curtain. "Back in your cell Rodríguez, you know the rules."

"*Bueno*," the woman said and scurried out of the cell.

"So, when you getting out of here?" her cellmate asked as if nothing had just happened.

"I guess we are just ignoring what just happened," Jade said.

"What just happened is a day in the life of an inmate. You get in where you fit in, and make things work for you. Hopefully you don't ever have to witness that again because you will go home leave that cheating husband of yours alone with his freak, and continue to live your life. Me? This is my reality too often. I'm a natural born fuck up with a pretty wealthy family that could care less that one of their own has a drug addiction. I don't want this life. I don't want to be a junkie, but it was the hand I was dealt and I play it well. This is my family," she said pointing outside of the cell. "People like you don't know how lucky you are."

The two chitchatted throughout the afternoon. Her

cellmate introduced her to her "family" and Jade was surprised at how welcoming the group of buff, and tatted women were. There were mothers, sisters, daughters, ex-teachers, and even ex-nuns behind prison walls. Their stories were amazing, yet staggering that one bad decision has twisted, and contorted then ultimately obliterated their lives. Jade talked to them about rebuilding and leaving the past where it belongs. For a brief moment it felt like they were in a criminal-infested camp.

"DeVoe, you posted bail," a guard said from behind Jade. She literally jumped for joy before saying her goodbyes, and being lead down to the lower level to await her release.

She stepped out of prison a new woman, and seeing Lani brought her to tears.

"I'm so happy to see someone I know," Jade said as she hopped in the passenger seat.

"You can take the girl out of the hood, but you can't take the hood out of the girl," Lani said while shaking her head at Jade.

"Can you just drive?"

Jade filled Lani in on Friday's events and how she landed herself behind bars. Of course Lani got a good laugh out of it, but Jade still had a court appearance to attend. Her freedom was still in the state of Maryland's hands, and she had no one to blame but herself. She knew that every action had a consequence so why did she go to Tamra's job in the first place? Now she had a list of apologies to dish out due to her absence. Her staff, her customers, and most importantly her children deserved apologies. She lost two business days, and now had a public record. She felt a strong need to assess her life, but she would start with a shower then going to her mother's to hug and kiss her children. She had to make a change.

Chapter Fourteen

"How would you like a little temptation to go with those morals?"

"Ok Courtni this is getting old," she spoke to herself as she sat at her desk staring at the piece of paper that contained Bo's phone number. After a few weeks of soul searching and prayer she decided to keep and raise her own child. She didn't know what to expect along this journey, but selfishness was not in her nature. Her initial shock has slowly turned to concern for her unborn child. Today she had an appointment for her first prenatal visit, and was trying to decide whether to invite Bo along. She knew the honest thing to do was to inform him of her decision, but it has been five weeks since she has heard anything from him and she couldn't help but to think he has moved past this, and does not want to be bothered. She tried bracing herself for rejection before calling, but couldn't manage to clear that hurdle. She sat tapping her fingers on her desk while biting her bottom lip. Her schedule was cleared for the rest of the day, and her appointment was an hour and a half away. The decision to call Bo had to be made soon before it was too late.

Her fingers dialed the ten digits slowly as she finally conjured up a bit of bravery. This was not the first time she thought about calling him, but it would be the first time she actually followed through with it.

"Hello," he answered quicker than expected, but that only confirmed to Courtni that he was indeed a hustler. Why wasn't he at work in the middle of the day?

"Hey, I mean hello," Courtni shook her head at herself.

"Hello, can I help you?" he asked.

She placed the receiver back down on its base. Lani was right, she was afraid of men; she had to be because her mind was telling her legs to run, and her heart rate had already began the race. She promptly stood up and grabbed her purse and keys from her bottom drawer, and headed for the door. That phone call would have to wait until she was feeling a little less cowardly.

She walked down the short hallway ready to leave that awkward moment behind.

"Ms. Jeffries you have a phone call on line one," her assistant said.

"For me?" Courtni asked as if there was another Ms. Jefferies standing behind her. "Did they ask for me?"

"Well no, but they did say they just received a call from this number, and I haven't made any phone calls," she said confused.

"Oh I see," Courtni paused.

"Here, you can just use my phone since you're right here," she said with her hand on the flashing red button.

"No, I'll take it in my office," Courtni said. She walked back down the hall and took a deep breath before answering the phone. "Courtni Jeffries," she tried her best to hide her nervousness.

"Hello Ms. Jeffries, I think we were disconnected." he said, and his deep voice filled her ears along with all of the noise in the background.

"Yes, but it's really not important at the moment. I shouldn't have called."

"It was important enough for you to finally call me, so fill me in," he said, and Courtni heard a door shut in the background and the noise diminish.

"Well, first I think I should tell you that I've decided to keep the baby," she paused trying to feel him out, but he said nothing, "and um, today I have my first pre-natal exam, and foolishly I was going to extend an invite to you but I know you wouldn't be interested. I don't know what I was thinking." She said the last part out loud but didn't mean to do it.

"Sure I would," he said, and Courtni smiled.

"Really? I mean I'm not trying to make anything out of this, and I'm not trying to trap you or anything. I don't date guys like you. I just figured if we are going to do this I should start by being cordial," she said.

"I understand."

"Good."

"I guess I should ask the time and place of the appointment," he inquired.

"Of course, it's at 2 pm at Greater Baltimore Medical Center."

"Great, you gave me less than an hour, but I'll be there."

"See you then," Courtni said, and took a deep breath after disconnecting the call.

She smiled from ear to ear as she made her way down to the garage. This was not the way she pictured things to be when she had her first child, but she had to make the best out of a very stressful situation. Life has been a rollercoaster for her lately. Between her unplanned pregnancy, Jade getting arrested, and Ira discovering Nick had a child outside of their marriage Courtni hasn't had much time to relax. As usual the shoulder everyone used to cry on was in her possession. She loved them to death and didn't mind helping at all, but it did bother her that none of them thought her situation was as severe as she did. Maybe they felt that way because they would not be the unwed mother of a slacker's child. A fine slacker he is, but his looks wouldn't help her raise a child.

She walked into her doctor's office, and did a quick scan of the room. Bo was nowhere in sight, so she tried to keep her thoughts on the positive side since it was only quarter til two. If he did show, she would be surprised. After all, she couldn't imagine being a man and having a child with a woman you do not know. Things on the opposite end were not very peachy either, but her experience would be different from his. She would feel this child, bond with this child, and without a doubt know that this child was hers.

The lobby was full of expectant mothers, and fathers. Courtni was glad that she was not showing since she was there alone, and probably would be throughout her entire pregnancy. She sat next to a young woman who appeared to be alone as well. To pass time, she picked up a *Time* magazine off the end table, and flipped through the articles, but her mind was elsewhere. She thought about all she was sure to endure alone. Her friends would be a tremendous help, but they wouldn't be the help that would fill her heart. It was her childhood and losing her mom all over again. That alone feeling she felt growing up would surely resurface. Although she has always appreciated the helping hands extended her way the only thing that truly comforted her was reading her bible. She knew her faith was all she had to lean on.

"Sorry I'm late," Bo said as he approached Courtni.

Her eyes followed him as he took a seat on the opposite side of the end table, and stripped her of her positive thoughts since she instantly wanted to jump his bones.

"I was doing so well," she said, referring to her previous thoughts of seeking refuge in her bible.

"What was that?" he asked leaning closer to Courtni.

"Oh nothing, I'm just surprised to see you here."

"Why is that when I told you I would be?"

Courtni stared across the table longer than she wanted to, but the man was captivating, and his cologne was immensely enticing. She definitely needed to keep her face buried in her bible. She was a weak woman.

"I thought you would have moved on with your life by now," she said.

"I did," he said, and Courtni broke her face down, "but that's the way of life. It goes on whether we are happy, sad, mad, or glad life goes on, and you have to roll with the punches right?"

Courtni looked away. His rash retort stung a little, and she was beginning to think this was the wrong thing to do.

"I am glad that you called though."

"Courtni Jeffries," the nurse called out, and Courtni gathered her things. She stopped when she noticed Bo was still sitting.

"Are you coming?" Courtni asked.

"Sure," he said getting up from his seat. "I thought I was going to wait out front."

They followed the nurse through the security door, and over to the scale. Courtni instantly felt uneasy and wished she could take her invitation back.

"I need you to step up on the scale, so that we can get your weight," the nurse spoke pleasantly, but didn't calm Courtni's nerves. She couldn't believe she was doing this in front of this fine ass man.

"Maybe dad can hold that for you," the nurse said as she removed Courtni's purse from her shoulder, and handed it to Bo.

That was awkward, but he didn't seem bothered. She wished he would walk away and give her some privacy for just one minute, but Courtni had his undivided attention.

"205," the nurse said softly, but it seemed as if she shouted it for everyone to hear. She was officially embarrassed. The last time she weighted herself she had yet to hit the two hundred mark.

"Ok, you two can follow me. I'm going to put you in room four," she said and they followed her around the corner.

"Hey Bo," a young nurse walking by spoke.

He squinted his eyes as if trying to remember the woman's face, "Oh hello," he said.

Courtni felt a little annoyed, but this was not her man so she had to check herself.

He took a seat in the empty chair while Courtni hopped up on the paper covered leather bed. The nurse recorded her blood pressure while she tried not to stare at Bo in his khaki cargo shorts and black T-shirt. His hair was pulled back into a ponytail so she could see that attractive face of his very well.

"I need you to undress from the waist down, and the doctor will be right in." The nurse smiled and exited the room.

Reason number two as to why she should have told Bo to stay out front.

"This was not a good idea," Courtni said.

"Oh yes it was," Bo said as he leaned back in his chair ready for a show.

"That's not funny," Courtni said and he smiled at her discomfort.

"I'll step out," he laughed as he opened the door.

Courtni rushed to undress and position herself back up on the bed before Bo or her doctor walked in on her.

"You can come in now." she said, and in walked Bo and her doctor followed.

"This is how you treat the father of your child?" her doctor asked playfully, but Courtni wanted to tell her she wouldn't understand.

The doctor made small talk, and updated Courtni's file before they reached awkward moment number three.

"Place both feet up on the stirrups, and we are going to

get your cultures done and out of the way," her doctor said as she sat on her stool and placed the bright light between Courtni's legs.

Courtni eyed Bo who was next to her and couldn't see between her legs from his seat. She smiled at his disappointment as he shook his head once the doctor covered her legs with the paper cover.

"Have you had an ultrasound yet?" her doctor asked.

"No ma'am,"

"Well, we're going to change that," she said as she handed Courtni a few napkins, and disposed of her gloves before leaving the two of them alone in the room.

"She just stuck a stick inside of you, three of them to be exact." Bo said.

Courtni laughed because he looked completely disgusted. "Yes, we have to endure quite a bit to ensure good health unlike men so you wouldn't know anything about this."

"You know one day I'm going to give you as much of my time as you need to get all of your insults and dislike for me out of your system, then after that, no more."

"Excuse me," Courtni sat up on the bed. "You do not dictate to me what I am going to do. I do as I see fit, and if you would have kept your behind away from me at that party then neither of us would be here right now. I wouldn't have to readjust my life because you decided you wanted to take advantage of a helpless woman."

"I see we are still playing the blame game," he said calmly.

"No, I wish this was a game, one that I could simply tap out of, but unfortunately I have to deal with a pathetic excuse for a man that relies on his looks to get him what he wants for the next eighteen years."

"Once again, you do not know me."

"Good," Courtni said and folded her arms.

"How about I just leave? You are getting yourself upset over something that is irrelevant." He stood from his seat and reached for the door knob, but her doctor was coming through from the other side pulling an ultra-sound machine and wearing a huge smile.

"Have a seat dad. We're going to see if we can check on your little one," the doctor said. "Now, I still want you to make an appointment to have a more extensive sonogram, but for now we can just take a peek," she said as she waited for the machine to load, and dimmed the lights.

Courtni looked over at Bo who was now sitting back in his seat. When he made eye contact with her she looked away. She felt terrible for her words, and he didn't deserve to be mistreated. Surely she eventually had to place some of the blame on herself, and let it go. She knew some of her anger came from a different place and that had nothing to do with him.

The doctor placed clear gel on the bottom of Courtni's stomach, and used the transducer probe to spread it around. Soon after an image appeared on the screen, but Courtni couldn't make out a thing.

"Ah, there you are," her doctor said, and Bo stood up and came closer. "There is the head, the torso, little tiny arms that were just nubs a few weeks ago, and you see that flicker there?" she said, pointing to the screen, "That is your baby's heartbeat." The doctor turned the volume up on the machine.

A rapid rhythmic sound entered the room, and filled Courtni's eyes with tears. It was the most beautiful thing she had ever heard. She couldn't describe the feeling and the amazed look on Bo's face added to her excitement.

"Wow," Bo said with his eyes still glued to the screen. "I see him moving. That's my son right there," he said, and the women laughed.

The moment was short lived since the doctor had a job to do and other patients to see. Bo stepped out as Courtni cleaned herself up, and redressed. Her heart felt so full at that moment, and she couldn't wait to see her baby again. The ultrasound changed everything, and she was grateful that Bo didn't leave. She reached the lobby and searched for Bo, but didn't see him. Her heart sank when she realized he must have left which he had every right to do. Since they would only be co-parenting if things worked out certainly she would not be of his concern, and their relationship would solely be for the sake of their child. She just hoped that he turned out to be a great guy that she didn't have to spend years fighting with.

She reached in her purse for her keys before stepping into the August heat.

"Are you hungry?" Bo asked as he stood next to his Porsche.

"I thought you were gone," Courtni said.

"No, I have tough skin," he smiled and Courtni dropped her head. He made her so nervous whenever things were calm between them. "I just don't think it's a good idea for you to get upset in your condition, so since I seem to be the problem I figured I should leave."

"I apologize for what I said in there. It was uncalled for, and you do not deserve the disrespect. I whole heartedly apologize. My troubles have nothing to do with you."

"Apology accepted. Now are you hungry?" he asked.

"No," Courtni said, but her stomach told a different story.

"Thirsty," he asked.

"I can use some bottled water," she laughed.

He walked over to the passenger's side of his car and held the door open. "I know a place that sells great bottled water."

Courtni laughed. "I'll just follow you."

"Oh, that's right. What do you think I have a car full of paraphernalia or guns or both?" he asked sarcastically.

"I didn't say that."

"But you are thinking it," he added. "That's fine you can follow me," he said. He looked like a man that was taking a verbal beating, but by no means was he going to truly strike back at a woman.

Courtni pushed her fears aside, "Ok, you drive," she said.

He smiled and opened the door again.

"So, on a scale of one to ten how much do you hate me?" he asked as he exited the parking lot, and turned onto the highway.

"I don't hate you," Courtni said.

He shot her a skeptical look with his lips twisted to the side, "Look at my lips," he said, and Courtni burst into laughter. That reminded her of her friends.

"I'm serious," she said, but he kept his lips twisted.

She was in awe of the beautiful red interior that covered the entire car including the steering wheel. This car was luxurious, and nothing Courtni was used to riding in. She has a really nice vehicle, but this car put hers to shame. He dropped the top as they cruised down the road, and enjoyed the tune of Anthony Hamilton's, "Sucka for You." He didn't strike her as the soul music type. She thought for sure they would be listening to rap music.

"You have a really nice car," Courtni said, trying to conceal her excitement.

"Thank you," he said as they pulled in front of Cami's Café. "Don't you touch that door," he said. He walked around the car and opened the door for Courtni then held the door to the café open for her as well.

He pulled out a chair for her over in the corner of the quaint artistry inspired café. Courtni surveyed the art that hung on the walls around her, amazed at the talent, and skill the artists possessed. The café had a vibrant feel to it, and its décor was intensely hued.

"These are all the work of local talent," the young woman said as she approached their table with a note pad.

"They are very talented," Courtni smiled.

"Can I get you two anything to drink? I know you haven't had much time to look over the menu."

Bo looked across the table at Courtni waiting for her to order, but she wanted way more than that water she mentioned earlier. "I'll have a lemonade," Courtni said, and looked at Bo who was smiling again, "What," Courtni asked.

"Nothing," he threw his hands up. "I'll take a glass of lemon water."

"Ok, I'll be right back," the waitress said.

"Have you even looked at the menu?" Courtni asked.

"I already know what I want. I've been here a few times," he said. "Have you changed your mind about being hungry?"

"No," she said again, although she was hungry after only having eaten crackers earlier that morning, but that 205 pounds that displayed on the scale at the clinic had her thinking twice about gorging, so something small would have to do.

"I hope when you are not around me you feed my child," he said.

"Fine I'll order something," she said as if she was being pressured into eating when she really couldn't wait.

They placed their orders with the waitress then got down to business.

"Ok I guess I'll start this off," Bo said after sipping his drink. "What are we doing here and how are we doing it?" he asked.

"Well, I'm glad you asked that," Courtni said. She pulled her note pad from her purse. "I wrote down a few questions I wanted to ask you," she cleared her throat. "Do you plan on signing over your rights?" She dove right in.

"No," he replied.

"Why not?"

"Why should I?" he asked.

"Do you plan on taking me to court? I just need to know if I should start saving for court fees and a lawyer," she said.

"No, I don't plan on it. I was hoping we could be adults about this."

"Do you have other children?"

"No."

"How old are you?"

"32."

"Will my child be in any type of danger while he/she is with you?" she asked.

"Not any more than he/she would be in with you."

"What kind of people do you associate with?" she asked.

"I don't know," he chuckled, "I guess it depends on why I am associating with them."

"What do you do for a living?"

"Rob banks, steal cars, cook dope, you name it," he said, and Courtni had a horrified look on her face. "That is what you are expecting for me to say right?"

Courtni sipped her drink trying to keep calm.

"Why do you think I'm incapable of being an upstanding citizen?" he asked Courtni as the waitress placed their sandwiches on the table.

"Did I say that? I asked a simple question."

"You judged me from the start. The day you came to Laurence's house you already had the preconceived notion that I was this menace that drugged you, seduced you, and probably raped you. Never once have you tried to detract from that, and actually get to know me for who I am, and not for whom you believe me to be. You think because I'm not wearing a suit and tie that I'm a thug, and the only thing I contribute to society is minatory ways," he left Courtni speechless as he continued, "I could make assumptions about you as well you know? I woke up that morning wondering what the hell happened just like you, and you know what I was told?" he asked, "You got drunk and fucked some hoe last night," he said, and Courtni felt as if someone had punched her in the chest. "I took that statement for what it was, and made myself an appointment to get tested a few weeks later. When I met you I got to form my own opinion of you, and it was nowhere near the immoral woman I imagined." He bit into his sandwich while Courtni sat there trying to take in everything he said.

"You're right," Courtni said. "I'm sorry, I should have just asked you the questions I wanted answers to from the start."

"Let me ask you this," he paused to swallow his food. "When you said you don't date men like me, what did you mean by that? What type of men do you date?"

"Well, I like—"

"No, I want to know what type of men you date, not like."

"I haven't actually been out on a date with a man." Courtni spoke to the table since she never looked up at Bo.

"I'm sorry I don't think I heard you. Could you speak up?" he said leaning closer with his hand behind his ear.

"I have never been on a date, ok?"

"How old are you?" he asked.

"27."

"And you have never been on a date?"

"No," Courtni said, embarrassed.

"So you are that picky?"

"I don't know," Courtni said. "Can we get back to the situation at hand?" she asked.

"Sure," he smiled.

She melted every time that smile displayed on his face. "So, when the baby is born you can come to my place to spend time with him/her. I can cover him/her under my insurance plan, and we can split all other expenses. When the baby gets a little older and is able to part from me we can talk about you taking him/her with you on the weekends or every other weekend or whatever we decide," she said.

"Ok, mother," Bo teased. He swallowed the last of his water, and placed his napkin on the empty plate.

"This is what bothers me about you. You aren't taking any of this seriously. This baby will be here before we know it. What is it that you want?"

"I want to get a blood test, just to be sure. Don't get upset with me."

"I'm not, keep going." Courtni said. That was the one thing she did understand.

"I want to get to know my child's mother, and I want us to work as a team in raising our child. I will always respect you, and I would appreciate it if you could do the same for me in return. That's it."

"You don't think this baby is yours do you?" Courtni asked, still stuck on his last answer.

"Actually I do," he said, surprising Courtni.

"Oh, I forgot to tell you while we are co-parenting out of respect for each other I will stay out of your love life and you should stay out of mine."

He laughed, "but you don't have a love life."

"I will someday," Courtni said. "You must think I'm very strange don't you?"

"Yes, but not in a bad way."

"I'm not strange. I just believe that God is going to send me my husband, if I just wait."

"God, huh?"

"You don't believe in God?" Courtni asked.

"Yes I do, I'm not a great representation of a believer, but I do believe. My mother would kill me if I didn't," he laughed. "Are you done? I want to show you something," Bo asked. He walked over to Courtni, pulled her chair out from the table, and helped her up. She walked over to the counter prepared to pay for her meal.

"Not on my watch," Bo said as he handed the clerk his bank card over Courtni's shoulder.

They got into the car and Courtni wondered where they were headed. She was pleasantly surprised by the person Bo was shaping up to be.

"Where are we going?" Courtni asked.

"You want to know how I make a living right?"

Courtni's take charge attitude was working overtime. She wanted to know where they were going, was it safe, and what time he going to have her back to her car? She could thank her grandmother for her panicky nature. Growing up she had to be in the house before the street lights were on, as a teen she could only work summers and not during the school year, and her grandmother drove her everywhere just so she would know exactly where she was. As an adult Courtni understood that she and her brother were all that was left of their beautiful mother, so their grandmother held on as tight as possible.

"Are you okay over there?" Bo asked.

"Yes, I'm fine."

"Are you getting too much sun?"

"A little," Courtni admitted. The sun was frying her forehead.

At that moment he put the top up, and they exited the freeway. They drove a few blocks before he made a right turn into a gated parking lot of a custom, auto body shop. There were people everywhere, and most of the guys had on grey and blue uniform shirts with a name on it that she couldn't make out. She observed quite a few women lingering around in miniskirts and halter tops, showing everything but the twins and their cousin. The custom cars that sat outside of the shop were impeccable, and there was rock and roll music playing from the speakers that hung from the building which Courtni thought was strange.

Bo was outside of the vehicle and opening her door before she even noticed he was no longer in the driver's seat. She climbed out and stood next to Bo.

"This here is my baby," he said pointing to the well-lit sign that decorated the top of the shop. The sign read Bo's Custom's, and Courtni looked over at Bo baffled.

He wore a proud smile on his face as he used his shirt to wipe off the custom car he stood next to. Initially she beamed with pride for him. This was a wonderful thing and looks like a lot of hard work.

"Come over here," he said and Courtni followed him through the lot to an adjacent building. "This is the auto body shop on this side. It's affordable, and my way of helping others that can't really afford to give an arm and a leg to have their vehicles fixed," he said.

"You have officially blown my mind," she said. "Now, I'm wondering how you financed all of this," she twirled her finger around to include the entire building. "Should I even be here? I don't need any trouble," she said looking nervous.

"You never stop do you?"

"Hi Bo," two dainty women dressed provocatively and carrying two boxes of shop rags spoke to Bo as they shimmied by.

"Hey ladies," he said, and the two woman giggled.

For some reason, that bothered Courtni.

"Whoa, whoa, whoa, man, watch the corners," Bo yelled at the fork lift operator, and no sooner than his rant was over there was another young woman approaching.

"Hey Bo, can you lend me a hand with something?" she asked. "Please?" she pouted and poked her lip out.

Courtni looked around at all the other men working on the lot. She could have multiple hands, but Bo's must have been something special. She was ready to go once she noticed the woman purposely drop her rag, bend over in her tiny jeans, and slowly come back up. The only difference between her and the others was she actually appeared to work there.

"Give me a minute," Bo said.

"Can you take me back to my car now?" Courtni asked with an attitude.

"Hold on, I wanted to show you something else," he said, as he began to walk in the direction of the needy woman.

"Now, please," Courtni raised her voice.

He glared at Courtni then pulled his keys from his pocket, "Come on," he said. She could sense a bit of an attitude, as she walked behind Bo. His normally confident stride was replaced by a fast pace as he headed towards his car with Courtni trailing behind. Even in the midst of his displeasure before thinking about getting into the driver's seat he proceeded to open the door for Courtni.

They sat in silence for a few minutes as they entered the freeway. Courtni's thoughts were jumbled, and her emotions were in disarray. Sure she thought Bo was by far the sexiest man she has ever had the pleasure of accompanying, but she didn't want him. She wanted a college-educated, suit-wearing, powerful, confident man that was established and hardworking not because he has to be, but because he wants to be. What she didn't understand was why he got under her skin without trying, and why did the sight of him make her heart flutter, and her palms sweat. So what other women lusted over him, he was physically a work of art, but that had nothing to do with her and was none of her business. She took pride in her self-control, but whenever he was around it seemed to wither away.

"Back in 1979, there was this beautiful young woman named Dena who was a freshman in college," Bo broke the prolonged silence, and grabbed Courtni's attention. "She became the object of her English professor's affection, and they began this secret relationship that lasted almost two years. One day the young woman announced to him that she was carrying his child, and he informed her that he was married with a family, and that she needed to get an abortion before she ruined his life, but she didn't. Dena gave birth to a baby boy, and kept their child a secret. She graduated from college two years later without ever speaking another word to him. Although he saw her pretty much every day, he never once asked about the baby." He paused. "He passed away twenty-three years later, and suddenly I receive this letter requesting my presence along with my mother's at his lawyer's office."

"The professor was your father?" Courtni asked.

"Yup," he looked over at Courtni and continued to talk. "We go to this lawyer's office and he hands over this box. Tells me that I was his beneficiary, and as soon as I sign the papers he placed in front of me I will be the new owner of his house, his lake house, his cars, his insurance money, and his savings."

"Wow," Courtni listened intently.

"I didn't want it. He didn't care about me when he was alive so I didn't want any parts of him, but my mother gave me this lecture about forgiveness, and how God saw to it that even in his absence I didn't need anything. He sent my mother a great man that married her, adopted me, and raised me as his own."

Courtni smiled.

"I did some research and I found his wife in a rehabilitation home. I wanted to see her and give her and her family what was rightfully theirs. When I got there the staff told me she was suffering from dementia, and I probably wouldn't get anywhere, but I walked into her room and she smiled so hard." Bo laughed out loud at the memory. "She said I look just like him when they first met, and then I told her why I was there, but she wouldn't take anything. She told me he told her about me years ago, and that I deserved everything he gave me. Then I found out that they lost their son years ago to leukemia." He paused, "I go to see her all the time now. Sometimes she's there mentally, and sometimes she's not, but I make sure to bring flowers so that she knows I was there."

"That is a wonderful thing to do Bo. You are a blessing to her." Courtni said, and that quickly he changed her mind set.

"You see, there's a lot more to me than meets the eye," he flashed that sensuous smile that penetrated her lady parts.

"I wouldn't take it that far," Courtni joked.

"I can be just as complicated as you, but that would only complicate things more. At least now you can stop calling me a hustler."

"So Mr. Bo, are you hands on at your business or do you sit around and watch the skimpy women parade around?" Courtni changed the subject.

"I'm very hands on Ms. 'I over analyze everything.'"

Courtni smiled, "What is your favorite thing to do there?"

"Graphic designing," he stated without thinking.

"You do that?" Courtni asked.

"Yup, I also hand paint if that's what the customer wants."

"If you say so," she smiled because she knew he would remember that saying.

"You don't believe me?" He asked, and took the next exit when Courtni didn't agree.

"Ok, I believe you. Just take me to my car," Courtni couldn't even get the words out through her laughter. She was thoroughly enjoying agitating him.

"I'm about to show you something I've only shared with my family," Bo said, "I'll have you back to your car before curfew." This time he was the agitator.

Courtni wanted so badly to ask a million different questions, but she didn't. She figured the more time she spent with him the more she would learn about the man she needed to form a co-parenting relationship with. She relaxed her shoulders, and laid her head back on the leather headrest as they coasted down the busy freeway. Her friends were not going to believe that she actually spent time with a man, and it was not work related. They would be proud of her since they have been pushing her to call him for weeks. This was the start of a very long process, and he appeared to want things to flow smoothly, if so they were on the same page in that aspect.

Bo pulled off the freeway, made a few turns, then headed down a long stretch of road. Courtni admired the scenery with its redbud trees and batches of dandelions covering the grass. The neighborhood had a rich country southern style feel to it with homes scattered about yards away from the road and sitting on acres of land.

They turned onto a long black top driveway with a beautiful French colonial style home at the end. Courtni's eyes started at the bottom of the home with its large gray, tan, and beige stones and gradually traveled up three stories to its grey siding and white trim. The front of his home had an amazing circular room that stood out from the rest of the house.

"Where are we?" Courtni asked.

"Cecil County," Bo answered, and turned the engine off. He took Courtni by the hand and helped her out of the car.

"Is this your home?" Courtni asked, as Bo held the tips of her fingers as they walked the gravel stoned path around the side of the house.

"Yup, my inherited home," he said.

"It's beautiful," she said as he let her lead the way up the white wooden stairs to a single white door.

"Thank you." Bo laughed as he unlocked the door. "You seem to like everything about me, but me."

Little did he know she liked him from head to toe. It was the situation she didn't like. She entered the room and many different odors invaded her nostrils immediately as Bo pulled a string and the blinds began to rise. The natural light lit up the circular room and shined on the canvassed paintings that covered the room. There were all kinds of painting utensils atop the long rounded table in front of the windows, and large paint stained cases full of paint brushes. Her eyes caught a glimpse of a bottle of turpentine which answered the question as to what the strongest odor was in the room.

She walked around the room on the paint speckled hardwood floors, and surveyed his undeniable talent. There were covered paintings that rested on easels in the middle of the room. She was amazed and felt as if she was drowning in this man's brilliant talent. The room was mind-altering for her, and she couldn't make out her blurred thoughts, so they escaped as tears.

"What happened? Did I do something wrong? Is it the smell?" Bo panicked.

"No," she cried.

"Well why are you crying?" he asked as he approached Courtni, and turned her around to face him.

"Because this is all so beautiful, I'm amazed, and I want a Whopper junior with cheese," she sobbed.

Bo couldn't contain his laughter, "Well lets go get you a Whopper junior with cheese," he laughed.

"But I don't eat beef," Courtni said which sent Bo into hysterical laughter that trickled down to Courtni. She laughed along with Bo as he used his shirt to wipe her eyes. "I think your hormones are making their presence known," he said.

"I'm so sorry," she said, trying to stop the tears, and control her breathing before it triggered her asthma.

"Come on, I'll make you something to eat."

"No, you don't have to do that. I'll grab something on the way home."

"I want to," he said.

Courtni followed him through a door and entered into the hallway of his home. They walked down the wooden spiral stair case that led to his chef's kitchen. She climbed onto a stool in front of the island, and admired Bo's muscular back as he rummaged through the fridge.

What was she doing here?

"So, what do you eat?" he asked.

"I'll just take a bottle of water," Courtni said.

"I don't have any bottled water that taste like a Whopper," he laughed.

"Don't do that," she said.

"I can make you a lunch meat sandwich," he said seriously.

"You can't cook, can you?"

"I can do a little something," he smiled.

"What were you going to eat for dinner?"

"My mother dropped off some of her baked chicken, garlic potatoes, green beans, and homemade biscuits this morning."

"Oh so, you are going to keep the good stuff for yourself?" Courtni asked.

"No mother, I'll heat you up a plate right away," he laughed.

They carried their food into the adjacent great room, and talked, laughed, and took turns yelling out answers while watching "Family Feud." She was really enjoying her time with Bo, and it was comforting to know that he was a very generous man. He was slowly changing her perception of him, and placing himself in a more positive light. She loved his sense of humor, and felt a lot better about their situation.

Courtni leaned back on the cushy, khaki sectional with a full belly. She was trying her best to act lady like and not unbutton her slacks and let loose one good belch. She watched as

Bo stood up, and removed his t-shirt. The little prayer warriors inside began to march, and she needed it. She felt her breathing picking up as he walked out of the room and disappeared behind a wall. The carpeted stairs creaked as he made his way up to the second level this time using a different stair case.

"Go home Courtni," she encouraged herself before Bo returned wearing black hooping shorts and a wife beater.

He sat next to her and she swallowed the lump in her throat. "Have you told your parents about your pregnancy?" Bo asked and silenced her hormones.

"I told my grandmother, and she claimed she already knew since she had been dreaming about fish," Courtni let out a fake giggle.

"Why haven't you told your parents? They are going to find out eventually."

She chose her words carefully before she spoke since she has never discussed her parents with anyone but her family and friends. "My mother is deceased, and my dad is incarcerated for it."

"Aw man, I'm sorry. I didn't know," he said sympathetically.

"I know and it's ok. What about your parents?"

"My mother was upset with me for about an hour," he laughed, "and my step father just told me to man up, and handle my business like a man."

"Do you have any siblings?" Courtni asked.

"Yes, twin sisters, and you?" he said.

"Just an older brother," Courtni sat in somewhat of a trance, staring at Bo as he gazed into her eyes as if trying to read her thoughts.

"I just cannot figure you out," he said in a moderate tone, never breaking his gaze.

"I'm not complicated. I just have big dreams," Courtni said while continuing to lust over Bo's full lips.

"Big dreams are good," he said in somewhat of a whisper.

Courtni nodded her head calmly but her heart was about to beat out of her chest.

"Why do they call you Bo?" she asked in a soft voice.

"It's been my nickname since I was a kid," he whispered back.

"What's your real name?" she asked and his smile stretched across his face.

"Bartholomew David Mitchell," he waited for Courtni to break her silence and laugh which she did within a matter of seconds. "Oh, you're just going to laugh in my face?" He leaned forward and began to tickle Courtni as she tried to shield herself from his skilled fingers.

The tickling subsided and she found herself inches away from his face. His warm breath brushed the tip of her nose, and awoke her pussy as it released a deep throb.

She inhaled his scent and briefly closed her eyes trying to gather herself.

"One day, you are going to like me. Mark my words," his whisper returned.

"I lips you, I mean, I like you now," she corrected herself.

He finally went in for the kill. His full lips devoured hers, and the initial contact was so intense it felt as if her heart was beating through her walls. She closed her eyes as she allowed him to explore her mouth with his tongue. Her moans were uncontrollable as he placed his hands on the sides of her face. She could feel the warm suction from his lips with each deep peck and she wanted more.

This had to stop, she thought. Bo interrupted the kiss, but Courtni's lips were still puckered up with her mouth open.

"We can't do this," he whispered. "Cause it's not what you want, right?" he asked, looking for confirmation.

"Yes, because this is bad, right?" Courtni responded.

"For you it would be. You're a good girl," he said with their faces nearly touching.

"Yes, and good girls wait until they are married to willingly do things like this, right?"

"Uh huh," Bo mumbled. He licked his lips then stood up.

Courtni's eyes grew when she noticed the front of his shorts extended, and full of wide- awake Bo Jr. "Oh my Lord," she whispered.

Granted she has never been in a situation like this, but she has also never witnessed a bulge that massive. Her friend's testimony echoed in her head about how well-endowed he was down below, and now she had almost witnessed it for herself, and surprisingly she wanted to see more, but not so surprising she knew that she shouldn't.

"I brought you one of those bottled waters you like so much," Bo said as he returned to the great room.

She cracked open the water and gulped half of it down. "So is this what you do?" she asked.

He sat back down beside her, "What's that?"

"Bring women home, wine and dine them, then make your move," she asked.

"No, I've only brought one woman to my home," he said.

She tried looking at his face but her eyes kept going south, and he noticed. "Can I ask you a question?" he asked.

"Yup."

"Am I really the only man that you have been with?"

"Yes, I have no reason to lie."

"I don't think you are lying. It's just a rare occurrence in this day and age."

He sipped his water.

"Well, we still exist." Courtni said. "I'm not lying," she declared when she noticed him still staring at her.

"I know you are not, because you are afraid of me."

"I'm not afraid of you," Courtni tried to sound confident.

Bo smiled and placed his water on the end table. He put his forehead on hers, and she tried to look away before he acted as Calgon and took her away again.

"See, what I mean?" Bo said without moving.

She looked up at him, trying to stand her ground.

"You know, that pussy you walk around with every day is mine, right?" he said.

"You don't have possession over anything over here sir," Courtni stated, but his words turned her on.

"I'm the only man that has been in it, and that's my baby in there? Oh, that's my pussy and my name is written all over it," he said.

Courtni's pussy practically begged to be put out of its throbbing misery.

He slide down on his knees in front of Courtni, and rubbed his hands up and down the side of her thighs. "Damn, I wish I could remember that night," he said.

"Me too," Courtni thought to herself.

He placed both hands on her belly, and smiled. She was still in shock that this was not one of her many fantasies, and that a man was actually touching her.

He slid his hands around to her back, and began to place soft kisses on her stomach. His actions cause her to shy away, and attempt to suck her stomach in. She was self-conscious about her small pouch on a day to day basis, so to have this physically perfect man kiss it made her want to run, but he was so sensual with every move, and every peck that it eased her concerns and made her forget that she was supposed to be a good girl.

Bo reached for the bottom of her shirt and pulled it over her head. Her black razor back bra held her mounds firm against her body, but they lithely moved up and down as she tried to calm her nerves. He observed her goodness from the outside before unlatching her front fastening bra, and releasing her glorious hefty melons. He marveled over her with that sexy smile for what seemed like forever.

There she was sitting in a strange house with her girls just hanging free, and catching a breeze. She didn't know what to say or do as Bo sat in silence.

"Beautiful," he said. He took them both into his hands, and drew her dark chocolate nipple into his mouth.

Courtni moaned and placed her hands on the back of his head. She grabbed a handful of locks as he sucked her nipples until they stood rock hard at attention, and the pulsating between her legs began to emanate heat.

"Bo, please stop," Courtni moaned, and he did as told.

She wanted to slap herself.

He came to a stance, and she was now eye to eye with the monster that was trying to make its way out of his pants.

"You're not ready for that yet," Bo laughed when he caught her looking.

"I want to see it," she blurted out before she even realized that she spoke the words.

Without hesitation he lowered his shorts and exposed the

most stout, robust, beautifully constructed magic stick she could have ever imagined. Although she knew it was wrong, and she knew they shouldn't be in the midst of such raunchy activity she knew only the Lord could create something so glorious, and she wanted to thank him from the bottom of her heart, but under the circumstances she decided against it.

"Yes, you are definitely telling the truth," Bo said as he covered his best feature, and flopped back down beside her.

Courtni sat still on the couch with her big brown boobs still exposed, and eyes still staring in the spot in front of her that Bo once occupied. Could it be the hormones causing her to hunger for something she has never consciously had? Could it be her curiosity egging her on, and providing her with ammunition or could it be that her long awaited sexual exploit was at her fingertips, and the gentleman in her midst was even more salacious than the men she fantasized about? Either way she knew she couldn't go all the way. She wanted to be someone's wife, and this was not the way to achieve that. No sooner than she came to her conclusion Bo was up out of his seat, and in front of her fastening her bra as she watched him struggle to contain her ample amenities.

"As much as I want you I just can't do it," he said.

Her feelings were hurt, although she was going to turn him down it didn't feel good for him to do it to her. Was it her? Was she too much woman for his liking? She saw the way he looked at the girls hanging around his shop, and she was nothing like them.

"I should probably go now," Courtni's voice was back to its low state as she spoke to Bo who was at eye level on his knees still fighting with the hooks.

"Stay with me tonight," he said.

"I can't. I have work in the morning," she said. Now it was her that was confused. Did he like her or not?

"I do as well, so we'll get up early, I'll take you to your car, and I'll go my way," he said finally hooking the latch.

"I don't know. I have to get home." Courtni said.

"Come on, you can sleep in one of my shirts, we can order some movies, and I'll hook us up some ice cream sundaes, we can pick out baby names," he laughed.

Courtni wanted to say no, but her lips wouldn't form the word, and on the other hand she wanted to say yes, but she knew what would go down if she stayed.

Bo took her silence as a yes, and pulled her up from the couch, "You can pick out your own shirt," he said as he led the way up to his bedroom. They stood in front of his armoire and she picked up a white t-shirt that sat on top of the folded pile.

"Can I take a shower?" she asked.

"Of course," he said and pointed to the master bathroom over in the corner.

She showered and lathered herself with masculine body wash since there was no other soap around. Her eyes scanned the marble shower looking for any trace of a woman, but she found nothing. She stepped out and searched the cabinets for lotion.

"Yes," she said after bypassing all of the men's products and picking up a bottle of cocoa butter.

She dressed then opened the bathroom door and stepped into the cold room. Hesitant to roam his home she walked slowly towards the door, hoping he would walk through it. The hardwood floors were cold against the bottom of her feet as she walked down the hall peeping in all of the rooms. She heard music playing softly from a room at the end of the hall, and she took her finger to push the cracked door open. Her dirty thoughts came flooding back as she stood in the doorway watching Bo do pull ups shirtless on his home gym. He exhaled with every extension, as his muscles contracted and beads of sweat covered his back around his long dreads. He hopped down once he reached seventy five, and finally noticed Courtni standing there.

"Sorry, I had to get my workout in tonight since I will not be able to do it in the morning messing with you," he smiled and turned the radio off. "Do you feel better now?"

"Yes, but you are going to find a pair of extremely moistened underwear in your trash can. I tried to hide them under some tissue, but I'm sure you will still find them," Courtni shamefully admitted.

"You pissed your pants?" Bo smiled.

"No, I didn't piss my pants."

"Just kidding," he said still smiling. "I'm going to hop in the shower. Make yourself at home," he said, "Or better yet you can go down to the kitchen and pick out what flavor ice cream you want. I'll be right down," he said.

They sat at the island in the kitchen eating ice cream with sprinkles, peanuts, walnuts, chocolate syrup, and whipped cream surrounding them. He made her laugh constantly throughout the evening, and listened to her ramble about how much she loves her job, how hard she worked to get there, and where she wanted to go from her current position. She loved that he complimented her, and praised her for her hard work and success.

As she lay on her side in his California King bed, wrapped in his arms, she felt loved. She knew he didn't love her, and barely even knew her but this is the safest she has ever felt. He toyed with her fingers as he held them up, and measured them in front of his. She smiled knowing that this was going to end soon, but at least she would have the memory and experience to savor. The flat screen TV played as they lay intertwined asking silly questions, and poking fun at each other. She mentally bathed herself in his affection as she took comfort in his arms. Tears ran down her cheek and landed on his bicep without her knowing. He sat up and hovered over her concerned.

"What's wrong?" he asked.

"Nothing," she answered.

"Are you scared?"

"I'm happy," she said.

Bo smiled and resumed his position. He held Courtni tight, and never let her go as she drifted off to sleep. Her dreams were as sweet as the sundae she devoured before bed, and her heart was as full as her belly. She made sure to say a silent prayer just to say thank you.

The sound of birds chirping infringed upon the cool room, and woke Courtni from her slumber. She sat up to view Bo's alarm clock then laid her head back down once she saw that it was quarter past five in the morning. Bo was no longer beside her, and she wondered if he had left her there alone since he hadn't disclosed what time he had to be at work. She laid back and examined Bo's room with its large flat screen TV mounted on the wall and black bedroom furniture. It was very cozy, but she could tell that it hadn't been touched by a woman. The walls were bright white and his room was very tidy from wall to wall, but it was plain compared to the rest of his home.

"Rise and shine sleepy head," Bo said as he entered the room.

Courtni quickly wiped her face, and wished that she had taken the time to run some toothpaste through her mouth. Her twist out hairdo was sure to be flat and dull so she sat up and quickly fluffed her hair as Bo approached the bed.

He placed the tray of food in front of her and smiled that gorgeous smile again.

"See, I can cook," he said. "That's turkey bacon also, so don't freak out."

"Thank you," Courtni smiled. "I've never had breakfast in bed or a man cook for me." She said shyly.

"I'm just checking off your list of firsts, aren't I?"

"Yes, but I need for you to save something for my future husband."

"I'll see what I can do," Bo said.

He climbed in the middle of the bed next to Courtni and ate a piece of her bacon.

"I'm sorry, but are we supposed to share this food?" Courtni teased.

"I've never had turkey bacon. I got up early and made a quick run to Wal-Mart to get it," he said. "Oh, and I picked you up a toothbrush. You woke me up this morning with that morning breath," he laughed.

"Shut up," Courtni laughed, and nudged him playfully.

She ate her food, and Bo took the tray and placed it on the dresser.

"What time should we leave so that you're not late for work?" He asked as he stretched out next to Courtni, and flipped through the channels on the TV.

"I don't know. I try to get there by nine, but my first appointment isn't until ten." Courtni said as she lay back on the fluffy pillows.

Bo placed his hand on her stomach, and part of her wanted to push it away since she was doing so good being "good," but his touch stalled that progress. He rubbed her stomach as he watched the morning news. His eyes were on the TV but her eyes were on him. She looked at his muscular chest and arms then down to where his bulge rested, and wondered what it must have felt like to feel him inside of her. The pain she felt the day after the party was now understood. Certainly he would be more tentative to her needs and her body while sober, but that's something she would never know.

"What are you thinking about?" Bo asked as he sat the remote down, and turned his attention to Courtni.

"Nothing good," Courtni admitted.

"For you to be such a good girl, you sure do have a lot of bad thoughts."

"Well, you aren't exactly helping matters any," Courtni said.

"What can I do to help you?"

"I don't know maybe put on a shirt, a mask, and a pair of overalls."

He laughed, "But you don't like guys like me," he mocked Courtni, and she ate her words.

"Where is that toothbrush?" Courtni ignored Bo.

He pointed to the bathroom and she went in and closed the door. She washed her face, brushed her teeth, and fluffed her hair again. When she walked back into the room Bo was under the covers, and still into the morning news. He watched her as she walked around the bed to the other side.

"You said your mother used to love lady bugs, right?" Bo asked.

"Yes."

"Let me show you something," he said and Courtni followed him down the hall, through the lower level, and out of the back door that lead to a white deck. They stepped down the four steps of the deck and on to part of the freshly cut acres of land. He walked over to the small garden against the house with a small wooden bench facing the open land.

"My mother took over my back yard," Bo said. "She planted these because she says they attract lady bugs and lady bugs bring good luck," he pointed to the patch of Queen Anne Lace plants. "Maybe I can spot one for you," he said as he stooped down, and came back up with a little red bug with tiny black spots covering its back.

Courtni smiled as the bug crawled from Bo's hand onto hers. The gesture would be simple to many, but special to her. She moved her hands around as she watched the small insect maneuver its way around before flying away.

"I'm not going to cry," she willed herself, and took a seat on the tiny garden bench next to Bo. Her bare cheeks rested against the wood as she laid her head on his shoulder and stared down at their bare feet.

The August humidity was at a minimum and the sky was grey with heavy clouds hiding the bright sun. Bo allowed her to have her moment, and sat silently as she waved her feet back and forth over the blades of grass.

"Have you ever wanted something so bad or yearned for something so much that it consumed you?" Courtni asked, "You yearn for it because it's appealing, but it goes against everything you have been taught to believe, and everything you have worked so hard to stand for. It's as if the devil says, "How would you like a little temptation to go with those morals?" Courtni said.

"Unfortunately I haven't been very successful in practicing the morality my mother raised me with, like you have," Bo smiled.

She stood up and grabbed his hand, "This meant a lot to me. I've never told anyone about my mother, besides my friends, and it felt so good to talk about her last night. Thank you for listening." She stood in front of him teary eyed.

Bo pulled her towards him and she straddled him on the tiny bench. For a while he didn't say anything. He just allowed her tears to fall as he reached under Courtni's t-shirt and caressed her soft skin from her ass up to her shoulders. Courtni leaned her head back and closed her eyes as she took pleasure in his touch. At that moment she was on a high and he was her drug of choice, keeping her head spinning, heightening her delight, and creating a thrill she longed for.

He pulled the cotton t-shirt over her head exposing her glossy dark skin, and she looked him in his eyes ready to receive whatever he wanted to give as long as he kept elevating her. She leaned in closer and kissed his lips. Not caring if anyone saw them, and not thinking about the opening clouds above. His dick throbbed between her legs, and this time she didn't falter. Courtni reached down, and grabbed a handful of goods through his shorts. The clouds finally released its moisture and the morning rain began to fall. She wanted him bad, inside of her, on top of her, holding her, kissing her, and loving her until she literally couldn't take anymore.

Courtni relished in the moment, as she fed Bo a handful of brown tits. He welcomed them with his mouth open before she sat up and ran her hands across his rock hard six pack as he continued to caress her body. The rain washed away her inhibitions, and rolled down her back as she looked Bo in the eyes and he smiled that beautiful smile. What a way to start her day.

Chapter Fifteen

"Hi Auntie Lani."

"Lani, I'm such a slut," Courtni spoke through the Bluetooth system in Lani's car.

"Join the club sister," Lani said to Courtni.

"No, I can't believe I did that, and I loved it. I need to be saved again."

"Weren't you just saved again like two months ago?"

"Yes," Courtni answered.

"Is there like a limit or something, if so I'm sure you're pushing it," Lani joked.

"No there is no limit."

"Was it as wonderful as I dreamed it would be?"

"Why are you dreaming about Bo?" Courtni asked.

"Did I say dream? I meant thought," Lani laughed.

"It was magnificent, Lani."

"I can hear it in your voice," Lani smiled. "You have to fill me in at ladies night."

"I will, and pray for me Lani. I was on top and in control the whole time. There has to be a miniature tramp living inside of me and I'm surprised we didn't go any further than foreplay." Courtni said.

"Wait," Lani said. "You sat on top of that beautiful monster and didn't insert it?" Lani asked.

"I'll see you later."

"I want a freak in the mornin' a freak in the evenin' just like me," Lani began to sing Adina Howard's song in Courtni's ear.

"I'm disconnecting the call now," Courtni shouted, and the line fell silent.

Lani laughed as she pulled into her driveway, and grabbed her bags from the trunk. She rushed into her house, washed her hands, and began cutting cucumbers for the salad she was preparing for her guest. Usher's "Confessions" played from her phone's playlist as she placed her garlic bread in the oven, and prepared her chicken alfredo. She danced around the kitchen as she pulled her good china from the cabinet, and cleaned them by hand. She dried them off and placed them on the table before removing her garlic bread from the oven. Once everything was prepared and covered she jumped in the shower, and slipped on a pair of blue leggings and a white blouse. There was no need for her to get all dressed up in her own home. She heard the knocker beating against the door, and headed down the stairs. She was excited to see Jackson, but a little tired of seeing Maya. They hit it off and all, but the plan was for her to stay her ass home sometimes, and that has yet to happen.

"Coming," she said as she reached the bottom of the stairs. She opened the door and Jackson's handsome face greeted her, with a dozen red roses. Lani searched behind him for Maya, but unless she turned into Mrs. Steinberg she was not around.

"Aren't you missing someone?" Lani asked as Jackson embraced her and kissed her neck.

"The sitter canceled, and her parents are out of town," he smiled.

Lani wanted to jump for joy, but she managed to release a, "That's too bad" before hopping up in Jackson's arms. He carried her over to the couch, and tugged at her leggings. He wasted no time pushing her legs towards the back of the couch and planting his face between her legs. She pulled his face closer as his tongue went a little deeper and grinded her hips against his tongue. He sucked the tiny barbell into his mouth and inserted two fingers in Lani's now moist kitty. She assisted by bouncing slowly on his fingers.

"I have been thinking about being inside of you all day," Jackson said as he stood up.

He dropped his pants and stepped out of them then pulled Lani up from the couch, and picked her up. He entered her with one quick thrust and Lani did the rest. She wrapped her arms around his neck and bounced up and down on the dick until the penetration erected her nipples and excited her soul. She bounced and grind and bounced and grind while Jackson moaned and groaned, but Lani couldn't fully commit. One of the most annoying sounds known to her seemed to be right outside of her door, and ruining her naughty mood.

"I miss you so much," Jackson said.

"Shh," Lani said still bouncing, but covering Jackson's mouth with one hand. "Do you hear that?"

"Hear what," Jackson's voice was muffled under Lani's hand.

Lani looked at Jackson as if he had x-ray vision and could see through the door, but he was just as perplexed.

"I want daddy," a kid said from the other side of her door.

"Oh shit," Jackson said as he dropped Lani on the couch and hurried to get dressed.

"What the fuck is that?" Lani asked as if she wasn't familiar with a child's voice.

"Maya must have brought the kids over with her," he said trying to zip his pants without catching his erect penis in the zipper. "Come on babe, get dressed please," he pleaded with Lani.

She stood up and slowly replaced her pants. "I guess I'll call you later," Lani said with an attitude. The last thing that was going down was an Andrew's family gathering in Lani's home.

Jackson ignored her and opened the door.

"Daddy," the kids screamed.

"There go my babies," Jackson scooped them both up in his arms. "Hey baby, what are you doing here?" he asked Maya.

"Oh hell fuckin' no," Lani said to herself.

"I promised to be here and I didn't want to let you two down so I figured I'd bring the kids along. It's only a quick dinner right?" She said as she entered Lani's house.

"Yes, we were just about to eat," Jackson said.

"Hey Lani, you're looking good." Maya said as she walked over to Lani and hugged her tight.

Lani stood there trying to hold in her harsh words. She couldn't believe what was happening.

"Hi, Auntie Lani," the little girl said as Jackson put her down and she ran over to hug Lani's leg.

"What the fuck," Lani said.

"Oh, I told them we were going to visit their auntie Lani. I just didn't know how else to explain it," Maya said in Lani's ear.

How about keeping your ass home, Lani thought. She looked over at Jackson who was sitting on the couch with the little boy. She patted the little girl on top of the head and wished they would all go away including Jackson at that moment. The only rugrats that ran rampant in her home were her friend's children, and that was only because she had permission to correct them when they were wrong. She didn't care if she never met Jackson's children. The situation was weird to begin with, but bringing your children and having them call the woman that is fucking their father "Auntie," was just wrong, even for Lani's foul mindset.

Lani checked the time, and it was seven pm. She had ladies night over Jade's house tonight so she would feed them and rush them out of the door. Shit, they could wrap their food up and go for all she cared.

"Well the food is in the kitchen if you all are hungry," Lani said unenthused. "As a matter of fact I have to get going soon, so if you could make your food to go that would be great."

"Is everything ok?" Maya asked.

"Just peachy," Lani said with a forced smile.

"You seem upset, is it the kids?" Maya asked with a hint of a smirk on her face.

"You think?" Lani said smugly.

"I'm sorry, I guess I took the whole "one big family" thing a little too literal," Maya dropped her head.

Yeah bitch you did, Lani thought.

"Come on kids let's take your toys into the kitchen," Jackson said. "I'll be right back." He said to Maya and Lani.

The two of them stood in silence then Maya walked over to the couch and took a seat.

"Honey, you have to understand where Lani is coming from," Jackson said when he returned. "She doesn't have any children of her own, and you should have told us you were bringing the kids."

"I didn't want to miss anything, and from the looks of that hard on you had when you came to the door earlier I almost did." Maya said.

"Baby, listen," Jackson said, and Lani drowned the two

of them out as she listened to their kids run circles around her kitchen table.

The kid's giggles and laughs turned to screaming and banging their toys on her table. Maya was so caught up in her feelings that it didn't even faze her, and Jackson was too busy trying to soothe her insecurities.

"Look, obviously this little arrangement isn't going to work, so why don't we all just part ways," Lani said.

"Lani baby," Jackson looked worried.

"Lani, this was my idea. Please don't take it out on Jackson," Maya stood from the couch that Lani and Jackson were just getting busy on. "I'll make it up to you at our place. Just say the word, but you have to understand this is still my husband and I told you I wanted in on the activities."

"You are not comfortable with this like you told me you were," Lani said to Maya, "The reason you came here with your children is to cock block."

"What is that?" Maya asked.

"You came here to make sure that you didn't miss anything," Lani stared her down.

"Ok, so I'm still working on things," Maya admitted.

"You said that you were willing to give me and Jackson our alone time."

"I know what I said."

"Well, if you are going back on your word just let me know." Lani said.

"She's not going back on her word," Jackson jumped in. "Right sweetheart?" he asked Maya.

"No I'm not," she hung her head. "I'll make it up to you. What would you like for me to do?" Maya asked Lani with that smirk on her face.

"Right now, just leave," Lani said and held the door open for them.

They gathered the kids, and began to leave Lani's house, but Maya stopped and leaned in close to Lani.

"I am by no means a bitch, but I am however the head bitch in charge when it comes to my marriage and this arrangement. Now, I have told Jackson this and now I am telling you, the bond or whatever it is that you two share leaves me with an uneasy feeling so I am trying to work through that, I—"

"I don't really give a damn what your issues are right now Maya, and by the way the only bitch that has ever been in charge of Lani is Lani, so sleep on that," Lani said.

"I'm trying to help you understand that I want this to work."

"Bye Maya," Lani shut the door in her face.

She was beginning to regret this decision, but she really didn't want to leave Jackson in her past. Honestly, before their proposition came about she planned on giving Jackson the goods eventually, but the drama was not for her. If Maya was going to share she had to play nicely, and in Lani's opinion it shouldn't be hard. All she wanted was to be gripped up, flipped, and thrown like The Roots mentioned from time to time since she was slowly beginning to understand that she would have to settle for only a fraction of Jackson. Like, every woman she wanted more, but what was a gal to do when she was head over heels for a sumptuous doctor.

She packed up her food that was sure to go to waste, and her bottle of Belvedere then headed to Jade's house. The girls would surely gobble it down without a problem, and she would most certainly be early, but didn't want to be in her own home after Maya completely ruined her plans for a quick fuck session.

Putting all of that behind her she looked forward to spending time with her girls. They have not had the time to get together with all that has been going on, and she couldn't wait to get her drink on, and laugh until her sides hurt.

Lani pulled in Jade's driveway and parked next to Trent's Range Rover. She was a little surprised to see his vehicle, but she knew he had been working painstakingly to save his marriage. Lani stepped out of her car and noticed Jade sitting on the front step of their home. Her eyes stared straight ahead as she placed something up to her mouth and a blue light illuminated from the tip. Lani couldn't make out what it was through the lackluster Friday evening light.

Once near Jade she made out the electronic cigarette which confused her because Jade didn't smoke. "Why the hell are you smoking that?" Lani said.

"Why the hell are you so early?" Jade said still puffing on the cigarette.

"I have troubles in my life, and I didn't want to be at home." Lani said, and took a seat next to Jade.

"Do you want to hit this?" Jade asked trying to pass the fake cigarette to Lani, and they both laughed. "This is Trent's old cigarette he used to quit smoking. I found it in the cabinet, and now I think I'm addicted," she laughed.

"Well not anymore," Lani said. She snatched the cigarette out of her hand and placed it in her purse. "Speaking of Trent, I see his truck is here. Are you guys back together?"

"Do I look desperate?" Jade said.

"A little bit."

"Yeah, it was a bad time for me to ask that question. I do look a little rough right now," Jade laughed. "He came to get clothes. He comes here every day to get an outfit to wear instead of just packing all of his shit, and get this—he brings the other clothes back. This is his second time here today. He came to get the kids earlier and claimed he forgot his clothes."

"Quit playing, you know you like seeing him every day," Lani said and Jade tried to conceal her smile.

The door opened and Trent stepped out of the house carrying his clothes in his hand. Lani stood up to give him room to get by, but Jade didn't budge.

"Hey Lani," Trent said.

"Hi Trent," Lani replied.

"Jade, our anniversary is in two weeks," he stopped and turned to address Jade, "I would love to take my wife out for dinner."

"I would love a faithful husband," Jade replied as Lani nudged her shoulder.

"If you would let me explain—"

"Explain what Trent?"

"Everything," he stated.

Lani watched Jade as she sat staring at Trent. It was her first time seeing Jade in that light. She was always so tough, but the Jade that sat in front of her looked untenable and drained. Lani could tell her friend was very unhappy, and she felt for her.

"Bye Trent," Jade said.

"Think about it please," he said before walking away.

"Ok, we can go in the house now," Jade said as she stood up and Lani followed her into the house.

"You can't even stand to be in the house with him?" Lani asked.

"Not without wanting to fuck him," Jade said as she plopped down on the couch, "I don't know how Courtni does it."

"Courtni is barely doing it, trust me," Lani said. "She had a little caress fest this morning."

"Are you serious?"

"Yup, and if you want to give your husband the goods than do so."

"I can't do that," Jade said.

The doorbell rang, and Lani looked at Jade who was looking at her as if it was her home and her guests arriving.

"Don't move, let me get that," Lani said sneeringly.

"Works for me," Jade said. She got up and headed for the kitchen while Lani answered the door.

"Wow, you beat us here?" Courtni said to Lani as she and Ira walked into the house.

"I told you I was working on my punctuality."

"If you say so," Ira said.

"Hey gals," Jade reentered the room with food and snacks piled in her arms. She placed everything in the middle of the table, and the girls wasted no time washing their hands and digging in.

"So, what's going on with your legal issues Jade?" Lani asked as she dug into a plate of pasta.

"Well let's see," Jade said as she munched on a cookie, "I've paid four hundred dollars in fines and legal fees, twenty-five hundred to my lawyer, and now I'm a free woman."

"I hope you have learned your lesson," Courtni said.

"I hope you are going to come up off of the details to your freak fest," Jade replied.

"Thanks a lot Lani," Courtni rolled her eyes.

"What freak fest?" Ira said.

"It was not a freak fest. It was actually really special at that moment," Courtni replied.

"Come on, give me something. I need some sort of details. A chick is going through a drought," Jade said.

She went into details about her experience and had them all smitten with Bo's charm. Lani has always known that Courtni would be a handful for whomever was up for the challenge, but it was nice to see her smile.

"So, does this mean you two are together?" Ira asked.

"No, I don't know what it means besides I'm weak," Courtni frowned.

"In your defense, that man is fine with a capital F, a capital I, a capital N, and a capital E." Lani snapped her fingers.

"Yes, but I feel as if I have pushed my goal further away, and let's not forget he's not my type."

"You really need to let that go," Jade said.

"No, I will not just let it go Jade. It's bad enough I'm having a child out of wedlock, and that was the one thing I have been trying to avoid."

"There could be something there between you two. He seems very provisional and that is hard to find in a man." Ira said.

"The key word being "seems," he seems very provisional, and that could very well be skill, but I have to hand it to him, he got me," Courtni said, "I came to my senses well after the fact."

"I see you are still scared of the dick." Lani said, and Jade laughed.

"I'm not scared Lani. I'll admit he intimidates me a little, but he is so dapper, and captivating, and…," Courtni paused.

"Yummy?" Lani said.

"Yes, and I know now that he was playing me, but in that moment it was so nice to feel a man's touch, and the intimacy was unbelievable," Courtni reminisced.

"So why are you still saying he is not your type?" Ira asked.

"He's rough around the edges and that is out of my comfort zone. I don't like dreads, I can do without all of the muscles, and not to mention, he doesn't have a college degree and you all know how much I rant about having a backup plan," Courtni said.

"Ok, but I'm sure you rubbed your hands all over those muscles, grabbed a handful of those dreads while he was licking and sucking, and probably didn't even ask if he had a college degree," Lani said.

Courtni sat staring at the girls, "Touché," she confessed and sipped her water, "I didn't exactly ask about the degree, and yes he is so very fine, and I am a little attracted to him, but I think it's because he is the only guy I have ever gotten that close to," Courtni said.

"I think you are picking and trying to find something wrong because you think he is a player and you want to ditch him before he ditches you," Jade said.

"I think it would be wonderful if you two happen to develop a personal relationship that leads to marriage. Your child will benefit from it tremendously," Ira said.

"Let's put Ira's positivity aside for a second and tell me something," Lani said, "Did you touch it? Did you taste it? Did you stroke it? Did you caress it? Can I?" Lani asked.

"Lani," Ira shouted.

"Just joking…geez," Lani laughed and shook her head "no" at Jade playfully indicating she was serious.

"Why do you think he was playing you?" Ira asked.

"He is irresistible, and there is no way this man doesn't have a line full of women waiting for him to court them," Courtni said.

"That may be so, but he obviously likes you." Ira said.

"Yes, and you are going to push him away which would be a big mistake," Lani said.

"Why would it be a mistake? I am more than capable of taking care of my child without him, and as we all know, I do not need a man."

"If you want what you got this morning you do," Jade said.

"Although it was beautiful, I do not need it, and it was wrong." Courtni said, and they all sat and stared at her, again. "Ok, I want it. I want it right now as a matter of fact I want more than I received this morning." Courtni covered her face and they all laughed, "I'm passing the torch because I'm through talking about this. Lani what is going on with you? Have you been in contact with Jackson?"

"Hmm hmm," Lani mumbled with her mouth full of cake, "I'm in a relationship with him and his wife."

"WHAT," they all shouted.

"Excuse you," Jade said with a mug on her face.

Lani shared her crazy story as they sat with their mouths open listening in shock.

"So you are fine playing second fiddle?" Jade asked.

"I'm not playing second fiddle, and do you see this ring?" Lani said as she held her hand out.

"Yes, we see the ring," Ira said.

"I'm sorry but this is unacceptable Lani. Do you know how many fish are out there in the sea, and you are giving your precious goods to someone else's man," Courtni said.

"Yes, you have to end this Lani. It's sad and ridiculous and Jackson is a loser with a few degrees," Ira said.

"I've known you to do some pretty stupid shit, but this tops the list," Jade said. "Are you afraid to break it off with him? Give me your phone,"

"No Jade," Lani said as she pushed her purse behind her back. "Besides, I have everything Maya has, the house, the car, the ring, with exception to the children, which I can wait on."

"How exactly will that work? Does his wife know that you would like to have children someday?" Courtni asked.

"No, she doesn't."

"Do you think that will pose a problem?" Courtni asked.

"I'm not sure, but if it does I'll just get you drunk and voila," Lani joked and Courtni gave in and laughed along with the girls.

"That is not funny," Courtni said.

"I'm sorry, that was too soon," Lani said. "Right now, I'm just not ready to let Jackson go."

"Well, I can promise you, this will not last very long, and his wife needs her head examined," Ira said.

"I'm with Ira on this one. Sleeping alone every night while she is snuggled in her husband's arms seems a bit futile," Jade said.

"Right now I am sticking with it. We have a few kinks to work out, but we will be just fine," Lani said, "Now, I'm passing the torch to Ira. Ira what have you been up to?"

"No ma'am, pass that torch back to her Ira," Jade said referencing to the imaginary torch they spoke of, "Give me your phone."

"No Jade," Lani said as she pushed Jade's hand away from her purse. "I'm an adult and I make my decisions. I appreciate your concern, but I am just fine. Now Ira—

"Hmm," Ira looked up from her plate in shock as if she was not expecting to speak.

"What have you been up to?" Lani asked again.

Ira sipped her soda and swallowed her food. "Nothing much, I had a dream that I was with Naomi sexually, and I did some things with Jonathan, sexually."

"WHAT?" they all shouted again.

They looked at Courtni who once had the biggest crush on Jonathan, but Bo must have expunged that. Ira told her story and left them all in shock as well. She has embodied so much strength that it was hard for them to believe that she was slowly falling apart.

"So, you want to bump coochies with your nanny?" Jade asked.

"No, I don't want to bump—I can't even repeat that. Just know that it was just a silly dream, and nothing more," Ira said.

"You have to remain strong Ira, and sex is not the way to redemption. I have to continue to tell myself that as well," Courtni said.

"I know, and trust me I'm in a better place now. I'm moving forward with the adoption of Nicah, and that's a start," Ira said.

"Wow really?" Jade asked.

"Yes, I feel like it's the right thing to do, so I have to meet with her grandmother, and I guess I should actually talk to the child," Ira said.

"She is a sweetheart." Courtni said.

"Naomi says the same thing. Honestly I have been hanging around the restaurant to avoid being at home, and having to see her, and talk to her, and just be reminded of the betrayal. My heart is hurting, but it's still fully functional, and I know that she needs a home. I'm doing a lot of soul searching, so pray for me."

"Do you like Jonathan in that way?" Jade asked.

"I don't know," Ira replied, "I was so caught up in my feelings and he was there; he's always there, and I appreciate him more than he probably knows."

"Give that man a chance Ira," Lani said.

Ira smiled, "I can't do that."

"Why not? He's single and you're single," Jade said.

"Yes, but don't you think that would be a little awkward?" Ira asked.

"Not at all, and the two of you are parting ways business wise. Perfect timing," Lani said.

"You two are trying to get me into trouble," Ira laughed.

"We're just trying to help," Jade said with a grin on her face.

"Now back to Bo," Lani said.

"Lani stop," Jade laughed.

"I'm kidding, but I honestly hope you make things work for the three of you Court," Lani said.

"Maybe you can do something nice for him," Jade said.

"Honestly, I think we just complicated things today. I just want us to get on track and understand the reasoning behind us getting together in the first place, and that is to co-parent not to indulge in anything sexual," Courtni said.

"Courtni, what are you so afraid of? The man treated you like a lady the entire day. So what if he doesn't fit the image you have constructed over the years. Maybe the image you have constructed is inaccurate for your future husband," Jade said.

"I just don't see anything happening there. I believe he is a playboy and loves to woo women and is very good at what he does. You should have seen how he looked at those twigs hanging around his shop."

"Ok, I must get this off of my chest," Jade said. "I need for you to stop talking about yourself as if you're obese. You have big boobs and that's it."

"Jade, everyone doesn't have the privilege of being well endowed around the backside like you, ok?" Courtni said.

"True," Lani said.

"Agreed," Ira said.

"That scale read two hundred and five pounds yesterday, in front of him," Courtni shook her head.

"And you still turned him on," Jade replied.

"We are focusing on the wrong things here. The baby is what is important and I for one need to keep that in mind when I'm around him. I don't want to be attracted to him, but I am and it sucks," Courtni said.

"When do you plan on seeing him again?" Ira asked.

"Yes, when?" Lani said, and everyone looked in her direction, "Ok, that was last joke I swear," She laughed.

"I will see him in about a month and a half at my sonogram appointment."

"That is too long," Ira said, "Why don't you call him and invite him to church? If you want to build your lives on a solid foundation, whether it's together or just for your child, church is a good place to start."

"I guess I can ask, but I don't think he will be interested," Courtni said.

"You will never know until you ask," Lani said.

"While we are on the subject of church I think we should all go. The decisions we have been making individually have been terrible. Sometimes we just need to hear the "Word" to get us back on track. I have been slipping lately, and it's funny how I feel lost now," Courtni said.

"That works for me," Jade said.

"Me too," Ira added.

"I need it, so I'm willing to try to get up early on Sunday morning," Lani said.

"How about we attend the evening service to start with?" Courtni said.

"Now we are talking," Lani said.

"Jade, you should invite Trent," Courtni said.

"Courtni you should mind your business," Jade said then laughed at the expression on Courtni's face. She knew she was thinking of something fresh to say.

"I'm serious. It's time for you to talk to your husband," Courtni said.

"I know, but I'm not looking forward to it," Jade said.

"I can understand that, but right now your life is at a standstill and you have to have some sort of closure."

"I know you miss him," Ira said.

"Like crazy," Jade said as she pushed the cake crumbs around on her plate, "It's been hard to digest, and I do want to hear him out, but you all know how hard it is for me to keep my mouth shut."

"Try harder," Courtni said.

"Ok mother," Jade replied.

"It was a shock to us as well. Trent adores you and always has. I just don't understand," Ira said.

"I want you to talk to him before you make any decisions," Courtni said.

"I will."

"That applies to you as well Courtni. You need to talk to Bo and you need to bring me along with you," Lani said and Courtni tossed a cookie at her.

They all laughed, cried, and danced until the wee hours in the morning, which is just what Lani needed. She could have done without the scolding, but she knew they were coming from a good place. If they only knew what it was like to love Jackson they would understand her decision. Thankfully they were not as harsh as she had imagined, but they would come around once they noticed how successful her relationship turned out to be. Jackson satisfied her in every way imaginable, even with a wife. The way she saw things she actually had it better than Maya. She didn't have to cook him dinner every night; she didn't have to wash his clothes; she didn't have to care for his children; and she didn't have to deal with the malarkey that came along with marriage.

She checked over her shoulder as she switched lanes prepared to exit the highway. The heavy rain altered her vision, and generated a stop and go affect amongst the drivers. Lani wondered why the traffic was so heavy at three a.m. in the morning. She stopped at a traffic signal, reached for her radio to turn the station, and jolted forward as a loud crash resonated from behind her. Her car drifted forward and stopped once she applied the emergency brake. The impact was hard enough to cause her neck to jerk, but not hard enough for her air bag to deploy.

"What the hell?" Lani said as she looked behind her trying to see through the rain.

"Are you ok?" A male voice asked as he approached Lani's car with a flashlight.

"No, I am not ok," Lani snapped, "and get that light out of my face," she shouted as she stepped into the pouring rain to survey the damage.

"I'm so sorry, here take this," the man said as he took his jacket and draped it over Lani's shoulder.

She sat back in the car and dialed 911, then tried to move her car out of the path of traffic.

"Damn," she said when the car barely moved.

"You need to get out of the road," the man said, "Here take my keys. You can sit in my car."

She looked through the window at the man and really couldn't get a clear view of his face. The last thing she wanted to do was hop in a stranger's car. There were vehicles driving through the grass to get around her car and her common sense kicked in. She had to get out of the car before someone slammed into her again, so she hurried to dial Jackson's number, and prayed he would answer.

"Hello," Jackson picked up.

"Thank God you answered. I really need you to come and get me. I was just in a car accident."

"Are you ok?" Jackson asked.

"Yes, but please hurry. It's raining and my car is in the middle of the road," Lani insisted.

"Ok let me grab a pen so I can get your location."

She gave Jackson the information then bolted from her car to the side of the road with the man's jacket covering her head.

"This is some bullshit," She said out loud.

"You can sit in my car while we exchange information," the guy said as he approached Lani.

"No thank you. I have your tag number that should be good enough," she replied.

"Here you can have the keys," he held them out for Lani

to take. "I really cannot watch you stand here getting drenched, and that jacket is already soaked," he yelled through the rain.

She looked up at the man and the collected rain from the man's jacket began to drip down the front of her face. The man stepped under the bright LED street lamp, and his face was finally visible.

"I will stand out here if that will comfort you, but please get inside," he said.

Lani weighed her options and looked down at her phone. Her clothes were soaked and she had no place to stick her phone where it wouldn't get wet.

Lightning bolts illuminated the sky and thunder roared around her. She looked around for the authorities then her attention went back to the man one last time.

"Fine," she said and snatched the keys out of his hand.

She looked inside of the man's Cadillac before hopping in the driver's seat. He stood in front of his car on the phone. His clothes were soaked and the baseball cap that covered his head dripped water from its brim. Lani watched as the man placed his phone in his pants pocket, and leaned against the hood of the car. She looked around for flashing lights or any sign of Jackson.

"I think you should get in." Lani yelled over the loud thunder.

The man scurried over to the passenger's side of his own car and hopped in. He removed his cap and reached into the glove compartment for napkins.

"Thank you," he looked at Lani and the dim light hit his gray eyes. "I can't believe I don't have any damage to the front of my car," he said and Lani folded her arms.

"I'm really sorry about this. I didn't realize we were coming to a signal, and before I knew it I slammed into you," he said. "If you need a ride home or anywhere it's the least I can do."

"Oh no, my husband, I mean my boyfriend, I have someone coming to pick me up." Lani said.

He laughed, "Ok," he looked over at Lani and she turned her head.

This man was a cutie.

"Here is my information just in case you need to contact

me," he handed Lani a business card from the center console.

The bright flashing lights behind them caught their attention. They climbed out of the car and received an accident report as the tow truck loaded Lani's car on the bed.

She looked around for Jackson as the cop hopped back into his cruiser, and the guy took refuge in his car.

"Are you sure you don't need a ride?" he yelled.

"No, he is on the way," Lani replied.

"Ok, sweetheart, but I'm not leaving until he comes, so if you would like to take shelter—" he said as he pointed to his car.

Headlights rounded the bend and the Mercedes Benz emblem glistened as it passed under the street lamp.

"That's him," Lani said excited.

"Ok, you be safe, and keep the jacket," he said as he eyed Jackson's car as it passed by him.

"Thank you," she smiled, but the smile was quickly wiped from her face as she approached the passenger's side of Jackson's car and noticed Maya, then looked in the back seat and saw sleeping children.

"What the hell is this?" she said to herself while still standing out in the rain.

"Are you alright?" Maya asked as she rolled the window down.

"I could be better," Lani replied.

"Come on babe, get out of the rain," Jackson said from the driver's seat.

Lani looked back at the man that hit her and thought about taking her chances. The stranger sat in his car with the interior lights on and still on the phone. He briefly looked up at Lani through the windshield, and mouthed the word "sorry." She wanted to tell him he could make it up to her by driving her home, but that wouldn't be very smart of her so she sucked her teeth as she walk around the vehicle to the opposite side. She couldn't believe she was actually sitting in the back seat of her man's car with his children while his wife sat in the front. If this was any indication as to how things were going to be she wanted out, and hated to admit it but her friends were right.

"Now, what happened?" Jackson asked as they drove away.

Lani turned around to check for the driver one last time, and turned back around when she noticed he was still sitting on the side of the road. She couldn't imagine what thoughts crossed the man's mind when he saw Jackson's entire family pull up after describing him as her man. Her insides were boiling, and as they neared her home she wanted to tell him to let her out and keep going.

"I don't want to talk about it," Lani said as she stared out of the window. When they pulled into her driveway, her hands were on the door latch before the car was in park. She wanted to bolt as quickly as possible before spewing anger into their spotless Benz, and awaking their children that would surely address her as Auntie. She hightailed to her door step with Jackson on her heels.

"Lani, wait," he said as he grabbed her arm and spun her around.

"What the fuck are you two attached at the hip?" Lani said.

"She woke up when she heard the phone ringing and volunteered herself and the kids to come. I didn't have time to argue with her baby. I just wanted to get to you," Jackson said with his voice low so Maya wouldn't overhear him.

"I do not appreciate sitting in the backseat as if I am your child. I am not doing this Jackson, so you better get your shit under control."

"Or what," he asked, and surprised Lani. "Or you are going to leave me? You wouldn't do that would you?" he said and leaned forward to kiss Lani's neck. He grabbed her face and planted kisses on and around her lips. She was upset with him, but her pussy had already forgiven him.

"I'm not happy Jackson," she whispered.

"I know and I promise I will make it up to you, just you and I," he said. He kissed her deeply before heading back to his car. "I have to be at the office in two hours so I have to run. I love you," he said before going in for another kiss.

"I know of a really good chiropractor if you wake up a little stiff in the morning," Maya said from behind Jackson startling both of them.

She must take Lani for a fool. She knew damn well Maya
didn't give a damn about how she felt in the morning or any
other day for that matter. It was driving her absolutely crazy that
her husband was in love with another woman, and Lani could tell
she was slowly beginning to lose it.

"Good night," Lani said before placing her key in the
door and disappearing into her house.

She was disappointed in herself and the way she handled
the situation. Why hadn't she addressed Maya in the car? Why
hadn't she stood her ground in front of Jackson? Denial is a drug
and she was slowly coming to the realization that she was
becoming a fiend. She knew the reason why she couldn't address
Maya was because she had every right to be there. Lani just
didn't want to face the facts. How badly did she want Jackson
and how much would she put up with?

*****

"Wait a minute here," Jade said as she drove Lani down
Pratt Street towards the rental car building early the next
morning. "You sat your ass in the backseat with the kids? Were
you stuffed in between two car seats?" Jade got a good laugh at
Lani's expense.

"I really wish you would take this seriously Jade. What
am I going to do?" Lani asked.

"I don't know Lani, maybe stop seeing him or them or
whatever you have going on over there, and haul ass away from
them before you are completely in over your head."

"You don't understand. I have a doctor, a young
successful doctor, on my hands." Lani stated.

"Correction, Maya has a young successful doctor on her
hands. You have successful doctor residue on yours," Jade said.

"See, you are trying to be funny."

"No Lani I'm not. You cannot honestly believe that you
have anything with Jackson besides a sexual relationship. I know
right now it all seems good when you have the man and the
money without life's relationship additives, but you are failing to
see the bigger picture. That man belongs to someone else
whether you want to believe otherwise is your choice, but if

something happens to him today or tomorrow, if you are lucky Maya may eat your pussy, but that is about all you will receive," Jade said.

"So I guess you think I should leave him."

"I think you should do what is best for Lani," Jade said. "Which is leaving him,"

"I believe you should do what is best for Jade as well, and I believe what is best for Jade is to one, not worry about Lani, and two, talk to your husband," Lani placed her phone in her purse and gathered her papers.

"You obviously do not know Jade." Jade insisted.

"I don't know what all happened, and I do not know why Trent did what he did, but I do know that the man loves you Jade. I may not know what I have going on, but that point I do know. I'll call you later." Lani said as she hopped out of Jade's SUV.

She had a few decisions to make, but she was not sold on leaving Jackson. He had everything she wanted in a man, and who knows what will happen in the future. She would just play things by ear and see how well Jackson handles the situation. For now all she wanted to do was receive her rental car and head to her mother's house.

Chapter Sixteen

"Do you hate me?"

"Hello, how may I help you?" the receptionist at Grover Oak nursing home asked.

"I'm here to see Agatha Ridgley," Ira said.

"Certainly, I just need you to sign in here," she said as she handed Ira a clip board with a pen attached to it, "She is in room A102, and that is straight down the hall, make a right and she is in the first room on the left."

"Thank you," Ira said.

She headed down the hall with papers in hand and nerves rattling her thoughts. The uncertainty as to what Nicah's grandmother would reveal had her stomach turning, but she knew it was the only way to receive closure. In her hands were the adoption papers she received from her lawyer for Mrs. Agatha to sign. Although she was not completely moved by the adoption she knew it was the right thing to do. Her boys enjoyed having their sister around, and thankfully they were too young to ask questions. The only thing they wanted to know was whether she could stay.

Now that her boys approved of the situation it was time to face the music and handle the final details before moving forward.

"Hello, Mrs. Agatha I'm Ira Meadows," Ira said as she crept into the woman's room.

She looked as if she had seen a ghost as Dr. Phil played on the tiny TV screen she sat in front of. She wheeled her oxygen tank around to the side of her chair, and smiled at Ira.

"Hello dear," she said, "Have a seat."

The woman's bed squeaked as Ira sat down on the edge just inches away from Agatha.

"I'm so sorry my dear," she said. Her eyes watered as she spoke to Ira, "Are you here about my granddaughter or your husband?" she asked.

"Well, both actually, I don't know if you know this or not

but Nicah has been staying with me for a few weeks now," Ira said.

"Where is Camille?" she asked.

"I don't know ma'am. She dropped her off at my restaurant and told me she couldn't take care of her any more. I had no idea about her," Ira voice tapered off as she held back tears.

"I'm sorry," Mrs. Agatha placed her hand on Ira's, "My daughter and your husband where stationed together and that is how they met. She said they had a brief fling and Nicah resulted from it. He told her about you and his son I believe."

Ira nodded her head because her youngest son was not born yet.

"He told her that he would always be there for Nicah, but there would be nothing between the two of them and he was a man of his word," she said, "My daughter passed away only a few months after he did. I did the best I could to raise her, and then my health started to decline and I needed money to care for her, so I thought maybe Nicah was entitled to some of her father's money. I didn't mean for all of this to happen."

"It's not your fault. My husband who was supposed to love me did this," Ira said.

"Oh honey, he did. We all make mistakes and you do not need the anger and animosity eating up your insides." Mrs. Agatha said, "You have to forgive him and please forgive my daughter as well. She has always respected your marriage and would have never in a million years revealed Nicah to you unless it was Nick's doing," she released Ira's hand and dug into her bosom. She pulled out a folded picture of Nicah and looked at it proudly. "Oh I just know she is so happy to meet her brother," she smiled.

"I have two sons now," Ira said.

Mrs. Agatha laughed, "Oh she will have a good old time with them."

"I have these papers for you to sign. They are adoption papers, but if or when you get out of here, if you would like to have her back—"

"Oh no honey, I'm too old to be raising kids," she laughed. "I thank you for taking her in. I can't believe that

Camille just dropped her off like that," a frown covered her face.

"I'm trying to adjust, but it's not the easiest thing to do," Ira said.

"The Lord will help you with that. He knows your heart my dear. You know, I have always told my daughter that God doesn't make mistakes, and my granddaughter was no mistake, given the circumstances. Now I know why she is here, she was meant for you." she looked at Ira, and those words sent a chill through her body.

If she were meant for her then why didn't she bear her instead? Why was she trying to convince herself that adopting her was the right thing to do instead maybe going shopping and doing all of the things she wish she had a daughter to get into?

"I can't believe he never told me," Ira said.

"He would talk about you and your oldest son with Nicah all the time. He would show her pictures, and tell her that someday she was going to meet you. He sat on that floor playing blocks with her in my home and told her one day he was going to take her to his family's house and show her off," she smiled at the memory, "You are my baby's blessing, and I am very pleased to meet you, and I'm sorry it had to happen like this," she said to Ira.

The selfish side of her was thinking what about me, and how I feel and what I want, but she knew as an adult she had to take a back seat to a child.

"You will be blessed, dear. I know it is a hard pill to swallow, but you start by forgiving your late husband, and everything else will fall into place from there. I don't think I will make it out of here any time soon, so I will pray for you."

"Does she have any family besides you and her aunt?" Ira asked, partially because she thought she should ask, and also because she was so afraid of this child, and didn't know how to overcome it.

"No honey, it's just me and Camille. My husband passed away ten years ago, and I don't have any siblings. Please just get to know her, she is a really good little girl. I don't want my baby bouncing around from house to house. If you need me to watch her sometimes I will ask if she can stay here a few days a week."

"No no, I was just asking," Ira said, "Do you mind signing these?"

"Not at all dear, could you hand me my eye glasses off that table over there?" Mrs. Agatha gestured towards the end table next to her bed.

Ira turned around and reached for the glasses, but the military portrait of a woman on Mrs. Agatha's night stand caught her attention. Her eyes locked with the young woman, and she finally had a face for the woman that gave birth to her husband's child. She was beautiful and closely resembled Ira. Her mesmerizing eyes peered into Ira's spirit with her beautiful cheesy smile that compelled Ira to freeze in place.

All of a sudden, she was real. The situation was real, and there was no more running. This woman's child was now in Ira's care, and she herself was no longer among the living. The thought of this woman and Nick reunited in the afterlife while she was still here to care for their child crossed her mind.

"Her name was Lia," Mrs. Agatha said after browsing through the papers, "She was a good girl, and felt so bad for what she had done that she never contacted Nick. He always made contact with her for Nicah. She told me she wouldn't be able to live with herself if she broke up someone's marriage."

Ira wiped the tears that gathered in the corners of her eyes and grabbed Mrs. Agatha's glasses.

"If you need time to read over the papers, I can come back for them," Ira said. She wanted to get out of there quickly.

"No, I just need a pen," she said as she held the papers far away from her face. Ira reached in her purse and loaned her a pen.

"I know everyone around you is feeding you their opinions, including myself, but ultimately it is your choice. All I ask is that you make that choice with your heart."

"I have Mrs. Agatha, otherwise the hurt and pain would have prevented me from being here with you today."

She smiled at Ira, "You are a strong woman," she said as she handed Ira the papers.

"That's what I keep hearing," Ira said as she stood, "I haven't been fully briefed on the whole adoption, but I do know that it is a process, so I will be seeing you again Mrs. Agatha," Ira said.

"All right honey, and you take care of those babies. Please tell my baby girl I love her," she said as she held Ira's hand in her hers.

"I will."

"If it's no bother could you bring her to see me while I still have a little bit of strength left in me?" she chuckled.

"No problem. Maybe I can have her call you as well," Ira said.

"That would be great," Mrs. Agatha smiled.

"You take care," Ira said, and exited the room.

She drove home in silence thinking about what lie ahead of her and the giant leap she was taking. Her agenda was cleared for the day and she had plans on giving Naomi a break and spending time with the kids which is something she was still nervous about doing. It has been two weeks since the girl's night, but her friends encouraging words still lingered around, and came in handy when needed. Today would be one of those days for her.

She has managed to separate herself from Nicah every day, and the longest exchange she has had with her was about a snack, so she didn't know how things would go when she was alone with her. If all else failed, her back up plan was to run to Jade's for pastries with the children just so that she wouldn't have to be alone.

Her thoughts shifted as she drove the twenty-minute route back to her home. It was a blistering Monday afternoon, and she really didn't want to spend her time out in the heat at the park, but she promised the boys she would and surely they wouldn't forget; plus although Naomi has been making almost double what she was making before Nicah came along she knew she would like a break to actually spend the money she has earned.

They all could probably use a break, including the children. She has had a plate full of responsibilities to handle over the past couple of weeks, and yearned for the day when she felt as if she had everything under control. Her constant worry about the restaurant since Jonathan left has caused daily migraines, but everything was going well. He did a really good job training the once assistant manager for his position, but Ira didn't know how to relax when her problems carried over to her home as well.

"I'm home," said Ira.

"Mommy," her boys shouted, but didn't move as she walked into the living room.

They were all gathered on the floor watching cartoons as Naomi sat on the couch behind them. Nicah sat up staring at Ira as if waiting for her to personally address her as Ira tried her best to administer a greeting to the bright-eyed little girl that notably resembled her late husband.

"Hi," Ira contrived. It was hard for her to even look at the little girl without wanting to look away.

Nicah's face lit up as she smiled and waved at Ira.

"Are we ready to go to the park mommy?" her oldest son asked.

"Yes, as soon as you get your clothes on."

"Yay," they screamed and ran up the stairs.

"I'm already dressed." Nicah said. She stood up to show Ira her pink tutu and white Hello Kitty shirt.

Ira had given Naomi money to buy Nicah clothes since she didn't have much.

"Yes, I see," Ira said nicely.

"I'll help the boys get dressed," Naomi said and headed for the stairs.

"No, I can do it," Ira said when she realized that would leave her alone with Nicah.

"Nonsense, I have to get dress myself so I'll do it," she said and disappeared up the stairs.

Ira walked around the sofa that Nicah sat on prepared to sit on the love seat nearby, but she couldn't do it. She hurried out of the room and walked into the kitchen. This was harder than she thought it would be, and she would love some of that courage and strength that everyone claimed she possessed. She pulled a soda from the fridge and sat down on the bay window seat that over looked the back yard.

"Lord, help me," she said as she broke the seal on the canned soda.

"Can I bring Lucy?" Nicah's voice came as a surprise.

She was carrying a cabbage patch kid with yellow hair.

"Yes," Ira said, this time staring at the little girl who was inches away from her.

"Ok, because I love her."

Ira smiled at her innocence, but didn't know what to say to her.

"Do you hate me?" Nicah asked and made Ira instantly feel two feet tall.

"No, I would never hate you." Ira said.

"I saw you in my daddy's wallet."

"You did?" Ira asked, intrigued.

"Yes, he said you are his beautiful wife, and someday I was going to meet you, but I never saw him again, and I never really saw my mommy either, only grandma Aggie and Camille."

"He said that?"

"Yes, but he said it was not a good time so I had to wait." Nicah said, as she played with her doll's yarn hair.

"I'm sorry about your mommy, and your daddy," Ira said.

"They are in heaven with Jesus."

Ira smiled, "I know,"

"My auntie Camille said I have to be on my best behavior so you don't give me away, so I made my bed and I cleaned up my toys. I don't want you to give me away. I like your house. It has lots of pictures of daddy," she said.

Ira fought back tears. It was surreal to hear her call Nick her dad.

"I'm not going to give you away."

"Thank you," she said and hugged Ira around her waist, "Can I take a picture with you and little Nick, and Tij like this one?" she asked and pointed to the family portrait of them that hung on the fridge.

"Yes," Ira replied.

"How come you are not my mommy?"

Ira continued to stare at Nicah unable to answer her question, "I don't know," she managed.

"I'm going to be really good so I can stay with you forever and ever and ever."

Ira smiled, although nervous Nicah infectious personality made it a lot easier for her to relax.

"Come on mom," the boys said as they ran past Ira straight to the door and Nicah followed suit.

"I'm right behind you," Ira said.

They ran to the car excited to spend the day with their always busy mother. She listened to them all talk in the backseat, and laughed at their conversation. It was as if Nicah was always around. They played Simon Says over and over and over again, and each time Nicah was the winner. Her youngest son was a sore loser and threatened to quit so she watched in the rearview mirror as Nicah purposely defied Simon and allowed Tij to win. He was so excited and not once did Nicah rain on his parade in fact she celebrated with him.

"Yay, we are here." Ira said, exciting the children.

Once out of the car they raced to the playground with Tij lagging behind. It warmed her heart to see them so happy and her talk with Nicah helped to ease her fears. She never took into account the girl's feelings and the heartache she has experienced in her short amount of time on this earth thus far. She did not ask to be here and Ira did not ask to be placed in this situation, but for some reason God placed the two of them together so she had to make the best of it.

"Jonathan?" Ira said as she approached the bench where he sat.

"Ira, how are you?" he stood and gave Ira a hug.

"I'm living," she stated and sat next to him on the bench.

"Well, you look great doing it," he said.

"What are you doing here?"

"I'm here with my daughter," he said and pointed to a little girl playing in the sand with little braids and barrettes in her hair.

"You never told me you had a daughter?" Ira said.

"You never asked."

"Yes, but you also never mentioned her or her mother."

"Well our relationship has always been business related, and her mother is long gone." he said.

"Long gone as in deceased?" Ira asked.

"No, long gone as in the parenting thing was not for her," he said. "Those were her words, by the way."

"Oh, I'm sorry."

"Don't be, she will always have me as long as there is air in my lungs." he said and Ira smiled, "I see you are still up a child."

"I am, and I'm in the process of adopting her," Ira said and this time he was the one smiling.

"I knew you would," he smiled and his stare lingered.

"How is business?" Ira asked.

"It's coming along. How about you?"

"Doing good, but we miss you," Ira said.

"I planned on stopping by very soon. I just didn't think you wanted to see me."

"Listen Jonathan, you didn't do anything wrong. I have to work on myself, and my short comings. I wish what happened between us never did. Not because I didn't want it to, but because it made things rather aberrant between us, and that is not what I want. I was only thinking about myself and what I thought I needed. I was wrong and I do apologize. It has been so long since I have had companionship that I think I got a little carried away, but that is not me. I don't like who I have become, but I'm working on that." Ira said.

"I know who you are, and I know you were just looking for a stress reliever, but I was willing to be that if it meant putting a smile on your face, and that was wrong," he paused. "I guess there is no time like the present so I'm just going to take my chances, cross my fingers, and do things the right way," he said and turned to face Ira, "I know you have a lot going on and you probably do not have the time to squeeze me in, but if ever you need a break I would love to take you out sometime when you are ready, and if you would like to," Jonathan said nervously.

"I would like that," Ira said.

"Really," Jonathan asked surprised.

"You should probably close your mouth before bugs fly in." Ira smiled.

"I'm a happy man and there is no reason to hide it," Jonathan replied.

"Maybe we can get together with the kids so that I don't force you to do something to me like I did the last time," Ira laughed.

"We can do whatever it is you want to do, and just for the record, I didn't mind being forced to do that," he smiled.

"You are not helping my growth."

"I'm sorry," he laughed.

She sat next to Jonathan in silence watching the children play. A few times she glanced over at him to view the inadvertent smile he held on his face. Ira imagined he felt a sense of achievement since he has been fond of her for years. She surprised herself with her speedy reply and readiness. Her life was changing, so she would adjust accordingly. Slowly it was becoming clear to her that there was nothing wrong with enjoying a little male companionship as long as she conducted herself as a lady.

"We are going to head to Jade's bakery for some snacks. You two should join us if you don't have other plans. I'll drive." Ira said.

"We would like that," Jonathan said, "Noma, come on honey," he called to his daughter.

"Let's go kids," Ira called.

"This is Ms. Ira, Noma. We are going to get snacks with her and your new friends," Jonathan spoke to his daughter.

"Ok, Daddy,"

Ira watched Jonathan's daughter run to the car holding hands with Nicah. They looked like they were around the same age, and the wheels in Ira's head started to turn. If ever Nicah needed a play pal, she knew who to call.

Ira and Jonathan actually had a chance to talk over all the noise in Ira's SUV. The kids were having so much fun and she missed the time she used to spend with her boys. They were growing so fast and she was missing out by allowing her issues to consume her.

"So what do I do with a girl?" Ira asked.

"They are the best. They are helpful, sweet, silly, and they have a way of tugging at your heart with just one simple pout," Jonathan held up one finger.

"I'm so nervous around her," Ira whispered.

"Don't be. Just imagine how nervous she is. She just wants to be loved."

"I'm trying," Ira said.

"You are doing just fine, my queen."

Ira smiled. As much as that used to annoy her when he worked for her, she actually missed it, and it excited her to hear him say it.

"Do you think you can pull yourself away from the restaurant tomorrow evening?" Jonathan asked.

"I don't know, why do you ask?"

"I have tickets to see *The Lion King* at the Hippodrome. I was going to give them to my brother and his wife, but if you are free, I would much rather take you," he said as Ira pulled into the parking lot at Jade's Sweet Treats.

"I think I can manage to pull myself away," Ira said.

"Wow, you really are changing," Jonathan joked.

They entered the bakery and hurried to pull two of the small tables together before the people in line were finished with their purchases. Jade had a packed house on this humid afternoon and she was nowhere in sight.

They sat the kids down and went over their choices as they waited for the line to go down. Thankfully most of the customers were getting their pastries to go.

"What do we have here?" Jade asked as she snuck up on them.

"Hey Jade, we're just here for some fatty foods," Ira said, and Jade stared at her looking for an explanation as to why she was out with Jonathan.

"Hi Jonathan," Jade said.

"Hello Jade," Jonathan responded.

"Are you always this busy?" Ira asked.

"It depends, but today I have a few specials going on. You obviously didn't pay attention to the giant sign outside," Jade said.

"Nope, I don't need to when I eat for free." Ira smiled.

"I don't know this is a lot of free," Jade said as she circled the table with her finger.

"Don't worry Jade, I will take care of it," Jonathan said.

"She is just playing Jonathan," Ira said and tapped Jade's hand.

"Hey there honey child," Arnie said as he joined the group.

"Hi Arnie, long time no see," Ira said.

"What can I get y'all? I'll bring it over instead of you coming up to order." Arnie said.

"Thank you. That's more than what Jade would have done." Ira joked and placed their order.

"Ooo honey, who is that fine piece of chocolate Ira done brought in here?" she heard Arnie say as he walked away with Jade.

She got to see another side of Jonathan as they ate and laughed along with the kids. He left her wanting to discover more, and he even disclosed that he had twelve siblings that shocked the hell out of Ira. There was a lot they never discussed, and Ira felt as if she had neglected someone she considered a friend all of these years.

"Do you smell that?" Jonathan asked.

"Yeah smells like smoke. Jade must have burned something in the back."

Ira looked around and noticed other customers turning up their noses and looking for any sign of smoke. She could see light grey smoke through the tiny window on the swinging door to the kitchen, and suddenly the sprinklers erupted showering everyone in cold water.

Customers began to panic and chaos ensued within the dining area.

"You take the kids out to the truck, while I find Jade," Ira shouted to Jonathan as they gathered the children.

"No, you take them outside, and I'll check on Jade," Jonathan insisted.

"Everyone, please do not panic and exit the building promptly," Jade said as she and Arnie emerged from the back before Jonathan made his way back there.

They all exited the building drenched in water and confused as to what happened. Jonathan began to hustle Ira and the children towards the car, but Ira wouldn't budge.

"I have to check on Jade," she said.

"Ira, I'm fine. Take the kids and go," Jade said from behind them.

Ira watched her friend tend to customers as Jonathan pulled her away, and sirens blared all around them. Even in all the commotion, the kids were unfazed. They cheered the firefighters on as Ira drove off feeling uneasy and worried about her friend's establishment.

Chapter Seventeen

"You know you are more trouble than you are worth."

"Lord, I'm gonna have a heart attack. What the hell is going on?" Arnie said. He had one hand on his hip and the other on his head.

"Do you need to see the medic?" Jade asked.

"No boo, I need to see the bar," he said, "Are you ok?"

"Yes, I'm fine. I'm just glad no one was injured," Jade said as she and Arnie stood across the street waiting for the firefighters to inform them of their findings.

She looked around at all of the onlookers and prayed that her bakery did not have a significant amount of damage. While in the back, she and Arnie couldn't figure out where the smoke came from. After turning all of the ovens off, the smoke escalated and filled the kitchen quickly. This was a strange occurrence and she wanted to know what happened and how to prevent it from happening again.

The firefighters began to migrate towards their trucks and round up their equipment, so Jade stood anxiously waiting to speak to someone and permission to enter the building.

"Are you the owner?" A firefighter asked as he approached Jade and Arnie.

"Yes, I mean she is," Arnie said pointing to Jade.

"Well this was your problem," he said as he held up a plastic bag with what looked like a can of spray in it.

"That isn't mine. What is that?" Jade asked.

"It seems that someone removed the screening from a vent outside, and placed this smoke bomb in it and sealed the vent. That explains why the smoke filled the room so quickly with no fire," he explained.

"What, who would do that?" Jade said.

"Some little young fools that's who and they better find them before I do because I beat kids too, and you can write that down officer," Arnie said.

"I'm actually a firefighter," he said.

"Well tell somebody to tell somebody that knows a cop that I'll whip a kid's ass," Arnie rolled his eyes.

"Ok, well, we have a witness giving the police a statement right now," he pointed to the cops that were standing over by Gerald, the homeless man. "From what I have gathered, the assailant was not a minor. Apparently it was a woman and she acted alone. You will learn more from the officer, but as far as your business, there is no damage, and we replaced the screen. It's a little smoky, but you can reenter now."

"Thank you," Jade said.

She was fuming and she had a feeling that she knew the perpetrator. Why was she still insisting on being a nuisance and disturbing her business? Now it was time for Jade to do some damage control, and try her best to stay out of prison. She really didn't need the added drama or legal issues if things escalated.

"You see, I done told you to let me sick Mooky and them on that heifer now look, you got this hussy on yo ass. I see I'm gonna have to take care of this myself 'cause you don't know how to be discrete and stay yo ass out of jail," Arnie said.

They splashed in water as they walked around the bakery. The clean-up would take hours, which infuriated Jade even more. She sat in one of the wet chairs and held her head in her hands. Angry that she was losing more money and pissed because she had no way of getting her hands on whomever did this, although she was pretty sure Tamra had something to do with it.

Arnie came from the back with a mop and bucket and tried to clean up the massive amount of water that covered the floor.

"Don't worry boo, we gon' get this place cleaned up, and we'll be back in action by Monday morning. If I see that wench I'm calling Mooky on the spot, but I still want to know what the hell her problem is. I mean, she is the scallywag not you," he said as he tried his best to mop the floor.

"That makes two of us and there is no need in trying to mop this water. I'm going to have to rent a wet vac," Jade said.

"Do you think the jump-off is going to try something at your home?" Arnie said as he sat across from Jade.

"Arnie if she does, she better pray her ass has nine lives."

The thought never crossed her mind, but he may be on to something. "I'm also not sure why she's plotting against me and not Trent. He's the one that fucked her not me."

"Hmm, well let me see, "Arnie said as he crossed his legs and looked towards the ceiling. "You have a fine ass husband, he's established, pretty wealthy, and she had all of that in her grasp, but just like that," he snapped his fingers, "It's gone. He uses her for what he wants and goes back home to his beautiful wife that he loves and spoils, while she rots in her tiny ass apartment. Now call me crazy, but if I were bitter, I would hate yo' ass too. You females are famous for hating each other when you should be hopping on another dick. In her case, the dick may be a downgrade, but still—"

"I don't know what to think, but I cannot afford to get in to any more legal trouble," Jade said.

"—and that's why I said I got you boo," Arnie said.

"Do you think I should call Trent? He may have some answers for me."

"Honey the only reason you want to call Trent is because you want him to put out that fire between yo legs. Shoot, you aint foolin' nobody, we all know you ain't gettin' none," Arnie said and Jade laughed.

He was partially correct, but she really did want to know whether he had any idea as to why Ms. Darkskn21 continued to make her presence known.

Jade received her report from the officers and went to rent a couple of wet vacs from the hardware store. They spent the remainder of the evening cleaning up water and airing out the bakery. She was thankful there was no damage and could rest a little easier tonight. Another awful thought came to mind as she and Arnie walked to their vehicles.

"Do you think Trent has other hoes?" Jade asked.

"Oh no boo," Arnie said as he put his bag in the back seat of his car. "He couldn't even handle one right," he laughed, "She wants to fuck your life up for one reason and one reason only, and that's because she saw something she wanted. She went after it and failed honey. You know a good man is a hot commodity. I know it's not 1999 anymore, but bitches still don't want no scrubs." Arnie said. "Let me check yo' tires." He did a quick circle around Jade's vehicle, "You're good."

"Thank you again for always being there," Jade said.

"I wouldn't have it any other way my big booty beauty," Arnie laughed.

Once in their vehicles Jade waved at Arnie, and he began to back out of the spot. She was glad it was the weekend and she was not on mommy duty. Her poor back was aching and her Jacuzzi bathtub was calling her name.

Her eyes almost popped out of her head and her anger returned. She glared through the windshield as her chest heaved and she tried to calm herself. Could this day get any worse? After placing her car in park, she unfastened her seat belt and hopped down out of her truck. She had to reframe from leaping forward and annihilating the figure that stood in front of her.

"You know you are more trouble than you are worth," Jade said with an attitude.

"I don't want any trouble," Tamra said. She put her hands up as she backed away from the hood of Jade's truck.

"Why the fuck are you here? Did you have something to do with this?" Jade pointed towards her bakery. She was slowly walking towards Tamra as she backed away from Jade. When Tamra dropped her head she had her answer. "You're a bold little bitch, but once again—"

"No wait," Tamra cut Jade off, "I'm through playing these games. If you just leave Trent alone all of this will stop."

"Let me think about that," Jade said sarcastically. She must have lost her damn mind. Jade could tell she was visibly afraid, but yet she was trying her best to intimidate her. She may be diabolical and devilish, but she didn't have an ounce of fight in her.

"Look, I wanted to get you back for what you did at my job. Obviously if I wanted to do any damage I would have set the place on fire or something like that," she said.

"And I would have set your ass ablaze," Jade said. "I'm not going to sit around and allow you to destroy my business like you have my life, so mark my words you better sleep with one eye open."

"No please listen, I have a proposition for you," Tamra said. "If you leave, I will not bother you again. All I want is

Trent. You obviously do not need him."

Jade laughed at her proposition and she could see that it angered Tamra, "Silly rabbit tricks are for kids," Jade said as she moved a little closer to Tamra, but she continued to back away. "Was that you that came into my bakery with the shades on?" Jade asked and Tamra nodded her head yes. "You know all of this energy you are putting into me, you need to put it into teaching yourself some fucking morals."

"I don't need morals, I need your husband," she said and Jade continued to laugh, "If you would just unclench your fist and listen to me, just for a minute we could talk woman to woman. I have to get this off of my chest."

"I would use that word lightly if I were you," Jade folded her arms. "Talk," Jade decided to entertain Tamra before she walked away because she was not spending any more of her time behind bars for whipping her ass.

"When I first met Trent I knew that he was married and I still pursued him."

"Ok, I've heard enough," Jade said.

"No listen," Tamra said, "I met this handsome successful man and from there I was hooked. I made it my mission to get as much information about him as I could and to see to it that he would leave you for me. Whenever I had to contact him about business I would make advances. One day I ran into him at lunch and I sat with him and we talked. I tried to convince him that I would be a good investment, but he would only laugh and mention his wife. I don't know what happened, but one day he came around and we started talking through emails. After months of this, I finally got him to come to my home," she paused. "You have to understand I have been fed this information my whole life. If you see something worth having you better go for it no matter who or what is in your way." Tamra made her confession in a pleading voice.

"If you are looking for sympathy, you are barking up the wrong tree," Jade said.

"I'm not, I'm looking for you to do the right thing and allow us to be together. Can't you see that you are the reason why he wants nothing to do with me?" Tamra said. "There was a video on that flash drive of him in my bed."

"Yes bitch I know," Jade stopped laughing.

"Yes, but what you don't know is that we didn't get a chance to make love," she said and Jade stood there confused. "He wouldn't, he couldn't," Tamra paused and Jade wanted to tell her to spit it out. "He couldn't get it up and he didn't want me to help." she said.

"Oh really, that's a first," Jade said.

"I kept asking him what was wrong and if it was me, but he said it was due to exhaustion. I knew the problem was that it was me next to him and not you and that infuriated me. He made a couple of jokes and tried to make me feel better. He fed me a bunch of lies then dozed off to sleep for about an hour then left. The next day he told me that he couldn't see me anymore, and that this was all just a joke that had gone too far. Everything was a lie."

"So you have never had sex with him?" Jade said.

"Not yet," Tamra answered, "I was crushed and I couldn't believe that I was a joke to him. After that talk he treated me as if I was just a business associate and acted like there was never anything between us. I tried my luck again and he told me he was sorry but he loved his wife and his family. I didn't take that too well and I went on this rant about wanting to see you, and wanting to know what it was that you possessed that I didn't, and he told me to stay away from you, but he doesn't understand I should have all of the things that you have, so you are officially my problem."

"You're fucking crazy little girl," Jade said.

"I am far from crazy, and for the record, I felt like shit watching those kids run from your bakery," she paused, "Just leave him alone," Tamra shouted and slammed her hand on the car she was shielding herself behind.

Jade stood unfazed and looking at Tamra like she had a third eye in the middle of her forehead. "If you so much as think about fuckin' with me or my family again I will gladly receive another charge for stomping a hole in your ass."

Tears rolled down Tamra's face as she pulled at the loose hairs that fell from her ponytail. "I can't do this anymore," she whined, "I need him, I have lost everything, my house, my car, my job thanks to you and even my best friend that you tased," she wiped her tears, "We didn't even get a chance to do any of the things a man that loves a woman does. He wants to be with me no matter what he says, he just doesn't want to upset you, so just leave."

"I'll tell you what," Jade said as she headed back to the driver's side of her truck. "I'll do that when hell freezes over, unfreeze, and freeze over again then maybe I will think about it, but until then you may as well have a seat with everyone else that's waiting for me to give a fuck."

"I need him," Tamra made one last plea.

"Go play little girl," Jade said as she opened her driver's side door. "Oh, and if you want to play, we can play, and I will find you."

"I just want a chance to be with him," Tamra cried.

"Well that's too bad, maybe you should go a little further downtown and try to snag you a wealthy businessman with your psychotic ass," Jade hopped into her truck and shook her head at Tamra's desperation. It seemed as if Jade could see her contemplating as calmness came over her and she rushed to her vehicle.

Jade kept her eyes on Tamra as she hopped into an older model Buick with handicap tags, and figured it must have been her parents or grandparents. She made a mental note of the vehicle just in case Tamra decided she wanted to act a fool again.

Her home looked like pure euphoria as she pulled into the garage. She entered her home and kicked off her wet flats then stripped on her way up the stairs. The warm water soothed her back, but not her disposition. Her hectic day was weighing heavy on her mind along with her conversation with MsDarkskn21. She was happy to learn that Trent hadn't been sexually active with Tamra, but he was still unfaithful. There was absolutely no reason for any married man to be in another woman's bed, and the game scenario was simply a façade. It was something he told himself to cover the truth, which she felt was that he was not happy. His change of heart was still up in the air. She couldn't figure out why he didn't go all the way with her, and why he begged her to let him come home every other day. It could possibly be because of all they have invested, but if they had split, Trent would still be pretty well off and wouldn't miss a meal.

She moisturized her body and walked freely out of the bathroom naked. This was one of the joys of being home alone. Her round ass jiggled as she made her way down the stairs to the kitchen. She stopped when she turned the corner and saw Trent searching the fridge. His loosened tie dangled low and the belt to his tailored suit was unbuckled. She hated that she couldn't tell him to get lost without him stating, "This is my home as well," but damn did he look good. This was the perfect time for her to release some tension and do a little teasing in the process.

"Where are my children?" Jade asked, and Trent turned his attention to the living room.

His eyes scanned Jade's naked body. "Our children are with my mother," he said with his eyes still on Jade.

"Why are you not with them?"

"I had a meeting. We just received a new account," he said.

"Why are you here?"

"I just wanted to chill for a second in my own home," he said.

"I guess I'm just supposed to chill with you as if everything is good?"

"I wish you would talk to me so we can begin to move forward."

She ignored Trent and turned to walk back up the stairs. He let out an "Mmm" when he laid eyes on his favorite part of his wife's body.

"When are you leaving?" Jade asked from the stairs, but he didn't answer.

She went into the bedroom to search the closet for her an accessory she could have fun with. After five minutes of digging in a box at the back of the walk in closet she made her way back down the stairs. Her body was freezing from the cool central air that filled her home, but she refused to put on any clothes until her mission was accomplished.

"Do you miss your girlfriend?" Jade asked as she made her way around the couch where Trent sat watching sports highlights.

"No, and she wasn't my girlfriend, so could you please stop saying that?" Trent said.

"Do you miss me?" Jade asked.

"Of course," he said. He brushed his hands together to rid them of the salt from his chips.

"Why did you step outside of your marriage?" Jade asked still standing in front of him.

"I don't know, I have been asking myself that question for a while now, but baby—," he reached out to touch Jade's hand and she whacked him with the black leather whip she had behind her back. "—Ouch, Jade what the fuck?" Trent shouted.

"You are naughty boy Trent," Jade said in a seductive voice, "but for some reason I still want to fuck your brains out," she said.

Trent turned his frown upside down and scooted towards the edge of the chair, "Baby I miss you so much," he reached out again.

The whip made contact and stung Trent's shoulder.

"Got dammit Jade," he shouted and tried to reach for the whip.

"Uh, uh, uh," Jade said waving her finger, "Do not touch the whip. You are a bad boy. Are you telling me you can't take a little whipping?" Jade said and swung the whip again.

"Ah," and again.

"Ah," and again.

"Ah, give me that damn whip," Trent said.

He wrapped his hand around the shingled material and pull Jade closer to him, "I love you Jade."

"I don't feel like you do," Jade stated

"Tell me what you want me to do and I'll do it."

"Eat my pussy," she whispered in his ear.

Jade climbed onto the couch as Trent leaned back and rested his head on top of the chair. She lowered herself down onto his awaiting tongue and her body shuddered from his touch. It's been so long since she has felt her husband's touch and her body begged for it. She grabbed the back of his head and slid her goods up and down his face. Her body began to warm and her pace quickened, but her thoughts alternated between loving her husband and her husband's infidelity.

Trent gripped her ass with both hands and worked his magic with his tongue. He flicked his tongue around, and sucked her clitoris into his mouth causing it to grow and emerged from under its hood, full and ready for more erotic stimulation that will lead to a delightful combustion. He knew his wife's body better than she did and at the moment she hated him for it. She was losing control of her sensibility and wanted to scream out in sweet delirium. Her body was leading the way as her pussy coated Trent's face with her sweet nectar. Her tears finally made its way outside of her body as Trent unfastened his slacks and slid them down to the floor.

He pulled Jade by her hips onto his hard dick and it pulsated as she squeezed her muscles on the way down. She took her time riding him slow and hard, as he kissed his wife's tears away.

"I'm so sorry baby," he said as he held Jade tight.

"I loved you Trent," Jade said.

"Don't stop loving me please," he said.

She extended her body to the top of his head, and began a pulsing motion with her PC muscle while sliding down slowly. Trent gripped her ass and sucked his wife's neck with a strong force trying to direct his attention away from her skill. She missed her husband, but was still unable to trust him. She didn't want another man when he was the only one that knew her as well as he did. The fact of the matter is if he wanted this to be over right at this moment, it would be. He knew exactly how to bring his wife to an uncontrollable orgasm in any position.

Trent grabbed two hands full of ass and grinded underneath Jade as she bucked hard and fast on top of him. He threw his head back and closed his eyes tight.

"Are you about to cum?" Jade asked, "Tell me you are about to cum?"

"Yes, baby I'm about to cum," he said through tight lips.

"Are you cummin'?" Jade asked.

"Almost there baby," Trent mustered.

"Now," Jade asked while still bucking.

"Yes," Trent grunted and Jade hopped up just before he reached his big "O."

"What the fuck? Why did you stop?" Trent asked while

jerking himself trying not to lose the feeling. He was in a panic as if Jade had gobbled up his entire dick with her pussy and walked away with it.

"I'm not quite over the fact that you fucked around." Jade said as she bounced her ass towards the stairs.

Trent stood from the couch looking confused. "Then what was this?" he said pointing to his still erect penis.

In all honesty she wanted to hop back on that bad boy as she looked down at it glistening with her juices still covering it.

"I wanted to fuck," Jade said plainly.

"That's it? Can I come home?" Trent asked.

"No," Jade said as she made her way up the stairs.

"Come on now Jade." Trent pulled his slacks up and rushed to the bottom of the stairs. "Can you at least do me one favor?" He asked and Jade turned around.

"What?"

"Will you go to marriage counseling with me? I'm not willing to just let this go. I fucked up and I just want to make it right Jade. Don't give up on me," he pleaded.

"We'll talk," Jade said, and turned towards the bedroom when a smile grew on Trent's face.

She shut the door and reached in her nightstand for her magic bullet vibrator. It did the trick quickly since Trent got her halfway there. Tomorrow, she was meeting the girls for church and hopefully that would help her start the healing process. She had to forgive her husband or simply let her marriage go, which at this point was unfathomable. Forgiveness is a step-by-step process and she was ready to start mending her marriage.

Chapter Eighteen

"Saints pray for me."

"You have to stop by and say hello," Lani said.

"I cannot just drop by his home unannounced, besides I said I think he lives in this area," Courtni said.

"Well, if something familiar catches your eye, you better tell me."

"Oh please, you just want to see him," Courtni said.

"That may be true, but you don't want to see him? You talk about him all the time, and the one day the two of you spent together was the best damn day of your life," Lani said.

"Says who Lani?"

"Says me, the chick that has known you your whole life, besides when is the last time you spoke to him?"

"He has left a few messages with my secretary," Courtni said.

"That was not the question."

"I haven't talked to him since that day."

"What," Lani shouted and looked over at Courtni.

"Keep your eyes on the road Lani. I hate it when you do that," Courtni said. She adjusted the seatbelt around her now protruding baby bump, "I'm supposed to see him next week at my ultrasound appointment."

"Why haven't you called him back?"

"I don't know, I'm trying to focus on what's important and that's the baby. The baby isn't here yet, so I have no reason to call."

"You're afraid he's going to fuck the shit out of you aren't you?" Lani asked.

"No, I'm afraid he's going to use me up, and toss me aside, so I think it will be best if I limited my contact with him," Courtni said.

She was glad that Lani volunteered to keep her company at the seminar this morning, but her bugging was beginning to annoy her. Although she wouldn't admit it she would love to see

Bo again, but she was holding strong and haven't contacted him even when the urge was strong. The only problem was that didn't stop him from invading her thoughts and dreams every day and night.

"Someday you are going to be honest with yourself," Lani said.

"Oh wow, that's the antique shop we passed," Courtni said.

"Which way, left or right," Lani said enthused, as they reached the intersection. She slowed down waiting to signal, "Which way Courtni," she rushed.

"Right," Courtni blurted out.

She reminisced as Lani drove down Bo's rustic road, except this time, things were a little different. The sun wasn't as bright and the October air was chilly enough for her to wear a thin cardigan. Her heart sank as they approached Bo's beautiful home.

"Lani, it's kind of early, maybe we should come back some other time," Courtni said.

"There's no time like the present," Lani said.

Courtni huffed, "It's the next house on the left."

"This is beautiful," Lani said as she pulled into Bo's driveway. "Are you going to go and knock on the door or sit here and marvel over his home with me?"

"I'm going," Courtni said. She unfastened her seatbelt, "How do I look?"

"Pregnant," Lani said.

"You're no help," Courtni stepped out and closed the door.

She tapped lightly on Bo's door and straightened her clothes as she waited for him to answer.

"He's not home," Courtni turned to yell at Lani.

"Good morning," a voice surprised her as she stood on Bo's steps.

"Oh hello," Courtni said, "I'm sorry I was looking for Bo," she said to the angelic older woman with her graying hair pulled back into a bun. Now she really wanted to turn around and run.

"He hasn't made it home yet. I have been housesitting for

him while he's out of town, and tearing the garden apart," she held up the trowel in her hand.

"Ok, thank you," Courtni said and turned to walk away.

"Are you the young woman carrying my grandbaby?" The woman asked, and Courtni turned back around.

"Yes ma'am," she dropped her head.

"I'm Dena, Bo's mother," she extended her hand.

"I'm Courtni,"

"Nice to meet you Courtni and this must be my little angel," she said as she placed one hand on Courtni's belly, "I'm glad you stopped by. Bo said he hasn't heard from you in weeks and you weren't answering his phone calls. I hope everything is well with you and the baby." She looked at Courtni genuinely concerned.

"Yes, I've just been a little busy," Courtni said.

"I understand," she said, "Well where are my manners? Would you like to come in? Bo should be home soon."

"No ma'am, I have my friend waiting for me in the car," Courtni pointed in Lani's direction.

"Well, it was nice to meet you," Dena said.

"Likewise," Courtni smiled and tried to walk normally since her nerves made her want to jog to Lani's car.

Midway there a black Infinity M45 pulled behind Lani blocking her in. Bo emerged from the passenger's side and a tall, shapely woman wearing shades with a mediocre weave emerged from the driver's side. Courtni wanted to disappear in that instance and wished she would have never bothered coming to Bo's house. She picked up her pace trying to reach Lani's car before Bo reached her.

"Looks like I arrived just in time," Bo said with a smile on his face.

Courtni came face to face with him before she could open Lani's car door.

"Excuse me," she said trying to get around him.

"What's wrong?" Bo asked.

"Are you kidding me?" Courtni shouted. She looked over at the woman who was now standing near Bo's mother on his porch. "Just move out of my way Bo, please."

"What could I possibly have done now when I haven't even been around?"

"Why did you do all the things you did with me if you had a girlfriend?" Courtni asked.

"I don't have a girlfriend," he said.

"Well, whatever she is," Courtni pointed to the woman.

"Like I have told you before, if there is something you want to know about me, just ask," he said trying not to raise his voice.

"I shouldn't have to ask you anything. You should volunteer that type of information," Courtni shouted in Bo's face.

"Courtni, calm down," Lani said as she walked around her car.

"No Lani, I'm going to clear the air and never bother him about this again," Courtni said then turned her attention back to Bo, "Is this what I'm going to have to deal with for eighteen years? Will my child meet a bunch of random women every time I drop him/her off over here?"

"She is not my girlfriend."

"So you go away with women that are just your friends?" Courtni asked.

"It wasn't like that and why do you care anyway? You want nothing to do with me outside of the baby, so why do you care about my love life?"

Courtni shook her head, "You know what, I don't. You two have a nice life."

"She is a married woman," Bo said.

"Whatever you say, I just want you to know that I will not play these games with you at all. You can see this baby when you get your shit together," Courtni said and tried to walk around Bo who was blocking the passenger's side door.

"Courtni," Lani said.

"What Lani?"

"You will not do this to me," Bo's stern voice halted their talking, "If you have an issue with me fine, but you will not use this baby against me because of your insecurities. When I receive the results from that test and it says I am the father, I will be a part of that baby's life whether you like it or not. All of this is unnecessary. I'm better than this and so are you," he glared down at Courtni, "Now I'm going to change my clothes and do some work at my shop which calms my nerves. I suggest you find some sort of retreat. You need it."

"Bo, calm down," his mother appeared next to him. Courtni hadn't even noticed her approaching them.

"I don't want to fight with you Courtni, but if that's what I have to do then so be it," Bo said.

"Let's go Lani," Courtni said, "Mrs. Dena I apologize for the disturbance."

"Just calm down," Dena said.

Courtni made eye contact with Bo as she maneuvered her way around him since he didn't move. His eyes weren't filled with anger like hers were. His seemed more pleading than anything.

"Do you think your friend could let us out?" Courtni asked when she rolled the window down.

They watched as Bo approached the woman and she tossed him the keys. He got in the car and put the car in reverse. The tires screeched as he backed down the driveway and turned onto the road.

"You were wrong Courtni," Lani said as they drove away.

"I was wrong?"

"Yes, you were wrong," Lani shouted.

"I wish I never went to that party. I wish I never met him and just cared for my baby by myself. I don't need him." Her eyes filled with tears that soon after rolled over her lower eyelids, "I knew he was a man whore and I still allowed him to get into my head."

"And your heart," Lani said, "You love that man and that's why you are acting the way that you are. You need to apologize to him ASAP," Lani said.

"No, I don't want to see or talk to him," Courtni pulled a napkin from Lani's glove compartment.

"Yes you are Courtni, what has gotten into you? I really hope it's just the pregnancy hormones because you have lost it."

"I just want to go home and get in bed. My stomach is cramping really bad."

"Because you are putting yourself and that baby under

unnecessary stress simply because you do not know how to express your love for this man. I've told you before it's time for you to be honest with yourself. If you love him, tell him you love him."

"In front of a woman he was out of town with?" Courtni cried.

"Yes, he told you she was not his girlfriend so that was your chance to put it all on the table," Lani said.

"If she wasn't his girlfriend than who was she?" Courtni asked.

"Don't you think you should have asked him that question?" Lani asked, "I know this is all new to you, and everything seems to be flooding in all at once, but you are going to miss out on something special if you continue on with that holier than thou attitude. He's rough around the edges, so what? He is a hardworking man that is sticking by you even in his uncertainty. His face lit up when he saw you, and then you opened your big mouth."

Courtni sat next to Lani allowing her to bombard her with the truth. It was true. She did care about Bo. She was bothered by the woman's presence. She should have asked him who she was, but all that came up was anger.

"That whole 'you can't see your baby' thing was way out of line and so not Courtni."

"I know," Courtni sniffled, "I didn't mean that Lani. I would never do that."

"I know you wouldn't, but you need to make sure that he knows that, and make up your mind about what you want from him. One minute you're only worried about the baby, and the next minute you're down his throat about the company he keeps," Lani said.

"This is why I chose to deal with children. They are a lot less complicated," Courtni wiped her eyes.

"You are making things complicated," Lani said.

"Lani, put yourself in my shoes."

"Ok, which pair of shoes am I in? The pair that wants Bo or the pair that doesn't?" Lani said.

"The pair that does, but is afraid that it isn't going to

work out, and then I'll be crushed and starting from scratch again."

"Girl, you need to get rid of those shoes," Lani said, "Now clean your face and let's grab something to eat."

Lani pulled into a diner's parking lot and they went in to order breakfast. Courtni was not hungry, but she was grateful for the extra time she had to prepare her apology to Bo.

"So when do you plan on going to see him?" Lani asked.

"I think I may just call or text him," Courtni said.

"You have to be thee most petrified woman I know." Lani said.

"I'm supposed to go to him and confess my undying love, and then what? What if he doesn't feel the same way about me?"

"Then you know where things stand between you two," Lani said while putting butter on her French toast.

"What about the woman he was with?" Courtni sipped her orange juice.

"What about her? He said she is married, so maybe she's a friend or something."

"A friend that is free to go out of town with a man that is not her husband, Lani?"

"Court, Bo has all of the answers you seek," Lani said.

"I need to prepare myself for whatever happens, I guess. What if he says she is in fact married, but he hits it every now and then, and is waiting for her to be a free woman?"

"Then you accept it, respect it, and move forward," Lani said, "I know one thing, you cannot continue to treat that man the way you have been with his fine ass."

"What if I make a fool of myself Lani?"

"Then you brush it off and try again," Lani said, "I'm not saying chase the man. I'm saying you cannot be afraid to express yourself with the next guy because of a bad experience with this guy. Every move you make is not going to be a safe move, but when you get knocked down, you get back up."

*****

Courtni checked the time on the dash and it read 6:15pm. She wondered how she would get inside of the gated lot, as she sat outside of Bo's shop. Her stomach did flips as she coasted forward and pressed the button next to the speaker.

"Welcome to Bo's, how may I help you?" A woman's voice sounded from the speaker.

"Hi, I'm here to make a payment," Courtni lied, "Lord, please forgive me," she whispered.

"Ok, you can come around to the office on the left," the woman said and the heavy black gates separated.

She drove past the office and parked near the garage since she knew that was more than likely where Bo would be. There were groups of guys all over the huge lot doing multiple different things, from giving their best sales pitch for the rebuilt classics cars to potential buyers, to guys sweeping the lot and transporting dented car parts.

No one noticed Courtni as she strolled across the lot and into the shop area. The sound of power tools pierced her ears, and sparks flew from the side of her as she made her way over to a group of guys working on a shell of a car. She saw Bo standing along the side of a car holding up a large piece of paper. A group of guys surrounded him and listened as he lectured them loudly over all of the noise. She swallowed trying to coat her dry mouth, and gather up the nerve to address him. There was no turning back now, it was time for her to face the music, spill her guts, and accept whatever the outcome may be. She stood there waiting for someone to notice her but they were into their work. Instead of yelling or screaming to get Bo's attention, she just positioned herself in one spot between two large oil puddles and assessed her surroundings.

"Are you looking for someone?" A young guy asked from behind Courtni. He lifted his safety goggles and held the welding torch away from her.

"Yes," she leaned closer to him and spoke into his ear, "I need to speak with Bo."

"Oh ok," he said. He placed two fingers in his mouth and released a loud whistle.

Everyone stopped what they were doing, and turned their attention to the two of them. That was not what she had in mind.

"Bo, you got a visitor," he said then walked over to the metal counter.

"Courtni, what are you doing in here?" Bo asked.

She could have sworn she saw him roll his eyes at the sight of her.

"Umm, I need to talk to you," she said and everyone looked from her to Bo.

"Yeah well, I'm busy and you don't need to be in here," Bo said, "Jim, could you see to it that she gets out of here safely?" he said to the young guy next to her and turned back to his paper.

"Sure thing boss," the guy replied.

"No wait," Courtni said. She stepped over a car frame in the middle of the shop and made her way over to Bo.

Lord knows she was shaking like a leaf and really wished she could do this in private, but now was her time, so she had to do this in front of everyone.

"I just want to apologize," Courtni said once in front of Bo and what seemed like half of his staff.

"Ok, now I really need to get back to work," Bo brushed her off.

"I love you Bo, and I'm finally able to admit that to myself. You have to forgive me because I don't know what that's like and you were so unexpected. I thought the man I would fall for would be a little more obvious. I thought he would tell me that he loves me and I would reciprocate then we would display our love and everything would be so amazing, but that's not what love is." She said and everyone gave her their undivided attention. "Love is—," she stopped again and looked Bo in his eyes. She couldn't believe she was doing this in front of a group of strangers. "Love is when you sit beside someone doing absolutely nothing yet you feel perfectly happy. I know I've been asinine and imprudent, but I promise you that is not the person that I am. I love you."

She stood there waiting for a response along with the rest of the group as silence lingered, and Bo rolled up the large piece of paper he held in his hand.

"Thanks," he said. "Now I really need to get back to work."

She now knew what it felt like to be punched in the gut with a massive fist. Her body felt as if it was deflating, and she had to push herself to move and hold back the tears that were rushing in.

"Ok," Courtni said in a soft tone.

She turned around and walked out of the shop in a hurry. Her hand fumbled around in her large purse for her keys as she neared her car. This had to top her list of the most heartbreaking and embarrassing moments of her life, but she only had herself to blame. Who would want to deal with all the theatricals she has displayed? She was damaged like many women, but that gave her no right to criticize anyone. Although she didn't get the results she wanted, she was still proud of herself. She was just knocked down, now it was time for her to get back up.

"Come on," she said frustrated with her search to find her keys. She had to get away from this place immediately before her eyes gave way and granted her tears the freedom they so desperately sought.

"Hey," Bo said from behind her.

She turned around and was taken aback by his presence as he walked towards her. Even though he just shot her down and her feelings had been lacerated, her first thought when she saw him walking towards her, with that tall confident walk that accentuated his broad muscular shoulders, was "Damn".

"I'm leaving, just trying to find my keys," Courtni forced a fake chuckle to keep from crying.

"I don't know why I cannot just let you leave," Bo said. He stood close to Courtni and pinned her between himself and her car door as he placed both hands on the top of her car.

Her fear of the old mighty alpha male took its place as she looked up at Bo's eyes.

"I don't know if it's those beautiful slanted eyes, that infectious personality of yours, that silky smooth dark skin you've been blessed with that the sun could have kissed all day and it still wouldn't come out as beautiful, or the fact that you cross my mind every day, I know that your hair smells like honey and you left me nostalgic, wanting to know more, see more, hear more, and become more, but I can tell you this, it's not your incredulous assumptions about me and my life, or your ambiguous state of mind. I like a woman that goes for what she wants, but I love a woman that knows what she wants. You...," he paused and placed his index finger on the tip of her nose, "You confuse me. I'm not used to chasing women. Although I know it's usually the man's job to hunt. Not to sound narcissistic, but I haven't had to do so in years."

"Love the modesty," Courtni managed through her daze.

Bo laughed but maintained his position in front of her, "See, that's what I'm talking about. You have something that I want, and it's not what you already gave me," he made a silly face, "I just wish you knew what it is that you wanted."

"You," Courtni said, "but if I can't have that then I'll settle for a respectful platonic relationship with you."

"Really?" he asked and she nodded her head yes.

"Even if that woman today was in fact my girlfriend, we could still manage a respectful relationship?"

Courtni took a second to digest his words and shake off the sting. "Yes," she said.

"Good, because she's not," Bo said, and Courtni let out sigh. "We could still manage a respectful relationship if I hit it off with someone and we married and had children as well?" he asked.

"Of course, and I would hope that if the roles were reversed, and I were the one getting hitched, you would be respectful of my decision." Courtni said.

He shook his head to Courtni's surprise, "I don't have to worry about that," he said, "because I want to continue becoming your first everything, and I have a lot of bases to cover, if you don't mind," he smiled.

"I don't," Courtni said.

"Then I guess I should do this the right way," Bo said and backed up a little, "Hello beautiful, my name is Bo, short for Bartholomew, and I would love to take you out some day. I like 40s and I see you like 40s," he touched Courtni's belly and she laughed at his silliness.

"I don't like 40's." Courtni laughed, "I actually don't even drink."

Bo broke his face down, "You're starting off wrong," he laughed.

"Ok, I sip a little something occasionally, but nothing like I did the day this happened," she pointed to her belly.

"You look gorgeous," he said and Courtni blushed, "So, can I take you on your first date?" he asked.

"I don't know, I have to check my schedule to make sure I don't have plans with any other guys beating down my door," Courtni joked.

"Yeah, well, while you're doing that, be sure to tell them that you're taken," Bo said.

"Ok, you be sure to tell them that you are taken as well," Courtni said pointing to the groupies scattered about his business.

"Hey," Bo screamed as he turned around, and everyone that could hear him outside over the music gave him their attention. "I just wanted to let everyone know that this is my woman."

"I was just kidding," Courtni hid her face in her palms.

"Hey Bo's woman," one of the guys said.

"It's too late now," he said to Courtni, and turned his attention back to the others. "I know that my guys aren't going to like this, but I'm making this decision with respect to my relationship so I'm going to have to ask all of you lovely ladies to leave the premises, and I'm sorry, but you are not allowed inside of this gate again unless you are making a purchase or on the opposite side getting your vehicle repaired."

"Oh come on boss." one of the younger guys said.

"You'll survive Lee," Bo laughed.

Courtni watched as the ladies exited the premises upset and a few of the mechanics hurried to get their numbers.

"Anything else?" Bo asked when he turned his attention back to Courtni.

"I'm so embarrassed," she said.

"I just want to put a smile on that beautiful face and keep it there, but you have to allow me to do that and trust me," he said.

"I know," Courtni said, "I'm thawing food out for dinner so I'm going to head home to cook, and I'll take you up on that date whenever you are free, but I would love for you to come to dinner at my house," Courtni said.

"I'm allowed in your house now?" Bo asked.

"Yes," Courtni laughed.

"Should I bring anything?"

"Just yourself," Courtni said, and felt the excitement starting to build.

"Ok, will I be riding with you?" he asked.

"Sure if you want to," taken aback, "I thought you were busy here?" Courtni said.

"I'm the boss remember?" Bo smiled. "Let me lock up my office and grab my bag from my trunk. Is it ok if I shower at your house?" he asked.

"Of course."

"Ok," he smiled again and turned to walk away but stopped and turned back around. "Pregnancy suits you well," he said.

Courtni sat in her car smiling from ear to ear. She texted Lani to tell her they were on their way to her house for dinner, and Lani expressed her admiration for Courtni's courage. Courtni was proud, as well and could now say that she took a leap of faith and landed on her feet. Certainly there were a few more things they needed to work out, and a few more questions to be asked, but at this moment she was truly happy.

Bo placed his gym bag in the back seat then joined Courtni in the front. This time instead of the citrus scent she remembered from being in his presence weeks ago, she was met with the scent of motor oil and even that turned her on.

"Are we having turkey and bottled water for dinner?" he asked as he fastened his seatbelt.

"No we're not," Courtni laughed.

"Good."

"Don't act like you didn't enjoy that turkey bacon," Courtni said, looking straight ahead.

"It was pretty good," Bo confessed.

The difference in the atmosphere made a difference in her demeanor; just being next to him in her car made Courtni hot and jittery. She made sure to keep her eyes on the road to direct her attention away from the masterpiece that sat next to her. If she could barely hold on to her sanity around him now, how was she going to cope in the long run?

"You should probably have a talk with your staff. I got

into your establishment fairly easy," Courtni said as Bo shuffled through his phone.

"How did you get behind the gate?" he asked.

"I told a little white lie."

"Hmm, you like being bad don't you?" he asked.

"Not at all," Courtni smiled.

They talked and laughed all the way to Courtni's home near the Inner Harbor. After he opened the door for her, she led the way up the stairs to her home. Colby rushed her at the door with his barking and wagging his tail.

"Hey Colby," she greeted her dog, "Make yourself at home," she said to Bo.

She sat her keys on the end table and stepped out of her shoes while Bo stooped down to pat her dog.

"Any house rules I need to abide by?" Bo asked.

"Not that I know of, but if I think of any I'll be sure to inform you."

Bo smiled and walked through the living room, then up the two steps to her bayside view. He pulled the string to her floor length drapes and unlocked the patio door as his face brightened at that sight.

"Now this is a nice view," Bo said.

"While you are out there freezing, and admiring the view, I'll start dinner," Courtni said.

"I should hop in the shower while you're doing that," Bo said. He came back into the house and locked the door behind him.

Courtni walked into the half bath and washed her hands with Sweet Pea scented soap and rushed to dry her hands.

"Oh, I almost forgot I—," she stopped when she walked back into the living room and Bo was shirtless, while digging in his gym bag. Her recollection of the day she spent with him flooded her head. Touching him in the rain and being wrapped in his arms was the best feeling she had ever had.

"What was that?" he asked when he stood up.

"Can you go to church with me?" Courtni asked while still enjoying the view.

"Sure," he smiled.

"Ok, because I feel like I need saving again."

"Or you could just control yourself," he flashed that beautifully corruptive smile again.

"I have to get you situated upstairs," Courtni pried her eyes away from him.

"Just tell me where everything is and I'll manage."

"The bathroom is the second door on the right and the towels are in the linen closet across from the bathroom," Courtni said.

"Got it," he said and disappeared up the stairs.

"Saints pray for me," Courtni said as she went into the kitchen and began to clean the chicken.

She seasoned her chicken and placed it in the heated oven, then decided to shower in the basement bathroom while Bo was upstairs. She went to her room and retrieved a pair of leopard print pajamas since they were two of the last items of clothing she could fit her belly into, then made her way down the stairs, and showered quickly before slapping on her vanilla lotion and wasting no time checking her chicken. She knew from the time she spent over Bo's house that he was long winded when it came to showering, so she wasn't surprised when he was not waiting for her when she arrived.

"What healthy dish are we having for dinner?" Bo asked as he entered the kitchen.

"Chicken Florentine casserole. I have to eat healthier since I am pregnant and you are eating it because you impregnated me," Courtni laughed as she stirred her sauce in a small sauce pan.

"I can't argue with that," Bo said, "Can I help you with anything?"

"You can cut these mushrooms," Courtni said.

She turned to hand him the cutting board, a knife, and a pack of mushrooms.

"Goodness," she said when she noticed him in his wife beater and briefs that weren't leaving much to the imagination. She could clearly see part of what had her acting a fool.

"You have to keep clothes on around me," Courtni said.

"I don't bite unless you want me to," Bo laughed.

Her thoughts shifted from the food to having male company in her home. He looked delectable as he sat there seemingly slicing mushrooms and looking like a chocolate fountain.

"You are the first man I have ever had in my home besides the plumber and my brother." Courtni laughed.

Bo looked up from the cutting board with a cunning smirk on his face.

"What is that look all about?" Courtni asked as she removed her chicken and placed her parmesan toast in the oven.

"I'm just wondering how I bumped into someone like you, that's all."

"You did a little bit more than bump into me," Courtni said and Bo laughed.

"It's very hard to believe you haven't had any male interactions that weren't work related."

"So you still think I'm lying?" Courtni turned away from the stove with her hands on her hip.

"No, I don't think you are lying. I'm just saying it's hard to believe," Bo said. He stood up from the table and placed the cutting board full of mushrooms on the counter next to the stove and playfully brushed past Courtni.

Yup, that deliciously smelling scent was back.

"You know there are things I question about you as well sir," Courtni said as she turned the burner off and placed a lid on her sauce.

"Oh really?" Bo said and took a seat back at the black pub style dinning set, "Well let's take care of that right now."

Courtni placed the spoon on the counter and hit the lights. "Ok, let's do that," she said. She reached for the contemporary-style chandelier above the table and pressed the button on the side. The bright light in the middle casted a spot light on the black table and made for a dramatic interrogation effect.

She sat across from Bo and intertwined her fingers. "Would you like to go first?" she asked.

"Ladies first," Bo leaned forward ready for her questioning.

"Did you rape me, honestly?"

"No, I did not. I would never do that," he said, "Did you have sex with anyone else that night?" Bo fired back.

"I sure as hell hope not, and from what I was told, I was

not apart from my friends very long. They actually couldn't believe that I had time to have sex so that says a lot about you," Courtni smirked and Bo laughed, "Who was that woman you were with this morning?"

"My sister's wife," he said.

"Your sister's wife?"

"Yes."

"Your sister is a lesbian?"

"Yes, one of them," Bo said.

"Why were you out of town with her?" Courtni asked.

"She's my art agent."

"What does her job entail?" Courtni asked prying for more details about the woman.

"She basically helps me sell my art work and this week she got me a showcase at an art gallery in New York."

"Oh wow," Courtni said excited, "How did it go? I wish I had known about it. I would have loved to drive up and purchase something."

"It was a success, to my surprise. I sold eight out of ten paintings and made a little over sixteen thousand dollars," Bo said.

"Wow."

"You would have known about it, but you were too busy avoiding me for some reason," Bo looked at Courtni, "Now, why did you act the way you did earlier at my house?" Bo asked and Courtni dropped her head in shame, "We are being honest right?"

"Yes, we are," she cleared her throat, "There were multiple reasons, the main one being I thought I didn't have a chance with you after seeing her. Does your mother hate me already?"

Bo smiled, "No, she took your side and blamed your actions on your hormones."

Courtni laughed, "I would never keep this baby away from you, just to be clear."

"I hope not," Bo said, "What made you change your mind about me?"

"Your charm, your honesty, your success, your old school chivalry, the list goes on. What is it about me that attracted you?" Courtni said shyly.

"Everything, you are nothing like any woman I have ever met. I love your shyness, I love your feisty attitude, and I love that you were saving yourself. I feel like unbeknownst to you, you were saving yourself for me, and that's the ultimate aphrodisiac for a man."

Courtni couldn't help but smile.

"Did you enjoy yourself at my house that morning?" Bo asked.

"Yes, it was like nothing I have ever experienced. It was more than a physical interaction," Courtni's hormones began a mini rage just thinking it. "Did you?"

"Yes, I don't know what you did to me, but I loved it," Bo said, "Do you like being pregnant?"

That question was a hard one to answer. "I honestly don't know. I pray that I have a healthy baby and I do venture off and wonder how he/she will look, and act, and sound, but I'm still afraid," Courtni said, "How do you feel about my pregnancy?"

"The closer I get to you, the more anxious I become. I was upset initially, but I was not going to run like my father did and now I'm to the point where I want to make things right between us, so all we have to worry about when the time comes is the baby. Could you see yourself being with me?" he asked.

Courtni used her pajama top to fan her face. These questions were getting hot.

"Yes, but I could really use some pointers on keeping my mind out of the gutter when I'm around you."

"You're a freaky novice," Bo smiled.

"Why do you excite me so much?" Courtni asked.

"I'm not sure, but the feeling is mutual. What size bra do you wear?"

"40DD."

Bo licked his lips.

"What size is your penis?"

"Ten and a half inches long, two inch girth," Bo said.

Courtni stiffened as she sat across the table from Bo absorbing the words that just came out of his mouth. Confusion engulfed her psyche as everything from the neck down began to harden, swelter, and leak, but apprehension entered her mind.

Yet and still, a soft moan escaped as she thought of the challenge.

"Your bread is burning," Bo said with a smile on his face.

"Darnit," Courtni said snapping out of it and rushing over to the oven.

She turned to look at Bo one last time and he sat there with a cocky stance as he smiled proudly. He knew the thoughts he provoked in her head and she tried to shake it off while she made their plates.

"So, what does Laurence do?" Courtni asked.

"Laurence does a lot of things, but why do you care?" Bo asked but smiled with the question.

"Just curious."

"He owns a few retail spaces that he rents out and he owns the audio system shop that we buy all of our audio equipment from."

"Oh ok, now why did you have groupies roaming your lot every day?" Courtni asked.

"They came with the cars," Bo chuckled.

"How many have you been with sexually?"

He looked up towards the ceiling in serious thought and Courtni had a change of heart. If he had to think about it, she didn't want to know.

"Never mind, here is your plate," Courtni said.

After dinner they made their way over to the couch to watch a movie. She sauntered as best as she could over to the movie rack to pick out a comedy. Hopefully that would keep her mind off of Bo's hefty member.

"Are you staying over tonight?" Courtni asked.

"Yes, if it's ok with you." Bo said. He leaned forward and picked up a book from the pile on her coffee table. "What do we have here?" he said.

Courtni turned to see what he was talking about and couldn't believe she left those books on her table.

"*The Ultimate Guide to Sexual Bliss* by Jenna Muriel, *Illustrated Sex Manual*…," Bo read off the names of the two books he picked up before Courtni snatched them out of his hand.

"Give me those," she demanded.

"Now I see why you are so concupiscent and eager. You sit around and read stuff like this, but don't practice it," he laughed.

"These are old," Courtni said embarrassed.

"Come here," he said and pulled her close to him.

Her bulging belly neared his face and an anxious feeling came over her body as he sat silently admiring her growing abdomen.

"Can I touch your stomach?" he asked.

"Yes," Courtni answered.

Bo carefully unbuttoned her blouse from the bottom up and exposed her heavenly expending belly with its emerging belly button in the center of her smooth skin. His hands rubbed the sides before he placed his soft lips on her belly. Courtni beamed inside and out. She didn't think she would have this experience during her pregnancy because of the circumstances, but Bo was unquestionably interested.

"This is incredible," he smiled up at Courtni, "Can you feel the baby move yet?"

"Yes, a little, but mainly at night," Courtni said.

"Does it hurt?"

"No," Courtni said.

"Hey baby," Bo spoke to her stomach, "This is daddy and I love you already." Courtni's heart filled with joy from his affection.

"I promise you'll never have to do this alone as long as I'm alive and well," Bo said to Courtni.

"Thank you," Courtni smiled, "I'm not going to cry," she recited her famous words.

"No, you are not," Bo laughed as Courtni sat beside him on the couch. "Let's read one of your books," he grabbed the book he once held in his hand and went straight to the page that was bookmarked.

"I actually would like to try that," Courtni admitted as she pushed her apprehension aside.

"I don't think that's a good idea," Bo laughed, "We can try this," he said flipping back to the beginning of the book that discussed kissing.

"No, I want to try this," Courtni said and got down her knees.

Bo was laughing uncontrollably. "Baby, I know you want to try new things, but this will be a disappointment."

Courtni didn't reply as she tugged on his briefs, "I've read this book a million times," she said.

She grabbed the book and placed it next to Bo on the couch where she could see it and took his limp dick into her hands. He looked down at Courtni as she puckered up her lips and went straight for his balls. She took her tongue and grazed the sensitive skin until it was nice and wet. Bo's dick grew with each flick of her tongue causing her grip to loosen as it filled her hands. Once Bo's dick became erect, Courtni quickly skimmed the book and took a minute to appreciate the beauty of his manhood. She took in every vein and the small, bell shaped birthmark at its base. It was truly a magnificent sight to behold and the pleasure he could bring was just as wonderful.

"Do you know what the Corpus Spongiosum is?" Courtni asked.

"No."

"Well, I'm about to show you," she said as she placed both of her lips and her tongue on the thick vein at the bottom of his penis. She licked and suctioned as she maneuvered up and down, and stopped at the tip. Bo's head was now leaned back on the couch, and she was turned on by seeing him turned on. Her tongue revolved around the head of his dick as it oozed a sweet tasting cream that she devoured. Flourishing in the moment she put all of the knowledge she obtained reading her books over the years to work as she opened her mouth as wide as she could to accommodate all of this amazing man. The corners of her mouth stretched as she sucked and glided up and down his dick repeatedly, and once thoroughly lubricated, she peeped over at the book then stood up on her feet with the dick still in her mouth. She extended her tongue a little past her bottom row of teeth and slid down as far as she could go. The back of her throat ached as she tried to force as much of him down as she could, but the pressure from her tactic made Bo's dick throb and he moaned out loud.

"Damn," he said as a mixture of saliva and pre cum

dripped and dangled from Courtni's mouth.

She came back up to the top then went back down this time consuming more than the last dive.

"Baby, come up, I'm about to cum," Bo said with his head held back and his hands over his face.

Courtni didn't stop; instead, she came up a little and repeatedly jammed the head of his dick against the back of her throat. She felt Bo's hands on the side of her face trying to warn her before he released a nice load into her mouth, but it was too late. The warmth cascaded down the back of her throat as remnants fell forward and was left in her mouth for her to either swallow or spit out. She swallowed without a problem.

"You are the best," Bo said out of breath as if he were the one doing all of the work.

He removed Courtni's pants and panties as he switched positions with her.

"My turn, but watch my baby," he said as he held Courtni's hand and she flopped down in the chair. "Oh, I see you liked that, huh?" Bo said when he noticed how wet Courtni was.

His large tongue sopped up the sweet juice before he turned his attention to her engorged clitoris. Every time his tongue landed on her clit an electric feeling shot through her kitty and Courtni twisted and turned and tried her best to get away from Bo's relentless mouth, but his grasp was solid. It took no time for him to give Courtni her first clitoral orgasm. She grabbed at him, pulled his hair, bit her lip, and trembled intently until her body calmed, but her goods continued to throb and excrete that tasty fluid that Bo seemed to be enjoying.

"You even taste different," he said as he came up licking his lips and wiping his face.

She lay stretched out on the couch with her belly exposed and fluids leaking, but she didn't care. Her mind and body was completely satisfied, but her throat hurt like hell. It was a pain she would gladly bear after seeing the pleasure it bought. She had a new talent that could only be shown behind closed doors which meant she really had to learn how to control her sexual appetite since she just couldn't stay on the holy road, but that wouldn't stop her from trying.

"Come here baby," Bo said as he did his infamous move

and pulled Courtni on top of his lap. "I'm having trouble believing that you are as special as you seem."

"I'm not special, just inexperienced," Courtni smiled.

"No," Bo shook his head as he looked Courtni in her eyes, "You are different, and I'm not letting you go."

Courtni smiled. She didn't know what to say, but it felt so good to hear those words after she so foolishly judged and condemned this man. He still saw through her to her heart.

"I hope not," Courtni said.

She placed both hands on the sides of his face as her puckered lips met his. The emotions he triggered and feelings that fluctuated throughout her body whenever he touched her was absolutely mind blowing and she never wanted it to end.

The throbbing between her legs returned, but this time it wasn't her. Her juices had never stopped flowing and her mental stimulation never languished as she reached around her belly and felt for Bo's heavy member. Never breaking their kiss, she stroked Bo's hard-on as clear fluid seeped from the tip of his dick and smeared across her belly.

"Are you sure you want to do this?" he asked as Courtni continued to place kisses along his cheek and neck.

"Yes," she answered.

"I don't want you to do anything you are going to regret after," he said.

She looked him in the eyes, "I need you inside of me right now."

Bo took his extensive hard on and rubbed it up and down Courtni's wet goods. When he stopped at the entrance, he gave Courtni one last chance to change her mind, but she declined as she slowly forced her body down onto his wide head. She flinched and wrapped her arms around his neck as the tip of his dick parted her lips and accessed her moist insides.

"Hold me tight baby," he whispered in her ear as he spread both of her cheeks, and gently thrust forward filling Courtni with the warm pleasure she has fantasized about for years.

"Are you ok?"

"Yes," she said through her moans.

"Do you want me to stop?" he asked.

"No Bo, please don't stop," she whispered.

Courtni bounced softly and begin to feel more pleasure than pain as Bo continued sucking the sensitive area on the side of her neck. She reached back to feel his dick and was surprised to feel about five remaining inches that hadn't reached her insides.

"I'm not going to hurt you," Bo whispered, succeeding in calming Courtni's nerves as she continued to hug and kiss this beautiful man that she almost chased away from fear of letting go. "I love you Courtni," Bo said.

The tears were back as she allowed Bo to make love, not only to her body, but her mind as well. She never knew that hearing a man speak those words would bring such joy, and she welcomed it with an open heart and looked forward to hearing those words more often.

*****

"So we're doing this? Me and you?" Bo said as they lay intertwined on the couch.

"What do you mean?" Courtni asked as she lay stretched out next to him with his arm wrapped around her.

"Dating. In a relationship. No more games," he said.

Courtni sat up excited and faced him, "I guess we are," she said with a smile on her face.

"That makes me your first man," Bo smiled and hugged her tight.

"So you are telling me that there are no other women lingering around and wondering where they stand in your life?"

"That's exactly what I am telling you. The women I have been with know where they stand. We only received one thing from each other then went our separate ways," he said.

"When is the last time you were with another woman?" Courtni asked, but wasn't sure if she wanted to know the answer.

"About two weeks before you stayed over my house," he answered honestly.

"Where is she now?"

"I have no idea. I call when I want it and she invites me over. I don't stay over. There's no kissing. It's always protected, and the number one rule, we do not leave her house. I'm very honest up front so there are no misunderstandings," he said.

"When was your last relationship?" Courtni asked.

"About a year ago, it lasted for three years until she moved to California to further her career."

"Ok, so what are you going to do about the bench warmers?" Courtni said.

"What's a bench warmer?" he asked.

"My friend Jade refers to women or men that you aren't in a relationship with, but you can call at any time and they come running, bench warmers, because they're always sitting around waiting for a chance to play," Courtni said.

Bo laughed at her reference then stood up to retrieve his phone. He sat back down next to Courtni. "I guess we should start deleting from the top," he said.

Courtni leaned in close as they sat back and started the process.

"Annalisa, man she has a big ole booty…"

"So she has to go," Courtni laughed and he deleted the number.

"Carissa, she can do some things with a Hennessey bottle," Bo said.

"De-lete," Courtni replied, and Bo laughed.

"Davina, oh she can work a pole like no other."

"Good bye Davina," Courtni waved her hand at his phone before Bo deleted the number.

He picked her hand up and kissed it as they sat there for hours reconfiguring Bo's contact list and enjoying each other's company in the process. She was excited to start this new journey, but hesitant about Bo committing. She finally had a good man so instead of stressing she was just going to live in the moment and see where things lead. She just needed to get herself and Bo on a more righteous path.

Chapter Nineteen

"It's just a matter of putting things into perspective."

"Will that be all for you tonight?" the clerk at the Wine & Spirits store asked.

"Yes," Lani said as she swiped her card to purchase the bottle of Red Berry Ciroc.

She was a few minutes away from Jackson and Maya's house, so she stopped to pick up a little something just in case their stock didn't consist of anything strong.

"I'm sorry," Lani said when she bumped into a guy entering the store.

"No, problem," the guy said, "Hey," he looked at Lani as if trying to remember why she looked so familiar. "BMW," he said, "Do you remember me?"

"Of course I do. Those gray eyes are hard to forget," she said to the wondrously tall guy she was involved in the car accident with. Today was her first time getting a good look at him besides what she saw in the dim lighting that night, and he was far more beautiful than she remembered.

"I'm Chris," he said extending his hand.

"Lani."

"How is the car?" he asked.

"Good as new. How many cars have you hit within the past two months?" Lani chuckled.

"I see you are comedian," he laughed.

"I try," Lani stated.

"Maybe you can tell me some of your jokes over dinner someday," he said rather abruptly, surprising Lani.

She let out a light giggle, "I would love to handsome, but I'm in a relationship."

"Oh, I didn't know what you had going on that night," he said.

Lani totally forgot he witnessed the fiasco of her squeezing into the back seat of Jackson's car and wished she could take back her words.

"It's complicated," Lani said.

"That's a shame. You are too beautiful to be involved in anything complicated."

"You are not exempt from hardship or adversity because you are beautiful," Lani said as she used her finger to place her hair behind her ear.

"I concur, but sometimes we welcome it when we don't have to. Life is all about choices," he said.

"If only it were that easy,"

"It is. It's just a matter of putting things into perspective, first thing being our self-worth. Once we realize how much we're worth and how much we have to offer, things tend to fall into place from there, and all of the seasonal people tend to drop from your life like leaves during the fall." he said.

Lani listened, but the entire time she felt as if this man knew her situation, and was speaking solely about her. Was she being pranked? Did someone set her up?

She looked around at the surveillance cameras in the store then back to him. "Are you sure you don't know me?" she asked.

"I would like to," he smiled.

She observed his face and demeanor as she contemplated his offer. The rock on her finger symbolized a sure sign of financial stability if ever she were in between jobs or decided she was bored with her current one. Jackson meant the world to her, but things were unquestionably different for them since they become a threesome. The little bit of time she did have alone with Jackson was spent wondering if Maya was going to appear with their damn children, and admittedly, Lani actually began to feel bad for Maya when she was alone with Jackson.

"I'll tell you what, if ever you would like to get away from all of the complications in your life and would like something a little more subtle, I would absolutely love to take you out. I was hoping you used my card when I gave it to you, but I've been given a second chance to give it to you, so I hope that you call," he said once Lani didn't respond.

She looked down at the card he handed her and immediately searched for his profession.

"Civil engineer, not bad," Lani said, but of course she automatically compared him to Jackson, and an engineer is no doctor, but she didn't know much about the profession.

"I do all right, but more importantly I love what I do," he said.

"Ok, well I have to get going." Lani said.

"Did the card turn you off?" he chuckled.

"No," Lani said, "Have a nice day." She exited the building.

She resumed her navigation and drove the last few miles to Jackson's house. This was her first visit and she felt aloof and disinterested. This relationship was turning into more of second job than the sexual hiatus she thought it would be. Seeing Maya's legs, ass, arms, feet, and tits in the air as Jackson smacked, licked, and fucked her was getting pretty old, but maybe this Ciroc would bring that spark back tonight.

Lani turned onto Littleminton Lane and made a right onto the red and brown quarry stones that covered the driveway. She drove down the driveway until she reached the three moderate size pine trees that accented the center of the circular end of the driveway.

"I guess I'll park here," Lani said once she rounded the trees and her car was facing the exit.

She grabbed her bag and exited the car as she took in their Spanish style residence that was painted an eggshell color with brown Spanish style tiles covering the roof. As she walked towards the L-shaped home, her thoughts altered to Jackson's condo she used to visit. She couldn't believe she actually fell for his bullshit and even considered that a doctor would live in any type of complex.

"Hello Lani," Maya said as she opened the door before Lani could even reach it.

"Hi Maya," Lani said and embraced her.

"What do you have there?" Maya asked referring to her vodka.

"Happy juice," Lani said.

"We have more than enough alcohol and Jackson picked you up a few things he said you liked."

"Is that right?" Lani said as she walked behind Maya admiring her home.

"Yes, that's right, he's in the kitchen. I'm not much of a chef so we had the food catered. I hope that's all right with you," Maya said.

Does it matter, is what Lani wanted to say. "That's fine," she said as she entered the kitchen and her eyes landed on Jackson as he picked up a piece of shrimp and stuffed it into his mouth.

"I told you to wait for Lani," Maya tapped Jackson on his shoulder.

"I was hungry honey and Lani is always late," he smiled at Lani, "Hey baby," he swallowed his food and kissed Lani passionately on the lips.

What was she saying earlier about being tired of him? She changed her mind.

"I'm not that late," Lani said and Jackson held his gaze on Lani until Maya interrupted.

"The table is set, so if you guys are ready to eat then follow me," she said and they did accordingly.

Jackson wrapped his arm around Lani and kissed her cheek as they walked into the dining room.

"You two have a beautiful home," Lani said.

"Thank you," Maya replied, "For you my lady," Maya said as she pulled out a chair at the end of the table for Lani.

"Thank you," Lani said.

She placed the red cloth table napkin on her lap and became a little perturbed when she looked up and noticed Jackson sitting across from her all the way at the end of the table and Maya in the middle. Lately she was getting the impression that Maya was purposely trying to keep the two of them apart, which Lani didn't fully understand. If she didn't want her around she shouldn't have agreed to the arrangement, and contrary to what she may believe, if she wanted to fuck Jackson she was going to do so whether Maya liked it or not.

"So what did you do today?" Maya asked Lani as they dug into their food.

"I had lunch with my friends, went home to shower, and prepared to come here but I made a stop and I ran into a gentleman I met a few months ago. That's why I was a little late," Lani said.

She looked up from her food and noticed Maya looking at Jackson and Jackson looking at her. He didn't like that last part.

"Is he an old friend?" Jackson asked.

"No," Lani said nonchalantly, "How has your day been so far?"

"My parents came to get the children this morning. We ran a few errands and came home to prepare for you," Maya said.

"You didn't have to do all of this. I'm easily pleased," Lani said.

They made small talk as they nibbled on the catered food and Maya attempted to pry into Lani's personal affairs, but she didn't get very far. Little did she know she had invested so much into Jackson that she didn't have any personal affairs. Her life consisted of work, her friends, and the two of them, so she ate alone, slept alone, and lived alone while they had each other, like her friends said. Originally, everything was just peachy, but lately it has become bothersome.

"I have to be honest with you two," Lani said as they sat in the great room drinking wine, vodka and champagne, "I am looking for a little more than I have been receiving."

"Like what?" Jackson said.

"I'm just not very happy with the amount of time I spend with you."

"Why haven't you mentioned anything?" he asked.

"I didn't want to impose,"

"Well, we are all in this together and if you are not happy, I know that Jackson will not be happy either, so what can we do to make things right?" Maya asked.

"I would like to have a few nights a month with Jackson for starters."

"Not with me?" Maya pointed to herself.

There she goes again trying to interject herself into the equation, Lani thought. "I figured you have him every night it's only fair that I get a few nights a month. I don't think I'm asking for much."

Maya looked at Jackson, "I guess that can be arranged."

Jackson smiled and sipped his champagne.

"Would you like that baby?" Maya asked Jackson. She placed her glass on the table and sat on Jackson's lap.

"Yes I would dear," he replied and tongued Maya down.

Lani guzzled her vodka down and poured herself another glass. This was going to be a long night and they were just beginning. She watched from across the coffee table as Jackson popped each button on Maya's pea green blouse and planted kisses all over her chest. She removed her shirt and bra and straddled Jackson as he sucked then gripped her nipple with his teeth. Her moans lifted and turned to screams before she stopped and stood up.

"Let's take this upstairs," she said pulling Jackson from the chair. Maya reached her hand out for Lani to take and Lani grabbed her bottle before latching on to Maya.

They climbed the staircase filled with family photos and Lani couldn't escape the guilt. She took the clear bottle to the head before they commenced to carnal pleasure. These days that seemed to be the only thing that made Lani happy.

"Let me see that body," Jackson said as he removed the vodka bottle from Lani's hand.

She pulled her pink shirt over her head, and slid out of her black jeans. Jackson pulled her close and kissed her deep as Maya undressed near the wooden king size bed. Jackson lifted Lani and placed her on the bed. As he hovered over her, it felt like no one else was in the room but the two of them. She looked into his eyes and saw the same man she fell in love with. All of the good times they had and hope for the future invaded her thoughts and she wanted more. He was the best thing that has happened to her and he has changed her life exceedingly. How could she let him go?

"I don't know what I would do without you," Jackson said.

"I love you," Lani replied and kissed Jackson's distinctive pink lips. He fingered her as he slid his tongue in her mouth and kicked off an erotic torrid that triggered tears in Lani's eyes.

She closed her eyes and submitted herself to Jackson fully. Not thinking about or caring what Maya was doing, the two of them entered a zone, their zone. As Jackson spread her lips and entered her with a deep thrust, never stopping his passionate kiss. His amazing mass of organ tissue rubbed against her moist walls, as it reached for her spot. It felt so good when he was inside of her. Her hands rubbed his back as she moaned and he kissed her neck.

She brought her hands up to the sides of his face.

"Jackson," Lani said with her eyes still closed.

"Yes baby?" he said in her ear.

"I just wanted to feel you inside of me one last time," Lani whispered.

Jackson continued to thrust and kept up his slow grinding pace.

"Yeah baby," he said not paying Lani any attention.

"I'm leaving you," she whispered.

He stopped mid-stroke and looked Lani in the face, "What do you mean?"

"I can't do this anymore."

"Well, tell me what you want and we can do it that way," he said in a panic.

"No, I mean I want more. I want my own man, my own husband, and someday my own children. I was willing to put that all on hold just to have you in my life, and that is unfair to me and her," Lani said as her eyes scanned the room as much as she could from her back looking for Maya.

Lani could feel Jackson's dick began to deflate inside of her.

"She doesn't mind, right baby?" Jackson sat up and looked over in the corner where Maya sat in a brown leather chair.

"No," Maya said, but the tears in her eyes and the somber look on her face only substantiated Lani's choice.

She pushed Jackson's chest so he would let her up from the bed. "I'm sorry," Lani said as she stepped into her pants and reached for her shirt.

"Lani, think about what you are doing," Jackson said.

"I have," Lani rubbed the side of Jackson's face, "Good bye Doctor," she said.

"No," Jackson said.

He grabbed Lani's arm as she passed him to get to the door. His grip was tight and his face was filled with anger.

"You are not leaving me," he stated.

"Jackson, you're hurting my arm,"

"I love you and I'm not going to let you go again," he said, "I need you."

Lani looked around him to Maya who now had tears streaming down her face as she listened, but stared at the bed.

"Tend to your wife." Lani said and snatched her arm away.

She walked out of the room and down the hallway bleak, but proud of herself. The money, the gifts, and the man would be missed, but she loved herself more than the material things he provided.

Dare she say she was slowly discovering her self-worth? It took her a while to see past the glamour and the glitz of Dr. Jackson Andrews and the life he provided, but things were becoming a lot clearer now. She didn't need him to provide for her, and she didn't need him to make her feel relevant. That was her job to do for herself, and the dick, well, let's be honest, a stiff dick isn't hard to come by.

"Lani wait," Jackson said from an upstairs window, "I'll be right down," he pulled his shirt over his head then disappeared from her view.

She placed her car in drive and pulled out of Jackson's driveway. Once she reached the end she looked in her rearview mirror and saw Jackson standing in the driveway watching her leave. Although tears fell, she knew there was no turning back. Jackson was officially a part of her past.

Epilogue

Six months later

"We cannot do this in here."

"Actually, I can do whatever I want in here," Ira said, "This is my office inside of my restaurant Mister." Ira unbuttoned Jonathan's shirt as she leaned against the front of her desk.

"I suppose this cannot wait until we are home," Jonathan said.

"I suppose you are right. I want you right here and right now," Ira smiled. She loved the new found freedom she discovered while with Jonathan.

He leaned in close to kiss Ira's full lips. She loved the way he looked at her with such desire every day, and had her thanking the good Lord above for sending him her way and finally opening her heart to love this remarkable man.

"I like it when you take control," Jonathan said.

"Drop your pants," Ira demanded and Jonathan unfastened his belt.

She dropped down to her knees in full office attire and looked up at Jonathan as she held his man meat firmly in her hands. This man was 100% prime beef, no additives, and no preservatives. All she needed was a tall glass of milk to top off the meal she was about to receive. Ira stroked his shaft as it grew towards her forehead. She softly kissed and licked the jewels that would probably produce her future children.

"I think I want to sit on my throne," Ira said as she smiled up a Jonathan.

"I don't know what has gotten into you lately, but I love it," Jonathan said.

He held Ira's hand and helped her up before escorting her around the desk to her leather chair. He sat down and looked to Ira for further instructions. She didn't say a word as she peeled her black, fitted skirt from her thighs and over her hips then slid her panties to the side. She took a seat on her self-proclaimed throne. Since he referred to her as his queen, it was only right that she had a throne. She slowly took a seat as she gradually received every inch of what he had to offer. Whenever they were together, she took her time. She wanted to savor every moment she had with the man she loved, the man who saw this emotionally-battered woman and took the time to tactfully mend her wounds.

Ira closed her eyes as she moved up and down. She welcomed the rising heat and energy that her body produced. Jonathan's soft moans coming from behind her only fed the fire that dwelled within. He wrapped his arms around Ira's waist and kissed her back through her white blouse.

"I want you to get on all fours on your desk," Jonathan said, turning the tables.

Ira did as her man said. Her onion booty sat up in the air as she arched her back and Jonathan jiggled both cheeks.

"Looks as good as it taste," Jonathan said before bending over and licking the goods.

He spread Ira's round brown cheeks and enjoyed the taste of the elusive woman he has lusted over for years. Ira covered her mouth to subdue her moans as Jonathan gorged on her juice and played with her nipples through her shirt.

"Come on babe before we are late," Jonathan said. He helped Ira to her feet then bent her over the desk.

Using his own saliva to lubricate his Nigerian wand, he gave Ira what she wanted as she lifted her body and leaned back to kiss him. He pressed hard and deep inside of her while he held her head, kissing her lips. Her walls reacted to the pressure and pulsated around Jonathan's dick.

"Mrs. Bello, you've been requested in the banquet room," one of her employees said through the door.

"Ok, I'll be right out."

"Looks like we will have to finish this up later Mrs. Bello," Jonathan smacked his wife's ass and gave her one last kiss before pulling out.

She loved being Mrs. Bello, although most people were apprehensive because things progressed so quickly between them and they married two months into dating. She never once questioned her decision. He was a phenomenal man that greatly appreciated his wife so she made sure to show him just how much she loved him each and every day. The support she received from him was overwhelming but welcomed.

As far as her mental and emotional growth it was a day-to-day process, something she worked vigorously on every day. She had too much to lose at this point, and as a wife and mother, she would do anything to protect her family and keep them smiling from ear to ear. It felt amazing to finally have the safety net she so desperately wanted and Jonathan was just that. He loved her and all of her faults and did so before she ever granted him the opportunity to know her on a personal level.

"Are you going home with me to change or will I see you there later?" Jonathan asked when Ira returned to the office.

"I am on my way out of here," Ira said.

"Good, you know how long it takes you to get ready."

"Are you kidding me Mr. 'Three or more showers a day'?" Ira teased.

"I sweat a lot, so I have to keep myself clean," Jonathan said.

"Whatever you say," Ira said and gave him a peck on the lips as they left the office and she locked the door. She teased him a lot, but she loved his cleanliness and masculine scent.

"Lara, don't forget I want the lamps wiped down tonight, and everyone needs to have their order in for the new uniforms by tomorrow," Ira said.

"I'm on it Mrs. Bello," Lara said.

"I know you are and please hand these out to everyone," Ira said as she handed her manager a stack of small envelopes filled with gift cards for her entire staff.

"You spoil them and me," Jonathan said as they exited the restaurant.

"It's only right," Ira smiled.

"See you in a bit," he said as he shut Ira's car door and pulled out of the lot behind her.

*****

"Could you zip this for me please?" Ira asked Jonathan as she rushed around their bedroom.

"You look beautiful," Jonathan said.

They were on their way to Bo's exclusive art exhibit in Annapolis, Maryland. She was so excited for Courtni and how far she and Bo have come, defying the odds and actually becoming a couple. Not to mention their beautiful new addition.

"All set?" Ira asked.

"I sure am," Jonathan said standing next to her as they gave each other a quick once over in the floor length mirror.

"Mommy, can we watch a scary movie while you are gone?" Nicah asked as she barged into the room without knocking.

"No you cannot," Ira said as she snatched the movie out of her hands.

"Aw man, why not?" she whined.

"Well, because the last time you all watched a scary movie, there were two adults and four little people sleeping in our bed for a week," Ira said.

"I forgot about that," Nicah said and Ira and Jonathan laughed.

"What time will you be back?" she asked getting comfortable on the bed.

"I'm not sure."

"Can I come?" Nicah said.

"Nope it's only for adults," Ira said and Nicah pouted.

The two of them were as thick as thieves and Ira loved having two little girls. Her blessings were continuously raining down and she was like a kid playing in the rain, allowing herself to become drenched, and basking in the moment.

Nicah addressing her as "mommy" was growing on her. She didn't want her to forget about her birth mother who brought her into this world, and actually suggested against it, but Nicah wanted so badly to fit in with the boys and feel like a part of the family, so Ira welcomed it. She also took her to visit her grandmother once a week which she loved.

"Come on," Jonathan said as he tossed Nicah over his shoulders and she giggled. "You and Noma can make cupcakes in the Easy Bake oven with Naomi while the boys play their game."

"Yay," Nicah sang.

"Naomi, I'm not sure what time we will be back, but

please call if you have any problems," Ira said as she stood in front of the door with Jonathan.

"I know the drill, but they never give me any problems. Have fun," she said.

Ira has mulled over the idea of telling Jonathan about the steamy tryst between she and Naomi in her dream since the day they started dating, but couldn't bring herself to do so. Although she was confident he wouldn't judge her, she didn't want him to look at her differently over a dream that she couldn't seem to forget about.

"Are all of the fellas going to be there tonight?" Jonathan asked as he drove down the freeway.

"Why, you don't want to hang out with us ladies?" Ira asked.

"Not really," Jonathan laughed and Ira tapped his leg.

"I am just happy that we are all getting together for once," Ira said.

"I agree," Jonathan replied

He rubbed his wife's thigh as he switched lanes on the highway. It felt good to be out and about just the two of them. No children in the backseat playing games, and no talk about their restaurants, just husband and wife enjoying each other's company.

*****

"So, how has things been going in the DeVoe household?" Dr. Lowery asked.

"Great," Trent said.

"That is wonderful. How about you Jade? Do you agree?"

"No," Jade said as she shook her semi-crossed legs.

"Why not? Talk to me," the doctor said.

"I'm still working my way up to trusting him again Dr. Lowery."

"Trusting me Jade?" Trent asked, "You don't seem to have an issue with me when you want some."

"What does that have to do with anything? If I need emotional support, I'm going to seek it from my husband. If I want to fuck, I'm going to fuck my husband. You should take note," Jade said.

"You see what I am still going through Doc?" Trent said.

"Well, it takes time for some of us to fully come to terms with the wrong that has been done to us. Tell me this…," the doctor paused and crossed his legs. His tight brown corduroys stretched as he shifted in his seat. They were nowhere near his burgundy penny loafers and didn't coordinate well with his rust colored sweater. "How were things between the two of you when you were separated?"

"We were never separated," Jade said.

"Jade, I stayed at my mother's house for four months," Trent said.

"Doc, what do you call a situation in which you go to the place that you own and where all of your belongings are every single day and sometimes multiple times a day?"

"I wanted my wife to know that I loved her and always will. That house is ours that we bought together, and that we planned on raising our family in and growing old in. I still tend to do just that. I fucked up and I'll say it as many times as it takes to get her to understand that I don't want anyone else but her." Trent said.

Jade sat next to Trent unmoved. She knew her husband loved her and she knew he didn't want to be without her, but what she still couldn't comprehend is why he did what he did in the first place.

"I went to jail for him," Jade said calmly.

"Jade, you went to jail because you tased a man with his own taser," Trent looked at his wife.

"For you."

"I didn't even know him," Trent said.

"He was an innocent victim doctor," Jade said.

"She's crazy," Trent said to the Doctor.

"Have you been practicing any of the exercises I gave you?" the doctor asked.

"Yes, we have been addressing all of our issues that come up instead of holding them in or arguing," Jade said.

"Is that true Trent?"

"No, Dr. Lowery, she uses me for sex and basically tosses me aside when she is done. Hence the belly," Trent said as he placed his hand on Jade's growing belly with a dignified smile on his face.

"Well dear," Jade said as she turned towards her husband with her knees close together. "That dick in your expensive slacks is mine. That tongue in your mouth…," she pointed to his mouth, "You guessed it, that's mine too. Just check the file cabinet at home, third row, first folder, second to the last paper in the file, and you'll find our marriage certificate that contains your signature and mine."

Trent mouthed the words "help me" to the doctor.

"Jade, do you love your husband?" the doctor asked.

"Yes I do."

"Trent, do you love your wife?" he asked.

"Yes I do."

"Good, that is all I want to hear, and from the first time you two walked into my office you have held steady to those same answers. You both look great, so I hope you are heading out for a romantic night to celebrate each other, and how far you have come, and how far you will go."

"That sounds good, but we are actually headed to our friend's art exhibit," Jade said.

"Well you two enjoy yourselves, and I will see you in two weeks if need be."

"Thank you Doc," Trent stood up and shook the doctor's hand and helped his wife to her feet.

"Thank you," Jade said repeating Trent's gesture.

She walked through the door her husband held open as he placed his hand on her lower back. Things were going better than she would have believed them to be six months ago, and she was not going to complain. Their children had their father back at home, and the way their little faces lit up the morning they woke up to their father, was worth the hard work she was putting into saving her marriage.

The scariest thing about the whole situation is that she had absolutely no clue her husband was seeing someone else, so she asked herself many times how was she going to stay aware and she finally came up with the answer. She was simply going to live her life and enjoy her family while doing so.

You can force a hand, but not a heart and one thing she has learned throughout it all is she had Trent's heart and that's the way it was going to stay.

"I would appreciate it if you wouldn't wear that dress out without me," Trent made his announcement as he turned the music down.

"Don't start Trent," Jade laughed.

"We're supposed to address our issues instead of holding them in, so I am addressing a matter that would potentially bother me if it came to head."

"What is wrong with what I have on?" Jade asked.

"I think you look drop dead gorgeous, but I can see every curve on your body and I don't want anyone else seeing it."

"Including the huge curve in the front," Jade said as she shuffled through Trent's playlist.

"That's alright, I don't want them seeing that one either. You know I think you're even more beautiful when you are pregnant," Trent smiled.

Jade allowed herself to smile at his comment. He has said those same words with each of her pregnancies and she loved hearing it every time.

"Jade, I know you will never forget about what I did, but I honestly hope that someday you sincerely forgive me," he looked over at his wife, "When I look back at what I did I can't even make sense of it. I know you don't believe me, but I swear I didn't have sex with her."

"I know," Jade said casually.

"You do?" Trent asked, shocked.

She never told him about her last run-in with Tamra.

"Yes I do, but I would love a real answer as to why you carried on this relationship with another woman."

"I don't know Jade. I think it was just the chase," he said, "She was constantly coming on to me and basically begging. I think a part of me enjoyed being desired, but when it came time to actually be with her I couldn't," Trent paused and kept his eyes on the road, "All I could think about was you at home sleeping alone after working all day and my kids. I couldn't even leave when I wanted to because I felt like shit, and I didn't know how I was going to face you so I waited until the early morning hours to leave."

Jade felt a bit of relief that his story corroborated with Tamra's, but she sure as hell wouldn't forget.

"I really just want to have a good time tonight so can we just drop it?" Jade said.

"Sure babe," Trent said and they drove the rest of the way in a music fog as they made their way down Route 97 towards Annapolis.

The historic art district was littered with all kinds of people as they navigated the narrow red brick road. The trees that lined the street of the charming area was lit up with tiny white bulbs and surrounded by little black iron fences. Trent found an empty meter and hurried to park before they were out of luck.

He held his wife's hand as he helped her out of his truck and onto her five-inch heels that he didn't think she should wear as she was five in a half months pregnant. The thin stiletto of her red pumps landed inside of each crack as they made their way to the front of the gallery.

"I take it you still don't know how to tie this thing," Jade said. She stopped in front of Trent and unraveled his dark blue velvet bow-tie that matched his dark blue velvet blazer.

"I only wore it for you. You know I hate these things," Trent said as he held his head back.

"Well, I think you look handsome," Jade said, "Damn near edible, if I must say so myself,"

She smiled as she looked into her husband's eyes. He was truly tantalizing with his long eyelashes and green eyes with a hazel ring around the pupil that he passed down to their daughter. Indeed, she missed these moments with him since they always led to a great night.

"The Davenport project launches on Monday," Trent said to Jade as she looped his bow-tie.

"Is that right?" Jade said calmly.

"I will not be in attendance for the meeting," Trent said.

"Why is that?"

"I gave Greg the account and stepped down a few months ago, so his team of guys will oversee the project," Trent said, "I love you Jade."

"I love you Mr. DeVoe. Now let's go." Jade said and turned to walk away, but he pulled her back and lustfully kissed his wife.

They stood outside of the glass front gallery, displaying a serious case of PDA as others walked by. His kiss reached beyond her lips, punctured her vascular organ, and seeped down to her freshly shaved goodies. This is the Trent that she knew and missed.

"Get a room," a passerby shouted.

"Get lost," Jade shouted back and continued lip locking with her husband.

"Come on, you're smashing my baby," Trent said as he took hold of his wife's hand and led her into the art gallery.

*****

"Aw, my sleepy baby," Courtni said in her baby voice as she rocked her two-month-old baby girl, Cami.

She was sincerely smitten with this beautiful new life. That distinctive new baby smell and chubby cheeks had her mesmerized each day. Coming home to such preciousness has put a lot of things in perspective for her. Something that began so wrong evolved into something so right.

Courtni placed her baby in the black round crib that sat in the middle of the posh nursery. Bo absolutely spoiled Cami and she had nurseries at both of their homes and his lake house, but his parents were worse than him. They called every day and were very much involved in their grandchild's life and Courtni couldn't complain. She was elated and appreciative of their acceptance after such murky details of the night she was conceived.

"The sitter is here," Bo said when he entered the room.

"Shh," Courtni held her finger up to her lips and smiled when she noticed Bo dressed in his best attire. His black Italian three-piece suit with a metallic pocket chain attached to his waistcoat only added to his magnificent physique, and his long dreads were pulled back into a ponytail, but his face looked troubled.

He held up a white envelope as he closed the door and walked in.

"What is that?" Courtni asked.

"The results," Bo said.

A sickening feeling came over her when he spoke those words. She was dreading this day, but partially wanted it to be over. Although Bo agreed he would always be there for the both of them no matter the outcome, she couldn't help but to think a change would come if it was determined that he was not her biological father.

"Are you going to open it?" Courtni asked.

"Not if you don't want me to," Bo said, "I will rip it up right now. Just say the word."

Courtni considered his idea, but it wouldn't be fair to him or Cami. They both deserved to know the truth even if it did ruin the wonderful relationship she used to dream of, but was now living. She had to take a backseat for the two of them.

"No, I want you to know," Courtni said.

"Are you sure?"

"Yes, but I don't want it to ruin your night if it isn't what you want to see."

"Nothing can ruin my night. If this paper says I'm not her biological father I will always be her dad. That's my baby over there," Bo pointed to the crib.

Courtni went over to the dresser to put out clothes for the baby as Bo opened the envelope. She seemed to be more nervous than Bo, and said a silent prayer while plugging up the baby monitor.

Bo approached her holding the paper out for her to read, but she read his somber facial expression first, and decided not to.

"I don't want to see it," Courtni said holding back tears.

"Here," he said shoving the paper towards her, "You need to see it," his voice was flinty and unyielding. It scared Courtni, but she took the paper any way. Her eyes skimmed the page and read along the lines:

Based on the genetic testing results below in the

combined paternity index, the probability of paternity is
99.99%+, meaning pursuant to the stipulations entered in this
matter, you are conclusively determined to be the father of the
child listed above.

She looked at Bo, who now wore an enormous smile on his face. He lifted Courtni and spun her around, ecstatic about the news.

"Thank you Jesus, thank you Jesus," Courtni said with her arms wrapped around Bo's neck. "No more questions," she said.

"That's right," Bo replied, "Do you love me?" He asked as he held her in his strong arms with his forehead touching hers.

"Absolutely," Courtni said.

"Good, because I love you, and I want to thank you," he kissed her lips.

"For what?" Courtni asked.

"For making me the proud father of that beautiful little girl over there," he said, "I don't know where I would be if you hadn't raped me that night."

Courtni laughed, "Well you better watch it before I strike again," she joked. He put Courtni down and began to take off his blazer.

"Oh no," Courtni said. She hurried to gather the baby's things to get away from Bo.

"One of these days, you're going to stop running from me."

"When the day comes that your "little friend" shrinks, I will gladly stop running." Courtni said as she opened the door and they headed down the hallway.

"You love it," he said when he came up behind Courtni and they walked simultaneously down the hallway to the stairs.

"You got me there," Courtni admitted.

She briefed the babysitter on the baby's to-do list and they headed to Bo's Porsche.

"Are you wearing a jacket or anything?" Bo asked as he held the door to the car open for Courtni.

"No, it's nice out. Why would I wear a jacket?"

"You are showing off my goods," he said and palmed one

of Courtni's breasts that were on display in her black, low-neck belted maxi dress.

"Is it that bad?" Courtni asked as she tried to stretch the fabric over her boobs.

"No, baby you look like a million bucks," he kissed her cheek then shut the door.

Her life has taken a drastic change for the better over the past few months and she couldn't be happier. Bo was truly the man of her dreams with a few added features and has opened her eyes to a whole new world of love and acceptance. Some days she would sit back in awe of this wonderful man that was all hers. They have spent every day together since the day she finally went after him, and the birth of their baby has only tightened their bond. Certainly she wanted to get married someday and have more children, but as of now, they would enjoy the healthy bundle of joy they have been blessed with and try not to rush things. She knew marriage would come soon because she was not letting him go.

"We will have to share with Cami the story behind her name someday, and show her all of daddy's paintings that spruced up the place." Courtni said.

The day she gave birth they decided to name their baby girl Cami after the café Bo took her to on the first day they spent together. A few months after their visit, he revealed to her that four of the paintings she admired around her that day were his, so their baby's name held significance with both of them, and of course, her mother's name was a mutual decision for the middle name. She was confident that little miss Cami was special indeed. She was God's gift to the both of them as undeserving as they were.

"Of course," Bo responded as he pulled into his reserved spot in front of the gallery.

"I'm so proud of you," Courtni said, and Bo smiled, which still had the same impact on her. She melted inside.

*****

"I'll be able to open a florist shop if you give me anymore of these," Lani said, "Come on in."

He walked in and followed her into the kitchen.

"I see you're learning how to care for them." he said as he leaned across the breakfast bar watching Lani cut the stems of her red roses.

"Yup, Jade taught me, and you look stunning by the way," Lani said as she looked at her handsome man.

"Thank you my love, and you look good enough to eat yourself."

"Don't start nothing, won't be nothing," Lani said as she placed the roses in a glass vase with water.

"I think I feel like starting something," he came around the bar and hugged Lani around the waist, "I've missed you," he whispered in Lani's ear and awakened the sleeping beast inside, but she was a different woman now and was learning how to build a relationship without sex.

"Please don't whisper in my ear," Lani said but did not change her position.

"You mean like this?" he whispered in her ear again.

She turned to face him, "You're bad," she said.

"That's all right. You're teaching me how to become a patient man and I love a good lesson," he kissed her neck and sucked a little before pulling away.

Her pussy did a quick throb and she was now aroused. She pulled him by the hand and led him into the living room.

"Here make yourself comfortable. I'll be right back," she said and handed him the remote control.

"Where are you going? We should be leaving soon," he looked at his watch as she forced him down on the couch.

"I just have to get something from upstairs really quick," Lani scurried off up the stairs.

She went straight to her closet and reached in the back for her goody box. Big Brown was calling her name once again for the third time today. Lani continuously wanted to answer, but held strong. Not this time. She has been celibate for six months, two days, nineteen hours, seven minutes, and about twenty-four seconds. She pressed her legs together to pull the tight skirt up her thighs and went into her bathroom. Big Brown made a small thud sound when the suction end connected with the cold marble floor.

Lani looked down at Big Brown with its veins protruding and waiting for her to pounce on it, but her damn legs wouldn't bend. She has been hell bent on staying true to her dedication of celibacy and was proud of her ongoing success, but right now she wanted nothing more than to be bouncing up and down on Big Brown.

"Lani," she heard from the other side of the door.

"Be right out," she replied as she finally kneeled down over Big Brown and slid her purple thong to the side.

"Baby, we really should be going. It's almost six," he said.

"Got dammit," Lani said as she stood back up.

She looked down at Big Brown one last time and thought about putting the head of it in her mouth. Anything sexual would suffice right about now, but she didn't have time for any naughtiness so she disappointingly opened the door.

"Were you in there doing what I think you were doing?"

"I'm sorry," Lani dropped her head.

He laughed at her appearance. "You know I would love to help you with that," he helped her pull her skirt down.

"I know it's just—"

"I know you want to wait, and I can respect that," he said, "Now can we go?"

"Thank you," Lani said, "By the way, I didn't do anything."

"Ok, so I'm not going to mention the size of that thing attach to the floor," he said as they walked down the stairs and out of the door.

"Damn, I was hoping you didn't see that." Lani said, "Don't get discouraged."

He chuckled as he pulled out of the driveway, "What if I told you when the time comes you will not be disappointed?"

"If you do I'll need you to turn this car around so I can hop on Big Brown."

"You named it?" he laughed.

"Can we talk about something else?" Lani said.

He slowed down as they reached the corner of her street

to let a pedestrian pass except this pedestrian decided to stand in the middle of the street. They both looked on confused for a second before Lani got a clear view of the man's face. Lani saw through his overgrown beard and brown flat cap, and instantly wished she could disappear.

"Do you know him?"

"I used to," Lani said, "I'm sorry, give me a minute," she said and climbed out of the car.

"Jackson what are you doing here?" Lani asked.

"I came here to see you. It seems that things are getting pretty serious between you two and I need for you to put an end to it. It's been six months Lani. How long are you going to make me suffer?" Jackson slurred his words and his breath reeked of alcohol.

"Go home Jackson and leave me alone," Lani said.

"Now you listen to me," Jackson said as he grabbed Lani's arm.

"Hey, watch your hands," her man stepped out of the car and approached the two of them.

"It's ok," Lani said, "Jackson was just leaving and never coming back," she looked at Jackson and snatched her arm away.

"You look beautiful," Jackson said.

"Go home to your wife."

"We miss you," he said.

"No, you miss me and she misses you. Now go," Lani said and grabbed a hold of her man's arm.

"Why is there a for sale sign in your lawn?" Jackson asked.

"I'm selling my home."

"I bought you that home and you loved it." Spit flew from Jackson's mouth.

"Yes I did, but I'm moving on and starting over. Goodbye."

"Lani please, what do I have to do, beg?" he said. He got down on his knees in the middle of the street as they climbed into the car.

Lani's heart ached for Jackson and it hurt to see him that way, but she couldn't help him. Her life was wonderful without Jackson, which was something she didn't think was possible. She resumed her post-baccalaureate courses and would soon take the Dental Admissions test. Lani was well on her way to becoming Dr. Lani Alona Wilkes D.D.S, and she didn't have time for Jackson's games. The man beside her was incredible and every bit worthy of her time. He was supportive and pushed her to excel every day, and embodied the motivation she needed.

"So is that why you are selling your home?" he asked as they drove down the street.

"Yes, and I'm not seeing him, I swear," Lani said defensively.

"I know," he smiled at her.

"I've seen his car in my neighborhood a few times, but I haven't seen him. I just want a fresh start and to build my own life without any hint of him," Lani said.

"I understand. Just be sure to include me in that life of yours, and please be sure to put it on me like you did him." he laughed, "I want to be strung out too."

Lani laughed, "Again, let's change the subject." she said.

"Ok, well I have been in Dallas, Texas for two weeks now, and I was wondering if you've missed me as much as I've missed you?"

"Of course I have," Lani said, "I hate it when you have to travel. You have me addicted." she smiled.

"Well I'm glad you brought that up, because I was hoping that you could take some time off to travel with me. Of course it's always work related, but I would love to have you around," he said.

"You want me to travel with you even though I'm not giving you the goods?" Lani asked with a serious look on her face.

"I don't care about that. I'll wait for you as long as it takes," he reached for Lani's hand and held it tight.

To hear those words were a dream come true. She didn't think a man would wait around long if he wasn't getting a taste of the box. Whether he waited around or not, she was prospering and no one was going to put a halt to that, but he most certainly made her better.

"You are not married, right?" Lani asked.

"Do you know how many times you have asked me that

in a six month time period? The answer is still no, unless you want to marry me," he said in a serious tone.

"You are silly," Lani said.

"I'm serious," he replied, and left Lani astounded as they drove the rest of the distance to the gallery. "We will continue this conversation later," he said as he opened the door for Lani.

"You really are serious?" Lani asked.

"Yes, I am beautiful," he held her hand as they walked up the street to the gallery, "I'm not getting any younger, and you are the most beautiful woman I know. You are smart, intelligent, freaky as hell, patient, and all I think about everyday all day."

"Yes, but you don't know what it's like to live with me. I can be a crazy woman at times," Lani said.

"I don't know," he stopped and sized Lani up, "I think I can take you," he said.

"We'll talk," Lani said before he opened the door to the gallery.

They entered the gallery and glanced around the room. Lani was sure they were both thinking the same thing since everyone was pretty much dressed in black and white. She noticed the bar in the back and knew exactly where she was heading once she located her friends.

"So what I'm late," Lani said as she snuck up behind her friends.

"Trust me no one is surprised," Jade said, "I see you finally bought Mr. Wonderful along with you."

"I sure did," Lani beamed, "This is Chris. Chris this is Jade and her husband Trent, Ira and her husband Jonathan, and Courtni. This is her man's little shindig," Lani said.

"Nice to meet you all," Chris said.

"So this is who has been keeping you busy," Ira said.

"Isn't this the guy that crashed into your car?" Jade asked, "I hope he didn't drive."

"Jade," Trent silenced his wife like only he could, but of course it wouldn't be for long.

"It's alright Trent. We all know she's a little slow," Lani said.

"I'm just kidding. It's nice to meet you Chris," Jade said.

"So where is the man of the hour? These paintings are

amazing," Lani said as she eyed the walls full of paintings.

"He's right over there," Courtni smiled proudly.

"We already have our bid in for this one, so don't even think about it," Jade said as she pointed to the abstract painting they all stood in front of.

"Baby I'm going to the bar. Would you like some water?" Trent teased.

"I'll head over with you," Jonathan said.

"No, I'm alright," Jade laughed.

"Is that who I think it is?" Ira said, and they all turned to look in the direction of her gaze.

"Excuse me for a minute." Courtni said. She made her way over to Bo who was engaged in a heavy conversation with an older man across the room. She stood back a few inches waiting for a break in the conversation before announcing her presence.

"Hey Baby," Bo said when he noticed Courtni next to him. "Mr. Raoul, this is my lovely woman," Bo slightly pushed Courtni toward the man.

"It's nice to meet you," Courtni said, "Bo, can I speak with you for a minute?"

"Go ahead, I have my eye on this painting over here, and I want to put my bid in." the man said.

"Thank you for the support," Bo shook the man's hand and walked away with Courtni. "What's wrong sweetheart?"

"I know you did not hire Uncle Marty as the bartender," Courtni said as they walked towards the back of the gallery.

"He said he needed a new gig," Bo smiled, "Look at him. He is in his zone."

"I don't care what zone is in. He's going to have everyone here highly intoxicated," Courtni said.

"Stop blaming Uncle Marty for your problems," Bo laughed.

"You young bloods don't know nothing about nothing," Uncle Marty said to Trent, Jonathan, and Chris, "Have you ever heard of a Slow Death? I'm gonna hook y'all up, no need to thank me,"

"No," Courtni shouted, and they all turned around.

"Look at you dark and lovely," Uncle Marty said. "Girl

the last time I saw you, you was drunk as a skunk, but you had a good time though didn't you?" he laughed.

"Uncle Marty, please no Slow Deaths for anyone," Courtni said.

"Oh that's what you had?" Trent asked with a grin on his face.

"Shut up Trent," Courtni said.

"Now I don't know how you expect for me to do my job if I can't make my specialty drink," Uncle Marty said.

"Do your thing Uncle Marty," Bo said.

"No, do not do your thing," Courtni said.

"I'll take one," a guy said from behind them.

"Well, alright. One Slow Death coming up," Uncle Marty did his infamous Temptations spin, and had the guys laughing at his entertainment.

"You think this is funny?" Courtni pointed her finger at Bo.

"Stop worrying," he kissed her forehead.

"Hey fellas, come with me," Bo said, "I'm Bo by the way," he extended his hand to Chris.

"Chris," he shook Bo's hand. "I'm with Lani," Chris said.

"I figured you were," Bo replied, "I have an idea for a couple's trip. I wanted to talk to you all about it," Courtni overheard Bo tell the guys as they walked off.

Courtni stood there and watched all four guys walk away. Uncle Marty made her extremely nervous with all that liquor at his fingertips. He was bringing forth severe flashbacks as he handed out Slow Death after Slow Death to the keen attendees.

"Courtni, step away from the bar," Lani said as the ladies approached her.

"Oh hush up, I'm not drinking," Courtni said.

"Oh that's right I forgot you can't handle your liquor. I just wanted you to move so I can get me a drink," Lani said.

"Should I prepare four Slow Deaths?" Uncle Marty asked while holding up four fingers.

"Hell no," they all said in unison.

"Where are the guys?" Ira asked.

"They walked off somewhere." Courtni replied. "We received the results from the paternity test today."

"And?" Lani said.

"He is the father," Courtni said excited.

"That's wonderful," Ira said.

"Can I have everyone's attention please?" A woman's voice sounded through the speakers.

"She looks familiar," Lani said as the woman she saw at Bo's house the day she was with Courtni stood up on the small platform.

"Don't start Lani. I have apologized to her months ago." Courtni said.

They all looked towards the front as the guys came from the back. His agent began her speech thanking everyone for attending and preparing to name the highest bidders.

"Hey Beautiful," Trent said as he came up behind his wife and placed his hands on her belly. "You want anything to eat?"

"Why do I get the feeling you are trying to fatten me up?" Jade asked.

"I love chubby Jade," Trent kissed his wife neck and she giggle.

"Can y'all take that outside somewhere?" Lani jokingly rolled her eyes.

Everyone began to applaud so they joined in unaware of what they were applauding. Bo took the stage and made a speech before the crowd began to disperse.

"We were talking about hanging around for a little while longer if you ladies don't mind. We can have Uncle Marty hook us up some drinks and just chill." Bo said.

"Not a problem for us," Ira said.

"I'm staying and she's not leaving my side," Chris said as he hugged Lani.

"I would argue with that, but you're right," Lani smiled and sank into his arms.

"Are we staying babe?" Jade asked Trent.

"Yeah, your mother has the kids for the night so we are in the clear," he replied.

"We cannot hang out to late, remember we all have church in the morning, and that includes you as well Chris. We have been doing so well, so welcome to the family, and let's not forget Cami will be christened as well," Courtni said.

"Sounds good," Chris replied.

"Let me shake some hands and say my good- byes," Bo said and walked towards the door to bid his guests farewell.

"Trent, are you going to show us your work or keep us in suspense?" Jonathan asked.

"Oh that's right it almost slipped my mind," Trent said. "Babe I'll be back I'm going to show the guys that new modern art museum we designed."

"Ok," Jade said and waited for the guys to leave before invading Lani's personal space. "Are you doing the nasty yet?"

"Please back up," Lani said while snacking on a Bruschetta hors d'oeuvre.

"Come on, I know you're not still going strong," Jade said as she continued to stand close to Lani.

"Your belly is invading my space," Lani said, "and for the record I am still going strong."

"Let me smell your breath," Jade said.

"No, for what," Lani asked as she looked at Jade who was all up in her face.

"Just wondering if you have dick breath," Jade said and Lani laughed.

"You two have very serious issues," Ira laughed.

"For the record I do not," Lani said proudly.

"Ok, I'll check back with you next week," Jade laughed.

"Hey ladies, what y'all drinking?" Uncle Marty shouted across the half empty room as all four ladies headed in his direction. "Well not you," he said pointing to Jade, "You look like you either can't drink or already had too many drinks," he laughed.

"I'll take a double shot of Grey Goose," Lani said.

"Oh, you're definitely getting it in tonight." Jade said.

"Nope, I got this," Lani smiled.

"I'll take a Coke," Ira said.

"I already know what you want," Uncle Marty said pointing to Courtni, "One Slow Death coming up,"

"Listen to me Uncle Marty and listen to me carefully," Courtni said as she leaned across the bar. "I don't know what you put in that drink, but it is not right. No human being should ever consume a Slow Death. It does not bring good results, so stop it," Courtni said.

"What you talkin' bout dark and lovely?" Uncle Marty paused and gave Courtni his best mean mug, "I've been making that drink since 1979. Do you know how many love connections I've made with that drink? Just look at you," he paused, "That man worships the ground you walk on and the last time we talked you couldn't even get a man to look your way," he said.

"Uncle Marty, I was impregnated and didn't even remember it happening," Courtni said.

"You're welcome," he said and burst into laughter.

"What's going on over here?" Jonathan asked with all of the guys standing behind him.

"Oh nothing," Ira said.

They all turned around to survey the empty walls. Bo had just about sold out of all of his paintings and made a heap of money in the process. The sound of Al Green's "Love and Happiness" sounded through the speakers and invigorated everyone in the room. They bopped their heads as Jade played the air guitar. She bounced her shoulders and used her fingers to call her husband out in the middle of the empty floor to dance, and without hesitation, Trent took his blazer off and joined his wife.

"What y'all youngin's know about this here music?" Uncle Marty said. He danced behind the bar as he made himself a drink.

All of the ladies began to kick off their shoes while the guys removed their blazers and loosened their ties. They all danced the night away to some of the greatest music ever made as love filled the room and optimism filtered through the hearts of each and every one of them.

*****

"Good afternoon family and friends," Pastor James spoke as they all sat in the sanctuary at the private ceremony.

"Good afternoon pastor," they all spoke.

"Amen," he said as he walked down the three steps covered in red carpet. "Today is a joyous day indeed, one to be honored and celebrated," he paused, "I often ask parents, have you given your child or children back to God? It's usually followed by, "I wish," he laughed and they all joined in.

"I ask that because we all need to understand that a child is a precious gift from the Lord that belongs ultimately to him first, not you. Giving your child to God is the best thing you can do. It shows that you understand that He is responsible for their ultimate design and already knows the purpose and plan of their future. We all know that it's easy to get lost along the way," he paused and scanned the faces of everyone in the room, "Oh we have all been there," he chuckled, "We try to stand tall, walk that righteous walk with our head held high, ready to take on the world, not knowing that the road separates at different points in our lives, and most times we choose the wrong path to continue on." he paused again, "but that's alright because when you are covered under the blood of our Lord and savior Jesus Christ, nothing can keep you. When you know where home is, you will be alright,"

"Amen," they all agreed.

They watched as the pastor called Courtni and Bo up to the front and blessed baby Cami and the parents as well. It's funny how you come to church for one thing, but receive something greater from your visit. Surely they knew that change within them wouldn't come overnight, and surely someone in the room would be getting it on tonight, but each day they were granted was another chance to make things right. No one knew what tomorrow would bring, but when life is good, you enjoy it. Live a little, laugh a lot, and most importantly you must find time for pleasure.